Jackie Kabler was born in Coventry but spent much of her childhood in Ireland. She worked as a newspaper reporter and then a television news correspondent for twenty years, spending nearly a decade on GMTV followed by stints with ITN and BBC News. During that time, she covered major stories around the world including the Kosovo crisis, the impeachment of President Clinton, the Asian tsunami, famine in Ethiopia, the Soham murders and the disappearance of Madeleine McCann. Jackie now divides her time between crime writing and her job as a presenter on shopping channel QVC. She has a degree in zoology, runs long distances for fun and lives in Gloucestershire with her husband.

www.jackiekabler.com
@jackiekabler
@officialjackiekabler

Also by Jackie Kabler

Am I Guilty?
The Perfect Couple

The Happy Family

JACKIE KABLER

One More Chapter
an imprint of HarperCollins*Publishers*
1 London Bridge Street
London SE1 9GF

www.harpercollins.co.uk

HarperCollins*Publishers*
1st Floor, Watermarque Building, Ringsend Road
Dublin 4, Ireland

This paperback edition 2021

First published in Great Britain in ebook format by
HarperCollins*Publishers* 2021

A catalogue copy of this book
is available from the British Library.

ISBN: 978-0-00-843398-7

This novel is entirely a work of fiction.
The names, characters and incidents portrayed in it are
the work of the author's imagination. Any resemblance to
actual persons, living or dead, events or localities is
entirely coincidental.

Set in Birka by Palimpsest Book Production Limited,
Falkirk, Stirlingshire

Printed and Bound in the UK using 100%
Renewable Electricity at CPI Group (UK) Ltd

Chapter 1

When I think about my mother, I mostly think about the crying. She cried a lot, my mum. Then again, so did I, because I lost her when I was ten years old. I don't mean she died; at least, I *assume* she's still alive. And when I say I *lost* her, I don't mean I lost her like you'd lose your mobile phone, or your purse. I mean, I can definitely be a bit forgetful at times, but even *I'd* struggle to mislay a whole actual person. When I say I lost her, I mean she just ... disappeared. Walked out. Abandoned me. Abandoned *us*.

I'm not sure why I'm thinking about her now, why she's come into my head unbidden on this busy Thursday morning as I lock my Audi and hurry across the car park. I try not to think about her at all and, generally, I succeed. But when Dad and I were chatting the other day he, who never mentions her either, suddenly remembered that next month would be her sixtieth birthday, and ever since ...

I stop to check for traffic on the road that separates our car park from the surgery building and shake my head to banish the pointless musing. What does it matter that she has a big birthday coming up? That is, if she really *is* still alive, because after all, who knows?

She hasn't been in touch for thirty years. *It's not as if I'm suddenly going to get a party invite in the post, is it?* I think, and sigh.

It's just started to rain, the weather chilly for March, the sky slate grey, and as I push the front door open, head through the still-empty reception area, and turn left towards the staff-room, I sigh again, remembering the long to-do list waiting on my desk. Then I smile as the sound of raucous laughter drifts down the corridor.

Ruth's in early.

I open the staffroom door and step inside. Our head receptionist is perched on one end of the long table in the centre of the room, still laughing, wearing a bright-green blouse with a string of coloured beads around her neck.

'Beth! Oh Beth, you've got to hear this!'

Ruth waves her coffee mug at me, then gestures at Lorraine, one of the practice nurses, who's sitting on a chair next to her.

'RUTH! Are you going to tell *everyone*?' Lorraine says, then groans and gives a resigned shrug. 'Oh, go on, then. Not going to be able to stop you, am I?'

'You're not. You know what she's like. And it *is* hilarious. Morning, Beth.'

Deborah, head of our nursing team, who's over at the kettle making herself a drink, grins at me. I dump my bag on the table.

'Morning. What's going on? You all right, Lorraine?'

Lorraine opens her mouth but Ruth doesn't give her time to answer.

'*She's* all right, but her dishwasher isn't. Menopause brain strikes again. Last night, our lovely Lorraine managed to put a whole Camembert cheese in the dishwasher instead of the fridge, Beth. And switched the thing on and went to bed. Now her entire house stinks of cheese, and as for the dishwasher ...'

She snorts and starts to cackle again. Lorraine rolls her eyes and turns to me. I'm grinning widely too now. Ruth's laugh is infectious.

'The whole bloody thing and everything in it is covered, Beth,' she says. 'And it's been through the drying cycle so it's all ... *hard* now. Like everything's been coated in cheesy plastic. Plates, cutlery ... I honestly might have to throw the whole dishwasher and everything in it away. How on earth am I going to get it all off? Honestly, don't have a menopause. It's sending me bonkers.'

'Oh, Lorraine!' I'm giggling too now. 'Too funny! Poor you!"

As I make myself a tea, Ruth regales us with one of her own many menopause-brain stories – something about putting her jewellery box in the fridge and a cooked chicken in her wardrobe. The laughter follows me down the corridor as I – feeling thankful that I'm still only forty and, therefore, hopefully have a few years yet before it's *me* sharing these stories – head to my office, pausing to wipe a smear off the smart brass sign on the door.

Beth Holland, Practice Manager

I've been here nearly three years now, and although it's madly busy – five GPs, three nurses, half a dozen receptionists and admin staff, and nearly eight thousand patients – I love it. The job, and these women – because they are mainly women – keep me going. On the tough days they make me smile, tell me I'm doing fine, remind me that life is too short to stress about payroll blips or IT issues. Today, although it's busy as always, turns out to be one of the better ones, and I'm humming tunelessly as I rush down the corridor again just after five.

'Fancy a quick drink, Beth? Ruth and I are heading up to Montpellier in a bit. Join us?'

Deborah, hearing me approaching, has popped her head out of her room, grey-blonde bob swinging around her face.

'Oh Debs, I'd love to, but I promised Dad I'd pop in this evening, and then the kids, you know ...'

I shrug, and she nods understandingly.

'We'll give you more notice next time. See you tomorrow, love.'

'See you. Enjoy. Have one for me. No, two. Have *two* for me.'

'Not a problem. Wouldn't do it for anyone else, mind.'

She winks and disappears back into her room, and I head for the car park. It won't be dark for nearly another hour but the sky is leaden and, while the morning was just wet, this evening is wet and windy, a sudden gust rolling a discarded Coke can across the slick concrete ahead of me and whipping a strand of hair across my face. I fumble for my car keys in the bag slung over my shoulder, and suddenly I see him out of the corner of my eye.

Again? Seriously? Oh, come on ...

I stop dead and push back my already-damp hair, trying to tuck it behind my ear. I feel a little wave of irritation. When it all began, I'd been wary, nervous, scared even. But then it seemed to stop again, and I'd almost forgotten about him. Almost. So if he's *back* ... I'm more than irritated now, I'm angry. What does he want, this weirdo who keeps turning up, hanging around? Has he nothing better to do than creep about, spying on me, following me? I turn, take a step towards the spot where he's standing, then blink. He's gone. It's raining harder now, heavy drops settling on my eyelashes, blurring my vision, and I stand still, my gaze sweeping across the almost-empty space. Where did he go? I can't see him; I can't see anybody. Only half a dozen cars remain, mine included. But no shadowy figures. Nobody watching me, lurking, waiting. Just my overactive imagination, playing tricks on me.

OK. Phew. Good.

I take a deep breath, look around one last time, and shiver. It's cold, and now I'm soaking wet. I need to get on. I climb into the car and start the engine.

Chapter 2

I'm still thinking about him though as I pull into the driveway at home an hour later, after popping in to see Dad. It was several months ago when I first began to get the feeling that someone was following me, that unseen eyes were watching me.

It was little things at first: a glimpse of a man on the other side of the road as I left the surgery, always in the same dark hooded jacket, but never approaching, never close enough for me to see him clearly, just standing there, statue-like, waiting until I got into my car and then scuttling away; the same silver Fiat appearing again and again, driving slowly past my house, following me into Sainsbury's car park – but again, never near enough for me to get a proper view of the driver. Now and again, I even thought he might be taking photos of me, because there was a phone or camera raised briefly in front of his face. Unsettled, I mentioned it to a few people – the girls at work, a couple of neighbours – wondering if maybe they'd noticed anyone hanging around too, but none of them had, and I could tell they thought I was imagining things.

'I mean, Cheltenham isn't a big place, not really, not when you think about it, is it?' Ruth said, when I confided in her in the staffroom one morning not long after it had started. 'You do tend to see the same people around. I see the same bloke passing my house with his black Labrador all the time. You worry too much, Beth. I haven't seen anyone hanging around. Nobody I'd be concerned about anyway.'

I nodded, somewhat reassured, but I still worried. As the weeks passed, though, I did try hard to convince myself that everyone was right and I *was* imagining it, because why would anyone want to follow *me*? The idea that I might have a stalker, some sort of crackpot secret admirer, is faintly ludicrous. I'm hardly a catch – a forty-year-old divorced mum of two, so frantically trying to divide her time between work, kids, and an elderly dad that she barely has time to drag a comb through her hair or dab on a bit of blusher. But still, every now and again, there he was, a figure on the periphery of my vision who seemed to melt away if I tried to get a closer look. I thought about marching over to confront him, to demand an explanation, but I couldn't pluck up the courage because ... what if I was wrong? What if I really *was* just being paranoid? And then, six weeks or so ago, it all stopped. He just seemed to disappear. No fleeting glimpses of hooded figures, no silver Fiats. And yet, today, there he was again, back in the car park. Except he wasn't. Or was he? I had been so sure, for a minute, but then ...

'MUM! ELOISE WON'T LET ME BORROW HER IPAD, MUM! TELL HER!'

I've only just pushed the front door open, key still in the

lock, and Finley is flinging himself at me, face contorted in frustration.

'Crikey, Finley, give me a second to get in out of the rain!' I say, and he pouts.

'But Muuuum ...'

'Shh.'

I close the door behind me, wipe my feet on the doormat, and drop my bag. Then I reach for him, ruffling his blond mop and pulling him in for a hug.

'Where is your sister? In her room?' I ask, and he nods, his head buried in my tummy.

'OK, well we'll go up and see her in a minute, but you need to learn to ask nicely, OK? You don't get anywhere if you're a grumpy little pup all the time, do you? Come on, I need to let Robin go first.'

I drop a kiss onto the top of his head and release him, and he follows, still muttering darkly, as I head into the kitchen where Robin is at the sink, wiping down the draining board. The room is warm with a delicious smell of cooked sausages in the air. She turns and smiles.

'Hi Beth. Sorry about the grump. He was fine until he decided he wanted to play that panda game he's obsessed with and Eloise told him she needed the iPad for her homework.'

'Oh gosh, don't worry, I'll sort him out in a minute. Go, Robin. Sorry I'm a bit late, I had to call in to see Dad and the traffic is dreadful. Not that that will bother you today, of course, you crazy woman.'

She's folding the dishcloth neatly, her grin widening.

'Nope. Running today. I know it's a bit damp but hey, there's no such thing as bad weather, right? Just the wrong clothes.'

She's a bit mad, Robin. She's my 'cleaner slash childminder', and she's definitely a bit of a funny one. Nice, obviously, and super capable and reliable or I wouldn't have hired her; the kids love her, but she's a bit ... a bit stand-offish sometimes, I suppose. Never reveals much about her private life, or her past. I mean, that's fine; she doesn't have to tell me everything, but I don't even know if she's in a relationship, has kids (I don't think so, as she's never mentioned any), or exactly how old she is, for example. Mid-fifties probably, lean and fit, with short, dark-blonde hair, and her skin is always pink and healthy and make-up free. And – and *this* is why I think she's a bit mad, because I'm slightly exercise-phobic myself – even though she lives a good five miles away, right across town, she quite often *runs* to and from work. If the weather's really terrible, or she's short of time, she'll drive her little yellow Smart car which delights Finley, who, at seven years old, has recently started reading Enid Blyton and thinks she's borrowed it from Noddy. But at least twice a week she'll turn up at 8am, red-faced and happy in her running gear, a backpack of fresh clothes slung over her shoulders, having spent an hour bounding across town and out to our place in Prestbury. Mad, right?

She's retrieved her backpack from its usual spot by the patio doors now and is heading for the downstairs loo to change out of the jeans, ankle boots, and jumper she's been wearing during the day.

'Oh, and Jacob popped in for a minute to drop off Eloise's trainers, the ones she left at his on Tuesday,' she calls over her shoulder. 'She needs them for school in the morning, I think. He said he'll see you tomorrow.'

'OK, great. Thanks, Robin.'

'Muuuum ...'

Finley is still at my elbow, pulling at my sleeve now.

'Darling, please, just give me one minute. Run up to your room and choose a book for your bedtime story later. I promise I'll be straight up as soon as I've made a cup of tea, and then we'll go and see your sister and see if we can borrow that iPad for half an hour, OK?'

He pauses for a moment, squinting up at me, considering my proposal. Then:

'OK!'

He scampers off and I give a small sigh of relief, yawn, and cross the room to put the kettle on. Robin's left the place spotless as usual, and for the umpteenth time I thank my lucky stars – or guardian angel or whatever other celestial being might just be out there looking after me – that it was she who answered the rather desperate plea I stuck on the noticeboard in the shop down the road about six months after Jacob and I split up.

Cleaner/childcare help needed for busy single mother.
School runs, after-school care, and light housekeeping duties Monday to Friday.
Please call Beth on the number below.

Days later, Robin was sitting in my kitchen, and twenty-four hours after that I'd hired her. It had been a miracle she'd seen the notice at all, living as she did across town, but she'd been in Prestbury visiting a friend and had popped into the village shop on her way home. She'd recently left her previous employer in The Park after the twins she'd been caring for had gone off to secondary school and didn't need her anymore. The reference she'd brought with her had been glowing, and when I called later to double check, the children's mother had urged me to snap her up.

'Honestly, I miss her so much,' she said. 'You'll have happy kids and a sparkling home. I'm jealous!'

She'd been right, and having Robin there every day to take them to and collect them from school, then feed them and supervise homework until I get in from work has given Finley and Eloise back some of the stability they lost when their father and I split. Eighteen months on, I do indeed (iPad-sharing dramas aside) have happy kids and a sparkling home, and although I couldn't exactly say we're close friends, Robin's certainly become someone I like, trust, and rely on. OK, so there have been, if I'm honest, one or two little ... well, I'll call them *incidents*, but I've let those go. They were minor, and not worth losing her over, and anyway, they were a while ago now. People like Robin are hard to find and I don't intend to part company with her any time soon – not if I can help it.

I drop a teabag into a mug and pour in the boiling water, yawning again. I'm not sure why, but I haven't been sleeping well recently; my nights are restless, my dreams more often nightmares. Nightmares like the ones I used to have years ago, way back in my teens.

Is it him, Mr Stalker, who's making me feel so strange? Is that why the nightmares are back? It's been so long ...

I stare into my mug, wondering, then jump as a voice shouts:

'Bye Beth! See you tomorrow!'

Robin is waving at me from the kitchen doorway.

'Oh gosh! Sorry, didn't mean to startle you,' she says.

I laugh and wave a hand dismissively.

'Oh, it's OK, I was in my own little world there for a minute! Bye, Robin. Thanks so much, as always. Have a nice evening!'

'You too.'

She smiles, waves again, and is gone. I turn back to my drink, fishing the teabag out, squishing it against the side of the mug, and depositing it in the food caddy that sits beside the sink. My heart is racing. How ridiculous. It was only Robin. What's wrong with me?

I walk slowly out into the hallway and make my way upstairs, bracing myself for the inevitable row I'm about to have with my strong-willed ten-year-old daughter when I try to persuade her to hand over the iPad to her little brother, and having a stern word with myself. Everything is fine. I'm fine, work is fine, the kids are fine. So I need to shake this nagging unease that keeps sweeping over me. There's no reason for it. I probably just need a hot bath and an early night – a decent sleep. Whatever it is, it'll pass, like everything does.

I take a deep, steadying breath and yet, even as I push open the door of my daughter's bedroom, I can feel that tight little knot of tension in my stomach growing. Because it's not working. No matter how sternly I talk to myself, how firmly I tell myself everything is fine, I can't entirely supress this creeping feeling of … *dread*. The clawing sensation that something that happened a long, long time ago, something I thought I'd managed to bury forever, might not be buried after all.

Chapter 3

'Do you think that poor woman is OK? It's freezing. Is there nothing we can do?'

I'm peering out of the window of the surgery waiting room. Across the street, in the doorway of the building adjacent to our car park, an old lady is sitting wrapped in a blanket, a big wheelie suitcase tucked in beside her. She has long, straggly grey hair and a brown felt hat pulled down low over her eyes, and she's reading a battered paperback, gloved fingers shaking slightly as she turns the pages. She started using the doorway – that of a closed-down Indonesian restaurant – as a daytime reading spot a few weeks ago, spending a few hours at a time there before neatly folding her blanket and trundling slowly off again, leaving a little nest of cardboard behind her. It's probably a lucrative spot for her – I've seen more than one of our patients stopping to drop a few coins in her lap as they arrive and depart – but it hurts my heart to see her there, alone in the cold.

'Nadia? I took her over a coffee earlier.'

Ruth is behind her reception desk, resplendent in red animal print today and sorting through some files. The waiting room is empty; the lunchtime lull before afternoon surgery begins at two.

'Nadia?' I say. 'Is that her name?'

Ruth looks up at me.

'Yep. She's a bit of a sweetie, actually. She doesn't say much, but I've started popping over with a hot drink and a few biscuits every time she turns up and I've built up a bit of rapport with her. She's staying in that shelter off the High Street, but they have to be out between breakfast and teatime, bless her.'

'That's pretty tough in this weather.'

'It is. But at least that doorway's quite deep, out of the wind. And she's got a hot water bottle, which helps. I top that up for her too, if she needs it.'

'That's kind of you. Poor woman. What's her story, do you know? How come she's homeless? She must be, what? Seventyish?'

I turn to look at Nadia again. She's buried even deeper in her blanket now, just her nose peeking out, the book close to her face.

'Probably. And I don't know,' says Ruth. 'Didn't like to ask really. She seems healthy enough at least. It's so sad though, isn't it? To be homeless and alone at her age. Well, at any age really.'

I turn away from the window with a sigh.

'It really is. I'm so grateful that Dad is safe and warm and looked after. He was in great form just now.'

'Oh good. Give him my love next time you see him. Tell him I'll pop in one day early next week, take him a slice of cheesecake. I'm planning a baking session on Sunday.'

'He'd love that. He always did love your cheesecake. Actually, so do I. You'll be bringing some into work too, right?'

Ruth grins.

'Of course.'

I smile back and head for my office. I called in to see Dad at lunchtime today so I could get home a little earlier; Jacob, my ex, is taking the kids tonight and Barbara and Brenda, my next-door neighbours and friends, are coming round for drinks and a takeaway, a Friday night treat. I try to see my father at least three or four times a week, but I don't always manage it. He understands, but it doesn't stop me feeling guilty. At eighty, he's been in a care home for nearly a year now, since he had a major stroke, but even before that he'd been struggling. He's got diabetic retinopathy, a complication of his diabetes which has gradually claimed more and more of his eyesight. He's not blind, not totally, but his vision is pretty poor these days, and that combined with the partial leg and arm paralysis caused by the stroke finally made it impossible for him to live alone. I considered, briefly, moving him in with us, but his need for full-time care just made it too difficult, and anyway, he refused point blank.

'I know a couple of lads who are about to move into Holly Tree anyway,' he said – his words were slightly slurred, the stroke having affected his face too, but only a little – when he first mooted the idea of going to see the newly built residential and nursing care home on Lansdown Road. 'Pretty fancy, apparently. Got a bar and everything.'

He'd winked and smiled his newly lopsided smile, and I'd felt a surge of relief, then immediately felt guilty again. But when we did the tour, we discovered it was indeed pretty fancy: a state-of-the-art modern building with a bar and restaurant, swimming pool and gym, games room and library. It was expensive yes, but Dad, a former accountant, had always been thrifty and had enough money put aside to cover the fees for the first eighteen months or so. After that, the proceeds from the sale of his house, a tidy three-bed in Shurdington which sold within days of going on the market, will hopefully be enough to pay for his care for as long as he needs it.

Today, when I popped in just after one, I found him sitting in his wheelchair by the window in the bar, nursing a glass of red wine in his good hand and snorting with laughter at something his friend Billy, another ex-accountant who was sitting in the armchair opposite, was telling him.

'Well, you two look like you're having a nice Friday,' I said. 'Wine at lunch? I'm jealous.'

Dad turned to look at me, squinting, trying to focus on my face, then grinned.

'Beth. Hello, love. Sit down. How are you?'

He looked neat and groomed as usual, wearing a dark-brown cardigan done up to the neck with his thin grey hair recently brushed. He may be almost blind, but he still has pride in his appearance.

'I'm OK,' I said. 'Tired. Ready for the weekend. Are you all right? And hi, Billy. How are you?'

Billy, a kind-faced old man in a blue checked shirt, raised his glass of what looked like gin and tonic and nodded.

'Grand, lass, grand.'

'I'm all right, love,' Dad said. 'We're going in for lunch at quarter to. Billy and I were just reminiscing about the old days. Some of the stories ...'

He laughed again, and I smiled. He's frail, but he's content here, I can always see that. We chatted idly for a few more minutes, Billy joining in to regale us with another half-forgotten memory of some notorious local businessman and his attempts at money laundering. My mind drifted a little, the overheated room making me sleepy, and random thoughts tumbled over each other.

Indian or Thai tonight?

Did I remember to put the bubbly in the fridge?

I need to put some clean pyjamas in Eloise's overnight bag.

Was that really him again last night in the car park, or was I imagining it? Who the hell is he? What does he want?

A shiver ran through me, despite the warmth of the room. I sat up straighter in my chair, trying to concentrate on Dad and Billy's conversation.

I really need to stop thinking about him. *Forget him, Beth.*

I've never mentioned him to Dad; it'll only worry him, and he'll try and make me go to the police, and what's the point, really? The man has never tried to approach me or harm me, after all. He's just been ... well, *there*.

'I was saying to Billy earlier about what we talked about the other day ... about it being Alice's sixtieth birthday next month. Seems strange to think of your mother as an older woman, doesn't it?' Dad said suddenly.

'I know,' I said. We looked at each other in silence for a moment, then I said: 'Well, wherever she is, I hope she has a good one. Sixty's a big deal.'

He shrugged, then grimaced.

'Not as big a deal as eighty.'

'True.'

I smiled, then leaned over to squeeze his hand. Dad turned eighty recently, with a Saturday afternoon knees-up here in the home, tea and cake and a few tots of whiskey, and a sing-song in the bar. The twenty-year age gap between him and Mum could well have been one of the reasons she left, I've sometimes thought on the rare occasions I've allowed myself to think about it. I could be wrong though – that's probably just me, as an adult woman, trying to make excuses for her. But a twenty-year age gap *is* big, isn't it, especially when you're young? Who knows, though; it's not something Dad and I have really discussed, not ever. She was unhappy, she cried a lot, and then she left. It was what it was; we suffered through it and then just got on with it, me and him. He was fifty when she went, she was just thirty, and already mother of a ten-year-old, me. Married at eighteen, to a man who was already nearly forty. My memories of her are hazy now – a vague image in my head of blonde hair, smiley eyes, the smell of the coconut-oil body lotion she loved, the tiny triple star tattoo on her collar bone.

One star for her, one for Dad, one for me.

She must have loved him once, must have loved me, to get that tattoo, mustn't she? Or did she know, even as she sat there in the tattooist's chair, the needle pushing colour into her skin, the smell of antiseptic in her nostrils ... did she know even then that she was going to leave us? Was the tattoo enough, a souvenir, a memory, of the family she no longer wanted to spend her life with? Over the years that followed – those dreadful teenage years when being without a mother led me to dark places I no longer allow myself to remember – I painted a picture of her in my mind, a picture of a free spirit, wild and beautiful, too wild in the end for marriage and children and suburbia, a woman who could not be tamed. But they were the romantic musings of a teenager, for I don't know why she went at all in truth, not really.

I have only one photograph of my mother, Alice, on her wedding day in the late 70s, Dad dapper in white trousers and a navy blazer, Mum in flowing lace with flowers in her hair. In a rare fit of rage – Dad *never* gets angry – he threw the rest of the photos, every album, every framed picture, on a bonfire a few months after she went, once it became clear she was gone for good, that it wasn't just a temporary thing, something that could be fixed. But I squirrelled the wedding photo away, slipping it under my mattress. I would take it out to look at, to weep over, when I was alone in my room at night, and run my finger across her face, whispering: *'Please come home, Mummy. Please, please come home,'* over and over and over again.

She didn't of course. The emptiness was so ... so *big*, at first. It got smaller over time, slowly shrank away over the years until I could barely feel it anymore, but now and again, even decades later and usually when I'm least expecting it, it returns, just briefly. That void, that pain.

'What're you doing tonight, love? Hitting the town?'

Dad was speaking to me again and I dragged my attention

back to him, to my father, the one person who's always been there for me. I smiled.

'Girls' night in,' I said. 'Jacob's taking the kids and Brenda and Barbara are coming round. An Indian probably, and a couple of bottles of wine. That will do nicely.'

'Sounds good. Enjoy, love. You deserve it.'

Now, back in my office, I think again of Nadia, the poor homeless woman, then I sit down at my desk and try to count my blessings. My dad is safe and happy and looked after, the kids are doing well, I have a secure job that I love, great friends and colleagues. I'm even on amicable terms with my ex. There's nothing to worry about. I tap my keyboard to wake up my computer and get back to work, but as the afternoon drags on one niggly, persistent thought repeatedly wriggles its way to the forefront of my brain.

Everything might be fine now. But that's only because nobody knows what happened back then. What if that changed?

That would be the end of everything, wouldn't it?

Chapter 4

'Right, got everything? I'm not going to get a call in two hours' time asking me to drive over with your nightie or your book or something else crucially important?'

I poke Eloise gently in the tummy and she squirms and slaps my hand away.

'Get off, Mum! No, I haven't forgotten anything this time. Check if you don't believe me.'

She points at her little rose-gold weekend case which is still open on the hall floor, and I shake my head.

'Nope, I believe you. Thousands of mums wouldn't, however.'

I grin at her and she rolls her eyes, then grins back and kneels down to zip up the case. I watch her, my heart twisting a little as it always does when she and Finley have to leave me. She's growing up so quickly, my little girl, fine, dark-brown hair swishing around her slender shoulders, long lashes like her dad's. She's only ten, not quite at the stage where she wants to start putting make-up on her smooth olive skin or punching holes in her soft earlobes, but I know those days are getting closer and I dread them. Finley, who's now trudging down the stairs, dragging his own bag behind him – THUMP! THUMP! THUMP! – is as like me in appearance as Eloise is like her father: blonder, paler, rounder of face.

'OK you two, let's get out of here. Give your mother some peace.'

Jacob is standing in the doorway and I drag my gaze from my children – *our* children – and I smile at him. Over his shoulder, I can see Crystal sitting in the front seat of his blue Land Rover which is parked in the driveway, long black hair pulled into a neat knot on top of her head. She's still in her business suit – he must have picked her up from work – and she's holding her phone to her ear, nodding, her face solemn. I meet her eye, raise a hand, and she waves back, flashing her perfect white teeth. We're OK now, Jacob and Crystal and I. Not close friends, but amicable, cordial, all three of us putting Finley and Eloise's happiness first. It took a while, but it's as good as it can be under the circumstances.

It was all so clichéd really: Jacob and I started dating at university, got engaged the day we graduated, and were married a couple of years later, both of us just twenty-four. Too young. We did, at least, wait a while before we had children, building our careers, buying a house. I had Eloise when I was thirty, Jacob's landscape gardening business finally making enough money for me to take extended maternity leave, and Finley was born three years later. On his fifth birthday, as we tried to restore order to the chaos our son and sixteen over-excited classmates had wrought on our living room, as I picked party popper streamers off the pot plants and wiped jammy fingerprints from the cushions, Jacob told me he'd been having an affair with one of his clients and was leaving me.

Our marriage was over, just like that. My happy bubble was popped like the deflated balloons lying limply on the sofa, my world falling to pieces like the cake trampled into the carpet. Of course there'd been signs – many of them, in the previous months – and more arguments. Jacob had worked late or at weekends more and more frequently, and there had been a general sense, unvoiced but felt by both of us, that we'd slowly grown apart as we'd grown up. But when the end came, it left me reeling. Crystal Williams, the woman now sitting in my driveway, waiting to spend the weekend with my children, is a beautiful thirty-five-year-old barrister with creamy caramel skin, a stunning home in Charlton Kings, and the most extensive shoe collection of anyone I know.

I should hate her – she shagged, and eventually stole, my husband as he worked on a three-month garden redesign for her, after all – and at first I did, with a passion. But the hatred slowly dissipated, and it has, miraculously, now gone completely. They're still together, she and Jacob, happy and settled in her gorgeous house, and the kids ... well, I'm still loath to say they *love* her, but I think they do, just a little. They fell for her accent first (she's originally from Barbados, and speaks, they say "*just* like Rihanna, Mum!"). But she's also kind to them, generous but not in an ostentatious or over-the-top way and, although she apparently has no desire to have children of her own, she has willingly accepted my offspring into her life and home as often as they want to be there, as part of Jacob, the man she genuinely seems to love.

A few months after the split she rang me, asked if we could meet, told me how ashamed she was, but also how in love. She was so humble, so deeply apologetic, so bloody *nice*, that despite myself I could feel the burning anger I felt towards her for hastening the end of our marriage begin to cool almost immediately. After all, if it hadn't been her, it would have been somebody else, eventually; it might even have been *me* who'd had the affair, who'd left first. That's the truth of it, and there's no point in pretending otherwise.

So now we rub along just ... fine. It's fine. I'm still single, of course, but that's fine too. For now, at least.

'Bye Mum! See you on Sunday.'

Finley has wrapped his arms around my waist, face upturned. I kiss his forehead and squeeze him tightly until he yelps and squirms from my grasp. Eloise takes his place and I kiss her too and then wave them off, the Land Rover pulling slowly out of the driveway just as Brenda and Barbara appear at the gate. They pause to wave and smile, then walk up the drive to where I'm still standing by the open front door. Brenda is clutching a bottle of cava and Barbara is holding a covered baking tray, which I very much hope holds some of her divine chocolate brownies.

'Evening! Brownies!' she says.

'Yesss!' I say. 'You never let me down! Come in, come in.'

I shut the door and we head for the kitchen, both of them talking at once.

'I'm ready for a glass of that bubbly, Brenda. Crack it open!'

'I'm starving. What shall we order tonight? Oh, Beth, the Kings Head is going to start doing a weekly quiz night next month, have you heard? The Busy Bees *have* to enter. We'd be brilliant, don't you think?'

I laugh, open the cupboard, and take out three glasses, then relieve Barbara of her tray. It's still warm to the touch and the contents smell mouth-watering.

'Indian? I'm easy though. We'll order straight away, shall we? I'm hungry too. And yes, a pub quiz sounds fun. Haven't done one in years. You're on for a Busy Bees team if I can get Robin to babysit.'

The Busy Bees is the name Brenda came up with for the three of us – Beth, Barbara, and Brenda – not long after we all met. As I stand at my front door, looking out, Barbara lives next door on the left and Brenda on the right. They're both a bit older – many of my friends are older than me these days, which doesn't bother me at all, although some would, I suspect, look for a deep psychological meaning behind the fact that I'm drawn to women of around my absent mother's age – and both are single, and we all just ... well, *clicked,* I suppose. They're kind, and good fun, and our regular get-togethers are always a hoot. We own three of just eight properties in The Acre, a small, new development just off the top of Prestbury High Street, where I moved after Jacob and I sold our marital home on the other side of town after the split. Brenda moved in just three weeks after I did, and Barbara about a month after that, so we've all been here a year or so now, and I love it. The house is spacious and bright and ultra-modern, four bedrooms and an open-plan kitchen and living area; outside, it has a smart paved driveway and a small but pretty south-facing garden, and it's perfect for me and the kids. Prestbury's great too, just two miles from Cheltenham town centre and a short drive from work, but with its own mini supermarket, a couple of hair salons, three pubs and, of course, the world-famous racecourse just down the road.

Now I smile as my friends settle themselves on the high-backed bar stools around my kitchen island, clinking glasses. Brenda, who will turn sixty this year, is sporting her trademark red-framed spectacles, her short stylishly cut grey blonde hair with its long fringe sweeping across her forehead. She manages a boutique in the trendy part of town called The Suffolks, one of those elegant little shops full of cashmere wraps and floaty silk dresses – lovely but way out of my price range. Barbara, who's always cagey about her age but who I suspect is a little younger than Brenda, is a hippy chick with long red hair and is fond of chunky jumpers she knits herself. She teaches knitting too, in courses she runs at the adult education centre in town, and although she keeps threatening to buy me some needles and wool and give me a free lesson, I've resisted so far. The jumpers are nice though. She's wearing one now – bright yellow with a navy zigzag around the neckline, teamed with a long denim skirt. I'm in black velvet joggers and a matching hoodie, my shoulder-length blonde hair pulled back into a messy ponytail. We're a mismatched trio style-wise, but none of us cares about that; it's our differences that make us interesting to each other, as Brenda once said.

We order an Indian and drink more cava as we wait for it to arrive, catching each other up on our news, although I don't have much – another busy week at work, Eloise landing a major role in the school's Easter play, Finley falling out of a tree in Pittville Park *again* but managing not to break anything this time. Brenda has been fending off the attentions of a would-be suitor, a gentleman in his seventies who's been dropping into the boutique on an almost daily basis, bringing her roses and offering to take her to jazz concerts ('I mean, he's too old, for a start, and I don't even *like* jazz. Why would he think I like jazz? It's just *noise*,' she says.) Meanwhile Barbara is trying to decide if getting a dog would be a good idea, and debating the respective virtues of poodles ('They're really clever, and they don't shed hair, and they don't need *too* much walking, apparently,') and pugs ('They actually quite like being indoors, I think, so it wouldn't mind me staying in knitting. Although they often snore. I'm not sure I could handle that; it would remind me of an ex ...').

Brenda has just launched into a story about a customer who tried to return a pair of palazzo trousers which she claimed didn't fit, but which had very clearly been worn ('There was this huge *stain*, and they stank of cigarettes. I mean, honestly ...') when the house phone rings.

'Probably the curry. Why can they *never* find us?' I say, as I jump off my stool and cross into the living area to answer the call.

'Hello,' I say breezily. I feel a little drunk already after two large glasses of cava on an empty stomach. There's a second or two of silence on the line, then a male voice says:

'Oh, hi. Is that Beth Holland?'

'It is, yes.'

I roll my eyes, waiting for the inevitable: *'I'm just trying to find your house. Can you tell me exactly where in Prestbury you are, please?'* Instead, there's another moment or two of silence, and then:

'Formerly Beth Armstrong?'

'Yes,' I say automatically. Then I pause. Why on earth would the curry delivery man be asking me my maiden name?

'Why are you asking me that? Who is this?' I demand sharply.

There's another couple of seconds of silence on the line and then, abruptly, the call is cut off. The dial tone sounds in my ear. I put the handset back in its holder and stare at it.

'What's up? Are they lost again?' calls Barbara.

I walk slowly back across the room, frowning.

'No, it wasn't the curry. I don't know who it was, actually. It was kinda weird.'

I sit down again and pick up my glass.

'Weird? Weird how?' asks Brenda.

'Well, some guy asked me if I was Beth Holland and then if my maiden name was Armstrong. And when I said it was – and don't ask me why I did; blame this stuff ...'—I wave my glass in the air—'When I said yes, he just put the phone down.'

'Hmmm. That is a bit odd,' says Barbara. 'I wonder ...'

BZZZZZZZ.

The doorbell rings and my friends let out a simultaneous whoop.

'Curry! Yesss!'

'I'll go,' Brenda says. She jumps up and Barbara turns to me.

'Shall I get the plates out?'

They've both clearly forgotten about the phone call already and I smile, trying to subdue my feeling of unease.

'Yes, you get the plates. You know where they are. I'll grab some cutlery,' I say.

I get up and head for the cutlery drawer, but my mind is racing.

Who was that? Why ask that and immediately hang up? What did he want? But ... well, there are plenty of organisations out there who know my maiden name, aren't there? My bank, car insurance company, credit card people ... so, probably nothing sinister, right? Maybe just a cold call from someone selling extra insurance or something, that got cut off? It's just that ...

I grab a handful of knives and forks and turn to see Brenda back in the kitchen brandishing a large brown paper bag, a delicious spicy aroma already wafting towards me.

'It smells amazing. Let's eat!' she says.

I smile and nod, but inside my stomach is flipping. My appetite is gone and my anxiety is spiralling again. OK, maybe I'm putting two and two together and making seventeen. Maybe there's a perfectly innocent explanation for that phone call. But suddenly it's all too much. As my friends chatter away, dishing out the food, I take a couple of deep breaths, trying to regain control, but I'm struggling. The fear is taking over, threatening to consume me, the fear that it's about to rear its head again, the thing I try never to think about, the thing I try to keep hidden in a tiny box in the far recesses of my mind. The thing I've tried to bury so deep it can never escape. Now I'm starting to think I'm *not* being paranoid after all.

I'm becoming convinced that finally, after all these years, someone's coming for me.

Someone who knows what I did.

Chapter 5

Creak, creak, creak.

I hear the sound and I know instantly that this is a dream. A dream I've had many, many times before.

No, not a dream. A nightmare.

I know this is a nightmare, just a nightmare, not real, but I still can't make it stop. I've never been able to make it stop, never been able to wake myself up once it starts.

And so I stand there, under the old wooden beams in the half-light, listening to the noise.

Creak, creak, creak.

The bedroom is cold. My breath hangs in the air in front of me, like little puffs of ghostly candyfloss. But I'm not cold; I'm sweating. My armpits are damp as the panic rises inside me again. My heart hammers painfully against the wall of my chest.

And yet, I know this isn't real, that I'm not really here in this room.

In fact, despite being able to see it in all its horrific detail in my nightmares, I've never been in this room.

And so I do what I do every time. I tell myself that

everything is OK, that I'll wake up in a minute, that this isn't happening.

That this never happened.

And for a moment, or two or three, I'll believe it, and great waves of relief will come crashing over me. My heartrate will slow, my muscles will start to relax, and the sweat begin to dry on my skin. But the relief won't last.

Because then I'll wake up.

And as I lie there alone in the dark, I'll remember again, slowly, agonisingly.

I'll remember that it is real after all.

It was the night that changed everything.

Every choice we make in life has consequences, doesn't it?

Chapter 6

'Let's just go up to Lonely Tree, then turn around, OK?'

It's ten o'clock on Saturday morning, and I'm up on Cleeve Hill with Ruth and Deborah from work. It's a semi-regular thing for us on a weekend morning – my few-times-a-month attempt to take a little exercise. This involves a brisk walk up the hill – the highest point in the Cotswolds – then some restorative (and probably benefit-cancelling) coffee and cake at the little hotel on the way back home. This is my happy place though, a thousand acres of limestone grassland criss-crossed with footpaths; the views are breathtaking. It's common land up here, with hundreds of sheep and cattle during the grazing season, but right now in early March it's just walkers – many with dogs – runners, and the occasional mountain bike or horse. We take many different routes, the three of us, during our weekend walks, but we often end up at Lonely Tree. Some call it Lone Tree, or Single Beech, but I prefer Lonely Tree because it really is lonely; a solitary, twisted, windswept beech tree, the highest tree in Gloucestershire, surrounded by a memorial wall with plaques dedicated to those who loved the hill.

'Race you to the top!'

Deborah is off, her long legs powering across the scrubby grass. Ruth and I roll our eyes and follow at a more leisurely pace. It's steep though, and if I'm honest I'm a little hungover from last night – a tad too much cava consumed – but I grit my teeth and keep moving. I've put on a few pounds recently. My size fourteen jeans are tight across my tummy and I know I need the exercise today – for my body as well as for my head. The exertion is helping me to forget the gnawing anxieties of last night and the nightmares that visited me yet again in the early hours. There's a chill in the air, but we've been walking uphill for the past fifteen minutes and I'm sweating, too warm now in my old navy puffer coat.

'Phew!'

Finally, Ruth and I are at the tree; Deborah is smugly waiting for us. We pause for a few minutes, reading some of the plaques.

1950-2018
John Evans, who walked his dogs here for 25 years.
Love you always, forget you never.

In loving memory of Ellen McDuff, 1944-2016.
Here forever, enjoying the view.

'I want one of these, one day. Make a note of that, Ruth, will you? You're the organised one,' I say.

'What do you want it to say? In memory of Beth Holland,

who used this hill as a hangover cure and an excuse to eat cake?' asks Deborah, and we all snort with laughter.

'Something like that,' I say. 'Come on, let's sit for a bit.'

There's a bench nearby and we slump onto it. There's silence for a few moments, as we take in the view.

'Rain coming. Not for a while though,' says Ruth. She's right; there are dark clouds gathering in the distance, but the sky above us is still a clear baby-blue.

'So how was last night? Have fun with the Bees?' asks Deborah. She's tied her barely shoulder-length bob back into a tiny ponytail at the nape of her neck for the ascent, and now she pulls at the hairband to release her hair, letting it swing round her face.

'Yeah, it was nice,' I say. *Apart from the phone call*, I think, but I don't say it.

'We should organise something for all five of us one of these days. A girls' night out. Fancy it?' I add.

'Definitely,' says Deborah, and Ruth nods too.

'That would be fun.'

It makes me happy that my friends all get on so well. I invited Deborah and Ruth, along with a few others from the surgery, to a house-warming drinks party a couple of months after I moved in last year when the decorating was mostly finished and I finally felt the place was ready to welcome visitors. As my immediate neighbours, I'd popped invitations through Brenda and Barbara's doors too, more to be polite than anything; I'd only spoken to Brenda a few times when we'd seen each other in the street, and Barbara had only moved in a fortnight or so earlier. That night though, we chatted like long-lost friends, and long after everyone else had gone home, the three of us, plus Ruth and Deborah, were still gathered around my kitchen island, drinking wine, polishing off the last of the cheese and crackers, and laughing until our stomachs ached.

As I've said before, it is maybe a *little* odd that all of my closest friends are twenty years older than me, but it's just the way it is. I do have younger friends, of course: old uni friends, although we've largely lost touch these days as a result of careers and families scattering us across the UK and indeed the world; there are 'mum' friends, parents of Eloise and Finley's schoolmates; and 'couple' friends Jacob and I made when we were together. But they're all ... more *acquaintances*, I suppose. We get together for coffee, discuss sleepovers and school events, have nights at the cinema or the odd dinner, but I've never really felt that I can talk to them, not about the things that really matter. I suppose that for years I had Jacob for all that – my teenage sweetheart, my husband, my best friend. I didn't need anyone else. When my marriage fell apart, it was Ruth and Deborah at work who saved me, who took me under their motherly wings, and helped me put my life back together. They're both married: Ruth is on her second marriage after her first husband died young, and Deborah, 'a late bloomer', in her own words, didn't meet her soulmate until she was forty-five. She doesn't have kids; Ruth has one son, now in his thirties and living in Canada. The three of us were already friends – they'd both joined the practice not long after I did and we'd hit it off straight away – but during those long, sad months they almost took on the role of surrogate mums too, doling out hugs and advice (and cake and wine, of course, on occasion) with unending patience and kindness.

Brenda and Barbara, who only knew me after the worst was over, have been equally kind, both more than happy to pop round and watch the kids at short notice if I need to go out, despite neither being mums themselves. Brenda, she confided once during a leisurely Sunday lunch last summer, was unable to conceive with her late husband, although I never got the impression that this was a great sadness in her life, rather something to be accepted and moved on from. Barbara, who's had several long-term female partners but never married, simply shrugged when I asked her if she'd ever wanted to be a mum.

'It was never a priority for me, no. And it all seemed so complicated, you know, with two women? I mean, I know nowadays there are lots of options, but you know ... I'm fine with it,' she smiled.

'How's Robin these days?' asks Ruth now. 'No more ... *odd* incidents?'

'She's great,' I say. 'No, nothing odd. I don't know, I probably read too much into that, you know? She's invaluable, to be honest. Can't imagine what I'd do if she ever left.'

'Good. Well, let's hope she won't then,' says Ruth. 'Right, shall we head back down? I need coffee.'

We stand up and start the descent, following the winding path that will take us back down to where we've parked our cars. Ruth and Deborah start chatting about some work thing and I tune out, my mind drifting back to one of the 'odd' incidents Ruth mentioned. The first was on a Monday morning a few months after Robin started working for me. I'd got halfway to work when I realised I'd left some files at home – stuff I'd been working on over the weekend – so I'd rushed home again to pick them up. I pounded up the stairs to my bedroom, which doubles as a home office with a small desk fitting snugly into an alcove by the window. When I burst in, breathless, Robin, who was wearing headphones to listen to music as she cleaned, was standing at the desk. She had a sheaf of papers in her hands and was leafing through them. When I tapped her on the shoulder she jumped so violently and whirled round to face me so abruptly that I almost lost my footing, staggering backwards.

'Beth! I ... sorry, I was just tidying these ... Is everything OK?'

She pulled the headphones from her ears and waved the papers vaguely at me, her cheeks glowing, then turned and put them back on the desk.

'Sorry,' she said again. 'I ... I wasn't ...'

'It's OK, Robin. Sorry to have sneaked up on you like that. I didn't mean to frighten you. I've just popped back to pick up some files. I forgot them and I need them today,' I said.

'Oh! Right, well ... I'll get out of your way. I'm pretty much done in here anyway,' she said, and, picking up her duster and polish, she scuttled from the room.

I stared after her for a moment, wondering. Had she really just been tidying up the papers, or was she flicking through them as I'd thought when I first walked into the room? I picked the pages up and examined them. Nothing particularly interesting – a few bills, confirmation from the council that I'd paid my green waste bin subscription. And to be fair, if I were cleaning somebody's house, I'd probably glance at papers left lying on a desk too. It's human nature, isn't it? She *did* have to move them to dust, after all. And so I'd let it go, forgotten about it. There'd been a couple of other things though, after that ... similar incidents when I'd walked into a room to find her opening drawers she had no need to open, when I noticed that my passport was on a different shelf in my bedside cupboard, and that documents were out of order in my in-tray. I'd let those go too. Robin was a treasure too valuable to lose over a little bit of nosiness, curiosity, whatever you wanted to call it. I needed her.

Half an hour later we're settled at a window table at Sunrise Lodge, the small hotel perched on the side of the hill, its coffee lounge famous for its homemade cakes. It's busy this morning. A steady stream of hikers and dog walkers wanders in and out, and the staff weave their way between tables, heavily laden trays held high. I've plumped for a slice of cheesecake, Ruth's gone for carrot cake, and the waiter has just put an enormous piece of Victoria sponge down in front of Deborah, vanilla buttercream oozing from its middle. It's making me wish I'd ordered that too, now.

When we arrived, I told the girls that today was my treat, only to realise when we sat down that I'd forgotten my purse, credit cards, the lot. So much for telling myself everything is fine. My head is so messed up at the moment it's a wonder I'm not leaving the house in my pyjamas. I can't say that though, even to my friends, so I just roll my eyes and apologise profusely for being such an airhead.

Ruth reaches over and pats my arm.

'Shush, it's fine. You've just got a lot on your mind, that's all. Work and the kids and everything else. You just need to chill a bit.'

Deborah nods.

'You've been more stressed than usual lately, Beth. Thinking someone's following you and all that stuff? Have you thought about talking to someone, maybe? Someone professional, I mean? I know some great counsellors. Just one or two sessions would probably be enough to help you with some relaxation techniques. What do you think?'

She picks up her cake and takes a big bite.

'Yum,' she mumbles, and licks a blob of jam off her lower lip.

I shrug.

'Maybe. I *have* been quite stressed. I'll think about it. Thanks.'

I probably won't, though. I've had counselling before, you see. Back then, back when the bad things happened. And it was fine – good even. It helped. But now?

They'd ask me to explain, wouldn't they? They'd try to get to the root of what's making me so anxious. It's what they do. And I can't do that, not now. I can't talk to anyone about that.

'I'll be fine,' I say. 'I've got the house to myself today so I'm going to go home, have a lovely hot bath, and spend the afternoon in front of the telly. That'll sort me out.'

I pause. 'As would some of that Victoria sponge. Want to share?'

I reach out a hand and Deborah bats it away with a squeal.

'No! Stick to your boring cheesecake! This is ALL. MINE,' she says firmly.

'Meanie,' I say. I sigh dramatically and pick up my own cake with a comedy pout, and we laugh. As Ruth launches into a story about Lorraine at work and her latest menopause-brain mishap, I start to relax. It's cosy here with the sun streaming in through the window and the smell of coffee and warm caramel in the air. I cup my hands around my mug of tea; its warmth is soothing.

Mindfulness, I tell myself. *Focus on the moment.*

I take a deep breath and join in with the conversation.

Chapter 7

'Yes!'

I sink deeper into the warm water with a satisfied grunt. I've just managed to turn the hot tap on and off again with my toes, topping up the bath nicely without even having to sit up, and this pleases me greatly. It's the little things sometimes, isn't it? I slide down even further, until the sweet almond oil scented bubbles are tickling my nose, and I feel the tension in my muscles easing. I love this bathroom. It's white and stylish, with a vase of fresh flowers on the window-sill and my favourite lotions and creams lined up neatly on the marble counter. This is my ensuite, so it's all for me; the kids share the main house bathroom. Even now, so many months after moving in here, I feel a surge of gratitude every time I use it. It's my own little sanctuary where it's always clean and smells nice, where there are no plastic boats to scoop out of the bath before I get in or suspicious little puddles on the loo seat. There are definitely advantages to not living with a man.

I've spent most of my life living mainly with men, when I think about it. First my dad, just me and him after Mum left.

We lived in Bristol at the time, but three years later, when I was thirteen, when everything started to go horribly, desperately wrong, when the bad thing, the really bad thing, happened, we needed a new start, and we moved the forty or so miles up the M5 to Cheltenham.

When I went off to uni in Manchester, I lived mainly with guys too, three of them from my business studies course plus one other girl, in a shared house. And then, of course, I met Jacob, and after a year or so we decided to rent a flat together for our final year – we were spending every night at either his or mine anyway by that point, so it seemed to make sense. From then on it was just us, first living in London and getting our careers established, and then moving back to Cheltenham to buy our own little home when we decided it was time to start a family. Jacob was from Worcester anyway, just half an hour's drive away, so we were close to both his parents and my dad, and for a while everything was wonderful. Until Crystal and everything that happened after that, of course. But things have a funny habit of working out, don't they? Yes, I'm feeling a little out of sorts at the moment, but when I have time to take stock, to look around me and appreciate what I have, I feel lucky. Really lucky. Jacob was generous when we sold our house, giving me the bulk of the cash to buy this place. He was, after all, moving in with Crystal, and I still have the kids for more time than he does every week. This house makes me happy, makes me feel secure. Yes, I'm very fortunate. Not every divorce is as amicable as ours was.

I spend a long time in the bath and when I finally wander

downstairs, snug in a soft cashmere jumper and my favourite stretchy sweatpants, I feel more relaxed than I have in days. It was lovely to see my friends this morning but it's equally nice now to have the rest of the day to myself, I think, as I put together a late lunch – a cheese and pickle sandwich, an apple, and a big mug of tea – and sit down in front of the TV. I smile as I pick up the remote, thinking about Ruth and Deborah suddenly appearing at the door earlier, a minute after I got home and a mere three minutes after I'd said goodbye to them outside Sunrise Lodge.

'Deb suddenly announced she needed an urgent pee just as we left the car park,' said Ruth, who'd driven them both. 'And that made me realise I needed to pee too, and we were already on the road, so we thought we'd come here instead as it's on our way back into town. Sorry!'

I laughed and rolled my eyes as Ruth rushed towards the downstairs loo and Deborah, who'd been dramatically hopping up and down on the doorstep, ran for the stairs. She took ages and Ruth was already back in the car before she scampered back down, but finally they were pulling out of the driveway again, waving at me, and I shut the front door with a sigh and headed up to run my bath.

Now I feel relaxed and contented. There are jobs I could be getting on with – a wall I've been meaning to repaint on the landing and some weeding to be done in the garden – but today I just need to recharge my batteries, rest, and take some time to do not very much at all. The kids won't be back until tomorrow evening so I have all of Sunday to get the chores done and visit Dad, and I refuse to feel guilty about it. But

I've just taken a big bite of my sandwich while a rerun of an old *Come Dine with Me* episode is playing on the TV, when the doorbell rings.

'Damn it!' I swear softly through a mouthful of sourdough.

Who on earth is that? Probably just a delivery.

I swallow and heave myself off the sofa, checking my face for crumbs as I pass the big mirror in the hall. When I open the door, a woman is standing there, a large red holdall slung over her shoulder.

'Hi,' I say. I don't recognise her and wait expectantly to see what she wants.

She hesitates for a moment, looking at me. Then: 'Beth,' she says.

I frown, starting to feel embarrassed.

So she knows me ... Is she something to do with the school, maybe? I have no idea. This is awkward.

'Erm ... yes, but sorry, I don't ... What can I help you with?' I ask.

Is she selling something, maybe? Is that why she has the big bag over her shoulder ...?

She's staring at me now, not saying anything, just looking. She's about my height, older though. Late fifties at a guess, with short blonde hair and a slick of berry-coloured lipstick. She raises a hand as if to shake mine, then seems to change her mind and drops it to her side again, and I suddenly realise that she's trembling slightly. There is a faint tremor running through her body and a tiny nerve twitching in her cheek.

'Beth ... it's me.'

She whispers the words, her face reddening, and I feel myself blushing too because I still have no idea who she is, and this is just so ... so *uncomfortable*.

'I'm sorry, I just can't think ...' I stammer, but now she's bending forwards slightly, sliding the heavy bag off her shoulder, and as she leans down to sit it on the ground the neckline of the loose jumper she's wearing under a dark coat slips forward and I see a small tattoo on her collar bone. Three little stars. Something catches in my throat.

Three little stars. One star for her, one for Dad, one for me.

I gasp.

But it can't be ... can it? It's not possible.

My legs suddenly feel weak and I grab the doorframe for support. She's straightening up now and I see there are tears in her eyes. She reaches out again, touching my arm this time. She's still trembling, her fingers sliding down my sleeve to grasp my hand, her skin warm on mine.

'Beth,' she whispers again. 'It's me. I'm so sorry.'

And finally, I say it. I say the word I've longed to say for so many years to the person I've longed so desperately to say it to.

'Mum? *Mum?*'

Chapter 8

We sit and stare, drinking each other in. The last few minutes are a blur: my mother on my doorstep (my *mother!*), me whimpering like a child, dragging her into my arms, both of us crying and laughing and talking at the same time. Me pulling her inside, the door closing behind us, the two of us collapsing onto the sofa, gripping each other's hands, touching each other's faces, unable to believe that this is happening, that this is *real*.

Now we have moved apart a little but our fingers are still entwined, our eyes fixed on each other's faces. She has changed – of course she has ... it's been three decades after all, and all I've had for all those years is one faded photograph and my own hazy memories of her face. I stare at her, looking for shades of the young woman I remember in this face that is looking back at me so intently, eyes still shining with tears. The blonde hair, flecked with grey now and shorter, the defined cheekbones. Yes, they're familiar. She was slender back then, and still is, even though she will be sixty in a few weeks' time. She still looks good, clearly looks after herself ... and that tattoo. The three stars, a paler blue than I remember them, worn by time, but unmistakable. I can't see them now – they're covered again by the neckline of her jumper – but the fact that they're still there, that she hasn't had them removed, has worn them on her skin for all this time, fills my heart with a soaring joy. *My mother. My mother's come home.*

'I need a tissue,' she says with a smile, and I hear the soft West Country accent that I remember so well from my childhood. My heart swells again.

She squeezes my hand and slips her fingers from mine, fumbling in her coat pocket. She finds a tissue and dabs at her eyes, then smiles at me again, a slightly wary smile this time.

'I'm sure you have so many questions,' she says. 'I'm sorry, so sorry, Beth. I'm going to try to explain, if you'll let me ...'

Her voice tails off, tears springing to her eyes again, and I leap to my feet.

'All that can wait, Mum, honestly. I'm just so ... so happy! I can't *believe* ... Look, let me take your coat, make some tea, get you something to eat maybe? And then we can talk. The kids are away until tomorrow and—'

'The kids! My *grandchildren* ...'

She lets out a little sob as she slips off her coat but she's beaming through her tears.

'I can't wait ... if you'll let me ...'

'Of course! Oh my goodness, they'll be so thrilled; they won't believe it either ... Right, I'm going to hang your coat up and put the kettle on, OK? Sit, relax. I'd just started a sandwich – I can make you one? And ... oh, I can't remember, do you drink tea, or do you prefer coffee maybe? How ridiculous that I don't know, I'm sorry ...'

I'm babbling, I know I am, and I laugh. She does too.

'I'm easy; either is OK. I'm not hungry, but tea maybe. Just a dash of milk. Thank you, Beth.'

I nod and head for the kitchen to make the tea. I bring it to her and sit as she sips it, looking at my half-eaten sandwich but not picking it up, my appetite gone. My head is spinning. The initial euphoria is wearing off a little now as reality begins to sink in. She's right. I *do* have so many questions.

What's Dad going to say? How will he react when I tell him she's back?

She caused him – caused *us* – so much pain ... Can we even let her just walk back in like this? Should I have been so welcoming? She left me, her own child ... The damage that caused, the anguish ...

But, it's her. It's my mother ... Isn't that all that matters?

The kids though, and Jacob, and my friends, and ... and everyone, everyone who knows she walked out on us so long ago. Will they welcome her, or reject her? How do I even tell them ...?

I don't know, I don't know ...

I take a deep, shaky breath and my mother looks up, puts her cup down, and dabs at her lips with her tissue. I'm sitting on the armchair opposite her now and we're both silent for a moment. Then she says: 'Right, well. Where to begin? I need to explain ... I would have come back sooner, you know? Years ago. But, well ... why I left, where I went ... there's so much. I don't know where to start. You must have been so angry. You must have felt so rejected ...'

Her voice quivers and I shake my head, holding up a hand

to shush her. Quite suddenly, I've made up my mind. Whatever's happened in the past, today is a new beginning. Recriminations, explanations, and everything else can wait. She's back. *She's back.* And today is for celebration.

'Please ... Look, don't worry about that now. We can talk about all that later; there's no hurry. I'm just so ... well, so happy, Mum. And so amazed you've just turned up on my doorstep! How did you even find me?'

She smiles and sinks back in her seat a little, her body visibly relaxing.

'Yes, let's start with that. It wasn't easy. I didn't keep in touch with anyone, after ... after I went. Well, you probably know that. So when I decided it was time, you and your dad had moved away and everything, so ...'

She shrugs.

'It sounds like something out of a movie but I had to hire a private detective, and it was only really last night, after he called you, that we were a hundred per cent sure ...'

Last night? He called me? But I didn't ...

'Ohhhhh!'

Suddenly, I get it, and a massive wave of relief, of understanding, rushes over me.

'Oh, *now* it all makes sense ... Oh thank goodness!'

The phone call, the man who asked me about my maiden name ... and, oh, of course! The man who's been following me too? A private detective, hired by my mother? Was that really who it's been, all this time?

I exhale and sink back in my chair, groaning and grinning at the same time.

'Honestly, you don't know how relieved I am to hear that! That explains so much. *So* much. A detective, of course! I mean, the thought never entered my head, and why would it? I suppose ... he's been following me for a while, hasn't he? Taking photos and all sorts? I thought ... well, I thought all kinds of things. Thought I had some sort of deranged stalker!'

She's shaking her head, her eyes wide.

'Oh love, I'm so sorry! Mike's his name, and he said you wouldn't even see him. Said it would all be completely discreet ... Did he frighten you? That's awful. Wait 'til I get hold of him ...'

But I'm laughing now, remembering all the times I spotted him, this clearly rather inept detective.

Nothing to do with the past, with what I did. Nothing to do with that at all. The relief ...

'He was rubbish!' I say. 'I saw him dozens of times!'

She starts to laugh too.

'Oh, Beth! I'm so sorry. It was just that, well, I didn't really know where to start on my own. I'm not very techy, you know, internet and all that, and I'd saved up some money, so I thought it would just be easier, you know ...'

She laughs again.

'Trust me to pick 'em, eh?'

I roll my eyes and smile.

'Don't worry. At least I know now. That's a huge weight off my mind, I can tell you.'

'Well, I feel dreadful. He was one of the cheapest I could find, and I suppose you get what you pay for, but he did track you down so he wasn't *all* bad. I'm not sure how he did it.

To be honest, I didn't ask. I just gave him all the details I had from the past – you and your dad's names, your school, previous address, stuff like that, and somehow he tracked you down. Public records, I suppose. I don't know. They have ways. Probably could have done it myself if I'd really tried, but you'd obviously changed your surname, so ...'

She takes a breath and I stay quiet, listening, watching her face, still scarcely able to believe she's really here. My mind is still racing.

My mother. Here in my living room. This is ... this is insane.

'... anyway, he said he was certain he'd found you, but I wanted to be absolutely positive, you know? So I asked him for photos. I knew I'd recognise you, even after all these years. You never forget your child's face, do you? But he said you're not on social media. Don't blame you really ...'

I'm not. I don't want the kids to be either, although Eloise has been nagging for a while about an Instagram account, and I'll probably have to give in at some point, but not yet. She's only ten, after all.

'... and there weren't even any photos of you on your practice website or anything, nothing he could find online at all, so he said he'd have to take some himself, and that meant hanging around where you work and stuff. When I saw the pictures, well ... I mean, I last saw you when you were a child, but I recognised you immediately, love. I did. Your eyes. Eyes never change, do they?'

Her voice breaks and she lets out a little sob. I instinctively rise from my chair, wanting to cross the room and comfort her, but she waves a hand and shakes her head.

'I'm OK, just a bit emotional. I'm sorry ...'

I nod and sit down again. I'm feeling a bit emotional myself.

I need to hear all this, and a lot more besides, but it can't be easy for her ...

I try to focus, realising she's still talking.

'The phone call last night just to check your maiden name ... that was just belt and braces really,' she's saying. 'You're in the phone book, you see, and he found your address on the electoral roll so that last bit was easy. He told me about the kids, and your divorce – I was sorry to hear that, love – but anyway, I was so excited. I'd already packed my bag. As soon as he rang me to confirm that you really were formerly Beth Armstrong, I knew I just had to get on a train this morning and come up here.'

She pauses, dabbing at her eyes with the tissue again.

'Train from where? Where do you live now? Did you ... did you have any more children? Oh, gosh, sorry ...'

I stop, feeling embarrassed at my eagerness, my *neediness*, and she smiles at the flurry of questions.

'It's OK. I get it. There's so much to catch up on,' she says. 'So, what was the first question? Where do I live now? Cornwall. Been there for the past ten years or so. Little place not far from Bodmin. It's so beautiful – the moor and everything. You been there?'

I shake my head. I've been to Cornwall a few times; Jacob and I used to take the kids for holidays. Padstow for the restaurants, Newquay for the beaches, but not to Bodmin or its famous moor.

'Can we do the rest later?' she says. 'I want to tell you

everything, I do. But I might need a little breather first. I'm kind of exhausted. It's been a bit of a day. All this ... and you ...'

She waves a hand vaguely and leans back against the cushions with a little sigh.

'Of course. I'm feeling a bit overwhelmed too,' I say.

There's silence for a moment. Outside, the earlier threat of rain has passed and the sun has come out. A few dandelions are already flashing yellow on the small patch of lawn outside the patio doors.

'Will you stay? For a few days? Stay here, I mean?' The words emerge in a rush, unplanned. I just know suddenly that I don't want her to leave again; that now she's back, finally here, sitting just feet away from me, that she *can't* go, she *can't* leave. I won't let her. And then, just as suddenly, my chest tightens, my heartbeat speeds up, and a little voice whispers a warning from far, far away.

Why did you suggest that? She'll say no, of course she will. She'll leave you again ... You don't deserve this. You don't deserve something this good to happen, not after what you did ...

But she's nodding, smiling, replying instantly, delight in her voice.

'Of ... of course! Love, I didn't expect ... I was going to check into a hotel, but if you're sure ... I mean, that would be *wonderful*, amazing. We could catch up properly, get to know each other again ... Really? I can stay here?'

I take a breath and the tension in my chest dissipates as quickly as it arrived.

'Of course. I've got a spare room. You're more than welcome, of course you are. Come on, I'll show you up now if you like. I'll give you a tour on the way.'

'I'd love that, Beth. Your house looks ... well, it's beautiful.'

She stands up, takes a step towards me, and reaches for my hand. I feel a surge of happiness. But even as I lead her from the room I start to worry again, my brain beginning to process what I've just learned. Processing the fact that my mother used a private detective to find me. Mike, a man who must surely, by now, know an awful lot about me. Does *he* know what I did, all those years ago?

And has he told her? If he doesn't, and hasn't, I have to stop her ever finding out, don't I? Because if she does, I'll lose her again. There's absolutely no doubt about that.

Chapter 9

Her name was Lucy Allen. We were in the same class at secondary school, but for the first year I barely noticed her. Our school, Fairbridge High in Bristol, was a big one, each year having about sixty pupils divided into two streams. Lucy and I were in different streams, so for that first year we were only together for morning assembly and annual events like sports day and the Christmas concert. It was only when we went back after the summer holidays to start Year 9 that she came to my attention, and even now, so many years later, I'm still not sure how it all started. The timetable was different that year; the two streams merged for some lessons, and the two of us ended up in the same Maths, History, and Biology classes.

Lucy was one of those quiet girls, clever and studious, mouse-like in her demeanour. She did have friends though; I remember a small group of similar girls, five or six of them, girls who spent their lunchbreaks at chess club instead of out by the tuckshop flirting with the boys like me and my mates. We had little in common. Before my mother walked out, three years prior to me going into Year 9, I'd been a hard worker at school too, but bit by bit all that had changed. Dad, struggling to juggle his job and me and housework and everything else, trusted me to keep my grades up with little intervention from him. At first, wanting to please him and terrified that he'd leave me too if I didn't, I obliged. But gradually, the anger and sadness inside me grew and by the time I was thirteen and hormones came into the mix too, I'd pretty much stopped caring.

When my body began to change, when my periods started one dreadful day in the school changing rooms and I thought I was bleeding to death until the kindly school nurse explained what was happening, the pain of the loss of my mother became even more acute. I loved my dad, of course I did, but how does a thirteen-year-old girl talk to her father about needing a bra, about buying sanitary towels? Friends' mothers were always offering to help, but it got to the point that year when I couldn't even bear to visit their houses anymore, to see those mothers fussing and cooking and hugging and just ... just being there. It hurt too much. And that was when it all started. I suppose, in retrospect, I was searching for a way to handle the pain. If only – dangerous though it might have been – I'd gone down the route that so many young people go down: alcohol, drugs, substances to take the edge off, to lessen the constant, aching sorrow. If only, if only.

But I didn't.

I didn't choose alcohol, or drugs, or even underage sex.

I chose something else.

And it all started the day I first sat next to Lucy Allen in Maths class.

I wish, so much now, that I hadn't.

I wish I'd never met her.

Chapter 10

'What a pretty churchyard. It's so nice here, Beth.'

'It is. I love it.'

I squeeze the hand Mum's looped through my arm. We've come out for a Sunday stroll around the village, stopping at the little shop on the High Street for a bag of mints and then wandering across the road to cut through the graveyard. The honey-coloured stone walls of the thirteenth-century church glow softly in the afternoon sunshine and a grey squirrel scampers across the gravel in front of us as we follow the path that winds its way among the headstones, pausing for a moment to admire the stained glass in the east window. As we walk on in companionable silence, I marvel once again at how bizarre all this is.

I'm walking around Prestbury with my mother. If anyone had told me yesterday, when I was up on Cleeve Hill with Ruth and Deborah, that I'd be doing this today I'd have laughed my head off. My mother ...

There's a bouquet resting on one of the new graves, blush-pink tulips and sunshine-yellow daffodils bound together with a blue ribbon, the colours vivid against the dark earth.

The flowers and their bright hues bring back a memory: me and Mum walking in a park – Brandon Hill, maybe, near where we lived in Bristol? I can't remember – when I was about five years old. I remember buttercups, vast swathes of them in the grass. Mum crouching down to pick handfuls and then skilfully weaving them into a necklace, draping it around my neck, keeping one tiny bloom aside to hold under my chin and telling me I *definitely* liked butter.

'Look at that glow!' she laughed, and I'd laughed back, loving being with her, my beautiful mother. Loving that today, she was happy. Aware, even at such a young age, that Mummy wasn't always happy. Learning to make the most of the good days.

I glance sideways at her now. I see the contented expression on her face and feel the gentle pressure of her fingers on my forearm. Such little things that seem so utterly remarkable when you've lived without them for thirty years.

Wow. Just wow.

I can't stop looking at her. Yesterday, after I'd shown her round the house and settled her in the guest bedroom, we'd returned to the lounge and chatted for hours. I'd forced myself to put aside my fears about how much she knew about my life in the years since we'd last been together. There was, after all, nothing I could do to change the past, and if she *did* know what had happened after she'd left, it hadn't stopped her wanting to find me now, had it? And if she didn't, well ... nobody else had ever found out, had they? My friends, my colleagues ... That realisation brought me some comfort, and so I vowed to put it out of my mind for now at least. There was so much – *so* much – to catch up on; three decades of life was impossible to sum up in the space of a few hours, and we had so many things to talk about, so many things to learn about each other. And to my great joy, just hours after our reunion, I already feel I have some understanding, some sense, of the sort of person my mother really was back then, and of who she is now.

Now, she works in a small art gallery near Bodmin, organising exhibitions and giving talks to visitors and school groups. Her face lights up when she talks about her work. The most recent exhibition – her 'favourite EVER' – was an extravaganza of blown glasswork, stone sculptures, and huge unframed canvasses. She's taken a sabbatical to come and find me.

'I can take up to six months, if I want to. Unpaid, of course, but I've put a bit aside over the years. They'll keep the job open for me until September, but until then ...'

She'd grinned, her eyes shining, and I'd grinned back. *Six months! Does that mean she might stay here, in Cheltenham, for six months?* The idea of it made me feel a little breathless with joy.

She likes to do yoga, and walks a lot, I learned. Maybe that partly explains her calmness now, her composure, so different from the younger version of herself, the one whose moods swung from elation to despair at a moment's notice. She's had boyfriends, relationships, over the years, some long term, others not, but she's never married again. How could she? She's still legally married to Dad, of course.

We talked about him, but only a little. He's had other relationships too, but nothing serious, and nobody ever moved in. I don't think he could do it, don't think he could let himself take a chance on opening up his home, his heart, to someone else, not after her. When I was a child, Mum's name was never spoken in our house. As I grew up I'd try, now and again, to make him talk about her, about what went wrong, about why she left. I'd wanted details, wanted the *story*, but I always got the same brief answer, his expression blank as he spoke.

'We just weren't compatible in the end, Beth. We loved each other once, but sometimes love isn't enough. She was too young, and she tried, but we were on different pages when it came to the book of life, as it were. She wasn't ready for any of it, being a wife, being a mother. So she moved on. Simple as.'

I stopped mentioning her to him eventually. I could see how much it hurt him. But when Eloise was born, when Dad came to the hospital to see us, his eyes wet as he cradled his first grandchild in his arms, I made the mistake of whispering: 'I wish Mum could be here, Dad. I wish my daughter could know her grandmother.'

Something had flashed in his eyes then.

'*No.* She's better off without her,' he said. 'I can forgive your mother for walking out on me, Beth. That is what it is. But forgive her for walking out on *you*? Never.'

I told my mother none of this last night, of course, and she didn't ask. No questions about how he was these days, or if he'd found love again. When finally, with a nervous flutter in my stomach, I began to ask her what had happened between them, she gave the same vague sort of answer he'd always given me.

'He was so much older, love. We were just ... just such different people, you know? I knew that if I stayed, it wouldn't be good for any of us, not for him or for me and certainly not for you. Growing up with two parents who hated each other? No child needs that. I know I hurt you so much, Beth. I know it must be so hard for you to understand, but I knew I couldn't be the kind of mother you deserved, and that's why I had to go. I'm so, so sorry. The shame of being a mother who abandoned her child ... it's never left me. I'll regret it for ever ...'

Her eyes had filled with tears again then and I'd wrapped my arms around her, telling her that it was fine, that I *did* understand. The past was the past.

She's here now. That's what's important, I told myself. It's what happens from here on that matters. We've both suffered pain because of what she did. I can see it in her eyes. What's the point in dwelling on it now, after so many years?

I did have one more question though.

'Why now, Mum? Why now, this year, today? Why did you come back *now*? What changed?'

She shrugged.

'I'd thought about it for such a long time, but I was scared, you know? And then I realised, well, I'm turning sixty soon, and who knows what might happen? Who knows how much time I might have left? I couldn't put it off any longer, Beth, scared or not. It was time. And I'm so glad I plucked up the courage. I'm so glad, so grateful. You could have slammed the door in my face and nobody would have blamed you for that, least of all me. But you didn't. Can I ... can I just ask one question too?'

'Of course.'

'Did he ... did he look for me? Did he try to come after me when I left?'

I hesitated for a moment, wondering what to say, and then decided to simply tell her the truth.

'He didn't. Not really. He never saw the point ... You left a note, after all, didn't you? Telling him you were leaving and that you wouldn't be coming back? At first I think he thought you'd change your mind after a few weeks or months, but even when you didn't, well ... it was your choice, wasn't it? And when friends would worry that maybe something had happened to you, I remember him always shaking his head. He always said he was a hundred per cent sure you were still alive out there somewhere. He did report it to the police eventually, but only because so many people nagged him about it. But he never thought anything bad had happened to you, and nor did the police, as far as I know. That's why they never instigated a search for you. It was one of those things ... well, she's an adult, she's free to go where she likes ...'

I left it there, realising she was nodding, shifting uncomfortably on her chair as if she'd heard enough. And then I forgot about it all together because a few minutes later she told me something that made my mouth drop open.

'You have a sister, Beth. Well, a half-sister, of course. Olivia. Liv. Her dad isn't on the scene. He was an artist. I met him when I lived in Newcastle for a bit, but he buggered off when I told him I was pregnant. Didn't bother me. I'd grown up so much by then. I was well into my thirties and I decided to do it properly this time. Be a mum, you know? Do it on my own. Oh God, Beth, I'm so sorry. That sounds awful ...'

She started to cry again and reached for me, pulling me into an embrace, hugging me hard.

'I'm sorry, so sorry. I thought about you all the time. I did, honestly,' she whispered, her face damp against mine. 'But I was so young when you were born, and after I left ... as I said, I thought you were better off without me, you know? Later, when I had Liv, when I was finally grown-up enough to be a proper mother, I thought so many times about coming back, about taking you to live with us, but ... well, I didn't know how you'd react. I didn't want to disrupt your life and your schooling and all that, all over again, or take you away from your dad ... I'm so sorry, love. I really am.'

I clung to her then. I'd thought for the past hour or so that I was OK, that the joy of having her back had somehow erased the pain of the past. But this news, the news that my mother went on to have another child, suddenly brought the old feelings of rejection, of abandonment, crashing back.

She left me behind, and then had another baby. And she kept this one. She didn't walk out on her. She stayed. Why her and not me?

And then, just as suddenly, yet again it didn't matter anymore. It should matter, I knew that. I should be demanding explanations, shouting at her, telling her how much what she did devastated me, how it ruined my childhood and took me to dark places I thought I'd never leave. But I just ... didn't. I didn't want to. Not now. Not when I'd just found her again. Maybe not ever. Because now not only was my mother back in my life but I also had a *sister*, for goodness' sake! A *sister*. I'd longed for a sibling as I grew up, and now ...

'Tell me about her. Tell me everything,' I said.

She laughed through her tears, wiped her eyes, and obliged. Olivia, Liv, my little sister. She's just twenty-four, sixteen years my junior. She has a degree in international business and Spanish from Edinburgh uni (*business studies, like me*!), and works for a big shipping company in Plymouth. I asked for a photo, and in it she smiled back at me, a pretty, blonde, petite girl in a black polo-neck jumper and tight jeans. I felt a shiver of joy.

My sister. I have a sister.

'We can call her, FaceTime or whatever maybe, during the week? I'll message her later and tell her I've really found you,' Mum said. 'She'll be beside herself. She's a sweetie. You'll love her. The spit of her father, facially. She's got our hair though.'

Our hair. My mother, my sister. My family.

We talked more about me after that – my career, Jacob, the children, the divorce. We opened a bottle of champagne the girls at work gave me for my birthday in February (I'd decided to keep it until I had something to celebrate, never *dreaming* it would be this), and we clinked glasses and laughed and talked until we were both exhausted. When we finally went to bed just before midnight, I couldn't sleep for hours, overwhelmed by such a gamut of emotions that I just lay there, staring wide-eyed into the dark. I was still ecstatic, of course, at my mother's return, and yet ... as the clock ticked round to 1am, and then to two, the thoughts swirled in my head and I began to feel panicky and bewildered, my fingers gripping the edge of the duvet so hard they ached as I tried to make sense of it all.

Yes, it was incredible, *incredible*, that my mother had come back. But could I really let her in, just like that, after all these years? Into my heart, into my life, into my *children's* lives? What if she disappeared again? I'd been so hurt, so angry, so damaged for so long. Somehow I'd finally managed to get past all that, to put it behind me and become the happy person I am today. Mostly happy, anyway. In many ways, what she did has made me more adaptable, more appreciative of the good people in my life, more empathetic, more protective of those I love. But her departure also left me with less welcome character traits ... I can be needy, insecure, oversensitive. And now she was back, but for how long? And what would happen if she disappeared again?

I slept eventually, the deep dreamless sleep that often follows a day of high emotion. And with the light of the morning came the sound of cups clattering in the kitchen, and my mother tapping timidly on my door, proffering a steaming mug of tea and kissing me gently on the cheek. In an instant, the lingering fears began to dissipate.

She's here. My mother is back. What does anything else matter?

After breakfast I rang Jacob, telling him briefly what had happened. I wanted to check what time he was planning to bring the kids back this evening and to ask him to break the news to them. He sounded, unsurprisingly, dumbfounded.

'Your ... your *mother*? What the hell? *How*? When? Are you serious? Good God, Beth, that's MAD!'

I told him I'd fill him in on all the details when I saw him and warned him not to mention it to Dad if, as he often did, he popped into Holly Tree with Eloise and Finley after Sunday lunch. That conversation was definitely *not* one I could delegate.

I'd called Brenda and Barbara too, remembering we'd vaguely discussed going out for a pub lunch today. On hearing my reason for cancelling, Brenda had shrieked so loudly that I actually dropped the phone, laughing as I scrabbled under the table to retrieve it, still hearing the little whoops and screams emerging from the speaker. Barbara had reacted completely differently, shocked into silence for a long minute before she stammered:

'I ... I just can't believe it, Beth. Your *mother*? That's ... that's *impossible*!'

'Apparently not,' I said. 'She's upstairs right now. Pretty amazing, eh?'

Now, as Mum and I start to head slowly for home again, crossing a field that borders the racecourse which is empty and quiet today, I feel another little rush of joy.

My children are going to meet their grandmother.

They've asked so many questions over the years, of me and of Dad, awkward questions both of us found tricky to answer. And now ...

'Hang on ... Mum? Look.'

I've stopped dead and I'm staring at a figure on the other side of the field. It's a man, dressed in dark clothing, standing still next to the stile that gives access to the lane back into the village.

'What am I looking at?'

I point, suddenly feeling that familiar agitation, anxiety pricking my skin.

'There. Is that ... is that your private detective again? Mike. It is, isn't it? What's he doing?'

She shrugs and starts fumbling in the small leather bag she's wearing across her body.

'Can't see that far without my glasses. Hang on ... but no, it can't be, Beth. His job's done. He's back in Cornwall now as far as I know. Must be someone else.'

I'm still staring. OK, he's a long way away, but he looks *so* like the figure I've seen so many times in recent months. As I watch, frowning, the man turns away from us, swiftly climbing over the stile and disappearing up the lane. Moments later he's out of sight. I stare after him for a few moments, then realise Mum's still rooting in her bag. I wave a hand at her.

'Forget it, he's gone. You're right. I probably imagined it. Ignore me.'

She smiles.

'You're *definitely* imagining it, love. Sorry, that's my fault for getting him to follow you in the first place. Worth it though, eh?'

She squeezes my arm and I smile back.

'Absolutely.'

We start walking again and I take a deep breath, trying to quell the butterflies in my stomach and silently talking myself down.

Of course it wasn't him. That's all over now. Stop it, Beth. It was just a bloke out for a walk ...

'Beth? I was just wondering ... do you need to go and see John later? Your dad? Because it's fine, if you do. I can amuse myself. I don't want you to change your routine just because I've turned up.'

The question comes unexpectedly. Her tone is casual and I'm so surprised I almost stop walking again. She didn't ask me last night about where Dad lives and now I'm wondering how much she knows. I hesitate, but she's still striding along, still talking.

'I know he's in a nursing home care facility, or whatever they call them nowadays. Mike saw you there a few times. Well, we assumed it's John you visit there?'

I glance sideways at her, eyebrows raised.

'It is, yes. And he must have been on the ball for once when he followed me there. Probably one of the very few times I didn't spot your defective detective.'

She laughs at that. She looks lovely today, I think. Her eyes are a dark green and I realise that's something I don't even remember, the colour of my mother's eyes. But they're smiley eyes, crinkled at the corners, and I do remember the warmth in them, the warmth I see now as she laughs at my silly joke. She's wearing a cowl-necked cream jumper and a blue angora wrap with an oversized silver necklace. She has the small brown leather bag worn across her body and her white-blonde hair is brushed back off her face. I can just picture her floating around her gallery, organising everyone, being all arty.

'How is he, health-wise?' she asks. 'He must be, what, eighty?'

I nod. 'He's OK. He had a stroke. His eyesight is bad – well, he's almost blind really – and his mobility isn't great, but he manages so well, with help. And his mind's as sharp as ever. He's the life and soul. I would have moved him in with us – I wanted to, but it would have been impossible, you know, with work and the kids and ...'

My anxiety is suddenly rising again.

She must think I'm awful, putting my father in a home, when I have a lovely house and a spare room ...

But she's shaking her head, frowning.

'No, no, you did the right thing. Gosh, you don't have to justify yourself to me, of all people, love. If he's well and happy, that's all that matters, isn't it?'

She squeezes my arm and my heart rate slows again.

'He is. He really is. I see him a lot ... Do you want to visit him, Mum? I mean, I haven't told him about you yet, obviously. I'd need to do that first, to see how he felt, but it would be so nice if the two of you could make some sort of peace, after all this time ...'

My voice tails off. Her footsteps have slowed and she's looking uncomfortable suddenly, her face flushed.

'I ... I don't know, love. I'd need to think about it for a bit. It would be so ... so awkward, you know?'

'Of course, of course. Ignore me. It was probably a stupid idea,' I say hastily. We're nearly at the house now and I take her hand and give it a little pat.

'I'll have to tell him you're back,' I say gently. 'But there's no pressure, OK? I suspect he might not be too keen for a reunion either, when I think about it.'

I smile at her, trying to diffuse the tension, and she smiles back.

'I suspect not,' she says drily. 'I doubt I'm his favourite person.'

As I turn the key in the lock, the house phone starts to ring.

'Damn,' I say. 'I'd better get that. Just close the door behind us, Mum.'

I run into the lounge and grab the receiver.

'Hello?'

'Mrs Holland? Hello, it's Anya here. From Holly Tree?'

'Anya, yes, hello. Is everything OK?'

There's a second of silence. Then: 'I'm so sorry, Mrs Holland, but I'm afraid it's your father. He collapsed about an hour ago. He's been taken into the General—'

'Collapsed? But he was fine ... What happened? What is it?'

I'm aware that I'm starting to shiver, that little tremors are running through me.

No, Dad. No. Please. Not now.

In my ear, Anya is still talking.

'... said it was most likely another stroke. But an even bigger one this time. I'm so sorry, Mrs Holland, but it's not looking good. I think you want to get over there as soon as possible.'

Chapter 11

He looks so small, so old, so frail. My dad, who just days ago was laughing and sharing a drink with his pal in Holly Tree's bar. Now he's a tiny white-faced version of himself, his mouth even more violently twisted than it was before, his breathing laboured. He's awake though, and when I bend down to whisper hello he mumbles, 'Beth. Shorry, love.'

His words are slurred, but the fact that he can say them at all is such a relief that my legs, already wobbly, almost give way. I lower myself onto the chair at the side of his bed and turn to see where Mum is. Dad's in a private room, and she's lurking by the door, her discomfort clear. She hasn't seen her husband for thirty years, and now ...

'Give me a minute,' I say quietly, and she nods, edging out into the corridor. I turn back to Dad. There's a reassuringly steady *beep beep beep* from his heart monitor, and I hope desperately that what I'm about to say won't change that. But what can I do?

I have to tell him, don't I? Just in case ... just in case he dies, and never knows ...

I sit there for a few moments, composing myself, trying to

find the words. They loved each other once, my mum and dad, I know that. And I remember those days too, sometimes, the days when they'd walk hand in hand in the park, when she'd drop a kiss on his head as she passed his chair, when he'd come home with flowers and she'd wrap her arms around him and then carefully select a bloom and put it behind her ear. But I remember the dark days more. The days when I'd come home from school to find the lounge curtains closed and my mum curled up on a corner of the sofa, sobbing. The days when she wouldn't even get out of bed, and I'd go to school and come home again and there she'd be, still lying there, staring at the ceiling, her eyes expressionless. The days, the weeks, when my parents would barely speak to each other, barely acknowledge one another's presence, both of them hurting but not knowing how to stop the pain. And then, one day, she simply got up and walked away. It probably *was* for the best, in the end. But on the way to 'the best' there had been so much destruction, so many repercussions. And now she's back and somehow I have to tell him, and I have absolutely no idea how this is going to go.

'Dad? Dad, something's happened. Dad, can you hear me?'

His eyes have closed, but he opens them again, blinks, and tries to focus on my face.

'Mmmm,' he says.

I take a deep breath. I can feel my heartbeat echoing in my ears, the clamminess of my palms.

'Dad ... it's Mum. I know this is going to be a lot to take in, especially right now. But, well, she's back, Dad. Last night. She just ... *appeared* on my doorstep. It's mad and it's a long story, but ... well, she's *here*, now. Can I bring her in, just for a minute?'

He's staring at me, frowning. He has deep creases around his eyes and his lips are dry and cracked.

'Mum? Alissh?'

He slurs the name but he's clearly understood.

'Yes, Alice. She's here, Dad.'

He stares at me for another moment, then his eyes close again. The room smells of disinfectant and over-bleached sheets. I reach for his hand. It's so thin I can feel every bone.

'Dad? I'm going to bring her in, just for a minute. Then we'll let you rest. Is that OK?'

I whisper the words, leaning in close to his ear.

'Mmmm,' he says again. He doesn't open his eyes. I turn back to the door and wave.

'Come in,' I say.

She's leaning against the wall just outside, her face tight and pinched. She takes a few steps into the room and then stops.

'Are you sure?' she whispers. 'I don't want to make things worse. I don't want to upset him. Are you sure about this?'

I nod. I have no idea if I'm doing the right thing. No idea at all. But if Dad dies and Mum was here, so close, and they didn't get to speak, to be in the same room just one last time after so many years ...

'Come on,' I whisper back. 'Sit here.'

I slip my hand gently from Dad's and stand up, moving aside so she can take my place. She swallows.

'John? John? It's me. Alice. Can you hear me?'

'Mmmm.'

His voice is weaker now but he opens his eyes again, even that small movement looking like an effort. He blinks, clearly trying to focus on her face, and my throat tightens.

How must he feel, seeing her again? Seeing the woman who broke his heart so long ago, who walked out and left him with a little girl to raise alone. Who made his life so very, very hard for so many years. Was it a mistake, bringing her here?

'Mmmmm.'

This time it sounds like a groan of frustration. He's squinting, his face contorted. Mum turns to me with a look of panic.

'What is it? What's he trying to say?'

I take a step closer.

'It's his eyesight,' I say. 'Lean in a bit closer so he can see you. He's just trying to focus on your face, don't worry.'

She turns back to the bed, shuffles the chair closer and leans forward.

'John? Is this better?' she whispers.

He's still squinting, and then, quite suddenly, his face relaxes.

'Shtill ... shtill got tat,' he says.

'What? Sorry, John ...'

I'm puzzled for a moment, and then I get it. I actually laugh out loud, relief flooding over me.

His brain can't be too badly affected if he's recognised that.

'He said you've still got your tattoo, Mum! He's remembered it, even now. That's ... that's amazing.'

She sits back in her chair, rearranging the neckline of her jumper which had dipped when she leaned closer to Dad, covering the tattoo again.

'Oh!' she says. 'That's ... well, that's good, isn't it? That's ...'

Her voice cracks, and a tear slips down her cheek.

'I'm sorry,' she says. 'I'm so sorry. And I'm saying that to him, as well as you, Beth. I'll never stop being sorry for what I did to both of you. If I could turn back the clock, if I could change things ...'

She sobs and buries her face in her hands. I look at Dad, but his eyes are closed again, his breathing slower and deeper. Asleep, I hope.

'It's OK, Mum. I know. He knows. Come on, let's go. Let's leave him to rest,' I say.

As I manoeuvre the car out of its space and look for the exit signs, she turns to me.

'Can I buy us a takeaway or something on the way home, to save you cooking? I mean, the kids are staying with Jacob tonight now after all, aren't they?'

They are. I rang him shortly after we arrived at the hospital and he agreed that it's best if they stay where they are tonight, just in case. And I really *don't* feel like cooking. It's been quite a day.

'Yes,' I say. 'There's a fish and chip place just down the road. We'll stop there. Good idea. Thanks, Mum.'

'Great,' she says. 'And don't worry. John's tough. He'll come through this, you wait and see.'

She reaches out a hand and pats my knee, and instantly I feel a little better. I'm still a little jittery after thinking I saw

Mike still following me, earlier, but things could be so much worse. My dad might be sick, but he *is* tough and he'll rally. And my mum is back. She's *back*. And we'll get through this together, won't we?

Chapter 12

'I can't find my keys. Where are my *bloody* car keys?'

I'm rummaging frantically through the pile of envelopes and fast-food delivery leaflets on the hall table. I'm *sure* I left my keys here when we got back from the hospital last night but they seem to have vanished and I should have left for work fifteen minutes ago, so I'm starting to panic. I have so much to do today, and I need to go and see Dad at lunchtime too. I haven't even called the ward yet to see how he is this morning, and ...

'Oh for goodness' sake, where *are* they?'

Exasperated, I stomp into the kitchen. There's every possibility that in my current distracted state of mind I've put the damn keys somewhere ridiculous, and I rush from microwave to mug cupboard, scanning their interiors and swearing under my breath. Robin, who arrived twenty minutes ago because I completely forgot to call her last night to tell her the kids would be staying with Jacob and therefore she wouldn't be needed for the school run this morning, watches me with a bemused look on her face.

'Erm ... aren't your keys more likely to be in your handbag, or on your bedside table, Beth?' she says, as I peer into the fridge, slam the door shut and open the oven.

'Already looked there. I've looked everywhere, Robin.'

I stop opening random doors and sigh.

'Oh sod it, I give up. I'm calling a taxi. I'll find the bloody things later. Mum will be here to let me in this evening and she has the spare front door key in case she wants to pop out. The kids won't be back until later. Jacob's going to pick them up from school and feed them so you can get off as soon as you've finished the cleaning Robin, thank you.'

She nods.

'OK. And I'll try to find your keys for you, don't worry. They'll turn up. Call your cab and I'll make you a quick cuppa to drink while you wait. It'll calm you down a bit.'

She turns to switch the kettle on and I take a deep breath.

'Thanks, Robin. You're an angel.'

I bring up the local taxi app on my phone and quickly book a cab. By the time I've finished, she's handing me a mug.

'I'm so sorry again about your dad,' she says. 'But it's such insane news about your mum. No wonder you're all over the place.'

I smile and nod as I sip. Robin still looks a bit shellshocked herself; I noticed her hand shaking a little as she scooped the teabag out of my drink. But as I wait for my taxi, I ponder the fact that it was actually *her* who made my day start badly. Mum had suggested that maybe I'd dropped my stupid missing keys on the driveway when I'd nipped down to the front gate to put some rubbish in the bin earlier, so I'd gone out to retrace my steps, and that was when I'd seen her, about twenty metres away down the street. My first thought had been: *bugger, I completely forgot to call Robin last night! There's no school run. She could have come later, dammit ...*

But as I quickly scanned the pavement by the bins, searching for my keys, and then looked down the road again, preparing to apologise, I stopped dead. Robin, in her running gear, was standing talking to a man, and laughing. And the man ... oh come on, *seriously*? It was *him,* wasn't it? I *wasn't* imagining it, not this time. It was Mike. It *was*. The private detective. What on earth was he still doing here, hanging around? He was in running gear too this time, dark knee-length shorts and a black T-shirt with a black beanie covering his hair, but it *was* him. I was certain of it. I'd seen him often enough over the past few months to recognise his build, the general shape of him. So what the hell was he still doing in Cheltenham? And, more to the point right now, why was he talking to Robin? Did she know him? *Or* ...

A cold hand of fear suddenly clutched at my heart. Had he stopped her in the street because he knew she worked for me? Was he telling her something? Passing on information? Passing on what he knew about me? I stood motionless, staring.

Please, no. Please.

And yet ... they were both laughing now. It looked ... Well, it didn't look as though a serious conversation was going on. Quite the opposite in fact. It looked friendly, casual. *Did* she know him? Then, as I watched, I saw Robin hand something to him, something small and square that I couldn't see properly. OK, what on earth was going on? Unexpectedly, the anxiety vanished, just like that, and instead I felt a rush of anger. Enough, now.

'OI!' I yelled. 'YOU! What are you doing?'

They both turned, wide-eyed, and I started to jog down the street towards them. For a moment, the man stood still, watching me approach. Then he turned abruptly and ran off down the High Street. By the time I reached Robin, he'd disappeared round the bend in the road.

'Beth? What's wrong?'

Robin was frowning at me and I looked at her and then down the road again, trying to catch my breath, panting even after such a short run.

'HIM!' I shouted, pointing in the direction he'd gone. 'Him. What did he want? How do you know him?'

She took a step backwards, looking startled.

'That bloke? I *don't* know him. I was running up the road to yours and he was coming in the other direction and as he passed me, he dropped his wallet. I called him back and gave it to him. That's all. Why? What is it, Beth?'

'No, you were chatting. Laughing. What was that all about?' I'd stopped shouting but I was still agitated, still breathing heavily. Did she think I was stupid? I'd *seen* them.

Robin's cheeks flushed.

'Nothing! He was kind of cute, that's all. And he's a fellow runner. We were just talking about how annoying it is to have to carry stuff, finding places to put everything so you don't lose it, you know? I don't understand, Beth. Why does it matter? Do *you* know him?'

I stared at her for a moment. Was I being paranoid? I hadn't slept well again last night, worrying about Dad, still trying to process the reappearance of my mother. Was it not Mike, after all? Was I going *mad*? I shook my head.

Oh hell. Robin must think I'm delusional.

'Robin, I'm so sorry. I just thought ... there's been a bloke hanging around a bit, that's all. I never mentioned it to you. I didn't want to freak you out ... I just thought it was him again. But I was obviously wrong. I'm really sorry. I've had rather a lot going on over the weekend. Actually, that's a bit of an understatement. Come on, let's go in and I'll tell you all about it. There's someone I want you to meet.'

We'd walked back to the house together and I'd apologised again, feeling like an idiot as I explained that the kids weren't even around today, and then filled her in. She'd been appropriately sympathetic about Dad, immediately telling me she'd be more than happy to take on extra childcare or whatever I needed while he was ill. And then we'd gone into the kitchen where Mum was drinking coffee at the island, and I'd introduced them. Robin nearly fell over with shock.

'Your ... your *mum*? But ...'

She was wide-eyed, staring from me to my mother and we looked at each other and laughed.

'Think you're going to get this a lot over the next few days, love,' Mum said wryly.

'I think I am! Are you OK, Robin?'

Robin swallowed and nodded, clearly trying to pull herself together. She knew, of course, that I hadn't seen my mother for thirty years; I'd briefly told her the story of Mum's disappearance as we drank tea together one day not long after she started working for me. It was bound to be somewhat surprising, therefore, for her to come to work on a Monday morning and find said runaway mother sitting in my kitchen.

'I'm fine, gosh. It's just ... well, it's a bit of a shock, isn't it? Lovely to meet you, Mrs ... erm ...'

She held out a hand and Mum smiled and shook it.

'Alice is fine,' she said.

'Of course. Lovely to meet you, Alice.'

Now, as I wait impatiently in the hall for my cab, I wonder if the two of them will be OK here in the house together while I'm at work. For the first few minutes Robin had simply stared at my mother; then, although she isn't usually one for long conversations, she began to bombard her with questions.

'So ... *where* do you live now? And *how* did you track Beth down? And how long has it been since you've seen each other?' I heard her say as I went into the downstairs loo for a quick pee, making me wonder if I should have sent Robin home today and let Mum have some space for her first full day alone in Cheltenham. I don't want her to feel overwhelmed, although I suppose it's only natural that people are going to have questions. I certainly did. I still do. But should I tell Robin to go home?

On the other hand, it's so nice to have a clean house on a Monday evening, and she's here now ...

I hear the toot of a car horn outside. *It'll be fine*, I think.

'Got to go! Have fun you two! See you this evening,' I shout, and there are answering yells from upstairs, where Mum's now gone to brush her teeth, and from the kitchen, where Robin's already started cleaning. So, still wondering where on earth my flipping keys are, I head for the taxi and work.

At lunchtime I rush to the hospital to see Dad, who I've been assured is stable and comfortable. He's asleep for my entire twenty-minute visit, but I chat quietly to him anyway, telling him about Robin's shock at meeting Mum, and the saga of my lost keys. I don't mention Mum coming to visit again though, as that, it seems, is a no-no. Over our soft-shell crab and chips last night I'd tentatively asked her if she wanted to see Dad again and about how she'd felt when she saw him.

She'd taken a bite of a large chip and chewed it slowly, contemplating her answer.

'It felt ... weird, to be honest. He looked so ... so *old*, Beth. I mean, I know he's got twenty years on me, but he seemed even older than that, you know? Like a really *old* man. I mean, I know he's sick and everything, but ... well, I'm not sure what I felt. It was just strange. And sorry, but I don't think I will go and see him again. I don't think it's a good idea, for either of us. I came back for *you*, not for him. I hope you understand that? And I hope you don't think it makes me sound cold, or unfeeling, or anything. But I have to be honest, you know?'

I nodded. I *did* understand. I wished things were different, but I got it. It was what it was.

And so I just promise Dad I'll pop in again on my way home this evening and race back to work, where I wolf down a ham sandwich in the staffroom while I hastily finish off the notes I've made for a meeting later with two of the GPs.

We're hoping to redecorate some of the consulting rooms later this year and we need to discuss timescales and budget and all sorts of other details. The meeting's scheduled for 3pm, but at five to Dr Johnson sticks her head round the door.

'Beth, I'm so sorry but can we delay a bit? I'm snowed under. Is four OK? I've asked Paul and he's fine with it if you are?'

'Of course. Any time this afternoon is fine by me, Gabby.'

I smile and she grins broadly, gorgeous white teeth flashing; she gives me a thumbs-up and disappears again. Gabrielle Johnson is probably my favourite of our five doctors, if I'm honest, although I'm rather fond of all of them. But Gabby is lovely. Born in Jamaica, she came to the UK with her family as a teenager and we always say she brought that Caribbean sunshine with her. It's rare to see her without a smile on her pretty face, and the patients adore her. I'm loving her even more now after my hectic morning, breathing a little sigh of relief that I've got some extra time before the meeting. I'm just about to start updating the surgery Facebook page – another one of my jobs – when Ruth walks in.

I sat her and Deborah down first thing this morning when I got in and told them the news about Mum – and Dad, of course – too, and their reactions were similar to Robin's. Sympathy and offers of 'anything we can do' for Dad, and: 'WHAT? But ... *how*? *When*? How on earth? But I thought ...'

This was Ruth, who had leapt from her chair when I described how I'd found my mother on my doorstep, and was clutching the chunky faux pearls at her throat as she gaped at me, wide-eyed. Deborah, meanwhile, was sitting stock-still, open-mouthed with surprise.

'Wow,' she said. 'Your ... your *mother*?'

'Yep. My long-lost mother,' I replied. I was rather enjoying all these reactions. I'd told them a bit more then, about how she'd found me, and about my sister (my *sister*! I'm still trying to take that in myself, and I can't *wait* to speak to her, to *see* her, when we FaceTime later this week). They'd both quickly recovered from their shock, hugging me and saying how excited they both were for me, how thrilled they'd be to meet Mum, before Ruth had to rush off to unlock the front door for early surgery. Meanwhile, Deborah had, to my amusement, got up and almost walked straight into the wall before wandering off back to her room still shaking her head and muttering under her breath, 'How extraordinary ...'

Now Ruth waves a battered thermos flask at me.

'This is Nadia's. She's over in her doorway again and I said I'd fill it up for her. I've got a packet of Hobnobs in my drawer. I'll give her a few of those too. Do you want one?'

I shake my head.

'No thanks. I'm not the biggest fan of Hobnobs. But listen, let me take those out to her. I haven't met her yet and Gabby's just moved our meeting to four, so I've got a bit of spare time.'

She shrugs.

'Yeah, if you like. She's a sweetie, but she might be a bit cagey with you at first. She's a tad wary, you know?'

'OK. I'll be nice. I just feel so sorry for her, even more so now that I've got both my parents again, for some reason. She must have nobody if she's living a life like that. It's tragic.'

'It is. But talking of parents, how are you feeling, really, about your mum suddenly coming back? I know it's fantastic and all that but ... well, it must be *so* weird too. Are you OK?'

She picks up the kettle, shakes it, and walks to the sink to top it up. I think for a moment and then say, 'I think so. It's really weird, yes, and honestly, if you told me this time last week that my mother would be back and staying in my spare room I wouldn't have believed you. I'd have said there was *far* too much water under the bridge to just let her back in. I'd have said I was way too angry and too upset about what she put us through ... but, I don't know. Somehow, when I saw her – well, it was just *joy*, Ruth. I'm not angry; I'm not anything negative really. That might change down the road, who knows. Maybe I'm kind of in a strange sort of honeymoon period. But right now, I'm just happy. I've got my mum back, and that's all that matters.'

Ruth nods slowly, and grins.

'Well, that's wonderful. It really is. I'm bloody delighted for you,' she says. 'Now, go and spread some of that happiness. I'm sure Nadia could do with a bit, bless her.'

As I cross the road to Nadia's doorway clutching the filled flask and three biscuits wrapped in tinfoil, I can see that she's engrossed in a book, a grubby paperback she's holding close to her face.

As I approach her, I call out, 'Nadia! Hi. I've got some tea for you!'

She looks up, a startled expression on her face. She's wearing the same brown felt hat I saw her in the other day, pulled low over her forehead, and although the day is mild she's bundled up in a thick padded jacket, fingerless gloves, and a tatty knitted scarf which is wrapped around her nose and mouth. Dark greeny-grey eyes squint up at me and she shrinks back a little, looking alarmed.

'Oh, I'm so sorry, I didn't mean to startle you,' I say gently. I bend down and put the flask and biscuits on the step next to her.

'I'm Beth, from the surgery?' I wave a hand vaguely in the direction of our building.

'I work with Ruth – you know Ruth? I said I'd come over with these. I was supposed to be in a meeting but it's not until four now, so ... Anyway, we've filled your flask, and there's some Hobnobs too ... Is there anything else I can get you? Anything you need? More books maybe? I've noticed you read a lot. Or maybe ...'

I pause, feeling uncomfortable. I'm waffling, and she's just staring at me.

'Sorry,' I say. 'I'll leave you in peace.'

I turn to leave, but as I start to walk away she calls after me.

'Beth? Thank you. It's nice to meet you. And some new books would be lovely, ta.'

Her voice is hoarse, as if she's smoked for decades, but her tone is polite – kind even. I turn back and smile.

'Of course, no problem. What sort of stuff do you like to read? What's that one? Oh, Agatha Christie, fantastic.'

I'm a big Christie fan myself, more at home with her cosy mysteries than with the darker, more violent crime novels some of my friends love. I peer at the cover of the book that's now resting on the blanket covering Nadia's legs. It's *The ABC Murders*, one of my own favourites.

'I've got loads of her books, if you want to borrow a few,' I say. 'What about *Crooked House*, or *Endless Night*. Have you read those?'

'Not for years, and I forget. That would be kind,' she says, and although I can only see her eyes, I can tell she's smiling.

We exchange a few more pleasantries and then she reaches for her flask. I say goodbye and head back to work, a little warm, fuzzy feeling inside me, and it's as if the encounter has turned my day around. My meeting goes swimmingly, with everyone in agreement about everything for once, and when I call in at the hospital on my way home, Dad is awake and responsive and has even managed to eat a little soup and toast for dinner. He doesn't ask many questions – he's clearly finding it hard to form words, his speech significantly worse than it was before this second much bigger stroke – but he nods and smiles as I chat. I don't mention Mum at all this time, and neither does he. It must have been *such* a shock for him to see her last night, and something tells me to wait until he's feeling stronger before I bring her up again. There is, I hope, plenty of time for that. He definitely seems better today, and the relief is immense.

When I get home, Mum opens the front door with a flourish. She's wearing oatmeal-coloured knitted lounge pants and a matching sweatshirt, and she looks relaxed and smiley.

'Darling! How was your day? I've been horribly lazy, I'm afraid. Barely moved from the sofa.'

'That's OK! You're on holiday, aren't you?' I say, and I follow her into the lounge where she's obviously been watching something on the Comedy Channel. She presses the mute button and beams at me.

'True.'

'Well, my day got much better, thank you,' I say. 'Hey, I don't suppose Robin found my keys when she was cleaning?'

'Ahh, yes. Kitchen island,' she says. 'As in, that's where they are now. I think she said she found them in the bathroom?'

I frown.

'The main bathroom? Not my ensuite?'

Mum shrugs.

'Think so, yes. Shall I open a bottle of wine? I noticed you had one in the fridge.'

'Erm ... yes, sure. That would be nice. Thanks.'

The bathroom? How on earth did they get there? I never use the main bathroom; it's just for the kids or guests.

Then I sigh.

Maybe I did go up there last night to replace the loo roll or something, after we got in from the hospital? I was so stressed and anxious, and I do tend to go into autopilot ...

I follow Mum into the kitchen and pick up the keys, slipping them into my handbag. I've got them back, that's the main thing. Mum's got the bottle of wine in her hand now, and she's looking around the kitchen.

'Corkscrew's in the drawer next to the cutlery one,' I say, and she smiles.

'Thanks, love.'

She finds the corkscrew and sets the bottle down, then starts picking the foil off.

'I'll need a glass of this before I meet the kids. I'm a bit nervous ... Isn't that silly?' she says.

I'm about to reply, to tell her it will be fine, that Jacob's told me the kids are thrilled at the news of her arrival and are dying to meet her, but she's still talking.

'... and by the way, Robin ... Do you really need her, love? Especially now I'm here, if I'm staying for a while? I can do the school runs and keep on top of the cleaning for you, if you like. It's just that, well ... I wasn't too sure about her, if I'm honest.'

'Oh!' I'm not sure how to respond. 'I mean, that's wonderful, if you still want to stay. I'd be absolutely delighted'—I take a step closer to her, feeling a little glow of happiness—'but honestly, I couldn't ask you to take on all that. It's too much. And Robin's great. What ... what did you mean about not being sure about her?'

She stops picking at the foil on the bottle and frowns slightly.

'Well ... oh, it's nothing, love. Ignore me. If you're happy with her ...'

She turns her attention back to the wine and I hesitate for a moment.

'No, go on, what is it?'

She shakes her head.

'Honestly, it's nothing. How long until the kids get here? I'm so excited. Do you want to go and change? I'll get this open and pour us both a glass, and then shall I stick the oven on for that lasagne you've got in?'

She's grinning widely now, and her sudden enthusiasm is infectious.

'Aww, thanks Mum. That would be great. I'll just be a minute.'

As I head upstairs though, my thoughts drift back to this morning, and the man Robin was talking to. Although by now I've pretty much convinced myself that it was a case of mistaken identity, that it wasn't Mike at all, that I'm just being paranoid, a tiny seed of doubt remains and it's just grown a bit bigger.

What if Robin was lying to me about him? I've seen her going through my stuff before. I trust her, but am I being an idiot? And what was Mum not telling me just now? Did she notice something today while they were alone here together?

There's a knot forming in my stomach, and I take a deep breath. Of course Robin is trustworthy. That was just a fellow runner this morning, she told me so. I have to stop being so paranoid, I tell myself firmly as I head back downstairs. If I carry on like this, I'm going to ruin everything. I take another breath and go and join my mother in the kitchen.

Chapter 13

'Eloise! Finley! Fifteen minutes, OK?'

I wait until I hear two voices shouting back at me from upstairs, then go into the kitchen where my mother is flicking through a magazine. At her insistence, we're taking the kids out for pizza – a rare treat for a Wednesday evening. She's been amazing with them since they met on Monday night, interested and interesting, helping Eloise with homework and reading Finley bedtime stories. They've been full of questions, of course, in the uninhibited way children are; I cringed inwardly when I heard Finley, just an hour after meeting his grandmother, ask her, 'Why did you leave Mummy and Grandad when Mummy was a little girl, Grandma? And why did you stay away for so long?'

She didn't miss a beat though.

'I was very sad back in those days, Finley. I had some grown-up problems, and I needed to go away and sort them out, because I didn't think it was fair to make your mummy and grandad sad too. And sometimes, when you go away, it's quite hard to come back, because you don't know if people will be happy to see you, or if they'll just be really cross with you. Do you understand?'

Finley thought for a moment, then nodded solemnly.

'Like when I broke my friend Luke's Nerf and I was scared to go back to his house for ages in case he was really cross?' he asked.

Mum looked bemused.

'Well, I don't know what a Nerf is, but yes, it sounds like a very similar situation,' she said.

'OK,' said Finley happily, and Eloise, who'd been listening intently from across the room, looked satisfied too.

'A Nerf is a stupid gun thing, Grandma,' she said helpfully.

And that was that. From everything they've said to me, the children seem to be smitten.

'Grandma is *dope*,' Finley told me when I went to kiss him goodnight last night.

'Yeah, she's pretty sick,' said Eloise, who was passing Finley's bedroom door on her way to the bathroom.

As far I know, dope and sick are pretty big compliments, and Mum cried with laughter when I passed them on to her.

'Oh, the youth of today,' she said, wiping her eyes. 'Whatever happened to cool and awesome, proper words?'

I could tell she was chuffed though, and now she turns to me and smiles.

'I'm really looking forward to this. I haven't been out for a pizza in ages,' she says. 'Oh, and you don't have to drive, love. I've booked a taxi. I didn't know which firm you normally use so I just googled local cabs.'

'Oh! That's kind. I don't mind driving, but I wouldn't mind

a glass of wine, actually. Thanks, Mum. You look lovely, by the way.'

She does. She's wearing a floaty floral top with some indigo jeans and a snazzy pair of red suede ankle boots; she looks stylish and youthful. I look down at my own outfit, a pair of denim jeggings which are just a bit too tight, white trainers, and a blue and white stripy shirt. I've tied my hair back and put some long silver earrings on, but suddenly I feel underdressed. Mum's looking me up and down too, and she clears her throat.

'Thanks. Thought I'd make an effort – first time out for dinner with you and my grandchildren. Are you ... are you ready to go?'

'Well, I was, but ...' I look down at myself again. *No, this won't do*.

'I think I'll lose the trainers and put some heels on,' I say. 'And maybe a blazer. What do you think?'

She nods.

'You look great as you are, but whatever you think, love.'

I'm already heading for the hallway.

'No, I'll change. Two minutes!'

As I force my feet into the uncomfortable stilettos, I suddenly decide I need to start making more of an effort with my appearance. Mum's so chic, and I'm ... well, I'm just *not*. I saw her looking me up and down just now, and although of course she's far too nice to say anything, I know I'm not stylish like her; I dress for comfort and practicality, not for fashion. And now my mother's back, I want her to be *proud* to be out with me, proud to tell people I'm her daughter.

I used to dress nicely when Jacob was around, didn't I? I've let things slip, I think.

He's another one who seems smitten with Mum. I smile as I wiggle into my blazer – also a little too tight these days. When he dropped the kids off on Monday night, he popped in briefly to be introduced, and ended up sitting and chatting with her for a good fifteen minutes. Shortly after he left, I got a text:

Wow! So nice to meet your mum after all these years! She's great. Very happy for you xx

It had been a while since I'd had kisses on the end of a text from my ex-husband, but I wasn't complaining. I wasn't reading anything into it – that ship has long since sailed – but it was still nice. Mum's reappearance, her sudden presence in our lives, just seems to be making everyone happy, and I'm damned if I'm going to do anything to spoil that. Desperate though I am to find out every detail of her life over the past thirty years, I'm trying to take it slowly, sensing a certain reticence on her part when I ask too many questions, and yet I think I know her well enough by now to realise that her reluctance to talk endlessly about the past is partly to protect me.

'I *have* had a good life, but that makes me feel so guilty,' she said at one point. 'I don't want you to think that my life was better because you weren't in it. It wasn't like that ...'

I shushed her, telling her I understood – and I think I do. And even though the feeling that she's less than impressed with the way I dress is just that, a feeling, it's something I can do something about. So, I muse, pulling at the sleeves of the blazer, if that means going out for dinner feeling all trussed up and uncomfortable then so be it. I take a deep breath and look in the full-length mirror that hangs on the bedroom wall. I look ... well, fine, I think. Better than before, anyway.

I stick my head around Eloise and Finley's doors as I head back downstairs, checking they're almost ready. I'm determined to enjoy this evening; it's going to be such a treat to be out for dinner with my mother and my children, and although I'm still worried about Dad, his condition continues to improve slowly.

Stop worrying, Beth. Stop worrying and enjoy tonight, OK?

'Taxi should be here in about three minutes. Everyone ready? And you look very nice, love!'

Mum has appeared in the hall where I'm transferring my purse and keys from my big work handbag to the small black patent-leather clutch I use for evenings.

'Thanks,' I say, just as there's the beep of a car horn from outside.

'Oh! He's early,' Mum says. 'Don't worry, I'll nip out and keep him talking while you get those two scamps sorted.'

'Great, thanks. We'll just be a minute,' I say, and she gives me a thumbs-up sign and heads for the front door, just as Finley and Eloise come thundering down the stairs.

'Erm ... shoes, Finley?' I say, pointing at his feet, on which he's wearing his favourite dinosaur socks and nothing else.

'Can't find them,' he says.

I roll my eyes.

'Finley, they're sitting on the floor next to your wardrobe. Eloise, can you go up with him, *quickly*, and get them on him please? The taxi's outside ... I'll go and tell the driver you're on your way. Make sure the front door is closed behind you when you come out, OK?'

Eloise sighs dramatically and grabs Finley's hand.

'*Such* a noob,' she says.

Like Mum with the Nerf, I have no idea what a 'noob' is, but trusting that my daughter is mature enough not to call her seven-year-old brother something *really* obscene, I decide to let it go. As they run back upstairs, I grab my bag and head out into the driveway. Mum's at the gate, standing at the open window of the cab that's parked there and chatting animatedly to the driver.

She turns as I approach.

'They're just coming, sorry. Missing shoes issue. Shall we get in?'

'Sure,' she says. I let her climb in first, and as I wait I notice that Brenda and Barbara are standing in Brenda's driveway next door, chatting to a man. I'm about to call out a hello when I pause.

Oh, bloody hell.

I move a few steps away from the taxi, eyes fixed on the tall figure. He's wearing a blue hoodie, denim jeans, trainers. It's the sort of casual gear you see on hundreds of men every day, and he has his back to me, but there's something about him ...

This is getting ridiculous. That's Mike, isn't it? What's going on? Why am I seeing him everywhere?

I'm standing there, staring, when suddenly Brenda notices me. She nudges Barbara and the two of them wave, smiling. The man doesn't turn round and I hesitate for a moment, then wave back.

'Just going out for pizza,' I shout.

'Lovely! Oh, can you just hang on one second?' Barbara shouts back, and then she turns to Brenda, says something, and scuttles off down the driveway, turning left at the gate and jogging along the pavement towards me.

'Hi,' she gasps.

'Hi. Erm, Barbara, who's that guy? The one you're chatting to? It's just ... well, he looks familiar?'

She turns and looks back to where I'm pointing.

'Him? He's just a gardener. Brenda's thinking of having some raised beds out back,' she says, then turns back to look at me, pushing a strand of her long red hair off her forehead. 'Look, Beth, I can't find my spare glasses anywhere and I'm just wondering if I left them at yours on Friday? Have you seen them?'

I shake my head. I'm still taking in what she's just said about the man being a gardener.

OK. Stop it now, Beth. Mike is not still hanging around telling people stuff about you. It's ridiculous to think that. You're ridiculous ...

'No, sorry,' I say. 'Haven't seen them.'

She sighs, then bends down to peer into the taxi. Her eyes widen and for a moment she just stares into the car's interior. Then she straightens up and turns to me.

'Oh gosh, is that your mum? Hello!'

She waggles her fingers, and Mum leans across and waves back.

'Hello. I'm Alice,' she says. 'Pleased to meet you.'

'Barbara, from next door,' says Barbara. 'Nice to meet you too.'

I smile at the pair of them – how lovely it is to see my friends meeting my mum! – then turn to frown at the front door, from which no children have yet emerged.

How long does it take to put on a pair of shoes?

'Beth, is it OK if I nip in and have a quick look around? For the glasses? Honestly, I haven't seen them since Friday and I've searched my place from top to bottom. I'm just wondering if they slipped down the side of your sofa. Do you mind?'

I turn back to Barbara.

'No, of course not, go on. And can you shout upstairs and tell my kids we're leaving in twenty seconds, with or without them?'

'Of course. Thanks, Beth.'

'Oh and Barbara – you and Brenda must come round for drinks to meet Mum properly. How does Friday sound?'

She hesitates for a moment, then nods.

'I think I'm free, yes. I'll check with Bren but she didn't mention any plans for the weekend. Thanks, Beth. That would be lovely.'

'Brilliant. OK, see you then. Hope you find your specs.'

'Thanks. I'm such a twit sometimes. Right, I'll send the children out. Have a great night!' she says, and I thank her and clamber into the taxi.

'Sorry,' I say to the driver. 'The kids are on their way.'

'No worries, love,' he says, smiling at me in the rear-view mirror.

'Your friend seems nice,' Mum says. 'When are they coming round? Friday?'

'Yes. Is that OK? You're definitely staying then?' I say.

'I'd love to. If that's OK with you, of course?'

'It's very OK,' I reply. 'You can stay as long as you like. Move in, if you want.'

I say the words lightly, as if in jest, but her eyes widen and she smiles broadly.

'Do you mean that? I mean, I'll have to go back to my job eventually, come the autumn. But for the next few months, yes. Yes, I'd love to move in. Are you sure?'

My heart leaps.

'Absolutely sure. That would be ... that would be wonderful, Mum! More than wonderful.'

I grab her hand and squeeze it, and she squeezes back.

'That's settled then,' she said. 'And right on cue, here are those gorgeous grandchildren of mine. Let's go and celebrate!'

Eloise and Finley finally wrench the taxi door open, bickering as they climb in next to us, and for a moment I think I'm going to cry with joy as all of my stupid anxieties evaporate.

She's moving in. She's moving in, and Dad's recovering, and everything's AMAZING. How did I get this lucky?

The evening's pretty amazing too. The food is delicious, and Mum and the kids are chatting away like old friends. I try not to eat *too* much; this new sense of wanting to dress more stylishly is also, for some reason, making me think about my weight. I know I'm bigger than I used to be, but until now I've been OK with that. As long as I'm healthy, what does the size label in my clothes matter? But now ... Mum's just so slim, so elegant, and I feel big and awkward next to her. At the same time, I'm feeling so happy, and it's such a treat to be out ... and the pizza is so hot and fresh and tasty and, well, I leave a *little* on my plate – the crust mainly. I blame the wine, which always makes me peckish; knowing we're calling another cab to take us home, I break my usual week-night rules and have a little too much of the perfectly chilled Sauvignon Blanc, and by the time we get back to Prestbury I'm definitely a little tipsy. Leaving Mum to watch the ten o'clock news in the living room, I shoo the children off to bed and go into my room to change into my PJs. I'll make some hot chocolate, I think, to finish the night off. But as I open the drawer to find a fresh pair of pyjamas I pause. Something doesn't look right. The little arrangement of cosmetics and perfume bottles that sit in regimented rows on top of my chest of drawers is somehow askew.

Why is that bottle of Obsession at the front? I haven't used that in ages; I've gone off it. And I didn't leave my eyeshadow palettes piled up like that. Or did I?

I frown, trying to remember, but the alcohol is making my head fuzzy. Slowly, I put everything back in its correct place, thinking. Barbara was in the house tonight, wasn't she? But she was looking for her glasses, and there's no way they would be up here, in my bedroom. She'd only have looked downstairs, in the kitchen or living room. Unless ... could she have thought that maybe Robin found the glasses when she was cleaning and thought they were mine? Might she have had a root around up here just in case? Maybe. I cast my eyes around the room, looking for anything else out of place, but everything seems in order.

I did get ready in a hurry earlier, didn't I? And all that wine ... I roll my eyes at myself in the mirror. It was probably me, then. I'm such an idiot at the moment. I'll be hearing voices next.

Stop it, Beth. Hot chocolate and a good night's sleep, that's what you need.

I give the now neat rows of cosmetics one more glance, then pull some clean pyjamas on and head back downstairs.

Chapter 14

It's Friday, and I've finally remembered the books I promised to bring Nadia. When we close for lunch, I peer out of the waiting room window to check that she's there – she is; she always seems to be there these days – and nip across the road. When I reach her, she greets me with a small smile. She's reading a newspaper today, *The Independent* I think, but her eyes light up when I open the bag I'm carrying and show her the selection of Agatha Christies I've selected from my bookshelf.

'I've brought *Crooked House*, *Endless Night*, and a couple of Poirots – *Third Girl* and *The Clocks*. Are they OK?' I ask.

'Perfect, thanks. Very kind of you,' she says, and smiles again. Her teeth are yellow and one upper incisor is missing.

'That's OK. Enjoy. And I don't need them back; my bookshelves are bursting at the seams, so just pass them on to someone else when you're done or leave them with a charity shop or something.'

She nods, eyes fixed on the books, and I feel a little surge of sympathy and sadness.

This poor woman.

I squat down beside her. There's a faint, stale odour of sweat and dirty clothes, but in her fingerless gloves her hands look clean and her nails are neatly clipped.

'Nadia, is there anything else I can do for you? What do you do at the weekends, when the surgery is closed? Do you still sit here or go somewhere else?'

She closes the plastic bag and pushes it into the big black half-open suitcase that's sitting next to her in the doorway. I can see clothes in it – a pair of denim jeans and a navy jumper.

'No, I usually go down to the Prom at weekends. Shoppers, you know. Some can be generous,' she says. Her throat sounds raspy, and she reaches under the blanket that covers her knees and pulls out a bottle of water. I wait while she takes a drink, unsure what to do next.

Give her some money? Would she be offended? Oh gosh, I don't know how to help her. I'm rubbish ...

'What are you doing this weekend? Anything nice?' she says unexpectedly. She wipes her mouth with the back of her hand and screws the cap back on the bottle with slightly trembling fingers.

'Nothing exciting really,' I say. I'm starting to wish I hadn't squatted down now; my left leg is starting to cramp.

'My mum is staying with me at the moment and I've got some friends coming round to meet her. We haven't seen each other for a long time – years, in fact – so none of my friends know her, you see. She lives down in Cornwall and we've only recently been reunited – it's a long story. But anyway, two of my neighbours are coming round for drinks later, which will be nice. I just have to decide whether I'm going to cook something or just get a takeaway. I won't have much time after work, so a takeaway would be easier, but it seems a bit lazy, you know ...'

Her eyes have widened and she's staring at me with a bewildered expression. I'm suddenly aware that I'm waffling, speaking far too quickly, and anyway, why on earth am I telling her all this, this poor old homeless woman?

Why would she care if I cook or get a takeaway? Talk about middle-class problems. *Shut up Beth …*

'Oh, heck, sorry Nadia,' I say. I stand up awkwardly, rubbing my leg. 'I'll leave you in peace. But do let one of us know if you want anything, OK? I'm sure Ruth will be out with some coffee in a bit. She usually makes some around now.'

She's still staring at me, but she nods.

'Thanks. And for the books. Thank you,' she mutters.

'No problem. Well, bye.'

I lift a hand in a half-wave and then turn and walk swiftly back across to the surgery, cringing inside.

What's wrong with me, going on like that? She'll think I'm bonkers ...

I'm just metres away from the door when a man emerges. He glances at me, then quickly looks right and left and jogs across the road towards the car park. I stop walking so suddenly that a woman coming towards me on the pavement has to step out into the road to veer round me. She tuts loudly, but I barely look at her, my heart pounding.

Is that Mike? Not again. Don't start this again, Beth. You know it's not him. You know there's nothing to worry about. Stop it, stop it …

But it's not working. My eyes frantically scan the car park but the man is already out of sight. I push the door open and walk into the waiting room. Ruth is behind the reception desk and Deborah is leaning across it, and they're having a conversation in low, urgent voices. Then Ruth spots me, and pokes Deborah in the arm with a manicured finger.

'Beth!' she says loudly. 'How was Nadia? Did she like the books?'

Deborah turns abruptly.

'Oh, hi,' she says. She looks a little flushed.

Why stop talking so suddenly? Were they talking about me? Was it him, after all? Did he ... did he tell them?

'Who was that?' I say and point over my shoulder in the direction of the door. 'That man, in the dark overalls? He just left. Who was he?'

I know I sound agitated but I can't help myself. Deborah frowns and looks at Ruth. Ruth hesitates for a moment, looking at me, then picks up a business card that's lying on her desk.

'He's a plumber. He just popped in to leave a card in case we need one at any point,' she says, waving the small white rectangle at me. 'Why? What's wrong, Beth? Are you OK?'

I take a breath.

A plumber. Just a plumber. And the other day with Barbara and Brenda it was just a gardener, and before that, with Robin, just a runner who dropped his wallet. It's not him. None of these men are him. He went home ages ago. I'm worrying about nothing. Nothing bad is going to happen. Everything is OK. Everything is fine.

I'm losing it, I think. *Literally* losing my keys, seeing people ... Is this stress? A result of Mum appearing so suddenly and Dad being ill? I need to get on top of it, and fast. I breathe in again, and out, slowly.

'I'm fine, sorry,' I say. 'I got cramp in my leg, crouching down talking to Nadia, and it's a bit ouchy, that's all. And I just thought I recognised him, that bloke, but I've obviously got him mixed up with someone else. You two OK?'

I smile reassuringly.

'Erm ... great,' says Deborah. She looks at Ruth, then back at me. 'Happy it's Friday, that's for sure.'

'Hear, hear!' says Ruth. 'Hey Beth, we were just talking about how we'd love to meet your mum. Why don't we organise drinks or something? Before she goes home again?'

Instantly, the paranoia is back.

Why were they just talking about me and Mum?

I hesitate, but they're both smiling, acting completely normally.

Oh, for God's sake, Beth. They're your friends, and you've just been reunited with your long-lost mother. Of course they'd love to meet her.

'She's not planning on going any time soon,' I say. 'So yes, that would be lovely. I'll run some dates past you later. Brenda and Barbara are coming round tonight, so maybe next week?'

'Ace,' says Ruth. 'Have you spoken to your sister yet, by the way? Weren't you going to FaceTime or something?'

'We did, last night. It was ... well, amazing,' I said.

It was. Once the kids were in bed – I decided it might be too much for Liv to be faced with all three of us at once –

Mum and I settled down on the sofa and dialled the number. I'd had butterflies for hours, but as soon as she answered the call and her smiling face appeared on the screen of Mum's phone, they vanished.

'Hey big sis,' she said.

She looked even prettier than in the photos I'd seen: long blonde hair a similar shade to mine falling in soft waves and framing delicate features. We didn't chat for long – she was at work, taking a coffee break during an evening shift at the shipping office – but she sounded exuberant, repeatedly saying how exciting all of this was and how she couldn't wait to meet me and her niece and nephew. She had, it emerged, known about me for years, but had rarely dared to ask about me, knowing I was a sensitive subject for Mum.

'When she finally decided to get back in touch with you, I literally ran around the room screaming,' she laughed. 'I couldn't believe it, could I, Mum? I've always, *always* wanted a big sister, and now here you are. It's mad, isn't it?'

When we ended the call, blowing silly kisses at each other and giggling like children, I felt elated, and went to bed dreaming of shopping trips, cocktails, and girlie weekends away – sisterly activities I'd always envied in my friends' lives, never imagining they could one day be possible for me.

As I relate this now to Ruth and Deborah, any residual feelings of unease fade. I need to pull myself together, I think, or I'm going to ruin this for everyone. This should be one of the happiest times in my life. I have to stop thinking about the past, have to stop being so terrified that it's going to ruin my future.

'Whoops, look at the time,' says Ruth suddenly, tapping her watch. 'The afternoon hordes will be here any minute now. Scoot, you two. Busy, busy.'

Deborah rolls her eyes at me.

'You'd think she was in charge here, not you,' she says.

'I know. What you can do, eh?' I give a dramatic sigh and we all laugh. I head back to my office feeling lighter, happier again. After work I go home via the hospital where I find Dad sleepy but still stable, and then race home. As I'm parking the car, Brenda's just getting out of hers and she waves to me across the wall.

'Looking forward to this evening!' she says. 'How are things though? Must be so odd for you ... Is it going well?'

I nod.

'It really is. You'd think it would be odd, and I suppose it is in some ways – we're still getting to know each other again, you know? But in other ways it just feels ... normal. Weird, eh?'

She shrugs.

'Blood's thicker than water and all that. That's brilliant, Beth. See you later then!'

She waves again and heads for her front door, and I lock the car and let myself into the house. I can hear music – is that the Bee Gees? – coming from the kitchen, and I walk in to find Mum twirling Eloise around the island, Finley perched on one of the high stools, laughing.

'What's going on here then?' I say. 'Party started without me?'

Mum stops dancing, pink-cheeked and breathless, and a beaming Eloise rushes over to give me a hug.

'We couldn't wait,' Mum says with a grin. 'Friday night and all that!'

Something's in the oven too, something savoury and fragrant. There's no sigh of Robin though, and I wonder if Mum's sent her home early.

'Grandma's giving me dancing lessons!' Eloise is looking up at me, arms still wrapped around my waist. She's still in her school uniform, her tie askew.

'Lovely!' I reply and kiss the top of her head. 'Rather her than me – two left feet here.'

Mum laughs.

'I've always loved dancing,' she says. 'And I'm glad you're home, love. I let Robin go, hope that's OK? She didn't seem to have much to do anyway. She was just hanging around, and with me here ...'

There's a disapproving tone to her voice and she pauses for a second or two then says, 'Anyway, I know we're getting a takeaway later but I popped out earlier and bought some ready-made canapés – they're in the oven. I thought the kids might be hungry. It's just little prawn blinis and some mini chicken kebabs. We can have them as an appetiser when your friends arrive?'

'Yum. Great. Thanks so much.'

I release Eloise and lean over to give Finley a kiss, and then Mum. This *is* great, I think. It's so nice to come home to a kitchen filled with noise and music and dancing, to see the children having so much fun with their grandmother, to feel ... *looked after*, I suppose. Looked after, by my mother. Food in the oven, wine glasses laid out on the countertop, a bottle in an ice bucket.

'Oh, and I got you something, a little present. Thought you might like to wear it this evening.'

Mum's waving a plastic carrier bag at me; it's from one of those chi-chi little boutiques in The Suffolks – not Brenda's but another even more expensive one.

'Mum! That's so naughty. You shouldn't have! You don't need to be spending your money on me, honestly.'

She shrugs and hands me the bag.

'Just trying to make up for all those birthdays and Christmases I missed over the years,' she says. 'And I have a very long way to go yet, so humour me. It's nothing much, just a little top.'

'Well, that's incredibly kind of you, thank you.'

I take the bag, and peek inside. I see leopard print and my heart sinks a little. I don't really do animal print. It's not my style – too 'out there', but I don't want to offend her, so I gasp appreciatively.

'Wow, that looks gorgeous,' I say. 'I'll run up and change. Brenda and Barbara will be here in a few minutes.'

'I'd better get those canapés out then,' she says. 'Eloise, darling, why don't you go and change out of your school uniform? And Finley, can you put your shoes away? Don't want Mummy's friends to trip over them, do we?'

The children leap to do her bidding and, wondering why they're never so well-behaved for me, I head upstairs to get out of my work clothes. I had wondered about asking Robin to stay this evening, to join us for drinks and dinner if she was free, but now I'm glad I didn't. I'm still getting the sense that Mum doesn't seem too keen on her, for whatever reason.

When I take my gift out of the bag it's even worse than I feared – a garish, leopard print jersey top with a flouncy, ruffled neckline. I pull it on and even though it's labelled a size medium it's far too small, flattening my boobs and clinging to my tummy. I stare at myself in the mirror and poke at the rolls of fat around my waist. I look dreadful, but I can't not wear it, can I? Not when she's gone to so much trouble and spent so much money.

I root in my wardrobe and find my stretchy black palazzo pants, which are high-waisted and help, I think, to conceal some of the lumpy bits, but I still feel horribly uncomfortable as I go back downstairs, my armpits already damp, the frills at my neckline scratchy against my skin.

'Oh!' Mum looks wide-eyed for a moment, then seems to recover herself and smiles.

'Well, don't you look pretty,' she says, but her eyes flick downwards to my stomach, to my thighs, and I feel again this new shame about my body, an acute sense of disappointment that I don't look nicer for my classy, fashionable mother.

I'm about to reply, to thank her again for the present, to apologise, maybe, for not looking as good as I should in it, when the doorbell rings. The next few minutes are a whirl of introductions and kisses, wine being poured, and glasses clinking. When we're all finally settled around the island, Eloise and Finley in the lounge nibbling canapés on the sofa, thrilled to be allowed to stay up for the takeaway, I wave my drink in the air.

'A toast,' I say. 'To Mum, and to friendship.'

'To Mum and to friendship!' they all echo, even Mum with

a grin, and we clink again and drink. We spend the next hour chatting and laughing. Brenda and Mum hit it off straight away with their shared love of fashion and the arts. But Barbara seems quiet, distracted, not her usual self at all. She's listening to the conversation, her eyes fixed on Mum and Brenda as they chat, but she's not joining in. Then she catches me watching her and seems to perk up a bit, clearly making an effort to smile and interject now and again, but she's not fooling me. It's pretty obvious that something isn't right. I need to find out what's going on, so the next time I stand up to refill the glasses I pull my stool over to sit next to her.

'You OK?' I ask in a low voice, as Mum regales Brenda with a story about a famous British artist she knows who had a threesome with two of his life models. I'm quite glad the children are in the lounge with the TV on, out of earshot.

'Fine, fine,' she whispers. 'Just a bit tired. Long week, you know.'

'You sure? You seem ... well, not yourself.'

'I'm fine, honestly. Just need a good night's sleep.'

I nod, but now I'm thinking about Wednesday evening when I let her into the house to search for her glasses and then thought somebody had been moving things around in my bedroom. It had slipped from my mind but I feel like I have to ask her.

'Did you find your glasses the other day? Were they here?' I ask.

She rubs her nose, frowning, then shakes her head.

'Oh, no, sorry, I should have said. Found them at home after all. I'd left them in the downstairs loo. Not sure why – I hardly ever use it. I'm so scatty at the moment. Must be my age.'

She smiles a wan smile and reaches for her wine glass.

'Good, glad you found them. You didn't ... well, you didn't go upstairs, did you? While you were here? It's just that ...'

But she's shaking her head, frowning again.

'No, I just looked around down here. Why?'

I pause.

It was probably me after all. Or maybe it was Eloise, borrowing some perfume or trying on my make-up without asking, I think. She's at that age, isn't she?

I pat Barbara's arm.

'No reason. Forget it. I'm as bad as you – head like a sieve – and I shouldn't be, at my age. Are you hungry? Shall I order the food?'

She nods.

'Go on. I'm *not* very hungry, to be honest, but the way those two are knocking back that wine they'll be getting the munchies about now.'

I laugh and place the order, and when it arrives we eat in the kitchen, the children taking plates into the lounge to eat off their knees in front of the television. I bundle them off to bed shortly afterwards, and when I come back downstairs, Mum and my friends have retired to the sofa, Barbara a little more animated now after several glasses of wine. I sink into the big armchair opposite them, pulling at the top which is now stretched even more tightly across my full tummy.

'Is that new? Don't usually see you in animal print.' Brenda gestures at my top.

'Yes. Mum bought it for me. It's good to try something different, don't you think?'

Brenda looks appraisingly at me for a few seconds, then nods doubtfully.

'Sure,' she says.

Mum's eyeing me too.

'It's a bit snug, love, isn't it? I'm so sorry. I thought the medium would be OK. You still look lovely though, doesn't she ladies?'

She smiles and Brenda and Barbara hesitate for a moment, looking at me in my gaudy, far-too-small top, then smile and nod too, but they look a little awkward and inside I'm cringing.

'I think it's me, not the sizing. Too much curry and pizza recently,' I say. 'Maybe the diet should start tomorrow, eh?'

'Well, not tonight,' says Mum. I realise she's not disagreeing that I need to lose some weight and I feel even more humiliated. But she's smiling encouragingly and she winks at me.

'I'll top us up,' she says.

She does, and I start to feel better again as we sit there in the warm lounge, drinking and chatting. Finally, my eyes start to droop and I sink back into the cushions and drift off to sleep, empty wine glass between my knees. I'm not sure how long I'm asleep for, but I wake with a violent jump to find the room empty and quiet, just one small lamp still on. I sit there, panting, disorientated, knowing I've been having another dream about Lucy Allen. Lucy, who changed my life when, that fateful day twenty-seven years ago, I sat down beside her in Maths class. Another dream, another nightmare.

Her face looming over me in the darkness, the sound of a distant wailing echoing in my ears.

Breathe, Beth. It was a dream. Just a dream.

I look around the room. Someone has taken my glass away and covered me with a blanket. The coffee table has been cleared, the television turned off, and the remote is sitting neatly on the sideboard. My mouth feels dry and my head is fuzzy; I know I've drunk far too much. How embarrassing to fall asleep when my friends are here, and leave my mother to see them out and tidy up. But right now, I'm too tired to care. Stiff and weary, I haul myself out of the chair and head up to bed.

Chapter 15

'What a beautiful morning.'

'It is, isn't it?'

It's the morning after the night before, and Mum and I are drinking tea and nibbling chocolate cake in the garden as the weather is surprisingly mild. I'm a little hungover, if I'm honest, but the fresh air and cake is helping. I probably shouldn't be eating it, not with my bulging waistline, but this is a celebration, of sorts – the one-week anniversary of our reunion – and Mum's making plans. She's just told me she'll write a list and email it to Liv later, get her to send on more clothes and bits and pieces.

'It's getting warmer every day. If I'm going to move in for a bit, I'll need more than I've got with me in that holdall,' she says. She pauses as a sparrow lands briefly on the edge of the patio table, considers us for a moment, then flies off again.

'Well, I'm seriously impressed by how much you managed to fit in it,' I say. 'You're obviously a lot better at packing than I am. Once when Jacob and I took the kids to Spain for a week I managed to take six pairs of shoes and no knickers.'

She snorts at that, and I laugh too, happy that I've amused her. I crave her approval, I've begun to realise; I yearn for it, like a child who wants to impress a cool, older school mate. Is that really sad? It probably is, but hey.

'So, what did you think of Crystal?' I ask. 'She's nice, isn't she?'

Jacob and Crystal had popped by to pick up the kids earlier, and this time Crystal had come into the house looking fresh faced and youthful in jeans and a Breton top, her hair pulled back into a ponytail.

'She's desperate to meet your mother,' hissed Jacob. 'I told her all about her and she's intrigued.'

'Everyone seems to be,' I hissed back, and we headed into the kitchen where Mum was helping Finley with his shoes as Eloise packed her homework books into her little overnight case.

I made the introductions and then left them to it for a couple of minutes, going upstairs to check Finley's bag and add pyjamas and a toothbrush. When I came back down, there were smiles all round. Crystal was perched next to Mum on the little kitchen sofa admiring the chunky brushed-metal pendant on a black suede cord she was wearing around her neck.

'I just love this, Alice,' she was saying. 'You look fabulous.'

Now, Mum nods and takes another sip from her mug.

'She's delightful,' she says. 'I can see why Jacob fell for her ... Oh gosh, sorry, love. That was tactless ...'

She groans and covers her face with her hands, peeping at me comically through her fingers and I laugh.

'It's fine, don't be silly! It's all water under the bridge, all very mature and amicable. She *is* lovely and I'm glad you liked her.'

Mum uncovers her face.

'Phew,' she says. 'Well, that's all right then. She seems very young. I suppose that's men for you though, always after a younger model.'

I shrug.

'Not that young. She's thirty-five, so only five years younger than me.'

'Oh.' Mum looks surprised. 'She looks great, then. She's so slender.'

I'm sure she glances down at my stomach as she speaks, just for a second, and I shift uncomfortably in my chair and pull at the fabric of my old grey sweatshirt which is pulled tight across my tummy. But she's smiling now and shaking her head.

'And that wasn't a dig at you, my darling. A bit of weight suits you. You're a curvy girl. Don't worry about it.'

She leans across the table and pats my hand but I know she's just trying to be nice. I need to get on top of this extra weight *soon*, before it gets out of hand. But ... I look at my cake.

Maybe not today. Tomorrow. I'll start tomorrow.

I'm about to start eating again when Mum says, 'Look, this is a bit awkward, but I just wanted to tell you ... well, just mention, something about last night?'

She's looking uncomfortable now.

'What is it?' I say.

'Well, it was just something ... something ... that was said. Something I thought you should know.'

'What? What is it?'

I'm suddenly feeling nervous; the cake is forgotten.

What's this about? Oh please, no ... Was that Mike talking to Brenda and Barbara outside the other day after all? Did he tell them about me? Was that why Barbara was acting so strangely last night? Oh God, I fell asleep ... Did they ... did they tell Mum? Did they all sit there talking about me, about that? But surely she'd have mentioned it before now, something so serious ...

I'm starting to panic. There's a tingling in my chest and my fists are suddenly clenched so tightly that my fingernails are digging painfully into my palms. Mum is still talking and I try to focus, try to listen.

What's she saying?

'... after you fell asleep? You were so exhausted, love, and we didn't want to disturb you, so we moved out into the kitchen again and, well, we were just chatting about you really, and how the three of you met after you all moved into your little estate. And I just happened to mention that they were both a lot older than you – more my age really – and then Brenda said, or was it Barbara, I can't remember, one of them anyway, well she said ...' She pauses, her eyes on mine.

I wait, my breath catching in my throat.

'Well, she said, and I'm paraphrasing here, but she said something like "yes, we always thought it was odd she hasn't got any friends of her own age. We just hang out with her because we feel sorry for her, really."'

She pauses again, and my eyes widen.

'They said ... they said they feel *sorry* for me? But ...'

She's nodding.

'Yes, and then she, whichever one it was, said "We always felt she was looking for a mother figure, and now you're back that takes the pressure off us. You can take over now." Something like that – I'm paraphrasing, as I said. "We can back off a bit now," she said. And then they both laughed. And I just thought, well, that's not very nice, is it? When you're meant to be friends? I just thought you should know, darling. I'm sorry. I know it's not a pleasant thing to hear.'

I'm staring at her, stunned. OK, a little bit relieved too, that she hasn't just said what I feared she might. But *this*?

Did they really say something so ... so horrible?

'I can't ... I can't believe that,' I stammer. 'We're friends. We have been since the beginning. Yes, they're both older than me, but so what? It was never about me looking for a mother figure. That's ridiculous. I just liked them. We're neighbours. We get on really well. I don't understand ...'

Tears spring to my eyes.

We're the Busy Bees; we're a little threesome. We're friends, aren't we?

Mum is handing me her napkin, telling me to wipe my eyes, and saying she's so sorry and she probably shouldn't have mentioned it, shouldn't have said anything, but my mind is racing.

Maybe they're right. All my closest friends are older than me, not just Brenda and Barbara, but Ruth and Deborah too, all of them closer to Mum's age than to mine. Maybe it's true.

Maybe that is why I was drawn to them. Maybe I'm a freak with some sort of mother complex. Have I just been subconsciously looking for my mother in every older woman I've met? Shit. No wonder they just feel sorry for me ...

'Are you OK, love? I feel so bad I've ruined our lovely morning now. I'm so sorry.'

Mum sounds as if she's on the verge of tears herself and I sniff, take a deep breath, and pull myself together.

'Mum, it's fine. If that's how they feel, honestly ... I'm fine. I'm glad you told me, seriously. Come on, let's forget it. Do you want to walk down to the shop with me? We're out of milk.'

'Of course. Sorry again, love.'

I wave a hand dismissively, but I'm fighting back the tears as we make the short journey down to the village shop and back. As we reach my front gate, my heart sinks. Next door, Brenda is standing at her open front door, chatting to Barbara.

'Uh-oh,' I mutter.

'Oh dear,' says Mum. 'Look, I'll leave you to it. I'll head in.'

She hurries towards the house and I hesitate at the gate for a moment, wondering how to play this. Do I pretend everything is fine and just give them a cheery wave across the wall? Or do I go round and say something, confront them about what they said? Do I just *ignore* them maybe? I'm hovering, still undecided, when Brenda glances across and catches my eye. For a few, horribly awkward seconds we just stare at each other, then Barbara's head turns too and now we're all looking at each other, and nobody's smiling and it's ... it's awful.

They must know, I think. They must know that Mum will have told me what they said about me. They must know I'm feeling hurt and upset. And they're not going to apologise, or even acknowledge it? Well, sod that.

Suddenly, I'm angry. I turn away abruptly and walk towards the front door and I don't look back.

Fine. If I'm such a burden, if they want my mum to take over now, fine. Just bloody fine.

I'm still upset though, although I do my best to hide it from Mum. In the end, we have a pleasant day – the afternoon is dry and sunny, and I potter around the garden, pulling up weeds and pruning some unruly shrubs, while Mum sits on the patio with her magazines. When it gets a little too chilly to stay outside, we go in and I settle Mum in front of the TV and then pop over to the hospital to check on Dad. He's fine – a little more alert than yesterday even, which lifts my mood – and when I get back I feel a tiny bit better. I join Mum on the sofa and we search the movie channels and end up watching *Gilda*. I've never seen it, but Mum's ecstatic.

'Oh, this is amazing!' she says. 'One of the classic black and white films. Rita Hayworth is just *stunning*.'

It *is* good – a casino, mobsters, and lots of 1940s glamour – although I'm finding it hard to concentrate and keep drifting off into my thoughts. I try to tell myself I'm OK but I'm still hurting. After staying up so late last night we decide to make tonight an early one, and I'm in my bedroom by ten. I wasn't in the mood for cooking anything elaborate for dinner so I raided the freezer and cobbled together a quick meal of oven chips, fish fingers, and salad, Mum insisting I had most of the chips and me not in the right state of mind to argue.

Now though, as I slowly peel off my clothes, I'm regretting eating so much; my stomach feels bloated and uncomfortable. As I walk past the full-length mirror on the bedroom wall after depositing my dirty clothes in the laundry basket in my ensuite, I pause, looking myself up and down. Is it that bad, really? My legs are OK – pale and a little blotchy but reasonably firm and shapely – *although* ...

I poke my right thigh and the flesh wobbles. Not so firm, then. My eyes move upwards to my stomach and my bum. Once (before children and, latterly, the comfort eating that came with divorce) flat and smooth, my tummy now has rolls of fat I can lift with both hands; when I drive over a speed-bump in the car, I can actually feel it bouncing up and down. And as for the rear view ... I turn my back to the mirror and peer over my shoulder at my bottom. Once high and pert, now it sags, the blubbery, untoned cheeks merging with the tops of my thighs. I stare at it, feeling disgusted. How have I let this happen? And why am I only feeling like this *now*? Yes, like almost every woman I know, I moan about my body all the time, batting off any compliments and vowing to lose a stone after Christmas/for the summer/before my next birthday, because that's what we do, isn't it? But actually, I've embraced my new curvier form of recent years, quite enjoying my larger breasts and the soft curve of my shoulders, so different from the thinner, flat-chested, bonier me of my twenties. I'm not sure what's changed, why I'm suddenly starting to feel so ... so *revolted* by my own appearance. *And yet* ...

I run my hands over my breasts, lifting each one up in turn, enjoying the weight of them. The nipples are pink and harden slightly in the coolness of the room. Yes, my boobs are still good, I think. That's something, at least. I stand there a little while longer, lost in thought, my hands idly caressing my breasts, my stomach, the tops of my thighs. Then, abruptly, I turn away from the mirror, pull my pyjamas on, and crawl into bed. I'm exhausted, but sleep doesn't come. My mind is racing, filled with thoughts of Brenda and Barbara, the women I thought were my friends but clearly, *clearly* weren't. And then I remember the panic I felt when Mum started to tell me what they'd said, and I'd thought for a dreadful moment that she was going to say something completely different, that she was going to tell me that they'd told her something about me, something they've only just discovered. I think about the fear that gripped me, the fear that's spiralled in the past few weeks. I think about the terror that one day the past I've tried so hard to forget is going to come back and ruin my present and destroy my future. The horrific thought of my friends, my colleagues, finding out what I did, what I *am*. I'm just so *scared*, I realise. So very, very scared. If Mike *is* still hanging around, if he *has* uncovered it, if he's told Mum, told *anyone* ...

I take a deep, shuddering breath, my hands gripping the duvet, my eyes wide and frightened in the dark.

If he has told her though, wouldn't she have mentioned it to me by now? And if he hasn't told her, then why on earth would he tell anyone else? He wouldn't; of course he wouldn't.

Could Mum know about it another way though? From somebody else? I need to know if she knows, or I'm going to drive myself mad. I need to find out, somehow, and I need to do it fast, because I can't go on like this. I can't.

It won't stop the nightmares though. Nothing, I think, will ever stop the nightmares.

Chapter 16

That first day, when I sat next to Lucy Allen in class, I barely acknowledged her. I was pissed off that the teacher, hoping for a quiet lesson, hadn't let me sit with my usual noisy gang, putting me instead with this dull little girl who blushed every time she was asked a question but still always knew the answer.

'Swot,' I thought viciously.

I was different then, you see, to how I am now. Now I've learned tolerance and patience, kindness. But then, when I was thirteen, puberty was kicking in and the pain of the loss of my mother was even more acute; the anguish and anger burned more fiercely inside me every day and I was, quite frankly, a little bitch. Now I know that the way I behaved back then was completely normal for someone who had experienced what I had; I had friends, girls I hung out with, but I fell out with them regularly, always pushing them away before we got too close. I had begun more and more to believe, even though my dad told me repeatedly that he loved me, that I was not worthy of love, that I was defective somehow, because why else would my mother leave me? Increasingly, I struggled to cope with any form of criticism, or the tiniest hint of rejection – even a dog bounding up to one of my friends in the park and ignoring me was enough to send me descending into a depression that would last for days and yet was impossible for me to understand or explain. Therapy, although I fought it and refused to go as a teenager, was what saved me in the end. At university, I finally realised I needed help, and the resultant year of regular sessions with a gentle soul called Rita finally taught me that it was safe to put down roots, that it was possible to work through issues with friends and partners instead of shutting down and walking away. That I didn't have to be so fiercely independent but could actually let people in. That I didn't always have to say yes to be accepted and loved.

I'm still a people pleaser, to a degree, still a little paranoid, a little needy sometimes. Still a conflict avoider. But without Rita, things would be very different now. She helped me heal, helped me become less insecure, less sensitive, less resentful. Become happier, basically. A normal person again, or as close to normal as any of us can get, for what is normal, after all?

But back then, at thirteen, I was so very different. The teenage Beth was manipulative, rebellious, callous. She looked at the quiet girl sitting next to her and she felt only scorn.

Look at her, I remember thinking. *She's so ugly and skinny and swotty and spotty. How can her mother bear to be related to her? Isn't she ashamed?*

She wasn't though. Because Lucy Allen's mother didn't walk out on her daughter. Lucy Allen's mother dropped her off at the school gate every morning at eight-fifteen and picked her up every afternoon at four-thirty. She was a pretty blonde woman smiling broadly, proudly, as her daughter climbed back into the car, chatting animatedly to her as she drove off. Lucy Allen's mother made her packed lunches with homemade Victoria sponge and freshly squeezed orange juice. Lucy Allen's mother sent her to school with shiny polished shoes and a jumper that smelt of Comfort. Lucy Allen had a mother and I didn't, was basically what it came down to. And I hated her for that. Hated her. Hated the fact that although I knew my dad did his best, he had a job to do and money to earn and so I got the bus to and from Fairbridge alone, and had neighbours watch me until he came home from work, and I made my own packed lunches.

It was horrible and it was lonely, and it made me angry, so angry. But I still don't know why it was Lucy I fixated on. Most of my friends had their mothers in their lives. It wasn't a blessing unique to Lucy. But fixate on her I did. Fixate. And hate.

It was the hate that ruined it all, in the end. Hate for someone who had never done me the slightest bit of harm. Hate that grew, rapidly and ferociously and completely irrationally. Hate that consumed me and began to fill my every waking thought.

Hate was where it all began.

Even now, I can hardly bear to think about where it ended.

Chapter 17

'Hey you two, Mum's coming into town to meet me for lunch. Do you fancy joining us?'

I've just walked into the staffroom and Ruth and Deborah are there, sitting close together at one end of the table, engrossed in quiet conversation. They both jump as I speak.

'Gosh, sorry, didn't mean to frighten you!' I say.

'Blimey, I didn't hear you come in,' says Ruth, hand fluttering at her throat. She smiles.

'What did you say? Lunch? Sounds great, yes please.'

'Amazing! Mum's dying to meet some more of my friends. Can you make it too, Debs?'

Deborah's not looking at me. She's frowning slightly, running a finger down a page of her big desk diary which is open on the table in front of her.

'Erm ... not sure. I'm quite busy today ...'

I peer over her shoulder. Her diary is pretty full all morning and again this afternoon, but there's clearly a gap between about 12.45 and 2pm.

'Not at lunchtime though?' I say. 'I mean, if we go out about one? I told Mum I could only be an hour max as I'm quite stretched myself today. You haven't got anyone booked in then, have you? Come on, it would be nice.'

Debs hesitates, looks at Ruth, and then back down at her diary. She shifts in her chair, looking uncomfortable, and suddenly I'm feeling anxious again.

Doesn't she want to come? Doesn't she want to meet my mother?

I tried, over the weekend, not to think too much about Brenda and Barbara and what they said to Mum on Friday night, but I'm still upset, and I was hoping lunch with my mother and my two best work buddies would help. But now ...

'OK,' Deborah says suddenly. 'It's fine. I have some paperwork and stuff to catch up on but it's not a problem; I can do it later. I'll come.'

'Great!' I feel a little wave of relief.

'OK, well shall we just go down the road to the coffee shop? I'll ring Martha and ask her to keep us a booth?' I say, and they both nod.

'I've brought sandwiches from home though, so I might just have a coffee. Is that OK?' Deborah says quickly.

'Of course! Brilliant. See you later.'

I wave a hand and leave the room. I wonder if I should tell Ruth and Deborah about what's happened with Brenda and Barbara – after all, they'd probably be as upset as I am – but I can't face it, not just yet. It's embarrassing, for a start, like being back at school when the girls you hang out with suddenly flounce off and say they don't want to be friends anymore. But I have other friends, I tell myself firmly now, and vow to forget about it.

'The Busy Bees can buzz off,' I mutter, as I settle myself at my desk and allow myself a small snigger at my own silly joke.

The morning passes quickly, and by the time we arrive at The Hideaway, our favourite local café, I'm feeling a lot better. Work is a good distraction and how close was I to Brenda and Barbara, really, I think, as we settle ourselves in our corner booth and start studying the menu. If they were really only hanging out with me out of some sort of sympathy, well, I can do without them, can't I ...

'Darling! Sorry I'm late, I decided to get a bus but then I had to find the way from the bus stop to here and I got a bit lost! I stopped and said hello to your friend Nadia on the way past. She doesn't say much, does she, bless her? Anyway, hello everyone!'

Mum has arrived, resplendent in a cobalt-blue jumper with some sort of fringe detail on the sleeves, her face carefully made-up, hair freshly washed and styled. Her bags arrived by courier last night, Liv somehow managing to pack them and organise delivery within twenty-four hours of Mum's email ('She's so efficient, it's scary!' Mum told me). The clothes filled two large suitcases and a vanity case, and she spent ages in her room, unpacking and arranging. She hummed happily to herself and it made me smile as I stood on the landing listening to her, my heart full.

My mother, here in my house. Actually moving in for a while. What does anything else matter when I have this?

I stand up and hug her, laughing at her noisy entrance and touched that she remembered to say hello to Nadia, who I'd only mentioned briefly to her the other day. I make the introductions and soon we're all gabbing away over toasted sandwiches and coffee. I say *we're* gabbing away, but it's really only three of us; Deborah seems distracted, sipping her coffee and nibbling on the sandwich she's brought with her (Martha, the owner, knows us well enough to turn a blind eye to us occasionally bringing our own food in as long as we buy *something*), while looking curiously at Mum but not really joining in with the conversation. It reminds me of Barbara the other night.

'Everything all right, Deb?' I ask, when Mum, at her insistence, goes up to the counter to pay for everyone's food and Ruth nips to the loo.

She nods.

'Just feeling a bit ... well, a bit guilty about coming out. I've got so much to do. You know what it's like. Your mum seems nice though. So interesting too. Great stories.'

I smile. Mum's spent the last few minutes telling us about an art gallery she visited a few years ago in Germany which hosted an exhibition of the work of a young artist whose work consisted entirely of the droppings of various animals moulded into sculptures and affixed to canvasses.

'I think he fancied himself as a sort of German Damien Hurst,' she said. 'But the place stank so badly they had to offer people facemasks drenched in perfume at the door. I mean, talk about shit art ...'

'She's had quite a life, yes,' I say. 'And she's quite the entertainer. Not shy, that's for sure.'

Deborah smiles and looks down at my still half-full plate.

'You're not eating much,' she says.

'Ah, just trying to cut down a bit. I've piled it on recently,' I say.

'Really?' She looks me up and down with a puzzled expression. 'You look fine to me,' she says.

'Thanks,' I say, but I don't really believe her.

Deborah smiles but her face looks strained. I'm looking at her properly now and she doesn't look great – dark hollows under her eyes, fingernails bitten. I'm about to ask if she's really OK, if she's not feeling well, but Mum and Ruth return and moments later we're back out on the street, Mum heading off for a wander round the shops while we rush back up the road to work. I don't get a chance to pop into Deborah's room during the afternoon and she's still with a patient when I clock off for the day and drive to the hospital to spend an hour with Dad before I go home.

I'm thrilled to find him wide awake and sitting up in bed. The little television on the wall opposite is switched on and some early evening quiz show is playing. I pull the well-worn plastic chair that sits by the bed a little closer to him and sit down, and for a while we make small talk, me asking what the hospital food's like, him wanting to know if Finley's been picked for the school football team yet. It's nice to just sit there with him, chatting about nothing very much, and I'm relieved to see that his face looks a little less twisted, to hear his words a little less slurred.

'So,' he says suddenly. 'Your mother. How ish she?'

I hesitate. I'm happy, so happy that Mum is back, but I wouldn't blame him in the least if he was angry that I'd welcomed her with open arms, although he doesn't *look* angry, just casually interested.

'She's ... she's fine, Dad,' I say eventually. 'She's in good form. She's going to stay for a little bit longer actually.'

I decide *not* to tell him it might be months. We can cross that bridge later. He nods slowly, then says, 'Whatsh she been up to then, all thish time? Go on, fill me in.'

'Are you sure? Well ... gosh. Quite a lot.'

I spend the next few minutes updating him, and his eyes widen with pleasure when I mention Liv.

'A sishter? You always wanted a sishter, didn't you?'

'I did. We chatted the other day. It was kind of amazing, Dad.'

He nods again and smiles his new, crooked smile, and suddenly I want to cry. I love him so much and he's sacrificed so much for me over the years, and here he is, old and sick but still here for me, still happy for me despite everything. I'm already holding his hand, the skin dry and thin, and I squeeze it, running my thumb over his bony knuckles.

'Ow,' he says.

'Oh heck, sorry!'

I release my grip and we both laugh.

'Passh me that water, will you, love?'

I hand him the plastic beaker that's sitting on the bedside table, and watch him as he drinks carefully, waving away my offer of help. The door of the room is half-open, and outside in the corridor a bed trundles past, its occupant a motionless mound under a blue blanket.

'Dad,' I say. 'Can I ask you something?'

'I don't want her to vishit me again,' he says quickly and firmly. 'I'm happy for you, but thatsh it.'

Oh. Well, that's good. They're on the same page with that one, at least.

'No, that's not what I was going to say, don't worry,' I say. 'I understand that. It was something else.'

I wasn't going to mention this to him; it's not something we talk about at all – haven't done for years. But now he seems happy to chat about Mum and suddenly I need to know, need to pick his brains, need to see what he thinks before I broach it with my mother. He's looking at me expectantly, still holding the water cup, and I take it from him gently, gathering my thoughts as I put it back on the table.

'Dad, do you think Mum might know? About Lucy? About what happened?'

His eyes have widened again, surprise and a little shock in them this time.

'I mean, she hasn't said anything, But I've been feeling really anxious, wondering if she knows, and I just wondered if you thought ... Oh, I don't know, sorry Dad.'

He's still looking at me with that surprised expression. He makes a little sound in his throat, opens his mouth, closes it again, and then finally says, 'I don't know, love. Unlikely, I think. How would she? Who would have told her?'

I nod, thinking. Putting Mike and his recent research aside – because that still worries me a *lot* – is there really a chance she could have found out about it from anyone else? Other than Dad and me, who else even knows about what happened? Lucy's parents, obviously, and the teachers, and at least some of the other pupils at Fairbridge High. Although efforts were definitely made to hush it up at the time, it was a school and things always get out, rumours go around. But who else? Some of Mr and Mrs Allen's friends, undoubtedly, some of the other parents I saw at the school gates. But, after the initial investigation, after those terrible early days when I felt like my whole life had fallen apart, it all just ... faded away. Nothing in the papers, no more visits by the police. Dad never breathed a word about it to anyone, not to friends, not to colleagues, not to family. He promised me he never would, and I had no reason to believe he'd ever break his word. Both of my parents were only children, so there were no aunts, uncles, or cousins who might have found out, and even if my grandparents had discovered the truth, they're all long dead now. Even – and to this day I wonder if this was the right decision, but it's far too late now – Jacob doesn't know what happened. My husband, left in the dark about such a big part of my life. Was that, I sometimes wonder, one of the reasons we grew apart, because I never fully trusted him? Certainly not enough to tell him and expect him to stay with me once he knew.

And as for Mum, well she had left years before I'd started at Fairbridge and didn't, as far as I knew, know any of the kids there, or their parents. Dad had wanted me to have a fresh start at secondary school, wanted me to go somewhere where nobody saw me as the poor little girl whose mother had abandoned her, and so he'd chosen a school on the other side of the city, one where none of my primary school friends were being sent. At first I'd been horrified, but when he told me I could make up my own backstory, tell the other children my mum had died, if I wanted to, I realised he was right. It would be easier, so much easier, not having to explain, not to be asked constantly if there was any news, if we'd heard from my mother, if she was coming home soon. And so that's what I'd done, and it had simply been accepted that I didn't have a mum. So, I think now, what were the chances of Mum knowing what had happened at Fairbridge, really? There was a tiny chance that someone she knew in Bristol might have got to hear about it, but she hadn't kept in touch with anyone, not as far as we knew.

Dad's right. It is unlikely Mum knows, because who would have told her?

I leave the hospital shortly after that, chatting to a nurse on the way out who says, to my great joy, that she thinks Dad will be well enough to be discharged and move back to Holly Tree in the next day or two. I'm equally relieved when I get home to see that Robin has fed the kids and is just finishing clearing up too, the big spaghetti bolognese pan washed and drying next to the sink, the dirty plates and cutlery neatly stacked in the dishwasher. Mum's eaten with the children and is in the lounge watching *EastEnders*. Once I've seen Eloise and Finley off to bed and wolfed down the portion Robin's kindly left for me in the oven, I take a deep breath and go and join Mum on the sofa.

'Has Robin gone?' she says immediately.

'Erm ... yes, a while ago. Why?' I ask.

She picks up the remote and hits the mute button, then turns to me, her face serious. I feel a little flutter of nerves.

Now what?

'Well, there was just something ... something I thought you should know. I mean, it might be nothing, but ...'

She shrugs, looking worried. She's wearing a soft beige sweater, a simple gold bangle on her right wrist.

'Go on, tell me.'

More bad news? I'm not sure I can take this, I think, but I don't say it.

'OK, well ... this afternoon, when I got back from town, I went straight upstairs to change and I heard some noise coming from your bedroom. It gave me a fright, silly me! So I sort of crept to the door and peeped in, and it was Robin of course, which was fine, just doing some cleaning before she went to get the children. But it was just ... well ...'

She pauses, her brow furrowing.

'What, Mum?'

I'm suddenly aware that my stomach is clenching uncomfortably and a bead of sweat is forming on my top lip. I wipe it away with the back of my hand.

'Mum? Go on.'

She gives a little sigh.

'Well ... she was in your ensuite bathroom, banging around in the cupboard you have on the wall. As if she was going through it, you know? I mean, it just seemed odd to me, Beth. You don't ask her to clean *inside* cupboards do you, to go through your stuff? And it's not the first time I've seen her behaving oddly in your room. I didn't mention it, but, well ...'

Her voice tails off.

'What? What do you mean? And are you sure she wasn't just dusting the bathroom cabinet?'

Mum's shaking her head.

'No, she was definitely going through it. And there've been other things. I heard her opening drawers in your room last week, on Monday before I'd even met the kids. I was going to tell you but, well ... and then on Wednesday, the day we went out for pizza, I was passing your bedroom door and she was in there again, looking through the stuff on your chest of drawers. She didn't even have her duster with her, so it struck me as strange, you know? To be in there and doing that when she wasn't even cleaning?'

I'm staring at her now. *Wednesday?* That was the night I noticed that my stuff in the bedroom had been moved, wasn't it? I hadn't even considered that it might have been Robin. I'd only thought of Barbara, looking for her missing glasses, or Eloise poking about. I frown.

'That's ... that's weird. Wednesday's not her day to clean the bedrooms. I'm not sure why she would have been in there ...'

'Oh darling, I'm sorry.' Mum shakes her head vigorously and rolls her eyes.

'It's probably just your stupid old mother being paranoid. I'm sure it's all perfectly innocent. Ignore me, honestly. I just worry, you know? A single mother, busy working woman, it's easy to imagine you being taken advantage of, that's all. You probably wouldn't even notice if the odd thing went missing, would you? Too much on your mind all the time. If you think Robin is trustworthy then I have absolute faith in your judgement. I shouldn't even have mentioned it. Don't worry at all.'

But I *am* worried now. It *does* sound like odd behaviour,

and after all, it's not the first time, is it? And maybe Mum's right. Maybe I wouldn't notice if little things went missing here and there. I'm always so preoccupied, especially at the moment ...

'Mum, look, thanks for telling me. I'm sure everything is fine, but I'll keep an eye on her, and on my things. I will.'

She nods and smiles, and I take a deep breath.

Now. I need to ask her now.

'Mum, while we're chatting, this is a bit random but, well, I was just wondering ... did you ... did you keep in touch with anyone from Bristol after you left? Anyone at all?'

She looks surprised.

'No. Nobody at all. I just wanted a clean break, I suppose. Why, love?'

'I was just wondering if ... well, if you ever tried to keep up with what I was doing, how I was ...'

There's a lump in my throat suddenly and I swallow hard, not looking at her now, my eyes fixed on my hands which are clenched together so tightly the knuckles are white.

'You know, how I was doing at school or ... anything else. If you knew what ... what I was up to, all those years ...'

There's a little gasp and for a few seconds all I can hear is my own heartbeat, loud and frantic, and then I realise she's speaking in a sort of strangled whisper.

'Oh, Beth. I'm so, so sorry.'

I look up and I see that she's crying, fat tears rolling down her cheeks, making streaks in her foundation.

'I didn't. I wish I could tell you something different ... I'm so sorry. So very, very sorry.'

She's shaking her head now and reaching for my hands, and I let her pull me into her arms. I can smell her light, floral perfume and I'm burying my face in the softness of her jumper and I'm crying too. I'm crying for all those lost years, for the little girl without a mother, for the mother who was so unhappy that she did the unthinkable and walked away and has never forgiven herself. But I'm crying with relief too, I realise, because she *doesn't* know, does she? She doesn't know about Lucy and what happened; she doesn't know about what I did. She doesn't know because she walked away and she didn't look back. And for once, just this once, that's a good thing. That's a really, really good thing because now I can stop worrying and forget about it. *She doesn't know.*

We sit there, wrapped in each other, for a long time. Eventually we pull ourselves together and, for some strange reason, start to laugh. And that's it ... We spend the rest of the evening drinking wine and tittering about silly little things until we're both worn out. At ten we head for bed, and I run a deep, hot bath, tipping in a generous dollop of lavender bath gel, and then peel my clothes off, dropping them carelessly on the bathroom floor, and groaning softly as I sink into the fragrant bubbles.

I soap my body slowly, massaging my legs and stomach, arms and breasts, enjoying the sensation of the warm water on my skin and feeling more relaxed than I have in weeks. Finally, I lie back and close my eyes, breathing deeply. *Bliss.* I'm almost asleep when I remember what Mum said about Robin and my bathroom cabinet. I open my eyes again and squint up at it. It's closed now, but I didn't notice anything out of place when I took the bath gel out.

I'm sure she was just dusting it. Robin wouldn't steal from me, would she? And surely I'd notice if things were going missing? Mum's just looking out for me, that's all. Trying to make up for lost time. I rather like it. It's kind of sweet.

I smile and forget about it, then reluctantly clamber out of the bath and head for bed.

Chapter 18

It's Saturday again, thank goodness. It's been a funny old week, my days madly busy at work and my head all over the place. I misplaced my keys *again* on Wednesday, and had to get another cab to work. Mum called me at lunchtime to say she'd found them outside on the patio table which puzzled me because I had absolutely no recollection of going out into the garden, not that morning or the previous evening. I tried to put it out of my mind, vowing to put my keys in a safe place from now on, but it's still worrying me now. I really need to get my head together, and being so tired isn't helping; I seem to have lost the ability to sleep properly in recent days and now my nights are replete with dreams. I don't remember the details, but despite that I know that most of them are about Lucy. I know just by looking at the sheets twisted around my legs and by the way I wake with my jaw clenched so tightly it hurts for hours.

Nightmares, not dreams.

But last night was, for the first time this week, OK. I've slept pretty well, and woken feeling alert and rested. I can hear chatter downstairs – *they're all up, already? It's only eight o'clock* – and when I come downstairs, hair still damp from the shower, the kids are bouncing around the kitchen with excitement.

'Grandma says the trampoline's arriving *this morning*!' shrieks Finley, and flings himself at my right leg, wrapping his arms around it. He's wearing his Spiderman pyjama top with a pair of jeans, his feet are bare, and his hair is a tousled mess.

'Is it? Great!' I say and bend down to give him a hug.

Damn. I'd forgotten about that.

Mum announced on Thursday that she'd ordered a trampoline for the back garden – '*A little something for my grandchildren to remember me by when I eventually have to go home. You don't mind, do you, love? It'll be SO much fun!*' – and Finley and Eloise immediately went into such paroxysms of delight that I didn't have the heart to say that actually, the garden wasn't really big enough and that I quite liked the little lawn space that we had.

Oh well. If it makes them happy.

Mum's sipping coffee, dressed in navy joggers and a blue cardigan embroidered with little red flowers. She smiles indulgently at Finley and then winks at me.

'You'll need to be properly dressed to jump on the trampoline, darling,' she says. 'Can't be going out there in half your pyjamas, can you? You'll need a jumper, socks, and trainers. And neatly brushed hair too. Think you can do that?'

'YESSS!' He lets go of my leg and tears from the room, and I grin at my mother.

'Nice work,' I say. 'Eloise, are you excited too?'

She's sitting opposite Mum, a book propped up against the milk jug in front of her.

'Yep,' she says, through a mouthful of toast. She swallows and looks up at me.

'I've been watching trampolining videos on YouTube. I'm going to learn *tricks*. Front flips, back flips, somersaults ...'

'OK, steady on! Just master jumping up and down safely first, please, before you start all the fancy stuff,' I say, and she rolls her eyes and goes back to her book.

'Yeah, yeah,' she mutters, but she's smiling.

I shake my head and exchange glances with Mum, who looks highly amused.

'Anyway,' I say, as I flick the kettle on. 'Did you say it'll need some assembly? I'll try and get it done before I go and visit Dad at lunchtime. Eloise, you and Finley are coming with me today, OK? Just for an hour. The trampoline will still be here when you get back.'

My daughter looks up with a frown, then her face clears and she nods.

'OK. Poor Grandad. I'm glad he's home now.'

'Good girl. So am I.'

The hospital discharged him on Thursday morning, and he's back at Holly Tree, to my great relief. He looked so much better when I saw him yesterday. His speech is improving already and he has a little colour back in his cheeks.

He'll be back in the bar with Billy in no time, I think, as I pop a teabag in a mug. Bless him.

'... only a bit of assembly,' Mum's saying. 'A few screws here and there, I think. Don't think it will take long. I can help, if you like?'

'No, don't worry,' I say. 'I quite like doing stuff like that. You can keep an eye on these two troublemakers while I sort it. At least the weather looks nice.'

'Yes, I was just thinking that. It's lovely. I might wander out for a quick walk in a bit, if you don't mind?'

'Go for it.'

I smile. I love how she seems to be feeling so at home here now, how she's slotted so effortlessly into our little family set up. The kids are with me until this evening, when Jacob and Crystal are planning to take them to the cinema and then to theirs until Monday, and although it's going to be a busy day, I suddenly feel a rush of contentment. OK, so I'm still sad, hurt, and confused by Brenda and Barbara's behaviour. But otherwise, everything's pretty good, isn't it? Dad being so much better, a weekend at home, the sun shining, no more sightings of bloody Mike – or no more *imagined* sightings, I should probably say ... Even the sodding trampoline will probably turn out to be a great addition to the garden, in reality. It'll be fun to see Finley and Eloise bouncing up and down out there, and much better for them than being glued to their screens, if I can manage to put it together without too much drama.

When it arrives mid-morning though, it actually needs a little more assembly than I thought. By lunchtime, I'm only about halfway there; one of the legs is almost impossible to attach. I finally do it, but I break two nails in the process and swear so loudly that Mum, who's popped out to drink a cup of tea in the garden after her walk, quickly ushers an impatiently hovering Finley indoors.

'Sorry!' I mouth, and she winks and waves a hand.

When we come back from seeing Dad (looking even better today, and so delighted to see his grandchildren), I take a deep breath, leave the kids to watch a film with Mum, and head back out into the garden. It's a beautiful afternoon. The daffodils along the fence are bobbing their golden heads in the gentle breeze and a bird is singing a sweet warbling tune somewhere nearby. I attack the damn trampoline with renewed gusto, but when I nip back into the house for a glass of water and a wee and then go back out again I can't find the spring puller – the tool I've been using to attach the jump mat to the metal outer rings – anywhere.

'Where the *hell* are you?' I mutter, as I search the lawn, and then, in growing frustration, the entire garden – although I can't imagine the stupid thing can have made its own way onto the patio or into one of the flowerbeds.

Did I bring it inside with me then?

I search the kitchen and the downstairs loo too, but no joy, so I go back out and scour the entire garden a second time.

Come on, things don't just disappear, I think. Unless ... could a cat or a fox or something have taken it and run off with it while I was indoors?

It doesn't seem very likely but it's absolutely nowhere to be seen and I can't finish the job without it. Infuriated, I give up and, bracing myself, go and face the wrath of Finley and Eloise, who've been poking their heads out of the patio doors every ten minutes to check progress.

'I'll have to go and get another one at B&Q in the morning,' I say. 'I haven't got the energy to go now and your dad will be here soon anyway to pick you up. I'm so sorry, guys.'

The disappointment on their faces is piteous.

'How on earth can it just disappear, Mum? That doesn't even make sense,' says Eloise.

She's right, it doesn't.

'I know, darling. Honestly, I don't know what's wrong with me at the moment. But I'll get it finished tomorrow, I promise. It'll be here waiting for you when you get in from school on Monday. Oh Finley, don't cry, come here.'

His little face has crumpled and I wrap my arms around him.

'I was just soooooo looking forward to it *today*,' he sobs, and I feel even worse. Mum, who's been searching the kitchen again just in case, grimaces at me then comes over and squeezes Finley's shoulders.

'These things happen, sweetheart,' she says soothingly. 'And just think, it'll be something to look forward to on Monday, won't it? They can try it straight after school, can't they, Beth? Even before homework?'

I nod gratefully. How does she always seem to know exactly what to say?

'Even before homework,' I say, and Finley looks up at me, his cheeks tearstained but a little smile playing on his lips now.

'But we always have to do homework *first*,' he says.

'Not on Monday,' I say, and the smile broadens to a grin.

'YAY!' he shouts, and leaps from my arms. Eloise grins too.

'Nice one, Mum,' she says.

Yes, nice one, Mum, I think, and give her a discreet thumbs-up. She returns the gesture and, calm and harmony restored, the rest of the afternoon passes uneventfully. After Jacob and Crystal have arrived and departed, kids on board, I tell Mum I'm going to have a bath and head upstairs. As I sink into the warm bubbles I find myself thinking, for some unknown reason, about Nadia. I popped over to see her again yesterday, with a cupcake from the box Lorraine had brought in to celebrate her birthday. We all met up in the staffroom at the end of morning surgery to toast her with tea and cake, although Deborah didn't join us, saying she had too much to do. She's definitely still acting oddly and I really need to find out why, but I've hardly seen her this week, apart from five minutes on Tuesday morning when I found her and Ruth chatting in the staffroom and finally told them what had happened with Brenda and Barbara.

They were gratifyingly horrified. Ruth pulled me into a bear hug and told me that if that's how they really feel, I'm better off without them.

'I mean, I'm shocked because they've always been so lovely, you know? They always seemed so fond of you, and of the kids too, Beth. I don't get it. But that's a really nasty thing to say. Your mum being back "takes the pressure off them"? Sod them. We'd never treat you like that.'

I felt better immediately and was about to ask Deborah if everything was OK with *her* when Ruth shrieked at us to

'LOOK at the time!' and they both ran from the room, Ruth to open the front door to let the patients in and Deborah to finish setting up her consulting room for the morning session. Since then, I've barely laid eyes on her, and every time I've swung past reception Ruth's either been talking to a patient or on the phone so I haven't had a chance to ask her if she knows what's going on either. As for Brenda and Barbara, I think they must be avoiding me; I haven't laid eyes on either of them all week, not even from a distance.

'A cupcake for you. They're yummy,' I said, as I crouched down to put the bag next to Nadia's suitcase. She was bundled up in her big padded jacket as usual; she had on a different hat this time, dark green with a sparkly metallic thread running through it. Her long grey hair was tied back, an untidy ponytail protruding from under the hat and tucked into the collar of her jacket.

'It's salted caramel. Do you like that? Love your hat, by the way.'

She nodded and smiled.

'Thanks. And yes, any cake is fine by me. How are you, Beth? And ...'

She hesitated then coughed a dry hacking cough and I watched her anxiously.

Is she ill? I hope not ...

'I met your mother the other day. Just briefly. She said she was meeting you for lunch.'

'Oh yes, of course! She said she'd stopped to say hello. That's nice,' I said.

She didn't reply, just gave a small nod, so I kept chatting, telling her that my dad had been ill but was out of hospital now, and about how busy work had been, and about the trampoline Mum had bought for Eloise and Finley. She looked at me intently as I talked, her eyes looking greener than I remembered them being in the afternoon sunlight. I could see the sadness in them and my heart twisted.

'How old are they? Your children?' she asked, then raised a finger and rubbed at a little sore on her top lip. Her hand was shaking a little and for some reason I suddenly wanted to cry.

'Eloise is ten and Finley's seven,' I said. 'I split up with their dad a while back but it's all good; we're still friends.'

She nodded slowly and I glanced at my watch. I needed to get back.

'I have to go but I hope you enjoy the cake. And let me know if you need any more books when you've finished those, won't you?'

I gestured to the Agatha Christie – one of mine – that was open on her knee and she nodded again and smiled, showing her stained, gappy teeth.

'I will, thanks. Bye, Beth.'

Now as I lie in my fragrant bath, I think again about how fortunate I am, despite my nightmares and silly worries of recent weeks. People come into your life for a reason – I've always believed that. And I'm wondering now if Nadia came into mine to help me appreciate everything I've got, and speculate again if there's some way I can help her, properly help her. I just don't know how.

Right now I need to go back downstairs and tidy up before

we eat though. It feels hot in the bathroom, I realise suddenly – uncomfortably so – so I wriggle until I'm half sitting up then fish around in the bubbles for my sponge and start quickly washing my body, running it across my chest and down my arms. Then I haul myself out of the bath, dry myself briskly and slather on some body lotion before heading back into the bedroom to pull on my favourite grey sweatpants and an old blue football sweatshirt – one that Jacob left behind. It's got the Manchester City logo on it, the team he began to support when we were at uni there and has carried on supporting ever since. I'm not remotely interested in football, but I like this top – not because it reminds me of my ex-husband but simply because it's soft and warm and a little too big for me, which is a rare feeling these days. Most of my clothes are unpleasantly snug. As I brush my damp hair back from my face though, I realise the bedroom is far too hot too. My armpits are already starting to feel moist and I pull the sweatshirt off again and put on a short-sleeved T-shirt instead.

Why is it so warm? Please don't tell me the heating's packed up now. That's all I need ...

When I walk into the kitchen, Mum's leaning against the island, fanning herself with a magazine, a half-peeled potato on a chopping board next to her.

'Phew,' she says. 'It's boiling in here. Have you turned the heating up, love?'

I shake my head, frowning.

'No, I haven't touched it! It's boiling upstairs too. Oh bugger. What's going on?'

I walk over to the patio doors and fling them open, which will help for now, but my anxiety is rising. I do a quick tour of the house, pausing in each room, feeling the radiators and pulling my hand away quickly when I realise that each one is almost too hot to touch.

What on earth? Is the boiler about to explode or something?

I check the little heating control panel on the wall in the hall but it looks fine, set as always to twenty-one degrees. But something is clearly wrong. The house is way, way hotter than that and for a moment I think I'm going to cry. I'm useless with things like this, and previously I would have gone round and knocked on Barbara or Brenda's door, knowing we all have the same heating system and hoping that one of them would be able to shed some light on it.

I can't do that now, of course, and I can't even ring Jacob because he's at the cinema. How much will a heating engineer cost? The emergency call-out charge alone, on a Saturday night, never mind the cost of repairing whatever the hell's gone wrong ...

I take a deep, shuddering breath, willing the tears away, and wipe my sweaty forehead with my forearm. First the stupid missing trampoline tool, and now this. The day started so well and now everything's ruined again.

'Beth? Honestly, I'm going to expire here in a minute. Have you worked out what's going on?'

Mum's calling from the kitchen and for the first time since our reunion I can hear a hint of ... well, not *irritation* exactly in her voice, but she does sound vaguely exasperated.

God. She must think I'm such a mess. Losing things all

the time, and now I don't even know how to work my own central heating ...

'I'm just about to call an engineer, Mum. I'm so sorry,' I shout back and, fighting tears again, I pull my mobile from my pocket and start looking for a number.

Chapter 19

It's Monday again, and as I sit down at my desk I feel a sense of relief. I'm actually glad to be here today, busy though I know it will be, because the weekend was, in the end, just one stressful incident after another. The heating problem was *weird*; by the time I'd finally tracked down an engineer, the house had started to cool down, and by the time he arrived an hour and a half later it was back to its usual comfortable temperature again. He listened patiently as I tried to explain that only a couple of hours earlier it had been unbearably hot, prodded the control panel for a minute, and declared it to be in perfect working order. Then he charged me a hundred pounds for the emergency call-out and left again with a wry smile on his face.

'He thinks I'm an idiot, doesn't he?' I said to Mum when I'd closed the door behind him and re-joined her in the kitchen.

'He thinks I imagined it. Thank goodness you were here, or *I'd* think I was imagining it too!'

Mum smiled, deftly chopping a potato into thin strips for chips.

'You definitely weren't imagining it. It *was* boiling. I thought I was going to pass out!'

She picked up another potato and began to peel it, then stopped and looked at me.

'But darling ... do you think it *might* have been you? After all, he said there's nothing wrong with the system, didn't he? Did you maybe turn the thermostat up and then forget about it? And then turn it down again? You know how forgetful you've been lately ... It's just that I certainly didn't touch it – I have no idea how to work things like that – and I doubt the kids did ...'

Her voice trailed off and I stood and stared at her for a moment, my mind racing. *Could* it have been me? I do sometimes turn the thermostat up and down as I pass the control panel in the hall if the house feels too warm or too chilly, but I had no recollection of doing that that day. And I'd never turn it up *that* high. And yet, Mum was right – the children had never, to my knowledge, fiddled with the central heating controls. So, *was* it me? *Did* I do it, and forget, and call the engineer out and pay him all that money for *nothing*? A little shiver ran up my spine. This was *bad*, if so. I really *was* losing my mind ...

'Or,' Mum said suddenly, 'and I hate to suggest this because I know how fond you are of her and I do seem to keep bringing her up in a negative way but ... well, what about Robin?'

'Robin? I don't understand.'

'Well, obviously I don't know how your heating works, as I said, but she seems to be a savvy kind of person ...'

She hesitated for a moment, putting the potato peeler down on the chopping board.

'Well, when she was here yesterday could she have set the timer for the heat to come on high this afternoon and then turn off again? Mistakenly, of course,' she added hurriedly.

'But why?' I said. 'She never adjusts the heating, as far as I know. Why would she even go near it? No, I don't think it was Robin.'

Mum shrugged.

'OK. But if it wasn't you, or me, or the children ...'

She picked up the peeler again and I stood watching her, thinking.

Robin? No! But again, Mum's right ... Robin *is* the only other person who's been in the house in the past twenty-four hours. But to fiddle with the central heating makes no sense. None of it makes any sense ...

I've given up thinking about it now. It's going to drive me crazy. Maybe it was nobody. Maybe it *was* just a blip in the system, despite what the engineer said. It all seems to be working fine now, and I don't have time to dwell on it any further. Yesterday, Sunday, was another busy one. I finally got the bloody trampoline assembled, after a trip to B&Q first thing to buy another spring puller, and I'm actually delighted with it. It looks good down at the bottom of the garden, and the children are going to be so thrilled to see it this evening, so excited to try it out. I visited Dad again in the afternoon, promising to record some video footage on my phone so he can see the children jumping. Then I had a nice movie night with Mum, nothing too strenuous, but I still feel exhausted this morning and I have so much to do today. It goes quickly though, and I power through my to-do list with the assistance of numerous mugs of strong tea and a large chocolate bar after my lunchtime chicken salad.

By four forty-five I've ticked off the final item on the long list and I sit back in my chair with a contented sigh, quite surprised and impressed by my own productivity.

'Not always a woolly brained twit then,' I say out loud to the cheese plant in the corner. 'Actually finished that lot *early*, don't you know.' Then I roll my eyes.

I'm talking to plants now. The plant really doesn't care. *Shut up, Beth.*

On the shelf to my left, my mobile phone starts to vibrate and I reach for it and check the display. It's a call from my house phone, and I answer with a smile, expecting it to be Finley or Eloise enthusing about the trampoline which they'll no doubt have been bouncing on for at least an hour by now, I think as I look at the clock on the wall opposite. But as soon as I hear the voice on the other end of the line my heart starts to pound. It's not either of my children. It's my mother. And she's crying.

'Beth, oh Beth, I'm so glad you answered. Something dreadful has happened ...'

I'm up out of my chair, grabbing my bag and running for the door before she's even finished trying to explain. It's Finley. Some sort of accident. Something to do with the trampoline. She's called an ambulance and she's telling me to meet them at A&E. And now I'm crying too, panicking, tearing through reception, shouting to Ruth behind the desk that I have to go, that I have to get to the hospital. I can hear her frightened voice and see the startled faces of the patients who are sitting there as I rush past, and then somehow I'm in the car and somehow I'm driving and somehow, *somehow*, I get to Cheltenham General.

It's a bad ankle sprain, nothing worse.

'I thought it was broken. He was in so much pain. Oh Beth ...' Mum whispers, her face tear-streaked, mascara puddled under her eyes, as I wrap my little boy in my arms and squeeze him so tightly that he whimpers.

'Muuuum! Stop it! I can't breathe!'

I release him, but only a little. He looks so small in the big hospital bed. He's still in his school uniform of a navy jumper and shorts, one leg now bandaged tightly from toes to knee. He's no stranger to A&E, this child, so full of energy and bravado that he's had numerous little falls and bumps over the years. But this time I wasn't there to pick him up, to kiss it better, and now I think this was *my* fault. It was the trampoline, the one *I* put together, the one *I* built.

'The leg just sort of went skewwhiff,' Mum says as I drive us home. Eloise is with Robin back at the house, Mum having travelled in the ambulance with Finley.

'Eloise had just climbed off to take a break, and Finley was bouncing happily up and down on his own, weren't you, love? Robin had been out there in the garden with them for a while, and then she said she wanted to go in and finish the cleaning, so she asked me to take over, which of course I was happy to do. It was so lovely seeing them enjoying it so much, you know? And so I was just standing there, keeping an eye on

Finley, and suddenly there was a sort of loud crack and one of the legs just ... *collapsed*. I hate to say this, darling, but I don't think you attached it properly. I mean, I'm not blaming you at all. Accidents happen and I know you were struggling with it so maybe the thing was faulty, but ... anyway, the whole jumping platform thing, whatever you call it, sort of tilted down really suddenly and Finley came flying off onto the grass. You landed really awkwardly on your ankle, didn't you, pet?'

She looks over her shoulder at Finley in the back seat, and in the rear-view mirror I see him nodding.

'It really hurt, Mummy,' he said. 'It feels better now though. And I like my crutches.'

'Good,' I say. 'But you need to take it easy for a few days. Remember what the doctor said? Be careful on the crutches. And definitely no more trampolining.'

He nods again, vehemently this time.

'Don't want to go on it anyway,' he says. 'Don't like it anymore.'

I've been feeling sick ever since Mum's phone call, and now I genuinely feel like I might throw up. The guilt is horrendous.

Mum's trying to be nice about it, but this *is* all down to me. I was so tired yesterday, and I thought I'd been so careful, but maybe I wasn't. Maybe I didn't tighten all the nuts and bolts. Maybe I missed one, missed something, because otherwise this wouldn't have happened, would it? And what if he'd landed on his head instead of his ankle? What if he'd broken his neck? My son could have died today, and it would have been all my fault ...

'Stop, Mummy!'

Finley's shouting at me from the back seat and I realise I'm about to drive past the house. I slam on the brakes. As I lean down to help him out of the car, Brenda suddenly appears on the other side of the wall.

'Beth,' she says hesitantly. I straighten up and turn to look at her, my heart sinking.

Not now. I really can't take it, not today.

But her face is creased with sympathy, her eyes anxious.

'It's my day off, and I was in the garden and heard the screaming, and then the ambulance ... Oh Finley, are you OK? Is he OK, Beth? I'm so sorry ...'

I think I'm going to cry again. Maybe, despite what she and Barbara said to Mum, she does care after all.

'He's OK, thanks. Just a badly sprained ankle.'

'Oh, thank goodness. Well ... I'll leave you to it. Take care, Beth.'

There's an awkward pause as we just stand there looking at each other. Then she turns away and hurries off towards her front door.

'Bit two-faced, if you ask me,' mutters Mum, who's been listening to the exchange, and I shrug.

'Maybe,' I say quietly, but she's already heading for the house. Brenda sounded genuinely concerned to me, but I'm clearly not a good judge of character, going by recent events, and anyway, I have more important things to deal with right now. Something's just occurred to me, quite suddenly, something to do with how Mum described what had happened with the trampoline and I need to get into the house. I need to talk to Robin, urgently, so I haul Finley out of the car and, groaning a little (when did he get so *heavy*?) carry him in and settle him on the sofa, where he proudly shows off his bandaged leg to Eloise and starts regaling her with tales from the hospital. Through the patio doors I can see the trampoline down at the end of the garden, one leg buckled, the platform at a sharp angle, and the nausea begins to rise again. *What the hell happened here?* I give Eloise a hug and then go and find Robin who's in the hall, putting her mobile phone into her backpack, ready to leave.

'Robin, did you see what happened? With the trampoline?' I ask, once I've reassured her that Finley's suffered no lasting damage.

She shakes her head. She's in her running gear, camouflage-pattern blue leggings today with a blue vest top and professional-looking white trainers.

'No, I didn't see anything,' she says. 'I was upstairs, vacuuming the landing. I didn't know anything had happened until your mum came in screaming that we needed an ambulance. It was awful, so scary. I'm so glad he's all right, poor little mite.'

I nod, not wanting to ask the question but feeling that I must.

I'm sure, positive, that she'd never do anything to harm the children, but even so, she was there this afternoon, and I have to ask, I have to ...

'Robin, you didn't touch the trampoline, did you, while you were out there with the kids today? Or before they got home from school? It's just that when I put the darn thing together yesterday I was so careful, and I'm sure it was fine. It was solid, you know? So I just don't understand what went wrong, how the leg could have broken like that. It doesn't make sense to me. So did you ...?'

She's looking at me wide-eyed, a shocked expression on her face.

'What? What do you mean? Beth, are you suggesting ...? I mean, why on earth would I ...?'

She sounds confused, *hurt* and confused, but I'm on a roll now and I can't seem to stop myself.

'And while we're here, Robin, did you touch the central heating controls on Friday, by any chance? Because something went wrong with that too over the weekend and it always seems to be when you're in the house, Robin, that things go wrong ...'

Her mouth has dropped open, her eyes fixed on mine.

'Are you serious? What are you accusing me of, Beth?'

I can see her eyes filling with tears. I should stop now, I know I should. I should apologise because of *course* Robin isn't behind any of this, is she? I can see it in her face. And yet ...

'Well, it's all just a bit of a coincidence, isn't it?' I say, and I can hear the bitchiness, the petulance, in my voice, as if I'm listening to someone else speaking, and I am helpless to stop it.

'And I don't know why you'd do any of this, no idea at all in fact, but you must see why I have to ask ...'

She's backing away from me now, shaking her head, her breath coming in shuddery little gasps.

'Beth, I can't ... I just can't ... I have to go, I'm sorry ...'

There are tears rolling down her cheeks and she wipes them away fiercely with the backs of her hands, then bends down to pick up her backpack from where she'd dropped it on the floor when we started talking. She marches to the front door, flinging it open and slamming it behind her so loudly that I jump. For a long moment I stand there in the silence, staring at the closed door. And then:

'Oh. My. God,' I whisper. 'What have I done?'

It's as if the noise of the slamming door has brought me to my senses and suddenly I'm horrified, mortified. Shame washes over me like an icy wave.

I've just accused Robin of trying to hurt my children. What's wrong with me? What's *wrong* with me?

Slowly, I sink to my knees on the cold tiled floor of the hallway and bury my face in my hands.

I've lost her now too, haven't I? Just like I've lost Barbara and Brenda. This should be such a happy time and instead I'm screwing everything up, ruining it all. If I go on like this I might lose Mum too all over again, and I can't, I can't bear that ...

I jump again as I hear a door opening upstairs on the landing and footsteps heading for the stairs. I know that Mum is coming down and I don't want her to see me like this so somehow I drag myself up and into the kitchen. I rip off a piece of paper towel from the roll by the sink, wipe my face and pull myself together. Somehow I get through the evening by painting on a smile. I call Jacob to tell him what's happened but tell him not to panic, because Finley is fine. I call Ruth to let her know everything's OK too and that I'll be back at work in the morning. But as I mechanically go through the evening routine – putting my broken little boy to bed, brushing the tangles from my daughter's hair, throwing together a quick carbonara for me and Mum, opening some wine, and making inconsequential chit-chat – there's a sick, hollow feeling in my stomach and no amount of positive self-talk is helping.

Normal. Act normal. Everything is fine. I'll apologise to Robin tomorrow, ask her to stay, beg her if I have to. It will all be OK. It has to be OK.

At ten Mum hugs me and tells me she's shattered and going to bed. I pour another glass of wine, turn the lights off, and sit there alone in the dark, the room growing cold around me. At some point my eyes close and I wake with a start sometime after eleven. A noise outside the patio doors rouses me from what is this time a dreamless sleep. As I sit there, my brain foggy, my thoughts confused, and my body stiff and aching, I hear the noise again, a sort of shuffling sound coming from outside. I stagger to my feet, expecting to see a fox or a hedgehog through the glass, a night-time creature on the hunt for food. But as my eyes focus on the wide expanse of glass, it's not a fox I see, nor a hedgehog, nor any other four-legged animal. It's a face. A human face, pale and round. And it's staring straight at me.

Chapter 20

It was just whispers at first.

'You're so ugly.'

'Those girls you think are your friends? They think you're ugly too.'

'Nobody likes you. You know that, don't you?'

Vicious, cruel little whispers. Words I spat into Lucy Allen's ear as we sat together in class, words that nobody but her could hear.

I wanted to hurt her; it was as simple as that. I wanted her to suffer. And why? Why did I want to inflict such pain on a girl I barely knew? At the time, I had no idea. It was simply a compulsion, something I had to do, something I couldn't stop myself doing, day after day after day.

Now I know that trying to hurt Lucy in the terrible way I did was my way of coping with the pain I was in. It was almost as if I thought that by increasing her pain I could dilute mine. That somehow it would make me feel better.

It didn't of course, but I carried on anyway. As I dripped my poison into her ear over weeks which turned into months, I could see her getting more and more withdrawn, becoming sadder, quieter. And instead of disturbing me, it was almost as if as she grew smaller and more diminished, I grew in stature. I began to rise above my pain, as she sank ever deeper into hers.

Then I discovered, quite by chance, that Lucy had a crush. She'd fallen in love with a boy in the year above us called Tony Fletcher. She'd confided in one of her swotty little friends, and they'd told someone else and, well, you remember what it was like at school. Soon everyone knew, even Tony.

And that was when I played my trump card.

I brought a Polaroid camera into school. This was, of course, in the early 90s, long before school kids had mobile phones, or mobile phones had cameras. I hid the camera in my gym bag, and after our Friday morning PE session I hid myself in a shower cubicle and I waited. I knew that Lucy, skinny and underdeveloped for her age was, like many teenaged girls, terribly self-conscious about her body – and even more so now that she had me whispering in her ear every day, telling her how hideous she was.

I knew she dreaded PE, and that afterwards she always waited until everyone else had gone before stripping off her gym gear and slipping her uniform back on. She rarely took a shower, muttering that she'd have one when she got home and saying that she didn't sweat much anyway.

And so that Friday I hid and I waited. And when, through the gap in the shower curtain, I finally saw her pulling her T-shirt over her head, unclipping her (unnecessary) sports bra, wriggling out of her shorts, and standing there naked for a few brief moments as she searched her bag for her underwear, I slipped quietly out of the cubicle, called her name and, when she whirled around, a horror-stricken expression on her face, took the photo.

'Beth ... NO! PLEASE!'

I was laughing as I ran from the room, the still wet instant photograph dangling from my fingertips. I was still sniggering as the picture developed and I studied the detail of the image I'd captured.

It was perfect: it captured Lucy's tiny breasts – little more than swollen nipples – the dark mound of her pubic hair, the curve of her bare buttocks, all there for all the world to see.

And I made sure they were seen. During the lunchbreak, before the halls and classrooms filled up again, I pinned that photo to the noticeboard right outside the door of the room in which Tony Fletcher was about to have his 2pm history lesson.

When the bell went to signal the start of the afternoon session, I waited again, my heart fluttering. It didn't take long. Did I feel bad? Did I feel any sense of guilt at all when they began, the howls of laughter, the jeers, the screeches of 'OH. MY. GOD'? Did I feel it when Lucy Allen walked down the corridor and realised what was going on, and started to run, tears rolling down her cheeks, the shrieks of her classmates ringing in her ears? I don't think I did, not then. Not that day.

But that was when everything changed. Because that was the day I went too far.

So cruel. So stupid.

I never saw Lucy Allen again.

Chapter 21

When I wake up on Tuesday morning I know I've been dreaming about her again. As I lie in bed, kicking off the duvet to try to cool my hot, weary body, I remember the face at the patio window, that small white outline, wide eyes staring at me, and my stomach clenches. It had vanished, melted away into the darkness as I took a step towards it, giving me no time to work out who it was, and I'd stood there, confused, heart pounding. Mike again? But he was gone, wasn't he? It didn't look like him anyway – too short, not bulky enough. A would-be burglar then? Or a figment of my imagination, once more? I'd gone to bed telling myself that's all it was, and now I'm not sure if I actually saw anything at all.

It felt real, but I'd been drinking and I was half asleep ... or maybe I saw the face later, in my dreams, and it's all got muddled up in my head. I don't know. I don't know anything anymore. Everything feels so strange ...

I feel better after a shower, and when I go into Finley's room to see how he is I find to my surprise that he's already out of bed and attempting to pull his school shorts on over his bulky bandage.

'I *want* to go, Mum,' he insists when I protest. 'And I can walk fine. Look! With my crutches it's fun!'

He's supposed to keep the weight off his ankle for at least three days and Mum said last night that she'd be delighted to look after him if he was staying home from school, but he's swinging quite happily up and down the narrow strip of carpet by his bed now, already a competent crutch user, and I don't have the energy to argue.

'Fine. OK. But I'm going to ring the school and ask them to keep an eye on you. And you must stay sitting down at break times. Deal?'

He shrugs.

'Deal.'

I'm pretty sure Robin isn't going to turn up for the school run, not after last night, and I'm right. Her usual arrival time approaches and then passes, and when, anxiety gnawing at my stomach, I call her number, there's no reply. I leave a message, but she doesn't call back. She's really angry with me, clearly, and I don't blame her. What possessed me to attack her like that? Now, in the clear light of a fresh morning, it's glaringly obvious that it's me who was responsible for everything I accused her of. It *must* have been me who screwed up the central heating settings, and it was *definitely* me who made such a cock-up of putting the trampoline together. I need to get hold of her, to apologise, to beg her to come back, but right now I don't have time.

'Mum, I'm so sorry about this, but Robin's obviously not coming today ... Would you mind doing the school run? Finley won't be able to walk so it'll have to be a cab. I hate to ask, but I can't be late for work, not today. We have too much on, and—'

'Shush, shush, of course!' She's raising a hand, smiling. I know she heard the argument with Robin last night but when she came downstairs she simply asked me if I was OK, then left it at that. I'm wondering if I should try to explain now but she's already bustling away, opening the cupboard where I keep the breakfast cereals and asking Finley and Eloise what they fancy this morning.

Finley requests 'a *huge* bowl of porridge, please Grandma' and, injured ankle clearly not affecting his appetite or his mood, starts chattering to his sister about something to do with Spiderman. Mum smiles indulgently, then her eyes meet mine across the room and she says quietly, 'And don't worry about Robin. I'm sure you can sort it out, whatever it was, if you really want to. But I did say from the beginning I wasn't sure about her, love. So if you want to let her go, I'm more than happy to step in and help, you know that. Now you get off to work and stop stressing.'

'Thank you so much. I really don't know what I'd do without you at the moment,' I say, and she blows me a kiss.

'Lucky you don't have to, then,' she says. 'Now, scoot!'

I scoot. I'm still feeling fragile, but the relief of knowing Mum's happy to take over while I sort this mess out means that when I get into the surgery I find myself able to focus on work; the job is once more a welcome distraction. I need to organise maternity cover for Ally, one of our part-time receptionists, so I draft an advert and send it to the local paper, then pop the details on the surgery Facebook page too.

At lunchtime I go into the staffroom to make a cup of coffee and find Ruth and Deborah sitting at the table, lunchboxes open in front of them. I saw them briefly first thing for just long enough to reassure them that Finley was well and cheerful this morning, but I have a few minutes to spare now so I sit down at the table, ready for a chat.

'Hey, you two,' I say. 'Mmmm, is that lemon drizzle?'

Ruth grins. She's wearing a black silk blouse today with a pussy bow tied neatly at the neck.

'It is. Made by my own fair hands. Want a bit?'

I'm tempted – the cake looks moist and delicious with a light lemon glaze on top of fluffy sponge – but I shake my head reluctantly.

'Better not. Too much cake going into this belly recently.'

I pat my stomach and Ruth raises her eyebrows.

'Shut up, you look fine. But hey, all the more for me.'

She picks up the slice of cake and takes a bite. I turn to Deborah, who's poking what looks like a tuna sandwich with a finger in a desultory fashion, a blank look on her face. She looks pale and tired; her hair is scraped back from her face in a tight little bun and her skin is free of make-up.

'You OK, Debs? Going to eat that or just irritate it?'

She looks up abruptly, as if surprised to hear my voice, then gives me a small smile.

'Oh, sorry, Beth. I was miles away. No, not very hungry. In fact, I might just head back to my room and get sorted for this afternoon. I'll see you both later, OK?'

She closes the lid of her plastic lunchbox, picks it up, and leaves the room. I frown.

'Ruth, what's wrong with her? She's been acting oddly for ages now. Do you know what's going on?'

Ruth opens her mouth as if to speak, then closes it again. There's a moment of silence, then she says, 'I think she's just knackered, needs a holiday, you know what it's like. And now I've got to go too, sorry. Want to get some filing done before the afternoon rush. I'm so glad Finley's OK though. And kids bounce back so quickly ... Oh, gosh, no pun intended. Probably a bit early for trampoline jokes!'

'A bit, yes!' I say with a grimace. She pats my hand and then stands up, gathering her belongings. Moments later she's gone too, and I sit there for a minute, sipping my coffee and thinking.

Why was Ruth being so evasive there, because she was, wasn't she? I don't care what she says, there's definitely something going on with Deborah, and it's more than her just being tired and needing a break. If she doesn't want to talk about it, though ...

I sigh and head back to my office. I've only just settled again, trying to get my head round the latest plans for the surgery renovations, when my phone rings. It's Jacob, and he's not happy.

'Beth, why has Finley gone to school? You said last night he's supposed to keep the weight off that ankle for a few days, but when I rang the house to talk to him your mother said you asked her to take him to school! And what's this about you falling out with Robin?'

I sigh.

'He didn't want to stay at home, and he's already a pro on

the crutches, honestly. He'll be fine. I rang the school earlier and the head promised they'd keep an eye on him.'

'Well, it doesn't sound like a good idea to me. And Robin?'

'It's nothing. Just a silly misunderstanding. I'll speak to her later and sort it out.'

There's a moment's silence on the other end of the line, then he says, 'Beth ... this thing with the trampoline. I'm trying not to blame you ... Accidents happen, but I'm sorry, you can't have put it together properly, and when our children's safety is at stake ...'

Well, I didn't hear you *offering to come round and put it up for them*, I think, and wonder if I should say that out loud, but he's still talking, his tone increasingly irate.

'And you seem to be away with the fairies recently, by all accounts. Eloise told me you keep losing your keys and having to get cabs to work, and that you've fallen out with your neighbours too ... What's going on?'

Shit. I hadn't realised the kids – or Eloise, at least – had picked up on the fact that something's happened with Brenda and Barbara. They bloody notice everything, don't they?

'Nothing's going on,' I say. I know I sound angry and defensive now but I can't help it. It's how I feel. Angry, defensive, and ashamed too.

'I've just had a lot on my plate, with Dad being ill and Mum turning up like that, but everything's fine now. Just leave it, Jacob. Finley will be OK, and if I think being at school is delaying his leg healing I'll keep him off, right? And now I have to go. I have work to do. I'll see you later in the week.'

He's still muttering, something about me 'needing to get

it together' as I end the call, and for a moment I sit there, staring at the phone, a sick, hollow feeling in my stomach. He's right, I do need to get it together. Why have so many things gone wrong recently? The past two weeks, since Mum reappeared in my life, should have been the happiest ever, and instead ...

I take a deep breath and then another. I just need to try harder, to concentrate on what I'm doing, to be more organised at home and to stop blaming other people for my own failings, I decide. I get back to work and an hour later I'm so engrossed in trying to sort out everyone's summer annual leave requests that when my mobile rings I jump. I grab it and instantly my heart rate speeds up.

Mum. Oh no ... Now what?

But this time, it's good news. The *best* news.

'Liv's coming to visit, darling! On Friday, is that OK? She's so excited to meet you all. She's got a half-day so she thought she'd get the train up on Friday afternoon. She has to go back on Saturday evening because she's working on Sunday but, well, it's wonderful, isn't it? My two girls, together for the first time!'

'Oh Mum ... that's amazing!'

I'm grinning from ear to ear.

'I'll move Eloise in with me and Liv can have her room. I'll ask Robin ...'

I pause, remembering.

'Well, anyway, I can sort that out. Mum, thank you, that's cheered me right up. I've got to go, but I'll see you in a few hours, OK?'

'See you later, darling. I'm off on the school run shortly. Is it OK to tell the kids their auntie is coming?'

'Of course. They'll be thrilled. See you all later!'

It's hard to concentrate after that. My head is full of plans for the weekend, what to cook for dinner on Friday, and what to wear when I meet my little sister for the first time.

'How much weight can I lose in three days?' I think, as I run a hand over the rolls of fat emerging from the waistband of my trousers, then grimace and vow not to worry about it. If Liv is as nice as she seemed to be during our FaceTime call, she won't care that her big sis is carrying a few extra pounds, and I have more important things to worry about. I need to patch things up with Robin, urgently now, and I leave another voice message, telling her I'm so sorry about last night and that I really want to speak to her. Then I remember the trampoline lying drunkenly in the garden and call the council to arrange a bulky item collection. It's a terrible waste – I'm sure it wasn't cheap, and I'm going to have to try to persuade Mum to let me reimburse her – but I can't bear to see it out there for much longer. To have it taken away is going to cost me twenty pounds but they can do it tomorrow, which is a relief.

The rest of the day passes quickly, and when I arrive home just after six the house is buzzing. Eloise – her school's Easter play is, it's emerged, a musical take on the life of Shakespeare, and she's playing the Bard's assistant – is boogying around the kitchen, accompanied by an upbeat dance tune (which, to my ears, sounds distinctly *un*-Shakespearian) blasting from the speakers in the ceiling. Finley is sitting at the island, his bad leg propped up on the stool next to him, tapping away at the iPad on his lap, engrossed in some sort of driving game. Mum is at the cooker stirring something in a big saucepan, and the room smells deliciously of garlic and spices.

'Making a curry, darling,' she yells.

'Amazing,' I shout back, and grab Eloise as she whirls past me.

'Eloise, fabulous dancing, but *please* can we have a little less volume on the music?'

'Be finished in two minutes. I can't dance if it's quiet!' she bellows, pink-cheeked and breathless, and prances off again. I sigh and give up. Leaving them to it, I push open the patio doors and wander out into the garden. It's a lovely mild evening and, trying not to look at the lopsided trampoline, I wander around for a few minutes, stooping now and again to pull a weed from a flowerbed, making a mental note that the birdfeeder needs topping up. There's a soft, sweet scent in the air, the promise of warmer days to come, and I feel my spirits lifting. I've always loved being outdoors, loved this time of year when winter finally gives way to spring. I love seeing new buds on old trees and watching the first flowers pushing their vibrant heads above the soil. There's something comforting about knowing that no matter what else is happening in the world, the seasons march on, gliding seamlessly into each other. Nature knows exactly what it's doing, even if nobody else does ...

What's that?

I'm still wandering up the garden, but now I stop abruptly and stare at the flowerbed that runs along the far fence, the one that finishes right outside the doors that lead out into the garden from the lounge. The spot where, last night, I thought I saw a face, outside in the dark, peering in at me.

But that wasn't real, was it? I was drunk, half-asleep, I imagined it ...

'Mum!'

I jump. Eloise has poked her head out of the kitchen door.

'There's an important letter for you from school. I've left it on the kitchen island, OK?'

I wave a hand, still distracted.

'Yes, OK. I'll look at it later. Be in in a minute.'

'Thanks, Mum.'

She disappears and I turn back to stare at the flowerbed again. I was so sure, this morning, so sure that the figure I'd seen out here had been part of my muddled dreams. But now, seeing what I'm seeing, a shiver like a bolt of electricity runs down my back. I take a step closer, and another, and now there's no doubt in my mind. Somebody *was* standing out here last night because there, in the soil, right outside the window, are two indentations, side by side. They're footprints.

And figments of your imagination don't leave footprints, do they?

Chapter 22

'It's tonight, isn't it? Have an *amazing* time ... Can't wait to hear all about it on Monday!'

I'm just switching my computer off for the weekend when Ruth pops her head round the door.

'Thanks! She'll be there when I get home. Her train got in about an hour ago and she was going to hop in a cab to Prestbury. I'm so nervous. Is that silly?'

Ruth shakes her head.

'Of course not. It's your long-lost sister ... I'd be freaking out! But it'll be fine; you know it will. And at least you've chatted on the phone. Stop worrying. Now go!'

'I'm going, I'm going!'

I scan my desk for any errant belongings, stuff my phone and diary into my bag, and make my escape. The Friday evening traffic is slow, and as I slam on the brakes yet again as I pass Pittville Park, I take some deep, calming breaths then check my face in the rear-view mirror, smoothing a stray hair and running a finger under my eyes where my mascara's smudged a little. It's been a long week, but I'm definitely in a better place now than I was on Monday, I think, as the car in front slowly begins to move again.

I've tried to put the footprints I saw in the flowerbed outside the lounge window firmly out of my mind. I still think I imagined, or dreamed, that face looking in at me, for who on earth would be standing in our back garden so late at night, and why? And although I didn't dream the footprints – they were there, right in front of me, clear as anything – well, anyone could have made those in the previous few days, couldn't they?

They were, if I was being really honest, too big to have been made by Finley or Eloise, unless they were messing around in adult's shoes, but I'm glossing over that in my head now. I'm glossing over the fact too that it's highly unlikely that my mother would have gone out into the garden and suddenly decided to stand in the flowerbed, and that I certainly don't remember doing that myself either – not there, in such a strange position, right up close to the glass of the patio doors. But I'm confused about a lot of things right now. Maybe it *was* me, maybe I stepped onto the soil when I was weeding, and didn't notice, didn't remember. I'm letting it go because I have other priorities. Robin for example.

Still sounding huffy, she finally called me back on Wednesday morning and she agreed to come round and see me after work. I apologised profusely for what I'd said to her, blaming the stress of Finley's accident on top of everything else that's been going on recently, and she eventually said OK, she'd come back. She was still a little grumpy with me yesterday though – not that I blamed her – but to her credit she was her usual cheery self with the children, for which I was deeply grateful.

'I'm glad you and Robin are friends again, Mum,' Eloise whispered, as I kissed her goodbye when I left for work.

'Me too,' I whispered, although I knew we weren't, not really. It was a start, though.

Mum had simply nodded and said, 'All right, if that's what you want,' when I told her Robin would be resuming her duties, but her mouth was set in a tight line for an hour afterwards, and it was pretty obvious she didn't approve.

But, much as I want to please my mother, I'm holding firm on this one, I think. I need Robin. It's OK now, with Mum here, but what happens when she goes home again in September or whenever? What do I do then?

Still, her disapproval stings a little, and her mistrust of Robin makes me uneasy.

I'm still not sure I entirely trust her myself, not after recent events, but she's back now, so—

BEEEEEP!

I jump as a car horn sounds loudly behind me and I realise the red light I've been sitting in front of has turned green without me noticing. I raise a hand in apology and move off again. I should be home in about five minutes now, traffic permitting, and my stomach rolls. I know the house will be immaculate – between them, Mum and Robin will have seen to that – and I've asked Robin to make up Eloise's room for Liv. We've pre-ordered some Thai food – apparently this is my sister's favourite – which will just need reheating, and there's champagne chilling in the fridge. Everything is perfectly in place.

But what if she doesn't like me? What if she thinks I'm fat and boring? What if ...

I lift my right hand from the steering wheel and firmly slap my left wrist.

'Stop it. She's going to love you. She's going to love all of us,' I say loudly.

I repeat the words like a mantra the rest of the way home, but it doesn't help much. As I put the key in the front door, my stomach is churning and my heart is beating so fast I actually feel a little faint.

Shit. Shit. I'm about to meet my sister. Is this even real?

And then I walk into the kitchen, and there they all are, my mum, my two children, and my sister. Our eyes meet and she smiles, the biggest, sunniest, most beautiful smile, and suddenly everything, *everything*, is OK.

'Mum! This is her! This is Auntie Liv!'

Finley launches himself at me and I hug him and laugh, and then Eloise is hugging me too, and across the room Mum's grinning ear to ear and Liv's getting up from her stool and coming towards me, arms outstretched.

'Hello, sis,' she says, and even though Finley and Eloise are still wrapped around me she just piles on too, and it's all four of us in a big, messy giggling cuddle, and it's wonderful. *Just. So. Wonderful*.

Eventually we extricate ourselves and I get a proper look at her. Her long blonde hair is tied back in a loose ponytail today, little wisps falling around her face, and when she smiles her teeth are white and even. She's wearing a buttery-soft navy leather jacket and tight jeans which show off long, slender legs. She smells of wildflowers and peaches, and her long nails are painted a chic nude colour. She's gorgeous, and I suddenly feel horribly self-conscious again – lumpy and wrinkly and unstylish, sixteen years older than her but looking much older. I am her frumpy older sister. And yet she's looking at me as if I'm the most exciting thing she's ever seen, grabbing my hands now and pulling me across the room, telling me how lovely the house is and how great the kids are and how fabulous it is to have a niece and nephew and how she just can't *wait* to get to know us all properly ... And now I'm starting to feel little bubbles of joy in my tummy. *My sister, here at last.*

For the next hour, we all just sit in the kitchen chatting. Mum opens the champagne and pours some lemonade for Finley and Eloise. We all 'cheers' and toast one another, and then we chat some more, Liv and I tripping over our words in our efforts to catch up on more than twenty years of life, twenty-odd years that we've been sisters without knowing a thing about each other. She's single at the moment, has had a couple of boyfriends in recent years but nobody serious. She loves her job but is keen to travel too, maybe take an adult gap-year and backpack around Asia. She's a keen runner with several marathons under her belt. This reminds me of Robin, who's not here – Mum must have let her go early again, but I'm not going to make an issue of it, not today.

At seven o'clock we decide we'd better eat, and Mum insists

she'll organise it while we carry on getting to know each other.

'It just needs heating up; it won't take long,' she says, and shoos us all into the living room. Finley and Eloise seem as smitten with their new aunt as they were with their new grandmother. Eloise in particular is hanging on Liv's every word. When my sister mentions loving drama classes at school, Eloise is ecstatic.

'Me too, me too!' she shrieks, bouncing up and down on her chair. 'I've got a big part in the Easter play. We're doing Shakespeare's life as a musical!'

'Well done, you!' says Liv. 'Must run in the family, eh Beth? Mum was into a bit of am-dram too, back in the day.'

She looks at me and winks, and I feel a warm glow.

The family. My family.

And then, predictably, it all goes wrong.

'I'm going on a school trip to London next week,' Eloise is saying now. 'We're going to see a matinee in a proper West End theatre, *Matilda the Musical*. I'm sooooo excited!'

'Sounds amazing!' says Liv, but I raise a hand, puzzled.

'Erm ... what? I don't know anything about this, Eloise.'

She turns to me, the smile fading from her face.

'Of course you do. I gave you the letter on Tuesday.'

'Tuesday?'

I think for a moment. Then I shake my head.

'Darling, you didn't give me any letter ...'

'I did, I did!' She interrupts me, starting to look anxious now.

'When you were out in the garden after work, remember?

I told you there was a letter from school and you said you'd look at it when you came in ... Oh Muuuuuum!'

I clap a hand over my mouth. I do remember her telling me about a letter now, the day I saw those footprints outside the window, but I can't remember seeing it when I came in from the garden. Where was it? And— Oh heck, does that mean ...?

'Muuuuuum!' She's wailing now, the tears starting to flow. 'You had to call the school and pay by yesterday. It was a last-minute thing, and if you haven't done it that means they won't have got me a ticket and I won't be able to go and all my friends are going and I was so looking forward to it and Muuuuuum!'

She slumps forward, hands over her face and sobs. Across the room, Finley is watching wide-eyed and Liv is staring into her champagne glass, clearly ill at ease.

'Eloise, darling, I'm so sorry. I just didn't see the letter. I've no idea where it went, and then I forgot all about it ... Look, let me call the school on Monday and see if I can do anything. Maybe they can still—'

'It's too late!' she howls. 'It absolutely had to be done by yesterday. Why are you so useless, Mum? You're always losing things and forgetting things and not doing things properly and falling out with everyone. And now you've ruined my *life*.'

She's risen to her feet and on the word *life* she turns and flounces dramatically from the room, still sobbing loudly. Moments later we hear footsteps pounding up the stairs and then a bang as her bedroom door slams shut.

'Oh dear,' says Mum mildly from the kitchen. Liv, Finley, and I look at each other.

'Liv, I'm so sorry. She's not normally like that, and I can't think what happened to that flipping letter ...'

'Oh honestly, don't think anything of it; these things happen,' she says, but she still looks horribly uncomfortable. 'Look, I'll go and help Mum with the food, you go up and sort her out.'

'I wouldn't bother. I don't think she'll talk to you,' Finley says darkly, his blond, barely-there eyebrows raised disapprovingly.

'I think you might be right,' I mutter, but I go upstairs anyway. I should have listened to my seven-year-old; Eloise is inconsolable, sobbing into her pillow (on her bed which, of course, has been freshly made up for Liv, and which now will be creased and tear-stained, I think ruefully) and she won't even look at me. And then, of *course*, Jacob arrives. He's not due to have the kids until tomorrow night, but he's decided to pop in on his way home from work to meet Liv and see how Finley's ankle is (healing beautifully, by the look of it; he's already hardly using his crutches). When he hears that Eloise is crying in her room, he runs upstairs, and comes down again twenty minutes later looking irate.

'Beth, can I have a word?'

Mum's about to dish out the food, asking Finley if he'll run up and try to persuade his sister to come down. I apologise and tell them to start without me, my heart sinking. Out in the hallway I brace myself. My ex-husband does *not* look pleased.

'How could you forget to contact the school about the London trip, Beth? She's heartbroken.'

'I just didn't see the letter, Jacob. I'm sorry. I don't know—'

'She says she left it right there in the kitchen for you, and you said you'd deal with it! It's not a lot to ask, is it? The poor kid. And it's not as if it's the first cock-up you've made recently, is it? What the hell's going on in your head at the moment? The trampoline accident, and now this? Seriously, Beth, it's not good enough. The kids are getting more and more frustrated and so am I. I said it the other day and I'll say it again. Get it together, Beth. Just sort yourself out.'

His voice has got louder and louder as he's speaking, and I'm sure Mum and Liv will be able to hear him clearly from the kitchen. I cringe inwardly. *Today of all days.*

'Jacob, please, shh,' I hiss, but he's finished now. He gives me an exasperated look as he turns and stomps out of the front door, slamming it nearly as loudly as Eloise slammed her bedroom door earlier. I stand there for a moment, guilt and humiliation washing over me.

How on earth have I messed up again? Where did that letter go and why didn't I look for it? Why didn't I remember?

I'm wondering now if I might have thrown it in the recycling bin when I was doing my usual pre-bed whizz around the house on Tuesday night, but it doesn't really matter now, does it? I *will* call the school on Monday and see if this can be salvaged, but if it really is too late for Eloise to get a ticket and go on the trip ...

I slink back into the kitchen. There's a moment of awkward

silence as Mum and Liv look at me, then at each other, and it's obvious they've heard every word.

'Dinner, darling! That will make us all feel better,' Mum says brightly, brandishing a large spoon.

The food smells amazing. Big bowls of green curry, pad thai, and spicy papaya salad are all laid out, waiting to be served, but suddenly I've lost my appetite.

'I'm so sorry about that,' I say, and they both tell me to forget it, that we're still going to have a lovely evening, but the atmosphere has changed and we all know it. Finley comes back downstairs and tells us that his sister will follow shortly. 'She's just washing the tears off her face,' he says to Mum, and glowers at me.

When she eventually reappears she's still sniffing loudly and refusing to look at me, picking at her food and giving brief, sullen answers when Mum and Liv try valiantly to draw her into the conversation. Then, when I finally send the children to bed, there's another row when Eloise refuses point-blank to sleep in my room, insisting on squeezing in with Finley instead. She won't kiss me goodnight either. As a result, and just to make things even worse, I come back downstairs and pour another large glass of wine – we've moved on from the champagne to Chardonnay – and then another, and another. At one point I suddenly decide it would be an excellent idea to tell my mother and sister about the face I saw outside the patio window on Monday night, complete with a full re-enactment which involves me running outside and squashing my face against the glass, then treading soil all over the kitchen floor when I come back in. They both laugh uneasily, clearly unsure whether I'm serious or just trying to be entertaining, and by then I've had so much wine I just laugh too, telling them it was probably just a dream. They look confused and so I change the subject, and thankfully they let it go and we start chatting again. I can tell they're both making a big effort to make everything feel normal, to recapture the happiness and excitement we all felt at the beginning of the evening, but more than once I catch them exchanging glances, and by the time we call it a night I'm drunk and miserable.

I tell my mother and sister to go up while I try, ineffectually, to make the kitchen look less like a bomb's hit it, then give up. I'm stumbling into my bedroom, feeling decidedly dizzy and a little bit sick, when Mum, passing my door on her way back from the bathroom, slips an arm around my waist.

'Come on, love, let's get you into bed,' she whispers.

'I'm so sorry, Mum,' I slur, as she half drags, half carries me. She squeezes my waist and tells me to stop apologising.

'It really doesn't matter, and don't you worry about Liv either; she's fine,' she says, as she lowers me onto the duvet. 'But I've been thinking ... Might it have been Robin who threw away that letter from the school? I mean, *I* didn't touch it, and if Eloise left it where she said she did on Tuesday evening it should have still been there on Wednesday, when Robin came round to see you, and on Thursday when she came back to work. It just seems to have vanished, which is a bit odd. I'm not saying Robin did it on purpose; I'm not suggesting anything sinister, but, you know ...'

She kisses my forehead and slips from the room, telling me to drink lots of water before I go to sleep and to have a lie-in tomorrow if I feel like it because she and Liv will sort the kids out. I lie back on my pillow feeling even more nauseous now, wondering if I even have the energy to get undressed and trying to focus my fuddled brain on what she's just suggested.

Robin wouldn't have thrown away a letter that was clearly from the school, would she? Even if she was mad at me, which she was? She wouldn't ...

I'm feeling too ill and tired to think about it anymore right now. The room is swirling around me. *It's not as if I'm going to confront Robin about it anyway*, I think, as I roll off the bed. I clamber unsteadily to my feet, pull my trousers and blouse off, and leave them on the floor where they fall, finally wriggling into my pyjamas. *Been there, done that, not risking it again.*

My stomach lurches and I know I'm going to throw up. I make it to the bathroom just in time, crashing painfully to my knees beside the toilet. I retch into the bowl over and over again until my stomach is empty. When I finish, I crouch there on the floor for a long time, tears flowing silently down my cheeks.

How can an evening that started so well have turned into such a bloody disaster? And what will Liv think of me now? Why am I messing everything up so badly? My brain doesn't seem to be working properly, I'm losing my friends, and even the kids and Jacob think I'm a mess. I am a mess, I am, and I don't understand why ...

Finally, I crawl into bed and dream of a cold, empty house, the sound of a little girl crying echoing around the lonely rooms. And at the window, a small white face stares in at me with eyes so dark and deep I feel like I'm drowning.

Chapter 23

I wake just after 4am, my head pounding, my lips cracked and dry, and my pyjamas damp.

Did I hear a noise out on the landing? Is someone up?

I groan and sit up slowly, pushing the duvet aside. I can feel sweat running down my back, plastering my hair to my scalp and stinging my eyes. The room feels like a furnace, so hot it's hard to breathe, and I whimper and struggle to my feet, staggering to the window to fling it open, breathing in the cool night air in grateful gulps.

Why is my bedroom so hot? Is it just me, is the hangover kicking in, or ... oh shit, have I messed up the heating again? Last night, when I was drunk? Did I ...?

There's another noise, right behind me this time, and I jump violently. The sudden movement jars my skull, making my head throb even more painfully. I turn to see Finley standing in the doorway.

'Mum ... I'm too hot to sleep. My room is *horrible*,' he says with a sob, and rushes across the room towards me, flinging his arms around my waist. He feels as overheated as I do. His skin is damp and his T-shirt is sticking to his back.

Oh God. What have I done now? Liv's here; she'll be awake too. They all will ...

'I'm going to go and sort it out, darling,' I whisper. 'It's just the heating playing up, I'm so sorry. You go back to bed and I'll open your windows to cool your room down, OK? It'll feel better soon.'

He sobs again, nodding with his head still pressed into my tummy, and I think I might be sick again. I lead him back to his room, grabbing a towel from the bathroom to mop him down with. Eloise is, thankfully, still asleep, curled up on one side of Finley's small bed. There's a sheen of sweat on her forehead too though, and I check the radiator and find it unbearably hot, my fingers barely grazing the white painted steel before I have to pull them away. My confusion growing, I open the windows wide, take another few deep breaths to try to quell the nausea, then creep down to the hall, flicking the light on then groaning again. My eyes feel as if someone's been rubbing them with sandpaper; they're gritty and painful, but I force myself to study the heating control panel on the wall.

Twenty-one degrees. My usual setting. This doesn't make sense ...

And yet I'm already feeling cooler, already sweating less profusely. I walk slowly around the ground floor, feeling the radiators. The rooms are warm – too warm – but the radiators seem to be cooling rapidly now.

I must have set a timer or something last night and now it's gone off again. But why? Why would I do that? And why don't I remember?

As I make my way slowly back upstairs, I think again about Barbara and Brenda and how I wish I could pop round later and ask them for their advice about this stupid problem, and about the face I saw outside the window, and about everything else that's been going on too. My heart twists with sorrow that I can't. And then I think about Robin and how upset she was with me, and I wonder.

Could Mum be right? Could Robin be behind all this? The heating, the missing letter? But why? What on earth would she gain from it? It just isn't logical ...

I'm back in my room now, fumbling in my bedside drawer for paracetemol, washing two down with some water from the glass that's somehow sitting by my bed – Mum, I assume. I strip my pyjamas off and go to the chest of drawers for a fresh pair, and as I do so I catch a glimpse of my naked body in the full-length mirror. I stop and look for a minute, watching a trickle of sweat running slowly down my chest, making its way between my breasts, and wonder if I have the energy to take a shower. I don't. I get back into bed and when I open my eyes again the sun is streaming in through the open curtains and somehow I've got through the night.

Remarkably, I don't feel too bad – a lingering feeling of mild nausea, a slight headache, and a raging thirst, but I've felt worse. I'm still dreading facing Mum and Liv though, and when I go downstairs they are, of course, already up and chatting in the kitchen, mugs of tea in hand. Liv looks fresh and lovely, dressed in a denim jumpsuit with pristine white trainers, while Mum's in slinky grey yoga pants and a cream sweater, her feet bare and her toenails painted scarlet. I glance down at my own ancient, creased T-shirt – a Minnie Mouse one Jacob bought me for a joke about five birthdays ago – and sigh inwardly.

Always, always such a mess.

'Morning!' I say brightly, and they both look round and smile.

'Morning, sis!' says Liv. 'Sore head this morning?'

She winks and I immediately feel a little better. Maybe she's not judging me after all.

'A bit,' I admit. 'Sorry about last night. I had a bit too much, I think!'

She shakes her head and pulls out a stool for me to sit down.

'Don't be silly. We've all been there, trust me. I only took it easy because I've got the long journey back tonight. Nothing worse than public transport with a hangover.'

I sit gratefully and Mum stands up.

'I'll make you a cuppa, love. By the way, did either of you notice how hot it got in the night? I woke up in the early hours and thought I was going to suffocate!'

'Gosh, yes. It was awful. I woke up too and it took me ages to get back to sleep.'

Liv puts her mug down on the countertop and turns to look at me.

'Is your heating on the blink or something?'

Shit, I think.

'I'm not sure what's going on with it,' I say. 'I'm really sorry. I woke up too, and poor Finley ...'

BZZZZZZZ.

The doorbell rings suddenly and, literally saved by the bell, I go to see who's there, hoping the conversation will have moved on from the damn central heating by the time I come back. To my surprise, Jacob's standing on the doorstep looking handsome in a blue polo shirt and jeans, his hair freshly trimmed.

He was at the barber's early, I think, then glance at my watch, and see to my surprise that it's already nine-thirty. I must have slept for longer than I thought.

'Beth, I'm here for the kids. Eloise rang me an hour ago and said she wanted to come to ours as soon as possible. The poor kid's still really upset, and what the hell's this about the central heating? She said she and Finley barely slept last night because the house was like an oven. I don't know what the hell's going on here at the moment, but if the children can't even get a decent night's *sleep* ... and what's wrong with you, anyway? You look dreadful ...'

'Shh, please, keep your voice down,' I beg. He's speaking so loudly I'm sure Mum and Liv can hear him from the kitchen, and next door I've just heard Barbara's front door opening and footsteps on her path. I don't want to see her right now, not with everything else that's going on. I grab Jacob's arm and pull him into the hall, closing the door behind him.

'The heating's been playing up. I'll get it sorted,' I say quietly. 'I didn't sleep well either. That's why I look dreadful, as you so kindly put it.'

'Sorry.' He has the good grace to look a little shamefaced, and I'm about to ask him more about his early phone call from Eloise when I hear footsteps on the stairs and turn to see the children making their way down, both lugging overnight bags.

'Eloise, Finley ... what, you've packed already?'

Eloise, shoes and red leather jacket already on, ignores me, not even glancing in my direction. Her eyes are fixed on her father.

'Hi Dad, thanks for coming to get us,' she says, her voice tight and prim with barely suppressed fury. I look from her to Jacob and then at Finley who's fully dressed too, and a sudden rush of anxiety makes me feel so lightheaded I reach out and grab the bannister for support.

Please, not another row. Not with my sister here ...

'Eloise, you don't need to go yet, do you? Your aunt is still here until this evening. I'm sure Daddy could come back and pick you up later?'

She's still ignoring me, opening the front door and wheeling her little case out into the driveway. Finley watches her uncertainly, then looks up at me.

'She wants to go now, Mum,' he says. 'She's in a bad mood. Can we go, Daddy?'

I look at Jacob in despair but he's nodding and reaching out a hand to take Finley's bag from him. It's still half-unzipped, the leg of a pair of jeans and the sleeve of a sweatshirt hanging out of it.

'Well, have you even packed properly?' I say frantically. 'I mean, have you got your homework stuff, and—'

'Eloise did it for me,' Finley says. 'It's fine, Mum. Don't fuss.'

He sounds so grown-up suddenly, so *patronising*, almost, and now I want to cry because he's walking towards the door too and neither of them is looking back. Neither of them has kissed me goodbye and now Jacob's leaving too, and giving me a strange look as he pauses in the doorway.

'He's right; don't fuss,' he says. 'Get yourself together and get that heating looked at. I'm worried about you, Beth. And, more to the point, worried about the kids. It's great that you've got your mother back, and your sister too, don't get me wrong. But it's starting to feel as if it's all about them at the moment and not about the children, and that's really starting to concern me now, you know?'

I open my mouth to speak, to defend myself, to tell him the children are fine, but he's turning away and heading for the car, and anyway, I know the children *aren't* fine, not really. They're not, and I'm not, and I just don't know why. I can't understand why everything's just so *awful* ...

'Everything OK, Beth?'

Mum touches me on the shoulder and I jump.

'Yes, yes. Jacob just came for the kids early. He's got something planned. Not sure what,' I say quickly, but she's frowning, peering out of the door and watching the car pulling away. The kids aren't waving and their heads are down in the back seat.

'But they didn't even say goodbye to Liv,' she says, and she sounds so hurt, so disappointed, that I almost can't bear it. I've hurt my mother now too, offended my sister, and I just want to slump to my knees right here in the hallway and bawl. I don't though. Instead, I force back the tears and tell my mother more lies, say I'm sorry and that they were just so excited about the day Jacob has planned, you know what kids are like, and I'll get them to call Liv tonight. I'll speak to Jacob later and get him on the case. And then we go back into the kitchen and I lie to Liv too, and tell her the same story. Bless her, she brushes it off and says she totally understands because there'll be plenty more times we can get together, won't there, and I smile and agree, but inside I'm angry and devastated. My children have *never* left this house without kissing me goodbye. Eloise has never treated me with such ... with such *disdain*, and it's killing me.

We sit in the kitchen for a while longer, the three of us. Somehow I manage to keep it together, manage to laugh and smile, and join in with the conversation. But then Mum and Liv decide to nip down to the local shop together so Mum can buy a newspaper, and when they come back Liv announces she's decided to leave early. To leave *now*.

'I was going to stay until this evening, but I've just been thinking about work tomorrow, you know? I have a really early start and if I don't get home until late tonight I'm just going to be knackered. Do you mind? We'll meet up again soon, I promise.'

She hugs me, and even though I don't believe her, even though I'm certain she's leaving because of last night and the row with Eloise and the stupid central heating and everything else that's happened, I hug her back and tell her that of course I understand, and that it's fine and we'll see each other soon.

She kisses me on the cheek.

'You're the best, sis,' she says, and skips off upstairs to pack her stuff, and for a moment I feel better.

Sis. I have a sister, and surely that's what's most important right now, the fact that we've found each other? All the other stuff, well, it's not ideal, but we can get past it, right?

But then I make the mistake of going upstairs to see if she wants a coffee before she goes. I'm about to walk into the room when I hear low voices and realise Mum's in there too. I hesitate for a moment, but I've already pushed the door open a little and the conversation stops abruptly.

'Beth! I was just helping Liv pack ...'

Mum's voice is bright and cheerful, but there's an awkwardness about her and I suddenly wonder what they've just been talking about.

'And I was telling her I'm not five anymore and I can pack by myself!'

Liv, kneeling on the floor next to her open bag, rolls her eyes and laughs, but there's definitely a strange atmosphere in the room and I'm certain, I *know*, that they were talking about me and are trying to pretend they weren't. I laugh too (*God, my little wannabe actress daughter would be proud of my Oscar-worthy performances today*, *if only she were speaking to me*) and ask what I came up to ask and go back downstairs again. Somehow I get through the next hour and there are more hugs and more promises to meet again soon. And then she's gone, and Mum and I stand at the door waving until the taxi goes out of sight.

'Beth ...'

I've just closed the door and I turn to look at Mum. My heart skips as I see the serious expression on her face and the concern in her eyes.

'Yes? Is everything OK?'

'Beth, look ... I just wanted to say something. I don't want to nag – God knows, I have no right to do that. I've only been back in your life for such a short time, but, well ...'

She pauses, and I can feel a flutter of panic in my stomach.

She's going to leave again, isn't she? She's finally got fed up with me, with everything that's been going on. I don't blame her, of course I don't, but ...

'It's just that, well, I'm worried about you, Beth,' she says.

'Wo-worried? Why?'

She sighs.

'You just seem ... so stressed. Last night ... well, you're drinking a lot, aren't you? And you seem so forgetful all the time – the stuff with the central heating, and seeing faces at the windows ...'

She hesitates, worried eyes searching my face, and I can feel my cheeks begin to burn with shame.

It's not my past that will drive her away, is it? Not what I did back then, not the fact that her daughter is a monster. She doesn't even know about that. It's how I'm behaving now that will make her leave ...

'Mum, I'm fine honestly. I've just had a lot on. You coming back ... well, it's amazing, wonderful ... but it's kind of a big life change, you know? And Dad being ill and everything ...'

I'm trying to sound upbeat and positive but she doesn't look convinced. She's still looking at me with those worried eyes, her brow creased in a frown.

'You're right. I need to watch the drinking though,' I say. 'I'll cut down. I just get a bit carried away sometimes, but I'll keep an eye on it, OK? And I'll call the engineer again about the heating later and get to the bottom of what's going on.'

She nods, smiles, and looks relieved.

'OK. Good girl. Come on, I'll make us another cup of tea.'

We head back into the kitchen and the conversation moves away from me and back to last night, but the good bits this time. We chat about Liv and how lovely it is that we've met now, how well we get on, how much we have in common, how she told Mum before she left how thrilled she was to meet me and how much she likes me. An hour later, I've begun to feel almost – *almost* – happy again.

I'll sort things out with Eloise, won't I? Mothers and daughters row all the time. This is just a little blip and we'll be absolutely fine once she calms down. And everything else ... I'm just overtired, that's all ...

The doorbell rings then and I run to answer it, my stomach flipping.

The kids, maybe, changing their minds and coming home again?

But it's just the postman with a parcel, so I take it and thank him, suddenly feeling tearful again. And then as he heads back down the driveway, a movement by the gate catches my eye and for some reason, a shiver runs through me. I stare, blink, but ... nothing. There's nobody there. I glance up and down the empty street, once, twice. Then I double-lock the door and go and join my mother.

Chapter 24

'Everything OK? Any issues I should know about?'

'All good thanks, Beth. Everything all right with you? How's Finley's ankle?'

Lorraine, her arms full of dressings and blood bottles, smiles at me and I smile back.

'Doing really well, thanks. He's in a walking boot now and pretty much running around on it. Should be fine in another couple of weeks. Kids recover so quickly, don't they?'

'They do. Right, must get on. See you later.'

She deposits her supplies on her desk and I tick her off the list on the clipboard I'm carrying and head back to my own office. I've just done the rounds, checking that all the staff are all right and seeing if any of them have any problems that need to be sorted out. The irony of this hasn't escaped me. Me, the practice manager, checking on everyone's welfare when I'm only just managing to hold onto my own wellbeing and sanity by my fingertips. What a weekend. Eloise was still barely speaking to me when Jacob brought the children home last night and this morning wasn't much fun either. Robin was still icily polite when she turned up to do the school run.

At least when I got to work I was greeted by a wide smile and a hug from Ruth who's in high spirits today, having been told by her son yesterday that he and his young family are hoping to fly over from Canada for a visit in June or July. Deborah, on the other hand, is still *definitely* not herself.

'That's great news, Ruth,' she said quietly, as Ruth bounced around the staffroom. Then, head down, she shuffled out of the door and headed off down the corridor, not looking back. I stared after her for moment, then turned to Ruth.

'Right, enough of this,' I said. 'Come on, Ruth. You *must* know what's up. I need to know – on a professional level if nothing else.'

Ruth stopped skipping up and down the room and, pink-cheeked, shook her head.

'She's fine, honestly,' she gasped, then clutched a hand to her throat and waved the other at me, signalling that she needed a moment to get her breath back.

'Really? I don't think so,' I said.

Ruth gulped in some air.

'Just feeling her age, you know. Now, I need to get reception sorted,' she said, and scampered off, leaving me feeling puzzled and a little left out.

What is it they aren't telling me? And why aren't they telling me? We've always told each other everything ...

The sense of being sidelined, of not being trusted with whatever is clearly going on, has made today's low mood even lower, but I force myself to keep going, deciding at lunchtime to pop across the road to see Nadia.

'Hey Nadia, how are you?'

She's been reading but she's already put her book down, having spotted me crossing the road, and she smiles her gap-toothed smile. She's still working her way through the novels I gave her, I notice with pleasure. *The Clocks* is her current read. There's a slightly more pungent odour wafting from her today and I wonder yet again if there's anything more that I, we, the surgery, could be doing for her.

There's always someone worse off than you, isn't there? I may be going through a bit of a bad patch at the moment but at least I have a roof over my head, I think.

I hand her the little foil-wrapped parcel of biscuits I've liberated from the jar in the staffroom and she nods appreciatively.

'Thank you, Beth, that's kind of you,' she says, and I feel a little shiver of pleasure that my small good deed has clearly made a difference. I perch on the step next to her and we chat easily for a few minutes, me telling her about Finley's ankle and his remarkably speedy recovery, her telling me about the woman she slept next to in the hostel last night who sang Abba songs in her sleep. It's a pleasant few minutes, and I find myself enjoying her company and mentally speculating again about the circumstances that led to such a genial, intelligent woman living like this, all alone in the world.

By the time I get back to my office I feel brighter, but the feeling doesn't last long. There's a note on my desk from Gabby, asking me to pop in and see her as soon as I can. I sigh, wondering if there's some new surgery crisis to deal with, and wondering how on earth I'm going to cope with it on top of everything that's going on at home. By the time I reach her room there's already a knot in my stomach, and when I see the expression on her face my chest tightens.

'Beth ... something very worrying has been brought to my attention,' she says.

She points to a piece of paper sitting on her desk, a note of some sort. I glance at it, puzzled, then look back at her.

'What ... what is it?' I ask.

'I've had a letter. An anonymous letter. And, well, it's about you, Beth.'

'About ... me?'

My voice sounds weird, too high, even to me. She nods.

'It's making some rather worrying allegations. We need to talk, I'm afraid.'

No, please no. Oh God, no, no, no ...

My stomach heaves.

This is it, isn't it? Finally. It's over. It's all over ...

'Beth? Are you OK?'

My knees buckle and suddenly Gabby is rushing out from behind her desk, telling me to sit down. I sink into the chair, my breathing fast and shallow, my legs shaking. I have a pain in my chest now too, as if something heavy is sitting on it, pinning me down. Suddenly my vision blurs and the room starts to spin around me. My hands are tingling, and there's a roaring in my ears. *What's happening to me?*

'Gabby ... help me ...' I gasp.

'Beth, oh gosh, calm down, all right? Breathe, come on. Deep breaths.'

She crouches in front of me, holding my hot, damp hands in her cool, dry ones, and I breathe, breathe, until the trembling begins to ease and my heart rate slows a little, my vision clears, and the pain in my chest subsides.

What was that? What's wrong with me?

'I'm all right, thank you,' I whisper. 'I'm so sorry ...'

'It's OK. I think you just had a bit of a panic attack. Do you get them often, Beth?'

Gabby stands up, moving behind her desk again, then seemingly changes her mind about sitting down in her big leather chair and perches on the edge of the polished oak tabletop instead.

I shake my head.

'No ... never. I mean, I get anxious, don't we all, but no, nothing like that. I'm sorry.'

She shakes her head but I see the concern in her eyes.

'Nothing to apologise for. Listen, Beth, this letter. It came in the post this morning and it's unsigned. But it came from someone who seems to mean well. They say they're extremely worried about you. And having seen the state of you, I'm worried too now.'

Worried about me? So it's not ... not about what happened back then, after all? I think. Relief sweeps over me for a moment but I'm still struggling to comprehend what's happening here. My head is fuzzy and my heart is still beating far too quickly. I take another deep breath and try to focus.

'I don't understand,' I whisper, and I raise a shaking hand and push my hair back off my sweaty forehead. I'm starting to wonder if I'm actually having another nightmare, if any minute now I might wake up, safe in my bed at home.

'I'll explain, but please don't get upset again.' Gabby leans forward, squeezes my knee, then straightens up again. She pauses, looking at me for a moment with her head tilted to one side, then picks up the letter.

'Right. Well, whoever sent this said they've been growing increasingly concerned about you for some time now. And they, for whatever reason, didn't feel they could speak to you directly so they felt maybe speaking to one of us, the GPs, might be the best way to deal with it—'

'Deal with it? Deal with what?' I interrupt her. I'm starting to feel frantic.

'Beth, please. Deep breaths, remember. OK, well they say they're concerned about a number of issues.'

She taps the piece of paper with her forefinger, the nail painted a creamy beige.

'They say they're worried you may have issues around food. Sometimes you binge eat and sometimes you eat virtually nothing. They're also concerned about your use of alcohol and say that your heavy drinking has been causing some problems. They're worried it's affecting your memory and concentration to a concerning level. You're very forgetful, apparently, losing your keys and various other things. They're also worried about the children, Beth. They say you're distracted and not doing things at home properly, possibly putting the children in danger, and citing Finley's recent accident as an example. They even think you might be having hallucinations. Apparently you keep seeing a man who you think is following you? And—'

'But I did! I do!'

I stand up and I'm shouting now but I can't help it.

'I *did* see a man. He was everywhere, and I saw somebody out in the garden looking in my window in the dark too. I even saw his footprints in the flowerbed. I'm not imagining these things! God, Gabby, some of this stuff is true, yes. I *have* been really stressed, and things *have* got on top of me at home. But the way you're saying it, it makes me sound ... makes me sound *unhinged*.'

I sink my face into my hands and I can feel the tears now, hot and angry, spilling out between my fingers. Gabby's hands are on my shoulders, moving me back to my chair, pushing me gently down until I'm seated again.

'You're not unhinged,' she says gently. 'Far from it. And I'm glad you feel able to confirm that these are valid concerns, Beth. That's a very positive step. If it helps, none of this has affected your work here, by the way, not as far as I'm aware anyway. You've obviously got an awful lot going on at home, and you've clearly been doing a marvellous job of keeping it together and not letting it impact on your job. But Beth, I wish you'd spoken to me, or to one of us. We all struggle at times, and maybe you just need to talk to someone, take some of the pressure off yourself? Maybe a bit of time off, a few duvet days?'

The kindness in her voice brings a fresh rush of tears, but I wipe them away and shake my head.

'I'm fine, honestly. I mean, what the letter says is largely true; all of those things have happened recently, but ... who wrote it, Gabby? Who would do that?'

She shakes her head and shrugs.

'I have no idea. But it was clearly someone who cares about

you very much, someone who wants to help you and just didn't know how. And that's why I'm going to do this.'

She stands up and walks quickly across the room, and before I've even realised what she's doing she's popped the letter into the paper shredder that sits on top of her filing cabinet and pressed the button. The machine whirrs and seconds later the letter has vanished.

'Gabby!' I gasp, but she's shaking her head again as she walks back to her desk.

'It's done. I don't want you anguishing over who sent it, OK? I'm just glad they did.'

'But Gabby!'

My mind is racing.

Who did this, who? Mum? After our conversation on Saturday, when she told me how worried she was about me, she seems the most likely suspect. But no. She did have the courage to confront me, didn't she? She told me she was concerned; she spelled it out. Why write a letter too? That wouldn't make sense, would it? So who else? Who was worried but felt they couldn't say anything? Jacob? Brenda or Barbara? Robin? Ruth or Deborah, even? They've all expressed some concerns over the past few weeks, haven't they? All mentioned my eating habits, or my drinking, or my forgetfulness, told me to stop worrying about someone following me. They all know about Finley's accident ... What if some of them got together, shared their concerns, and decided telling Gabby was the way to go? But that seems so unnecessary, so strange ... and surely they'd know this could get me into big trouble? If Gabby thinks I'm not fit for work, I could lose my job ...

I'm feeling panicky again. I need to convince Gabby that everything is OK, that I'm fine. I take a deep breath and sit up straight.

'OK, you're right. Who sent the letter doesn't matter,' I say. 'But I'm on top of this, I promise. Yes, I *have* been drinking a bit too much recently. With Mum suddenly back in my life, and Dad's stroke, and Finley's accident ... well, all of it. It's just become a habit, and I'll stop. I will. And the rest of it, well, I've just been a bit scatty. I don't need any time off, honestly. It's helped just having this chat with you. I'm OK, I promise.'

Gabby is looking at me with a doubtful expression, clearly not entirely convinced, but she nods slowly.

'All right, we'll leave it for now. I am concerned, Beth. However, I know you're a strong and sensible woman, and I'm going to take you at your word that you have all this under control. But we're here to help. And I want you to promise me that if you're feeling overwhelmed, or have any more panic attacks, or if you're struggling to control your drinking or anything else, you'll come straight back here and talk to me, OK? Promise?'

I give her a little mock salute.

'Promise, ma'am!' I say, and she laughs her lovely melodic laugh which always somehow makes me think of sunshine and honey. I leave her then and I go back to my office, and I sit there for a long time, wondering. Wondering who wrote that letter, and whether it really was written by someone who cares about me, or for some other reason. Wondering if I'll ever have the guts to confront anyone about it. Wondering why everything's changed so much, why *I've* changed so much. Why, when I should be so happy right now, I'm really, *really* not. Why, increasingly, I have this low-level, nausea-inducing feeling of pure dread deep inside.

And, most of all, wondering why, despite Gabby's reassuring words, I have this awful sense that something even worse is just around the corner.

Chapter 25

BRRRR. BRRRR.

It's after nine on Saturday morning and I'm still in bed when my mobile rings. The kids are both away – Friday night sleepovers with friends – and Mum insisted I make the most of it today, telling me to sleep in as long as I like and promising to bring me breakfast in bed. I didn't tell her anything about the anonymous letter Gabby received; I'm almost certain it didn't come from her, and I simply couldn't face having a conversation about it with her – or with anyone. Not right now. I keep telling myself that whoever sent it did it out of genuine concern, but that feeling that it may have been written with a more sinister motive in mind keeps creeping in and it makes me feel sick. I can't let myself think that, I just can't, because if I do it will mean I can't trust anyone, and that's unbearable.

So this morning I'm focussing on all that's good and positive, and I have a lot to be thankful for. Mum, for example, who knocked on my door half an hour ago with a tray of tea and smashed avocado on toast, and a tiny vase with a soft-pink camelia bloom freshly picked from the garden. It's nice, so nice, to feel loved and cossetted like this. And overall, despite the new anxiety about the letter, I'm feeling so much better this morning than I did a week ago. OK, so I've lost Brenda and Barbara, and that still hurts horribly if I let myself dwell on it. And at work, Deborah's behaviour is still bothering me – on a professional level as well as a friendship one – but no doubt I'll get to the bottom of that eventually. But at home things are pretty good right now. Robin's still working for me, which is good enough for now. Eloise, after a frosty few days, seems to have forgiven me for the missing letter and school-trip debacle; all her focus now is on the school play in a couple of weeks' time, her little face glowing with excitement at the prospect of her parents, her grandmother, and her auntie all being there to support her. Because yes, to my delight and relief, and despite what happened on her first visit, Liv has promised to come back up to Cheltenham for the occasion. She was bright and bubbly as ever on the phone during the week, saying she wouldn't miss it for the world. So I'm feeling OK on this Saturday morning, nibbling my toast and sipping my tea. The duvet is cosy around my legs, the radio is tuned to Classic FM, and the calming strains of Grieg's piano concerto in A minor fill my room as the morning sunlight streams in through the window.

When the phone rings, it's like an assault, an unwanted intruder, and instantly my heart begins to thump.

A call this early on a Saturday morning can't be good news, can it? Has something happened to one of the children?

I grab my mobile from the bedside table, but to my relief

it's Ruth's name on the caller ID and I hit the button to accept the call.

'Hey, you. You're up and about early.'

I settle back on my pillows, expecting a gossipy catch-up, maybe a suggestion to meet for a walk or lunch over the weekend. Instead there's a pause, and when she speaks her voice sounds sharp and tense.

'Beth, what on earth is that on the surgery Facebook page?'

I frown. I haven't looked at the page since yesterday morning when I did a quick post; some of our patients have begun dumping their cars on single yellow lines on the street outside the surgery recently instead of using the car park across the road, and I wanted to warn them that traffic wardens have been patrolling the area around us with greater frequency and to be careful or risk a ticket. But that was early, around ten, and I haven't logged on since.

'Why? What's up? Someone said something offensive on there?'

Another pause.

'Beth ... look, I don't know what's going on, but ... Oh heck, come on, you know what I'm talking about!'

I've just picked up my mug of tea again but now I put it back down on the tray. I'm starting to feel alarmed.

'I have *no* idea what you're talking about. What's going on?'

There's a groan on the other end of the line.

'Oh bloody hell, Beth. Were you pissed or something when you posted it? Look, I'm not an admin so I can't delete it, only you can do that. But I'd advise you to do it as soon as possible, OK? Because *so* many people have already seen it,

Beth, and commented, and ... well, it's not good. You could lose your job. What were you thinking? And who's Daphne Blake?'

'Lose my ...?'

For a moment, two, three, I'm stunned into silence. I've never felt so confused in my life.

What's she talking about?

'And Daphne who? I've never heard of her. Ruth, honestly, I have no idea what this is about. What's going on? Seriously, you're scaring me now.'

She sighs.

'Shit, Beth. Were you really that drunk? I'm talking about the ... I can hardly bear to say this, but ... the porn videos. The ones of you in your bedroom and bathroom. You posted them last night? You wrote, "a tribute to my friend, Daphne Blake", whoever she is, and then added a link to a porn site ...'

A ... a WHAT?

I laugh. This is a joke. It has to be.

'Oh come on, Ruth. Don't be ridiculous. That's impossible. I've never made a porn video in my life and there hasn't been anything to film anyway, not since Jacob, so stop it. You're freaking me out—'

'It's not sex, as such,' she interrupts. 'It's a link to a video on one of those amateur porn sites. And it's just you, on your own, naked and ... and touching yourself. I couldn't watch much of it, to be honest. But Beth, are you saying you *didn't* post these pictures? That someone else did? Because they've been posted from your account, that's all I know. I think you need to have a look. And then bloody delete them, for God's sake. Look, I have to go, I'm sorry. Speak to you later.'

She ends the call abruptly and for a few seconds I stare at the phone. But now I'm not laughing anymore; shivers are running up and down my spine and a hard knot is beginning to form in my stomach.

Naked? Touching myself? Pictures of me in my bedroom and in my bathroom?

With shaking hands, I open the Facebook app. I see it immediately, just as Ruth described it: a post, ostensibly by me, the words 'a tribute to my friend, Daphne Blake', and a clickable link.

Daphne Blake?

Something about the name is suddenly familiar. Something is pinging in the furthest recesses of my mind but I can't grasp it. I look at the words again and the link beneath them. And then I look underneath the post at the comments. Dozens and dozens of them.

Disgusting. How inappropriate on a doctors' Facebook page.

Wow! Who's this?

I think that's the practice manager, Beth Holland. My sister had to see her once when she wanted to make a complaint.

Hey Beth, fancy a date? Looking a bit lonely in those videos.

Could do with losing a bit of weight, LOL! The doctors are always telling us to drop a few pounds, maybe they should try telling their own staff first.

What a sight! Put me off my dinner.

I stop reading, hot tears filling my eyes.

What is this? What is it?

Terrified, I click on the link and wait an interminable three, four seconds while the page loads. There's a screenshot, a blurred image of a figure, and I swallow hard and press play. The video begins and the image comes into focus.

'Oh God. OH MY GOD!' I gasp, horrified.

I didn't post this. Of course I didn't. I've clearly been hacked; someone, somehow, has got into my account. But ... these pictures, these videos. *How?* It's me, very obviously me, standing right here in this bedroom, reflected in my full-length mirror, naked. Running my hands over my breasts, over my nipples, turning slowly to reveal my buttocks, then jiggling up and down. And then the scene changes and it's me in the bath, in my ensuite, again seemingly caressing my body, my stomach, between my legs ...

'NO! NO!'

I'm sobbing now, flinging the phone across the room and hearing it crash against the wall.

How, HOW? I remember standing in front of the mirror a few weeks ago, studying my body, feeling fat ... The bath ... I remember all of it. It's real footage but this looks so sleazy. It wasn't like that. It wasn't, and that's not even the point ...

'How? How have you done it? And who the *hell* ...!'

I'm screaming now, jumping off the bed, grabbing the ornate wooden frame of the mirror and pulling it off the wall with such force that chunks of plaster come away too. I throw it on the floor and crouch down, running my hands across the wood, into the crevices and swirls.

A camera. There must be a hidden camera, a tiny one, there must be, but where and who. *Who?*

I can't find anything, nothing. I look frantically around the room but I can't see anywhere else that could hide a camera either, not one that could take shots of me from that angle. The panic is building now and I'm panting like a dog on a hot day, gasping for air.

The bathroom. Check the bathroom.

I stumble into the ensuite, looking at the bath, thinking about how the footage seemed to have been shot from directly in front of me but slightly above. I look at the bathroom cabinet on the wall opposite, painted an innocent mint green.

There. It must be there.

I run my hands over the wooden door as I did with the mirror, again finding nothing, then wrench it open, grabbing bottles and tubes and packets of headache tablets, flinging them onto the floor until the cabinet is empty and the shelves are smooth and bare, and still I've found nothing, nothing at all.

'Darling! What's going on? What's wrong?'

I spin around, my breathing laboured and my chest tight. Mum's standing in the bathroom doorway, staring wide-eyed at the mess, at the broken glass, and at the shampoo oozing out of an upended bottle onto the black and white floor tiles.

'Oh, Mum ...'

My voice cracks and the tears come again. She takes two careful steps towards me and opens her arms. I stagger into her embrace.

'Darling, what is it? It's OK. Whatever it is, we can sort it, OK?'

She's murmuring into my hair, arms wrapped tightly around my waist, and I bury my face in her neck. Suddenly I'm five again, falling over in the back garden and running to my mummy to kiss it better, and for a moment, just a moment, I feel a wave of pure happiness. And then reality comes crashing back and I think about all the patients, hundreds of them maybe, who've seen that footage, that horrendous, humiliating footage. My naked flesh on display, out there on a porn site. *Oh my God, a* porn site. I start to panic again.

'Mum ... Oh Mum, something terrible's happened.'

I take a step back, out of her arms, and I tell her. She listens, her concerned frown turning slowly into a look of horror.

'But I don't understand. How did someone get pictures of you, here in your own house? And it's on the *internet*? Can't you do anything? Beth, this is awful. Who would do such a thing?'

'I don't know, Mum. I just don't know.'

Why didn't I delete the post immediately? I think suddenly. I push past her and grab my phone and, hands shaking, delete it all. Then I sink onto the bed. My legs feel weak and my mind is racing. Mum's still hovering, watching me uncertainly.

'Mum, I'm OK, it's OK, it's gone,' I say. 'You go on down. I won't be long.'

She hesitates, then nods.

'Well, if you're sure. I'll put the kettle on again. You look like you need a strong coffee.'

'Something like that,' I say, and try to smile. She smiles back and leaves the room but I feel sick. Yes, I've deleted the Facebook post, but the video's still out there, isn't it? Still on that disgusting website, still there for anyone to see. How the hell do I get it taken down? Do I go to the police? A solicitor? I don't know. I need to look it up. I've just picked up my phone again, wondering what on earth to type into Google, when the phone starts to ring. Jacob.

Oh no, please. Not now.

'Good morning!'

I try to sound upbeat, cheery, but I've barely got the words out before I have to move the phone away from my ear. He's *bellowing*.

'JESUS CHRIST, BETH. WHAT'S GOING ON? WHAT ARE YOU PLAYING AT? I'VE ONLY GOT A LINK TO A FRIGGING PORN SITE ON MY COMPANY FACEBOOK PAGE.'

My heart almost stops beating.

What? It's on another page? Jacob's landscape gardening company page? Oh shit, shit ...

'It's not ... I didn't ...' I stutter, but he's still yelling.

'PICTURES OF YOU, BETH. A FORTY-YEAR-OLD MOTHER. WHAT IN BUGGERING HELL WERE YOU THINKING? WHAT'S WRONG WITH YOU? AND WHO'S DAPHNE BLOODY BLAKE?'

'Jacob, listen, please ...'

'CHRIST, I MEAN I COULDN'T EVEN WATCH IT ... WHAT POSSESSED YOU, SERIOUSLY? ARE YOU THAT DESPERATE FOR ATTENTION?'

'JACOB! CAN YOU SHUT UP FOR ONE MINUTE AND LET ME SPEAK?' I scream down the phone at him, and finally he stops shouting, his breathing heavy and angry in my ear.

'Jacob, listen.'

I take a breath, wondering how on earth to explain something I don't even understand myself.

'It wasn't me. I mean, the footage is obviously me, and I'm ... just so ashamed, so mortified, but I didn't shoot those pictures, and I certainly didn't post them. I've obviously been hacked. And I don't know who Daphne Blake is. I don't know how it's happened, Jacob. Somebody must have put hidden cameras in my bedroom and bathroom. I don't know who or how. I've searched everywhere and I can't find anything, but you have to believe me, all of this is nothing to do with me. I would *never* ... The link was posted on the surgery Facebook page too, Jacob. It's a nightmare, and I just don't know, I just don't *know* ...'

Hot tears are flowing down my cheeks again. There's a long silence on the line, then he says: 'What the *fuck*?'

'Jacob, I—'

'Beth, you're making no sense. You're telling me that

someone, what, broke into your house, fitted hidden cameras and then recorded video of you naked and put it on a porn site? Seriously? Why would anyone do something like that? And who? That is just *ridiculous*.'

'I know,' I say helplessly. 'I know it sounds ridiculous. But it's what's happened, OK? Maybe not someone breaking in, I don't know; we haven't had a break-in. Maybe it's someone I know, someone who's been in the house. Maybe someone did it for a joke, and obviously it's not funny; it's horrendous, but—'

'Oh, for God's sake.'

He sounds so scornful, so full of contempt, that I actually wince, as if he's just punched me in the stomach.

'Jacob, I'm telling you the truth ...'

He isn't listening.

'I've deleted the post, OK? And now we've just got to hope that the kids and their friends never get to see those videos, haven't we?'

'Oh God, Jacob. You have to believe me. I don't know—'

'Well, I don't know *anything* anymore. I don't know *you* anymore, that's for sure. All I know is that you've been acting so fucking weird recently that I'm now seriously worried about the kids' welfare. I'm picking them up from their sleepovers later and then they're staying with me, Beth. I'll come round later and pick up some of their stuff, but I'm not bringing them home. I'll take a couple of weeks off work and you need to sort yourself out, OK? This can't go on. Get your shit together, Beth. Act like a proper mother, or they'll be living with me permanently, OK?'

'Jacob, no! Please, let's talk about this—'

But the line's gone dead. I stare at the handset for a moment, horrified, then fling it on the bed and start to sob.

Not the children, please ...

BRRRR.

The phone's ringing again. This time the display says *Holly Tree*, and my hand's already started to shake as I accept the call.

'Mrs Holland? It's Anya, at Holly Tree. I just need to ask, did you post something on our Facebook page? Some ... well, *footage*?'

And the calls keep on coming.

'Mrs Holland? It's Rachel from Pitt Lane Primary School ...'

'Is that Beth? Hi, my name's Sarah and I work with Brenda Welch, you know, your next-door neighbour, at Evolution boutique in Suffolk Road? She's just checked the shop's Facebook page ...'

I try to explain it to all of them, denying any knowledge, telling them someone's clearly hacked my account, apologising anyway, and begging them not to click on the link, to delete the posts. When the calls finally stop I'm exhausted, limp, but I stay in my room, ignoring Mum's pleas to come downstairs and have something to eat. I can't bear it. I have visions of Jacob, and Finley and Eloise's teachers (*and oh God, my dad, could my* dad *have seen it?*), and Brenda and her staff, and everyone else, all watching that video, seeing me like that, naked and exposed. I have to find out what's happened here, I *have* to, so I search the room again, every little bit of it this time. I search the bathroom too, running my hands increasingly frantically over every inch of the walls, the pictures, the furniture, and still I find nothing, *nothing*. I slump to the floor and sit for a long time after that, my head in my hands, my nails clawing at my scalp.

I need to get the room swept. That's what they call it, isn't it? I think. I look it up and find a bug-sweeping service based in west London, a company that can send someone up here as soon as Tuesday. It's going to cost me hundreds of pounds but I don't care. I don't care about anything right now other than stopping this, whatever it is. Stopping it and getting my children back. My brain is whirring. The name Daphne Blake is still niggling me. Something about it is triggering some distant memory but it's still too faint, too vague, just a whisper, and I push my fists into my eye sockets, trying to make myself think, *think*. Who would do this? *Who?*

The face outside the lounge window floats back into my mind. Could whoever that was have been here before, have broken in somehow and planted the cameras? And then I think about Mike, the private detective, and I wonder about him too. *Was* it him, hanging around long after he should have been, after all? *Was* it him talking to my friends, pretending to be a runner, a gardener, a plumber, or was that all, as I'd finally started to believe, in my imagination? Does he know about my past, about what I did, and is he trying to punish me for it for some reason, or is that all in my head too? Although, if I didn't imagine it, could *he* have somehow got in here? Tiny hidden cameras are probably part of a private detective's arsenal, after all, aren't they? And yet there's been no sign of a break in, nothing at all to indicate that someone's been in my house uninvited. But is it possible? Because *someone's* been in here; that's abundantly clear. And if it wasn't a stranger, then that means it's someone I know, and that doesn't bear thinking about.

With a shudder, my face flushing, and sweat running down my spine, I go back to the porn site page and make myself watch the video footage again, properly this time, trying to pinpoint when each segment was filmed. The first appeared to be the Saturday after that Friday night when Barbara and Brenda came round for dinner, the night Mum bought me the new top that was far too small. I remember being upset that following evening, remember standing in front of the mirror naked after going up to bed, remember scrutinising my body. All the other footage is more recent: me in the bath on several different occasions, me pulling off my clothes in the bedroom, clearly drunk, and collapsing on the bed, legs splayed, showing the camera everything. There's more, but I can't watch it.

My stomach contracts and hot waves of shame and humiliation wash over me. I have to get this footage removed, somehow, but now all I can think about is who, *who* ... Faces start to race through my brain, faces and dates and horrible possibilities. I think about the day Mum first came back, the day I spent the morning up on Cleeve Hill with Ruth and Deborah, and about how they knocked on the door on their way home wanting to use the loo. I think about Deborah rushing upstairs to use the bathroom, and taking ages, much longer than normal. Deborah, who's been acting so oddly in recent days, with no real explanation. And then I remember the night before that, when Brenda and Barbara came round, when we were still friends, when we got drunk on cava, when I wouldn't have noticed at all if one of them had nipped upstairs for a few minutes, when it wouldn't even have occurred to me to be concerned. And then I think about the night a few days later when Mum took us out for pizza, and Barbara asked if she could slip into the house to look for her glasses, and how I happily said yes and let her come in here alone. Brenda and Barbara, who've now drifted away, who've cut me off.

Could Mike have persuaded one of them, one of my friends, to hide cameras in my home for him? But wouldn't they have told me if someone had asked them to do something like that? Why would they agree? Why would any of them do something so vile, so cruel? They've all had the opportunity, the access to my home, it's true. But ... really? Why would any of those women, women I love and respect, treat me like that? I've never exchanged so much as a cross word with any of them. It doesn't make sense; it just doesn't make *sense* ...

And then I think about Robin. I think about the times I've suspected her of rooting through my stuff, the rearranged cosmetics in my bedroom, the time Mum saw her nosing in my bathroom cabinet. If Mike had approached *her*, maybe, just maybe. And then, of course, there's Mum.

My stomach lurches and I sit there and think about Mum for a long time. About how, wonderful though it's been to have her back in my life, it's only been since she returned that everything's begun to fall apart. And about how, as far as access goes, she's the one who's had the free run of my house recently, the one who's been in it alone for hours every day while I'm at work and the kids are at school. I'd be an idiot if I didn't consider her being behind this, wouldn't I? But ... no. Ridiculous. Why on earth would she want to hurt me like this? She's done everything, *everything* she can to show me how sorry she is for leaving all those years ago; she's shown me nothing but love. She looked almost as horrified as I felt when I told her what had happened today. Whoever this is, it's not Mum. But who, then? *Who?*

I groan, my head spinning. I can't work it out, any of it, and now my phone's ringing again. I don't even look at the display this time. My eyes are swollen and sore from crying and my voice is weak and weary even to my own ears as I say hello.

'Beth, it's Gabby from work.'

She sounds cold, brisk, so unlike her usual warm, smiley self that a chill runs through me, and I suddenly realise that what has happened today isn't just about embarrassment and humiliation. Hundreds, maybe thousands, of people have seen Fairfield Surgery's practice manager naked on the internet.

This is serious, isn't it? As Ruth said earlier, I could lose my job over this, my livelihood. And what then? Jacob will never let me have the kids back, never ...

Gabby's still speaking, her tone terse and business like.

'Beth, I know Ruth spoke to you earlier, and that you're claiming your Facebook account has been hacked. To be honest, I'm not entirely sure what to believe, especially after the concerns about your mental health raised by that letter earlier in the week. It's something we need to talk through with you in person, and we'd like you to come in for a meeting at seven-thirty on Monday, so we can discuss it before morning surgery, so please put that in your diary. But I also have to tell you that I received a telephone call earlier from a tabloid news reporter who somehow tracked down my home number and who told me he'd received a tip-off that our practice manager was "moonlighting as a porn star", as he put it. I managed to put him off and told him it was all a misunderstanding, but I'm not sure he'll drop it, Beth. These people can be very persistent, and there's every chance he'll run a story anyway. The link to the website appearing on our Facebook page was bad enough, but if the practice ends up in the papers, well ...'

'Oh God, Gabby! I'm so sorry, but I don't know. I have no idea ...'

I'm crying again, great gulping sobs now, and on the other end of the phone there's a pause, a few seconds of silence, before Gabby speaks again, a little more gently this time, telling me to calm down and asking me if I've eaten today, if I'm alone.

'No ... no ... Mum ... Mum's here. Downstairs,' I manage. She tells me to go downstairs, to stop sitting in my room dwelling on it, and to try to distract myself.

'Put a movie on – something funny. Don't drink any alcohol,

and make yourself eat, OK? Promise me, Beth? I'm very, very worried about you. I'm going to call you again tomorrow and I'll see you first thing Monday, right? I'm going to go now, but do as I've said, OK?'

'I will. Thanks Gabby. I'm so, so sorry,' I whisper, and she says goodbye and ends the call. I think about going downstairs but Mum seems to have finally given up calling me to come down so instead I just sit there, huddled on my bed, my mind blank and my cheeks still damp with tears. And then, quite unexpectedly, there's a little pop in my head, like a light coming on, and it comes to me, clear as a summer sky, as I remember again those words on the Facebook post: *a tribute to my friend, Daphne Blake*.

Daphne Blake. I know who Daphne Blake is.

I grab my phone again and type the name into Google. And there it is.

Daphne Blake is a fictional character in the Scooby-Doo franchise ...

Daphne Blake. Daphne and her friend Velma. And her friends Fred and Shaggy, and Shaggy's dog Scooby-Doo. Daphne Blake is Daphne from *Scooby-Doo*.

I stare at the page, fear prickling my skin. You see, Daphne isn't *just* a cartoon character. Back in the day, back at school, it was somebody's nickname. Just an occasional nickname, but a nickname, nonetheless. A nickname for a girl who, now and again, wore her shoulder-length hair pulled back with a purple headband, just like Daphne did in the cartoons we'd watch at home on Saturday mornings.

'Hey, it's Daphne!' people would say, and laugh, and she'd smile shyly, enjoying the unaccustomed attention.

Daphne. Daphne Blake.

Daphne Blake was Lucy Allen's nickname.

Chapter 26

I killed Lucy Allen.

Well, that's what I always believed, anyway. I still do. The official inquest verdict was, of course, suicide. But I knew that I'd killed her just as surely as if I'd put that noose around her neck myself and pulled it tight. She did it because of me. She died, at thirteen years of age, because of me. Because of the things I said, the things I did.

Years later, when I was in therapy, talking it all through with Rita, she suggested that maybe I didn't know the whole truth, that maybe there were other things going on in Lucy's life, that maybe what I'd done to her at school was just a tiny part of a bigger, darker whole. Rita was right about many things but I disagreed with her on that one. I knew she was trying to tell me that unless I knew all the facts, I shouldn't shoulder the entire burden of guilt myself; that it may, after all, not have been entirely my fault. But I knew it was. And I knew that, no matter what I did, I could never fix it. Instead of directing my anger and frustration at my mother for leaving me, I directed it elsewhere, and that was my choice. That was down to me.

The only person I ever told was my dad. In the days after she died, after the headteacher sent letters to all the parents telling them what had happened, I fell apart. And when my poor, puzzled father finally realised that this couldn't just be grief, that it didn't make sense for me to be so desperately upset about the death of a girl I barely knew, when he sat me down and made me talk to him, I told him everything. I think I confessed because I wanted to be punished, because I felt I should be made to suffer for what I'd done.

He was horrified, of course, horrified and ashamed. And then, hours later, while he was still processing it all, still trying to work out what to do, he got the phone call. The phone call from Lucy's distraught mother, screaming at him. Lucy had left no note but they'd found her diary. And in it she'd detailed it all. The things I'd whispered in her ear, the photograph I'd pinned to the board. And the family were, she said, taking it straight to the police.

'Your little bitch of a daughter is going to pay for what she's done,' she said.

And I did. I paid for years, knowing what a vile, worthless person I was, watching every word I said, terrified of hurting someone else. Avoiding getting close to anyone, convinced I didn't deserve happiness or love. Even believing, for a very long time, that I didn't deserve to have children because I'd caused the death of another woman's child and how, then, could I ever be worthy of motherhood myself? Yes, I paid. But ... officially? Formally? Publicly? No. No, I didn't. I didn't pay at all.

The Allens did go to the police and I was questioned. I

know now that I was lucky, that taking and pinning up that photograph of Lucy was actually a criminal offence; I shared an indecent image of a child, and if it had been today, if I'd put it on social media for example, I may well have been prosecuted. But it was a long time ago and I was a child myself; it was one photo, pinned on a noticeboard for a short time, and I was let off with a warning. Mrs Allen wanted me to be charged with manslaughter, but in the end no charges were ever brought. Lack of evidence that it was actually my bullying – and that of course, is exactly what I was: a nasty, vindictive little bully – that tipped her over the edge. Lucy's diaries, although they detailed what I'd done to her, were full of all kinds of teenage angst: how stressed she was about exams, how sad she was that Tony, her first crush, seemed to have no interest in her, all the usual stuff. There was, it was concluded, no proof that she'd taken her own life because of me; that although my behaviour probably did play a role in her death, it was impossible to know how significant that role was.

It was exactly what Rita tried to tell me when I finally sought counselling all those years later, but I didn't believe it at thirteen and I still didn't believe it then. I knew it was me. And her family knew it was me too. I still remember their faces when we saw them, her dad and a woman – an aunt maybe – in the corridor at the police station after I was questioned. I remember the malevolence in her father's eyes as he stopped dead in his tracks, his gaze following me as I shrank behind my dad and shuffled past him; I remember the venom in his voice as he said, 'That's her, look.' I remember the way she glanced at me too then, and immediately averted her eyes, as if I was something disgusting, too loathsome to look at for more than a second.

When the entire school filed into the church for the funeral, I was told I wasn't welcome. I never went back to Fairbridge after that. We moved away, Dad and I, started over yet again at another new school in Cheltenham where nobody knew me, or what I'd done. And, although for years I feared that one of Lucy's family or friends would come after me, would make me pay, they never did.

'They'll want to put it behind them,' Dad told me. 'They'll want her to rest in peace, Beth. And you need to find some peace too.'

And I did eventually. Although I never stopped worrying that one day my past would find me, over the years I did find peace, of a sort. Rita's counselling helped; she never made excuses for me, for my bullying behaviour, but she helped me to understand why I'd done it, to understand that it was all a horribly misguided attempt to banish my own anger, my frustration, my jealousy. And so, as time passed, I healed. I changed. I left it all behind me.

Or I thought I did.

Chapter 27

Somehow, I sleep until after seven. I wake with a dull headache because, despite Gabby's advice on the phone, I did drink last night. I opened a bottle of red wine with dinner and downed the entire thing myself while Mum contented herself with one gin and slimline tonic and watched me from across the room with concern in her eyes. When I finally emerged from my room yesterday I made light of it all, telling her I was fine, that everything had now been deleted, and that the videos were obviously someone's idea of a silly joke which had backfired somewhat. I even managed to laugh as I told her that one of my friends was going to be in *big trouble* when I found out which of them had planted the hidden cameras.

'Ooh, I'll get them back,' I said. 'They've hidden them so well I can't even find them, can you believe that? I'm going to have to get someone in. Best practical joke ever, isn't it!'

She raised an eyebrow and shook her head disapprovingly, telling me it wasn't *her* idea of a joke and that she wouldn't have taken it so well if anyone had dared to do that to *her*. But she left it at that, offering to cook dinner. She rustled up a salmon and pea pasta which smelled delicious but which

I pushed aside after two mouthfuls because I was still feeling sick.

I excused myself from the table and called Ruth. I told her again that my account must have been hacked, described how everything had snowballed after her call, and mentioned the meeting Gabby had demanded. She was hesitant at first, but she finally sounded as if she believed me and wondered aloud who on earth could have been behind it, finally telling me she was there for me if I needed her. I didn't tell her about Jacob and the kids though. I didn't trust myself not to break down, and I knew that if I started crying I simply wouldn't be able to stop.

Jacob had appeared at the door just before we ate, pushing wordlessly past me and marching upstairs to fill bags with extra clothes and toys for the children, grimly muttering, 'Just leave it, Beth. I can't talk to you, not now. I can't even *look* at you,' when I tried to reason with him.

He wouldn't even let me help pack the bags, and by then I was too tired, too mentally exhausted, for another row. When he'd gone again, I fobbed Mum off ('They're going to stay at Jacob's for a few days. He's decided to take some leave so he might as well have them; they're off on Easter holidays this week anyway ...') and opened the wine. It went down better than the food, taking the edge off the anguish and helping me to fall into a restless sleep. There was no way I was sleeping in my own room, not while those cameras were unaccounted for, so I moved into Eloise's. Her small single bed was strangely comforting, like sleeping in a soft cotton cocoon. Her pink starry duvet cover smelt of cherry-blossom shampoo and of her. As I lie here now, slowly coming to, unwilling to get up and face a Sunday with just me and Mum and knowing that I'm going to spend it feeling ill and anxious about my meeting at work tomorrow, I think about Daphne Blake again, and I shiver. My nightmares last night were more like hallucinations, dark and twisted, my body paralysed with fear. Images of Lucy Allen and Daphne Blake flashed through my mind, their faces merging and blending, until I woke, screaming, as if a demon were being unleashed from my soul. My mother must have been deeply asleep because she didn't come, and I lay there panting, bathed in a cold sweat. I wondered if the scream had been part of the dream, although the ache in my throat made me think otherwise.

And now, now that I can think more clearly, now that the daylight is streaming in through the gap in Eloise's fuchsia velvet curtains, I'm starting to work it out.

Daphne Blake. The only reason anyone would use that name would be if they knew about Lucy Allen, knew that Daphne Blake had been her occasional nickname. And I took a photo of Lucy, didn't I? Twenty-seven years ago, I took a polaroid photo of her naked and pinned it up at school with the sole object of humiliating her. Now somebody's basically done the same to me, only it's not noticeboards but the internet. Now it's online, for the whole world to see. My punishment, finally.

I sit up slowly, pushing back the duvet and swinging my legs over the side of the little bed. What I don't know yet is why *now*? Why wait so long? But I almost don't care about that because what I need to do, and do urgently, is find out *who*. Because it's now become abundantly clear that somebody I know, someone with access to my home, knows all about

Lucy Allen. Knows all about me, about my past, about the thing I've tried so desperately to keep hidden from everyone I've met, from everyone I've loved, for nearly three decades.

I'm on my feet now, walking slowly to the window. My limbs are heavy as I draw the curtains open. Eloise's room is at the front of the house and the road outside is empty and quiet this early on a Sunday morning. I watch listlessly as a squirrel scampers across the small square front lawn of the house opposite and spirals itself up the trunk of the nearest tree like a tiny grey acrobat, then I lean my hot forehead against the cool glass and close my eyes.

Who then? Of those who've been in my house in recent weeks, who could it be? They must be responsible for the anonymous letter and the videos, mustn't they? And maybe some of the other things that have gone wrong recently too. And – the thought strikes me suddenly, my eyes snapping open – is it because Mum's come back that they, whoever they are, have chosen now to do this? It's perfect timing after all, because this should be one of the happiest times of my life – my mother back with me, my family reunited. If you want to punish someone for destroying your family, or the family of someone you're close to, why not pick a time when they're extra happy? It makes watching them fall apart even sweeter, doesn't it?

But who? *Who?* Right now, I think I've narrowed it down to the three most likely suspects, and I run through the names in my head.

Deborah. Barbara. Robin. They're the ones who've been acting strangely recently. But could one of them really have some connection with Lucy or with her family?

None of them have contacted me since the videos went online, and while Robin, *if* she's innocent, may not know about the Facebook post, the other two surely must – Ruth will have told Deborah, and Brenda will have told Barbara – and their silence has been deafening. But if it *was* one of them, that means they've known all about me and what I did to Lucy from the very beginning, doesn't it? It would mean they came into my life deliberately and then bided their time, waiting for the perfect moment to strike, to take their revenge. They waited months. *Years*. The thought of that makes me shiver again, and I wonder if this is all just too far-fetched. There must be some other explanation, but I can't think of one, can't think of anything else that could explain this. Barring a break-in, of which there's been absolutely no sign, only a handful of people have had access to my bedroom. And whoever did this used the name Daphne Blake, which can only be a reference to Lucy Allen. There's nothing else that makes any sense. Unless ...

I think about Mike again. He's the only other possibility, but if he knew about Lucy he'd have told Mum, I'm pretty sure of that. Even so, I'm wondering now if it's time to confront him, to ask him straight. Time to take control of it before it takes control of me. Before it destroys me. I shiver again and turn away from the window.

Yes, I did what I did to Lucy Allen. And if someone's decided to punish me now, properly, all these years later, fine. Well done, you've done a bloody good job. My reputation, my livelihood, my friends, my family, my sanity ... but enough. Enough, now. I can't take any more. Somehow, I have to make it stop.

Chapter 28

I sacked Robin last night. I'm driving to work, feeling sick at the thought of my seven-thirty meeting, and even sicker about Robin. I had a long chat with Mum yesterday afternoon and that was the outcome – a phone call to the woman who's been my right arm for the past eighteen months to tell her I no longer require her services.

'So you're not going to the police about it then?' Mum said, and my stomach flipped. We were sitting on the sofa, mugs of tea and a plate of chocolate biscuits on the go. No booze yesterday, because although by the evening I could have murdered a drink, I knew it would be a dreadful idea, especially with what I'm facing this morning.

'No! No need for that; it was just a prank,' I replied with a smile, as inside my head a little voice issued a stern warning.

No. No police. How can I report this to the police when now I know exactly why it's happened? I can't go to the police and I can't talk this through with anyone either. Nobody can find out about Lucy, nobody ...

'OK, whatever you think,' she said, and I thought she looked at me rather strangely for minute, but then her face cleared and she sighed. 'I've told Liv, by the way. She sends her love and sympathy. She's furious about it, on your behalf.'

'That's nice of her.' It is, but the thought of my new-found sister seeing those pictures – *oh, please, don't let her look at them* – makes me feel ill.

'Anyway, I've been thinking, really thinking about all this nonsense,' Mum continued. 'And I know you don't want to believe anything bad about her, but honestly, love, I think it can only have been Robin. I mean, it seems such a silly, childish thing to do for a joke, and potentially really damaging too, for your career and your reputation'—she shook her head, a flash of real anger in her eyes, and it made me happy, briefly, to see that outrage, that maternal defensiveness, the lioness fighting to protect her cub—'but there's no way your work friends would do something so stupid, and as for your neighbours, well, they may not be true friends. They made that pretty clear ...'

She rolled her eyes, then carried on.

'But I just don't see how they'd have *time* to fit cameras if they were just nipping upstairs to the loo or whatever. I mean, I don't know anything about that sort of thing really but surely that would take a while? And I've seen her, remember? Robin, acting oddly in your bedroom *and* in your bathroom. She's the only one with the time, here in the house on her own. It *must* have been her, Beth. I don't know why; that's the only thing. It doesn't make sense to do something like that, but I can't work out how it could have been anyone else.'

I thought long and hard after that. Thought about how

Robin, even though she didn't live anywhere near me, just happened to see the card I'd put up in the village shop looking for help with the kids and the housework.

Could she possibly have some connection with Lucy's family and have known who I was all along? And yet, despite the occasional hint of slightly odd behaviour, she's always been so ... so *great*. So incredibly helpful, a rock, and someone the kids adore. It seems so unlikely that she'd come here with the sole purpose of trying to destroy me, and why wait so long anyway? It just didn't seem logical to wait until I was really happy, with my mum back in my life, because who could have foretold that? She could have been waiting for years, for decades, for something like that to happen.

Could my past have been something she found out about later, though, *while* she was working for me? Again, so unlikely. There's nothing in this house to link me with Lucy Allen and what happened. Nothing. No diaries, no newspaper cuttings. The only other possibility was that somebody told her. But who, and why? The only person in Cheltenham who knows about it is my dad, and she's never even met him. And if it were me, if I discovered something that awful about my employer's past, I'd be horrified, yes; it might even make me reluctant to work for them anymore. But would I take it upon myself to wreak some sort of revenge, to punish them for what they'd done to someone I didn't even know, so many years before? No, of course not. No sane person would do that.

I couldn't have this conversation with Mum, of course. Instead, I tossed the arguments back and forth in my mind for hours until my head was pounding. I thought about the other stuff too – the central heating, the accident with the trampoline, all of it. And even though it still didn't really add up, I finally decided that the unease I've been feeling about Robin recently was something I could do without. I was struggling as it was, and if Mum was happy to take over Robin's duties for now ...

'Of *course*, darling! I'll even help you recruit someone new before I have to leave. You're doing the right thing,' she said and hugged me. I clung to her, muttering my thanks. I made the phone call immediately, knowing I'd chicken out if I waited a moment longer, but when Robin picked up, still sounding curt with me, I lost my nerve a little. I knew I should confront her about the letter, the videos, all of it. But I still wasn't *sure*, was I? And frankly, I was feeling too fragile, too exhausted. And so I kept it short and to the point.

'I'm sorry it's such short notice, Robin, but I don't think you've been very happy here recently, and it seems silly employing someone when Mum's here now and can help me out. I'll pay you to the end of the month, obviously. I hope you understand.'

There'd been a long silence on the other end of the phone, and then she'd simply said, 'Fine. Say goodbye to the children for me. Bye, Beth.'

Her voice had cracked as she mentioned the children and I wondered if she was crying, and whether I'd made a terrible mistake, but it was too late. And now, as I pull into the surgery car park, clamber out of the Audi and slowly, reluctantly, make my way across the road and into the building, I try to put

Robin out of my mind. Today, my focus has to be on keeping my job because if I lose it, if they don't believe that making and posting those videos was nothing to do with me, what then? How will I get another job with that disgrace hanging over me? What will Jacob do? He might actually try for full custody of the kids, and that ... well, that doesn't bear thinking about. I swallow a sob as I push open the door to my office, hang my coat up, run a brush through my hair, and dab on some lip balm. And then I take a deep breath and go and face the music.

An hour later, I'm back in my office, tears running down my face. I haven't been sacked; instead, I've been told to take some time off work – a month or so. They're still going to pay me too, and they told me it's to help me, to give me a break, but it still feels like a punishment.

'We've become increasingly concerned about your mental health, Beth,' Gabby said gently. 'After that worrying letter, and now these videos ...'

She paused and exchanged meaningful glances with Dr Andrews and Dr Wilson, who were also sitting at the big round table in the doctors' meeting room. The room was warm and the sickly smell of too much furniture polish mixed with coffee from the pot sitting inches away from me was not helping my still present nausea.

'The good news is that we haven't heard anything else from the newspaper reporter who got in touch with Gabby so hopefully that worry's gone away at least. But the problem is, we don't know how many of our patients saw those ... well, those *images*,' Dr Wilson said, shifting uncomfortably in his chair. He's young – in his early thirties – but dresses like a sixty-year-old, all tweed jackets and white shirts always buttoned to the neck, even on the warmest of days. Today the jacket is brown and his neatly knotted, skinny tie is red. He looks like Mr Bean.

'But I think we can assume from the ... the, erm, *volume* of replies and reactions that it was many hundreds,' he continued. 'And we know your role isn't patient-facing, but even so ... we just feel it's better for everyone if you keep a low profile for a while.'

I gave a little nod, my eyes fixed on a puddle of coffee on the table, trying desperately not to cry. I tried, when the meeting first began, to explain again that I'd known nothing about the post or the videos, that somebody, somehow, must have hidden cameras in my home and hacked my Facebook account, that the first I knew of the pictures was when Ruth phoned me.

'So you found these cameras then?' Dr Andrews asked, frowning and rubbing his untidy grey beard.

'Well ... no. I searched everywhere but I couldn't find anything. I'm getting a specialist company in this week to do a proper sweep ...'

My voice tailed off as the three doctors exchanged sceptical looks.

What's the point? They don't believe me and I don't really blame them. It sounds crazy. I sound crazy.

I gave up after that, and let them deliver their verdict. I was, they'd decided, clearly having some sort of mental health crisis and my time off would be deemed sick leave.

'Try to get your drinking under control, Beth,' Gabby said. 'If you feel counselling might help we can organise that for you, OK? But above all, just take some time for *you*. You've been through some big life changes in the past couple of years – your divorce, your dad going into a home, your mum coming back into your life. It's all just caught up with you, that's all. It'll all be fine, and we're here if you need us.'

Somehow, I managed to get back to my own room before the floodgates opened. Now, I sit here and cry for a good ten minutes, feeling wretched.

I love my job; I don't want to take a month of sick leave. Who's going to run things here? And what if they decide not to let me come back at all?

The thought of having to leave altogether brings a fresh rush of tears, and when I eventually pull myself together it's after nine. Feeling unable to face anyone, and knowing the waiting room will, by now, be full of patients, I gather my belongings and slip out the rear fire door, then make my way down the alleyway that runs along the side of the surgery building. As I cross the road I hear someone calling my name, and turn to see Nadia gesturing at me from her usual doorway.

Oh, no. Not now.

But now she's waving at me too and I don't have the heart to ignore her. Horribly conscious that my face is still red and tear-stained, I make my way over and attempt a smile.

'Hi, Nadia. Are you OK? What can I do for you?'

She's squinting up at me, one hand shielding her face from the sun that's suddenly decided to make an appearance. Her eyes are watery and blood-shot in the clear morning light.

'Are *you* OK?' she asks. 'You look as if you've been crying.'

The concern in her voice almost makes the tears start again, but I swallow hard, refusing to release them.

'I'm fine. Just a few issues at home so I'm taking some time off, just a few weeks. Nothing major, don't worry.'

She stares at me, looking almost as sceptical as my colleagues did earlier, but she lets it go.

'Right, well I just wanted to give you your books back. I've finished them and I know you said to give them away or to charity but it seems a shame. They're in such nice condition and I've taken care of them. Look.'

She holds out a plastic bag. The books are neatly stacked inside and I want to tell her to keep them, that I don't care about books right now, that I don't have time for this, that I need to get home, need to curl up in a frightened ball somewhere and lick my wounds like a dog, but I can't. I can't be mean to this poor old lady, sitting here on her little pile of cardboard in her stale-smelling clothes. Instead, I force a smile and take the bag from her.

'Well, thank you. And I'm so glad you enjoyed them. As I said, I'll be off for a few weeks now, but I'll sort some more out for you for when I come back to work. If you're still here, that is. Do you think you will be?'

She nods.

'No plans to move on. I like it here. Town is nice, people are nice, hostel is clean. For now, anyway.'

'Good,' I say, and realise I mean it. I've got used to seeing her out here and I enjoy our little chats. I'd miss her if she went.

'Well, bye for now, Nadia. Take care of yourself, OK? See you soon.'

She raises a hand encased in a grey wool fingerless glove.

'See you, Beth. Hope you sort it out, whatever it is.'

'I will. Bye.'

But as I walk to the car, I suddenly feel more alone, more scared, than I have in a very long time. I have no idea how to 'sort this out'. None. Because I don't even know what this *is*. I've got rid of Robin, but I still don't know if she truly has anything to do with it, and I feel another little shiver of doubt. Was it her, really?

My life's falling apart, I think. And I have absolutely no idea who's responsible

Chapter 29

'Nothing, Mrs Holland. Nothing at all,' says the man.

He bends down, snaps his little black case shut, and straightens up again.

'So I'll be off then. You'll receive an invoice by email in the next day or so. Thanks again for the tea.'

I see him out, shut the front door, then lean my forehead against it for a minute, my mind racing.

How? How can there be nothing? This is ... this is ludicrous.

He'd turned up a couple of hours earlier and I'd shown him up to the bedroom. It had been tempting to have the entire house swept for bugs and cameras but the cost would have been eye-watering, and after yesterday, and my paranoia that this 'sick leave' I'm now on might end up being something more permanent, I'm too scared to deplete my bank account any further than is absolutely necessary.

'I think it's just my room and the ensuite,' I explained. 'Video cameras of some sort. I took both rooms apart, but I couldn't find anything. I know they can be really tiny these days though, and I didn't really know what I was looking for, so ...'

He nodded. He was a small, wiry man in a short-sleeved black shirt with *Bugsweepers* in yellow embroidery on the breast pocket.

'Don't worry, Mrs Holland. If there's anything here, I'll find it. Don't you worry about that.'

He hadn't asked any more questions, for which I was grateful. *Discretion's probably a big part of a job like his*, I thought, tuning out as he started talking about radiofrequency detectors and infrared scanners. I didn't care *how* he was going to do it, I just wanted it done, and so I went back downstairs and left him to it. But when he finally emerged, he told me the room was clean.

'All safe, you'll be glad to hear,' he said, and I thought I heard a note of disappointment in his voice.

Now I feel more confused than ever.

How could he have found nothing? There were, very obviously, cameras in my bedroom at some point. And now there aren't. So what does that mean? That someone fitted them, then took them away again?

I jump as my mobile phone vibrates in my pocket. It's the solicitor I called as soon as I got home yesterday to ask for advice on how to get the porn site to remove the video. It's not straightforward, apparently. Obviously, the first step is to contact the site and ask, nicely, if they can take it down, but they don't have to oblige.

'They probably get a lot of takedown requests, and if a video's popular they may well ignore them,' she said. 'But if you can actually speak to a human being and make an eloquent case, well, you never know. Humanise it. Make them empathise with you. They may well have a partner and children themselves, so try to make them see how embarrassing it all is for you, how the video was made without your consent, how it may even affect your job, that sort of thing. You need to make that contact yourself. If that doesn't work, come back to me and we'll see what else we can do.'

I'd forced myself to go back to the website immediately but found no contact phone number, just an email address. I'd spent the next hour composing a heartfelt email, but when by this morning there was still no reply I was too anxious to wait any longer. I left a message with Anna Reid, the solicitor, begging her to do something, *anything*. It was going to be more money I couldn't afford to spend, but there was no way I could live with knowing that video was still out there. We had to get it taken down; we simply had to.

'I'd wait a bit longer before giving up, Beth,' she says now. She has a lovely voice, calm, warm, reassuring. I've never met her – I found her on Google yesterday – but I'm picturing a soft bun, tendrils falling around her face, and a crisp white shirt.

'It's been less than a day and they may not check their emails regularly. But if we don't hear anything after, say, a week, then I'll put the pressure on a bit. If they still ignore us, or point-blank refuse to remove the footage, we can suggest some alternatives. We can ask them to blur your face, maybe. That might be a good compromise. It's a tricky one, but don't despair, all right?'

I thank her and end the call, but I *am* close to despair. Mum's gone to a yoga class in the local W.I. Hall, and the children are, of course, still at Jacob's. The house seems so quiet, so sad, that I almost can't bear it. I know I need to keep busy or I'm just going to collapse in a messy sobbing heap, and so I try to focus on some housework. I flick a duster around the living room and wipe down the kitchen surfaces. But there's a buzzing in my head, a fuzziness, and I can't seem to organise my thoughts. Images of tiny vanishing video cameras flash through my mind; I know I barely slept last night and wonder if I'm starting to hallucinate. I go upstairs and lie down on Eloise's bed, then remember my room is safe again so get up and go to my own bed instead. I'm just drifting off when I get a text from Mum telling me she's nipping to the shop on the way home and asking if I need anything.

Cameras all gone now, I assume?

she adds, and I tap out a reply.

No cameras to be found! I'm so confused. Not sure what's going on. Robin (if it was her) removed them again, maybe? Having a little nap. See you later xx

I do fall asleep then, too exhausted to even crawl under the duvet. I wake with a start an hour or so later, feeling cold and woozy. It's lunchtime and I'm thirsty, my lips cracked and dry, so I make myself get up and walk stiffly down the stairs. But when I get to the hall I pause. I can hear voices in the kitchen. It's Mum, and it sounds as if she's chatting to ... Ruth?

Yes, it's Ruth. What's she doing here?

'She's not in a good way at all,' Mum's saying. 'I'm so worried, Ruth. I went out this morning to give her some space, you know? I don't want her to think I'm watching her all the time. But I think she needs medication, at the very least. She's all over the place, and now Jacob doesn't even trust her with the children. He's taken them to stay with him. Did you know that?'

'Gosh ... no, I didn't! That's awful. Poor Beth,' Ruth says.

Out in the hall, I'm squirming.

They're talking about me. Oh shit ...

'Oh, please don't say anything,' Mum says. 'She's so upset about it and she's trying to hide it. I'd hate for her to think we've been gossiping about it. She tried to pass it off as Jacob having some holiday and wanting to spend some of it with the kids while they're on Easter break, but it was pretty obvious what was going on. I think he was really angry about that awful video. I mean, I don't blame him I suppose ...'

'Well, no. God, poor Beth. It's all so embarrassing for her, and when I heard yesterday the docs had decided to send her home, well ... has she got to the bottom of it yet, the video?'

'Well, this is the thing.' Mum's lowered her voice and I take a step closer to the kitchen door, straining to hear.

Mum's not stupid. Of course she's worked out that I lied to her about the true situation with Jacob and the children. Why did I do that? Why?

'She had a man in this morning from some electronic bug-sweeping company,' she's saying. 'And apparently he found absolutely nothing. No cameras. And do you know what, Ruth? I really hate to say this, but I'm starting to think all this hidden camera stuff is all in her mind. She's so confused at the moment, and I'm now wondering if she filmed herself, and posted it herself too. All these allegations she's making, they just don't make any sense, you know? And did you know she's fired Robin over it all? They've had a few fallings out recently and she thinks it might be her idea of revenge. I thought that might be the case too, at first, but now I'm suddenly changing my mind. I think it might be a sort of attention thing, a cry for help. I mean, it makes sense when you think about it. All the pages the link was posted on, they all belong to people she wants attention from, don't they? Or people she's not on great terms with. Jacob, her friend Brenda ...'

'NO! NO!'

I burst into the room, horrified. They're standing at the patio doors and they whirl around, both with shocked, guilty looks on their faces.

'Darling ...' Mum says, eyes wide. She takes a step towards me but I'm still shouting and she shrinks back again.

'THAT IS NOT TRUE! I DID NOT FILM THOSE PICTURES MYSELF. WHY ON EARTH ...? I MEAN, EVEN IF I DID, WHY WOULD I POST THEM TO THE SURGERY PAGE? THAT'S RIDICULOUS!'

'Beth, calm down!' Ruth is moving towards me now, hand outstretched, but I can't seem to help myself.

'I DON'T KNOW WHY THERE AREN'T ANY CAMERAS. IT DOESN'T MAKE SENSE TO ME EITHER, BUT IT WASN'T ME, OK? IT WASN'T, AND I DON'T KNOW HOW YOU COULD EVEN ...'

And then, quite suddenly, all the rage dissipates and I look at their stunned, worried faces and burst into tears.

'I'm sorry … I'm so sorry … Ruth, Mum … I shouldn't have lost my temper. I'm sorry …'

Ruth takes another step towards me and wraps her arms around me, pulling me close, and I let her. She's wearing a soft, fluffy jumper today, baby pink, and I bury my face in her shoulder.

'It's all right, it's all right, let it out, that's it. Of course we believe you, don't we, Alice? My poor Beth. It's all going to be OK, I promise you,' she murmurs, and I stand there for a long time, crying, her palm making soothing circles on my back. When I eventually stop weeping and look up, Mum's standing next to us with a box of tissues. Wordlessly, she offers me one and I take it, nodding my thanks. I wipe my eyes and blow my nose loudly.

'I sound like a seal,' I say, and that makes us all laugh, just a little.

'I'm so sorry, darling. I shouldn't have said any of that. I'm just trying to make sense of it, and you know how worried I've been about you. But Ruth's right, of course we believe you. Forgive me?'

I hesitate, just for a minute, then nod. *She's just as confused as I am about all this, isn't she?* I think, and I can't blame her for speculating.

'Of course I forgive you, Mum.'

'Thank goodness. Look, come and sit down,' she says, and I do. Ruth pulls out the stool next to me and sits down too.

'I need to get back in a minute,' she says. 'I just wanted to zoom out in my lunchbreak and see if you were OK. Gabby told me about what happened yesterday and I didn't want to just call; it seemed too impersonal. Deborah was going to come too, but, well ...'

She shrugs awkwardly, and I wonder again about Deborah, but Ruth's still talking.

'Anyway, do you really think it was Robin? You've actually fired her? Why would she do such a horrible thing though? I don't understand.'

'Oh Ruth. I just don't know. But she did have the most access, the most time ...'

Even as I say it, the Robin thing still isn't ringing quite true. There's something just not right about it being her, even if she did have the best opportunity.

Unless maybe Mike paid her to do it? She can't be very well off, and maybe she needed the money ...

That makes more sense again suddenly, and I remind myself to get his number from Mum. And then I think about the face at the window again and a shiver runs down my back.

'Or maybe someone broke in,' I say lamely. 'Someone who wanted to ... to mess with me.'

That *is* still a possibility, but I can't explain any further without telling them about Lucy, and now they're both looking at me with sceptical expressions.

'But why would anyone want to do that?' Ruth says. 'I can understand you suspecting Robin – I mean, you've had a few issues with her – but why would anyone else want to hurt you like this? What have you ever done to anyone? That doesn't make sense, sweetheart.'

She says the words soothingly, like a mother trying to calm a child having a tantrum, and I give up. There's no point in having this conversation, not with either of them, not when I can't tell them what I really think's going on here. And anyway, Ruth's looking at her watch now, jumping off her stool, and saying she's going to be late for afternoon surgery and that she'll call me soon.

'Rest, OK? Make the most of this time to yourself. You look knackered.'

She gives me another hug and then she's gone. Mum kisses my cheek and tells me to go and relax and she'll bring me some lunch shortly – fresh mushroom soup and sourdough bread that she picked up on the way home from yoga. I thank her and wander aimlessly back upstairs and into my room, where I stand by the window gazing down at the quiet street, at my neat paved driveway, flanked on either side by Brenda's and Barbara's. I think about them, the two women I thought were my friends, and feel a little wave of sadness. I remember the early days, just after we'd all moved in, the way we hit it off immediately and how lucky I'd felt to have neighbours like them. And then I remember something else, something which strikes me with such force that I gasp. Something I'd totally forgotten about.

I take a deep, jagged breath.

It would have been easy for Brenda or Barbara to nip in and install those cameras after all. To remove them again too. All they'd have to do is watch the house and make sure it was empty while they did it. Because what I've suddenly remembered is that back at the beginning, back when we first became friends, we all decided it made sense, as we lived next door to each other, to exchange door keys, just for emergencies. We've never needed to use them, and so I'd forgotten all about it. In fact, I'm not even sure where their keys are now – probably in one of the kitchen drawers. But the fact remains: I have keys to both Brenda and Barbara's houses.

And, more importantly, they have keys to mine.

Chapter 30

I dreamed about Jacob last night. He was here, in my bedroom, and he had a tool kit with him. He was over there by the mirror, screwing something into the wooden frame. I called out to ask what he was doing, but he didn't hear me.

I woke with a start, in a panic, jumping out of bed and running to the mirror to check, but of course there was nothing there; there was no tiny camera blinking at me. It was just a dream. And yet, as I crawled back under the duvet, I began to wonder again. Did I have this all wrong? The fact that I'd now remembered that Barbara and Brenda have keys to my house seemed to have blown everything open again. My trust in everyone except, probably, my mother and Ruth, was trickling away. Was it so ludicrous to think that Jacob might have been involved in this? I'd already wondered if he'd written the anonymous letter, and he was always popping up and down to the kids' bedrooms when he was here – Crystal too, on occasion. Could it have been him, or her, who'd fitted those cameras? He'd seemed so furious, so disgusted, about the video, but what if he had a grand plan? What if they were scheming all along to take the kids away from me permanently? To make me seem like an unfit parent would surely strengthen their case hugely. But the thought that this misery, this hell I'm going through, could have been brought about by Jacob, the man with whom I spent so many happy years, the man I still, until recently, had such a good relationship with, made me feel ill. And Crystal is a barrister, for goodness' sake. She wouldn't, would she? Somehow, I convinced myself I was being ridiculous and fell back into a fitful sleep. But now, as I spread butter on a slice of toast in the quiet kitchen – Mum's already gone out for a walk – the doubts are sneaking back, wriggling their way into my thoughts even as I try to bar them entry.

I don't want *this to be anything to do with Jacob*, I think, as I pull out a stool and sit down, flicking the TV on to catch the end of *BBC Breakfast*.

I don't want it to be anything to do with anyone I know because how do I move on from that?

I'm starting to think it doesn't even matter who's behind it all. The damage is done, and all I can do now is hope things turn around, hope that whoever is trying to hurt me feels they've done enough now, finally. Hope that those pictures, which may have had tens of thousands of views by now for all I know, will eventually be taken down. Hope that I'll be allowed to go back to work. Hope that this nightmare will soon be over.

For now, I have this period off work, unwanted though it may be. I need to be constructive with it, use it to clean up the mess I've found myself in. I haven't seen Dad since the pictures went online, and while I'm almost certain the care home staff won't have told him, won't have shared the juicy news that his daughter's naked body is out there on the internet for anyone to ogle, I can't be sure that one of his friends hasn't seen them, or one of his care home buddy's relatives. The thought of him hearing about it and then, horror of horrors, taking a look for himself, petrifies me. I've spoken to him on the phone over the past few days, just briefly, telling him I'll be in soon and that everything's been a bit hectic, and he's given me no indication that he knows anything's amiss. Even so, nerves are beginning to flutter in my stomach as I get into the car to drive to Holly Tree.

When I walk into reception, Anya is arranging some flowers in the big vase that sits on the round table in the centre of the entrance lobby. I can smell the fragrance from several feet away; it's a heady mix of lilies, freesias, and irises, sweet and powdery.

'Mrs Holland!'

She sees me and smiles. Her official title here is Client Liaison Manager, which always makes me think of a bank, but she's charming and excellent at her job, a reassuring link between anxious relatives and clinical staff.

'Hi, Anya. Just popping in to see Dad. Look, I'm so sorry about ... well, you know. I'm still trying to work out what happened.'

I can feel myself blushing but she's grimacing, moving closer, and putting a sympathetic hand on my arm.

'Don't worry, honestly. We've all taken pictures we regret, but to be hacked ...'

She's keeping her voice low, glancing over at the desk where

Ben, the head receptionist, is chatting to a well-dressed couple and pointing to something in a colourful brochure.

'But I didn't …' I begin, then give up. *What's the point?*

'Anya, do you think …? I hardly dare ask, but do you think Dad …?'

She's shaking her head.

'It's lucky we're staffed twenty-four-seven, to be honest. I think the night crew spotted the post on our Facebook page pretty quickly and deleted it before too many people saw it. We haven't had any comeback at all, as far as I know. There's a *possibility*, of course, that some of our residents know, but nobody's said anything. So I think you might be in the clear, as far as John goes, fortunately.'

I want to kiss her but instead I thank her fervently, apologise again, and go and find Dad. He's sitting by the window in the bar, clearly engrossed in some programme that's playing on the little digital radio that's sitting on the table in front of him. I pause in the doorway for a moment, watching him. He looks content, and I feel a rush of gratitude; I'm so thankful that he's still here, that he's well and safe and happy. As I cross the room towards him though, I see out of the corner of my eye heads turning and eyes following me; I hear a little snigger and my throat tightens. Do they know then, some of them at least, despite what Anya said? Or is this my paranoia taking over again? It's just natural curiosity to look round to see who's getting a visitor – nothing more than that, I tell myself. But the snigger has bothered me and the thought that the eyes following me now have also lingered on images of my unclothed body turns my stomach.

I sit down opposite Dad and swallow hard. He looks up, squints, and smiles his crooked smile.

'Hello, love. Mished your face.'

'Missed you too, Dad. You look well.'

I leave an hour later feeling lighter and ignoring what I'm sure are fresh stares as I depart. He doesn't know, I'm sure of that, and if some of the other residents do, then all I can do is hope they've got the decency to continue to keep it to themselves. Dad was in good form. He's feeling stronger every day and happily swallowed the lies I told him about taking some time off work because I have annual leave to use up, and about Jacob taking the children off my hands for a while to give me a proper break.

'You desherve it, love,' he slurred, and squeezed my hand, his wrinkled fingers soft as tissue-paper. I kissed him and nodded, and told him I was going to make the most of it, almost starting to believe it myself. As I drive home though, I start to worry again. Mum gave me a number for Mike last night and calling him is next on my to-do list.

'I mean, I'm not sure how much good it's going to do,' she said doubtfully as she scribbled the number on the back of an envelope and pushed it across the table to me.

'I know you think you saw him all over the place but honestly, I'm a hundred per cent sure he went back to Cornwall before I even got here, love. He's got nothing to do with those silly pictures, mark my words.'

I told her she was probably right, that calling him was just a box-ticking exercise, but the more I think about it, the more it makes sense to me that it *was* Mike I kept seeing, that he *is* involved, that he somehow found out about my past while working for Mum and is now working for Lucy Allen's family, helping them wreak revenge. But how? How did he do it all?

Whoever he got to help him, he could have given them the camera equipment and instructions on exactly what to do with it, couldn't he? I think. I saw him – thought I saw him – with Robin first, didn't I? And then chatting to Barbara and Brenda outside, and then at the surgery? What if he offered them all money to mess with me, to tamper with my central heating and the trampoline, to write that letter to Gabby? Between all of them, how easy it would have been! Robin with her daily access to the house, Brenda and Barbara with their keys ...

I cross the roundabout onto Prestbury High Street and consider Deborah, who *doesn't* have a key to my house.

But she could easily have nipped into my office when I was in a meeting and taken my keys from my bag. There's a key cutting place just a few doors down, for goodness' sake. She could have made copies in minutes and put them back before I'd even noticed they'd gone. All she'd have to do is call my house phone from her mobile, and if Robin or Mum didn't pick up, she'd know the coast was clear ... I mean, it would be risky, but still ...

My mind is racing as I indicate right to turn into The Acre. My heart's racing too, and I sit in the car for a minute after I've parked, my hands gripping the steering wheel, trying to calm myself. I wonder if I really have stumbled on a possibility here or if all this is just wild, nonsensical speculation. Am I really starting to believe that a complete stranger was able to convince my closest friends and colleagues to turn on me, en masse? Would I do that to them, if the tables were turned, even if vast sums of money were offered? Of course I wouldn't. So why am I even entertaining these thoughts? It's ludicrous, I know that, and as I finally get out of the car and go into the house, I'm talking myself out of it again, discarding the ridiculous scenario I've just dreamed up. OK, I'm still going to call Mike. But there's some other explanation; there must be.

I just don't know what it is yet.

Mum's back and is pottering around the kitchen, a mixing bowl and bag of flour on the counter.

'Making biscuits,' she said happily. 'Nice woman at yoga the other day gave me a recipe. Pistachio and cranberry. We can have one with our afternoon tea later.'

'Lovely,' I say, then, 'I'm going upstairs for a bit. Call me if you need anything, OK?'

She shoos me out of the room, telling me to go and rest, and I head upstairs and close my bedroom door firmly. I find the envelope with Mike's details on it and sit down at my little desk, wanting to feel business-like and in control for this call, even though my mouth is dry and my hands are tingling as I dial the number.

'Mike Langton, hello?'

'Mike ... erm ... hello, this is Beth Holland. Alice Armstrong's daughter, in Cheltenham ...'

Five minutes later I end the call and stare at the phone, not sure how I'm feeling. Mike Langton was, I'm pretty sure, telling the truth. He sounded bemused, baffled even, when I asked him why he'd been hanging around town after Mum had dispensed with his services.

'I'm looking at my diary right now and I promise you, Beth, that the last time I was in Cheltenham was Thursday and Friday the fifth and sixth of March,' he said.

He has a nice voice, deep with a soft Cornish burr, which threw me a little. I'm not sure what I was expecting a private detective to sound like – a New York drawl maybe, like in the films? I tried to concentrate on the dates he was giving me, feeling a little foolish.

'I was outside your workplace on the evening of Thursday the fifth – sorry about that by the way, but part of the job and all that – and left Cheltenham the next day; got the lunchtime train back to Bodmin.'

Thursday the fifth. I remembered that evening, just a few days before the Saturday when Mum suddenly rang my doorbell, when my life changed forever. The shadowy figure in the car park. It *was* him then. At least I wasn't imagining that.

'It was the 12.52, if you want precise details,' he was saying. 'The 12.52 from Cheltenham Spa to Bodmin Parkway, changing at Taunton. So, I don't know who you've been seeing hanging around talking to your friends and neighbours, but it wasn't me, I can assure you of that. Maybe I've got a lookalike, eh?'

He laughed, and I found myself laughing too, telling him I was sorry to bother him, that some odd stuff had been happening and that I was trying to do a little detective work of my own. I end the call before I can embarrass myself any further. I stay in the bedroom for a while after that, my head in my hands at my desk, plunging back into despair.

I'm so confused. I know, without any doubt, that somehow what happened all those years ago with Lucy Allen is behind all this. But who, for God's sake? *Who*? I can't even talk to anyone about it; there's nobody who can help me. Nobody ...

I stand up, knowing I need to go downstairs and act normally, but how much longer can I pretend to Mum that I'm OK? Despite her outward cheeriness, I keep catching her watching me with an uneasy expression, her face a little paler and more drawn these days than it was when she first arrived. I wish desperately that I could confide in her, but I can't, can I? She's all I have now, and I can't put that at risk. The kids are gone, Jacob's gone, my friends are slipping away, and I can't even talk to the few people who *are* still speaking to me, not about this. And now I have even less idea about the truth of what's happened here than I did when I woke up this morning. I'm back to square one, and all I know is that somebody's out to get me.

And, until I find out who, I can't trust anyone.

Chapter 31

'I'm going to nip out to the supermarket, love, and do you know what? I'm going to buy us some Easter treats. Cheer you up a bit.'

I look up. I'm on the sofa, half watching the cookery segment on *This Morning*. The chef's decorating a batch of Easter cupcakes, adding tiny white chocolate eggs to the vanilla buttercream icing.

'You don't have to, Mum.'

'I know I don't have to; I want to. All those Easters I missed, Beth. All those Easter eggs I didn't buy you. Let me, please.'

She looks pale again, tired, but so wistful and so eager to please that I haven't the heart to argue. And anyway, I'm feeling a little more cheerful today because it's the Thursday before Easter weekend and tonight is Eloise's school play, finally. I may not have the children for Easter, but at least I'll see them tonight. I bought their eggs weeks ago – big, fancy ones from the posh chocolate shop on The Prom, personalised with their names. I can't wait to hand them over this evening, can't wait to hold my babies again, to kiss their soft cheeks. I miss them so much it's like a physical ache.

'Oh, go on then. Do you want a lift?'

I smile at Mum and she beams.

'No, no, I'll walk. I can manage a couple of shopping bags; it's not that far.'

She heads for the door, waving over her shoulder.

'See you in a bit.'

When she's gone I switch the TV off. I'm still feeling low, but the thought of tonight's keeping me going; I need to find something to wear to the concert and wash my hair. I'd been so looking forward to Liv coming up for tonight, as she'd promised, but she called yesterday apologising profusely, saying someone had gone sick and she now had to work over the holiday weekend instead. I wondered, briefly, if this was a lie, if the real reason she wasn't coming was because she was ashamed to be seen with me after the porn site debacle, but I let it go, more worried about how Eloise is going to react when her aunt doesn't show. I couldn't bring myself to tell her when I called last night. I didn't want to upset her before her big day, and anyway our phone calls have been so brief and so perfunctory for the past couple of nights. She knows *something's* up, that much is clear.

'There've been rumours at school,' Jacob said gruffly, before passing the phone to the children on Monday night. 'Nothing specific, just something about embarrassing video footage of you on Facebook. Eloise isn't happy. She wants to know what's going on. I've managed to fob her off for now, but she may well find out sooner or later. Nothing I can do about that.'

I'm trying to stop dwelling on it all now, just trying to look forwards. Mum was, I think, relieved when I told her what

Mike had said, and that I'd now accepted I was imagining seeing him all over Cheltenham colluding with my friends.

'Just as I told you, love!' she said. 'Now, no more worrying. Whoever did it will get their punishment one day, you'll see. And nothing else has happened since Robin left, has it? So it probably was her, wasn't it? It's all over now. Just forget it. We'll have a nice Easter, and then hopefully you can get back to work, and the children will come home, and we'll have a wonderful summer together. It'll all be fine, OK?'

And maybe she's right. It's true, nothing else bad has happened since I fired Robin. So maybe it is really over after all, I think now. It's just that something still doesn't feel right about it being Robin, and yet ...

BRRRR.

My mobile phone is ringing. Jacob.

'Hello?'

'Beth.'

Just one word, yet already he sounds so ... so angry, and my throat constricts.

'What is it?'

'I've just got back from the school. I had a call just after ten saying that Eloise was terribly upset and that I needed to come and pick her up.'

'What? What's wrong? Is she sick?'

I'm starting to panic, clutching the phone so tightly my fingers are hurting.

'No, she's not sick.'

He practically spits the words into my ear.

'Well ... what, then?'

'It's you, Beth.' A pause, a heavy breath. 'She's finally found out. One of the boys in her class somehow got his hands on that video of you. He was showing it around in the playground before lessons this morning. Ten-year-old children, Beth, looking at videos of you naked, touching yourself. I can't even ...'

He sounds like he's struggling to form the words.

Oh no. Please, no ...

'And Eloise? She's ... she's seen them too?'

My voice is a strangled whisper.

'Yes, she's seen them. She's mortified, Beth. She says she doesn't want to go back to school and is refusing to take part in the play tonight. She's upstairs now, crying her little heart out ...'

'Jacob, I need to see her. I'm coming over, now, please ...'

I slump down onto the nearest chair. I'm feeling so dizzy I might actually faint, but I have to get to my daughter, I have to comfort her.

'Please, Jacob, is that OK?'

'NO!' He shouts so loudly I jump. 'No. You are not to come over, do you hear me? She doesn't want you anywhere near her. She doesn't want to see you, or speak to you. She made that very clear in the car on the way back here.'

'But—'

'*Listen*, Beth. The answer is no. Our daughter is very, very upset, and you're the cause of it. All that work, all those hours of rehearsal ... She's devastated, but she says there's no way she can go on stage tonight with everyone laughing at her. Laughing at you ... Do you see? Do you see now the awful consequences of your recent behaviour?'

He's angrier than I've ever heard him and that's scaring me, but it's *what* he's saying that's scaring me more.

Eloise, my darling girl. I can't bear this, I can't ...

'But Jacob, please ... It's not my fault; it wasn't me. I didn't ... Please, can you just tell her?'

I'm suddenly sobbing so hard I can barely speak.

'No. And I can't talk to you anymore, not now. We'll be in touch. Goodbye, Beth.'

And then he's gone, and now I feel as if my world, already so fragile, is crumbling around me. Blackness is creeping ever closer. I think about Eloise, and about Finley – my children, my life. I think about Lucy Allen and how her mother must have felt when she lost her, and now, for the first time, I realise that I truly understand. I can feel her pain, her agony.

My children may still be alive, but I've lost them, haven't I? I've lost them, and now I get it. This is it. This is my real punishment. It's what I deserve, I know that, but how can I survive this?

BRRRR.

The phone's ringing again. For a moment, numb with fear and grief, I just stare at it, sitting there on the arm of the chair. It's a private number this time. I consider ignoring it, but it's still ringing, ringing, ringing. It might be important, might be something to do with Eloise maybe, and so I force myself to move. I reach slowly for the handset, my finger fumbling for the button to accept the call.

'Hello?'

My voice sounds hoarse, thick with tears, and I couldn't care less. Nothing matters now.

'Beth Holland?'

The voice is male, brisk, business-like.

'Yes, this is me.'

'Hi, Beth. My name is Miles Cranford. I'm a reporter on the *Daily Star*? I just wanted to let you know that we're going to be running a story about you on Saturday. We spoke to your boss a few days back – she might have mentioned that?'

Oh God, oh God, oh God. No, no, no ...

'But ... Oh, please, no, don't do this! She said ... Gabby said you hadn't been back in touch. She thought ...'

My heart is pounding so hard I can feel it hammering painfully against the wall of my chest.

'Ah well, she wasn't too helpful,' he says, with a little laugh.

A laugh? He's laughing about this?

'I believe you claim you were hacked, but the footage is definitely you, isn't it? So, you know ...' he's saying. 'We have that, and some of the comments from your patients. Someone forwarded me some screenshots, you see, before it was all deleted. Some very complimentary remarks, I have to say. I think you've got some fans out there now, Beth.'

He laughs again as I listen, aghast. I think I'm about to vomit.

'Somebody filmed that footage without my knowledge. You can't—' I splutter, but he's still talking.

'It's a great story. GP manager in X-rated video storm. Imagine it! But Beth, while we were doing a bit of background research, you know, for the story, well, we came across something, and I just wanted to run it past you, maybe get a comment? I'm going back a bit here, quite a few years, and it may be something hard for you to talk about, but I need to ask ...'

His voice has softened a little, taken on a more wheedling, questioning tone, and I feel a shiver down my back, an icy finger of fear moving slowly along my spine.

'It's about something that happened back in the early 90s, when you were a pupil at Fairbridge High School in Bristol. A fellow pupil very tragically took her own life, and a source tells us that you had some involvement in that, Beth? I mean, I know there were never any charges brought, don't worry'—again, he lets out a light laugh, and I'm frozen now, a sort of paralysis creeping over me; the only moving part of me is my chest, pumping up and down, up and down. I'm starting to hyperventilate—'but a source tells us that there were allegations of bullying, before this girl killed herself? Bullying by you, I mean. Do you have any response to that, Beth?'

I sway in my chair, black spots dancing before my eyes.

This is it then. This is it. It's all over, isn't it?

'No comment,' I whisper. 'No comment.'

Chapter 32

It's worse than I ever thought it would be.

I was down at the local shop before it even opened at eight, hovering on the pavement as the door was unlocked. I rushed to the newspaper stand, folding the paper in half as I paid, too terrified to look. Now, back in my kitchen, with Mum still upstairs in the shower, I open it with shaking hands, turning the pages until ...

Oh. My. God.

And there I am, naked in a national newspaper. OK, not completely naked; they've put little stars over my nipples and over my crotch. But I'm still *largely* naked, no pun intended. Two photos – big photos – that are stills taken from the video footage. There's one of me standing in front of my mirror, slightly side-on, hands stroking the rolls of flesh on my stomach, wobbly thighs and bum turned towards the camera. The second shows me in the bath, breasts visible above the bubbles, hands under the water somewhere. And the headline ... I read it again, my cheeks burning.

SCANDAL OF COTSWOLD GP MANAGER'S STEAMY SECRET VIDEO

I'm breathing so fast that my chest is starting to hurt, but I force myself to read the article, my feeling of desperation growing with each sentence.

A GP practice manager from Cheltenham has shocked patients after a link on her surgery's Facebook page took them to a porn website, where she's currently starring in a saucy video. The steamy shots show Beth Holland (40) frolicking naked in her bedroom and enjoying a spot of solo underwater fun in her bathtub

Frolicking? Solo underwater fun? But I didn't … I wasn't … Oh shit, shit, shit …

I read on, eyes skimming the text now, seeing mentions of 'the curvaceous mother of two', 'eye-popping cleavage', 'recently divorced', and 'generous derriere', my hands gripping the kitchen counter for support. This is horrendous. *Horrendous*. It is a carefully worded article, with no mention of the footage being obtained without my consent, or my account being hacked. And then I read further and I freeze. This is it; this is the bit I've been terrified of seeing since Miles Cranford, whose by-line now sits under that hideous headline, rang me on Thursday.

Beth's sizzling X-rated video has now been enjoyed by thousands of randy web surfers, but it's not the first time she's been in the spotlight. Back in her schooldays Beth was the focus of attention for a very different reason, after being linked to the suicide of a troubled pupil at a Bristol secondary school. No charges were brought, and Beth's family moved away from the area after the scandal.

Her latest racy antics have plunged her into the spotlight again, and although she's currently 'on leave' from work, patients are hoping she'll make a return very soon. 'Maybe they should put her on reception instead of hiding her away in the back office,' said one horny chap. 'That would cheer us up when we're waiting to have our piles checked, wouldn't it?'

Beth declined to comment when contacted earlier this week.

I stand there, staring at the page, and I realise that I'm whimpering; little involuntary noises are coming out of my mouth. I can't even process what this means, what impact this story being printed in a newspaper is going to have on my life. I just know that it's going to be enormous. Huge. Today is going to change everything. I take a deep, shuddering breath, then another, trying to quell the panic. I need to move, need to do something – call my solicitor maybe? – but it's as if my mind has disconnected from my body and all I can do is stand there, eyes fixed on the newspaper, the words dancing in front of me, bouncing across the page.

'Beth? Beth, what's that? Are you OK?'

It's Mum, crossing the kitchen towards me, hair still damp

from her shower. A towel is draped across her shoulders, concern etched on her un-made-up face. I swallow.

'The pictures. Someone sent them to the papers, Mum,' I manage to say, and I push the newspaper along the counter towards her. She frowns, fumbling in her dressing-gown pocket for her glasses and starts to read, and I stand there numbly, watching her. When she reaches the last couple of paragraphs she looks up at me, eyes wide, and I know she's read the bit about Lucy. A fresh wave of horror washes over me, because how do I explain that now? What do I say, to her, to Jacob, to *everyone*?

'Mum ...'

My voice is croaky, my throat tight and dry, but she doesn't respond. Instead, she shakes her head and then, to my surprise, picks up the newspaper and very slowly and deliberately begins to tear it up. She rips it into long strips, dropping each one on the floor as she completes it. When she's finished, when the entire thing is in shreds, she bends down and scoops it up, marches to the recycling bin in the corner, lifts the lid, and stuffs the bundle of paper in. Then she turns to me.

'There. That's dealt with that load of nonsense,' she says, sounding satisfied. 'Shall we have a cup of tea?'

Stunned, I stare at her for a moment, and then, surprising even myself, I laugh.

'But ... don't you want to talk about it? The article? What it *said*?'

She shrugs.

'Maybe later. First, my darling, you need a hot drink and sustenance. One of your so-called friends has clearly been at it again, talking to the press. I'm furious and upset, but I'm more concerned about you. You look dreadful, and I want you to sit down and let me look after you, all right? We're having tea and *pain au chocolat* because it's Easter Saturday after all. And after that, if you still want to, we can talk. OK? Now sit.'

She gestures to the nearest stool and I stare at her for another few moments, marvelling, then do as I'm told. The tea is hot and strong, the *pain au chocolat* sweet and flaky and delicious, and as we sit there, the morning sun warming the room as it floods through the patio doors, I feel a strange sense of calm descending.

The very worst has happened, and yet maybe it's not as bad as it could be after all, is it? Yes, there's a mention of something bad happening in my past, a link to a suicide, but it's vague, and it even says that no charges were brought. There'll be questions, yes. But maybe, just maybe ...

'So. Do you want to talk about it now?'

Mum's pushed her plate aside and she's cupping her chin in her hands, waiting.

I nod and clear my throat. Since Thursday, since that phone call from that bloody *bastard* Miles Cranford, I've been in hell. I decided almost as soon as I put the phone down not to tell anyone about Miles and his story, hoping against hope that it might not materialise, that some massive incident – a terrorist attack or a Royal death ... anything – might come along to fill the pages of the newspapers, that my story might be postponed or even forgotten about altogether. Then I spent an hour berating myself about wishing for a terrorist attack or a Royal death and felt more dreadful than ever. I say I told nobody but

I did call Anna Reid. I thought I already knew the answer to this, but I wanted to check, just in case – was there any way I could *stop* a newspaper running a story about me?

'Sadly, no,' she said. 'It's called freedom of the press. At least they've contacted you, given you the chance to comment, to state your case, even if you've declined. They're very careful, Beth; they police themselves really, to a degree. They don't want to be sued, so they're generally very careful not to libel anyone. So as long as there aren't any actual untruths in his story, well ...'

'Oh, Mum.' I sigh and push my plate away too.

'I know. I can only imagine what it was like to see yourself all over the newspaper,' she says. 'And I don't even want to talk about those pictures; we've been there. I'm horrified they've ended up in the paper, just absolutely disgusted, and if I ever see that nasty little ... that *evil* little ...'

She narrows her eyes, looking furious, and I know she still thinks it was probably Robin, but I say nothing, for maybe it was Robin and maybe it wasn't. I just don't know anything anymore, and if I think about that too much on top of everything else today I might actually go mad.

'The only thing I want to ask you about, darling, is ... well, what was that bit about the incident at your school? A suicide?'

She casts her eyes around the room, as if looking for the newspaper, then looks at the recycling bin.

'It implied you were involved, somehow?' she says.

'It was ... well, it was a girl I knew – not a friend exactly. A girl called Lucy,' I say.

I'm trying to remember the exact wording in the newspaper article. All it said was that I'd been linked to the suicide of a troubled pupil at a Bristol secondary school', didn't it? That no charges had been brought and that we'd moved away from the area?

Mum's wrinkling her brow. The towel is still hanging over her shoulders and she pulls it off, draping it over the back of her seat.

'Lucy? I don't remember anyone called Lucy in your primary school class.'

'No. We met for the first time at Fairbridge.'

I pause. For a moment, I'm teetering. To tell or not to tell?

What I should do now is tell her everything, for surely I'll have to, one day? I think. She's my mother, and now she knows that something happened, all she's doing is showing concern. She's not running from the room, she's not shrinking away from me in disgust, and maybe I should have told her about this at the very beginning. Maybe I should have told Jacob too. Maybe I should have told everyone ...

It's part of my story, my history, part of me, I know that. And now half of me feels it's been ridiculous – *I've* been ridiculous – to even think that I could keep this massive secret for my whole life, that nobody would ever find out. But then there's the other half of me, the half that's screaming: NO! DON'T TELL HER! WHAT CAN YOU POSSIBLY GAIN FROM TELLNG HER NOW, YOU IDIOT?

And, predictably, that half wins.

'She was being bullied, or that's what her parents thought,'

I say. 'We were thirteen. And after she ... after she died, there were diaries, or something, and they thought ...'

My mouth is dry, my tongue thick and heavy. I reach for my mug and take a slug of the now-cold tea and grimace.

'They thought I might have been involved. In the bullying, I mean, because I sat next to her in some lessons. The police investigated and there was no evidence, so that was it. But, well, I was really upset by it, you know? Everyone at school was; it was horrible. And so Dad decided it might be better to move me away. That's it, really.'

Mum's listening silently, her eyes boring into mine. I look back for a second or two longer then drop my gaze, shame sweeping over me.

I'm lying, Mum. I did bully Lucy. It was my fault. She died because of me. And I'm sorry, so very, very sorry. I've been sorry every day of my life since and the burden of this dark, abhorrent secret has dragged me to the very depths of despair more times than I care to remember. And now I'm sorry again, sorry for lying. But I've lost so much. I can't lose you again, and if you knew ...

Inside, I'm howling the words, but I sit here, silent, waiting for her to react.

'OK,' she says simply.

I look up, puzzled.

Is that it?

She stands up, all efficiency again. She picks up my pastry plate, putting it on top of hers and adding the mugs before walking to the dishwasher.

'Stupid little hack trying to cause trouble, making something out of nothing,' she says, as she starts stacking the dishes in the machine. 'You'll probably want to explain that to the surgery? They're bound to ask. Now, why don't you go and have a nice bath? And don't you worry about that.'

She's turning on the tap to wash her hands now and gesturing towards the recycling bin with her head.

'Tomorrow's chip paper,' she says.

Still feeling slightly stunned – *is it going to be that easy to get away with this, to keep this secret?* – I go upstairs, strip off, and (I've gone off baths, for some reason) get into the shower. I stand there for a long time, letting the powerful jets of hot water pummel my tense shoulders. As I'm drying myself my phone rings. It's Jacob and I sigh. I put him on speaker as I slowly get dressed. He has, of course, heard about the *Daily Star* piece, and I stay silent, letting him yell, letting him tell me how appalled he is, how this is the final straw, how the entire school is going to know about it by the time the children go back after Easter, how Finley and Eloise are going to be a laughing stock, and my heart breaks all over again.

'I'm sorry,' I whisper.

But he's still shouting, and now he's demanding to know what the reference to the school suicide was about and why this is the first he's heard of it. I tell him the same story I told Mum, but he's still so angry, so livid. He wants more detail and I fall silent again.

I can't do this, not now. Maybe not ever.

'I can't believe I was ever married to you, Beth. I don't know you at all, do I?' is his final scathing comment before he puts the phone down.

I call Anna again then, on the mobile number she kindly gave me. She's at home, a baby crying in the background. I realise she's a mum and for some reason this surprises me. I tell her about the article and she goes online and reads it, her child still wailing. I wonder if she's a single mum like me, with nobody else there to help her juggle her job and her baby, but I don't ask.

'OK, I've had a quick read, and honestly, Beth, there's not a lot we can do,' she says. 'Everything in it is factual, I assume? What's this thing from your school days he's talking about?'

I give her the same spiel and she tells me that the inclusion of that was a little unfair.

'But it doesn't appear to be libellous. Everything in the piece is true, right? It must be awful for you, seeing it in print like that, and if you run into any issues at work because of it, get back in touch with me. We can carry on trying to persuade the website to remove your video in the meantime, but that may be harder now, with all this publicity; it's going to drive even more people to the site, I'm afraid, and they're going to love that. My advice is just to try and forget about it and get on with your life, Beth. People have short memories. And now I have to go; this little one's acting like he hasn't been fed in days. Speak soon, OK?'

I go back into the kitchen then and sit down next to Mum who's writing a shopping list. She looks up, and slowly puts her pen down.

'Beth?'

'Yes, Mum?'

'I just wanted to say ... to say I'm sorry.'

She reaches over and takes both of my hands in hers. I look at her, puzzled.

'I'm so very sorry that I wasn't there,' she continues. 'When you were at secondary school, when your friend ...' She pauses, takes a breath, and now she has tears in her eyes. 'When your friend died, and you had to go through all that. I'm so sorry.'

'Oh, Mum, don't. It's ...'

But she's pulling me towards her, wrapping her arms around me. She's crying properly now, great heaving sobs, and I realise I'm crying too. We sit there for a long time, until finally she moves away, wiping her eyes and smiling a watery smile.

'Gosh, what are we like? Emotional wrecks, both of us,' she says, and I smile too. It amazes me that I *can* still smile when I know there's still so much to come; when I know with absolute certainty that the aftermath of this day is going to be bloody. And sure enough, I've just gone upstairs to wash my face when my phone buzzes with a text.

It's Jacob, who clearly can't even bring himself to speak to me now.

Please don't attempt to call the children this weekend. Both know about the newspaper article. Eloise distraught. They don't want to see or talk to you. I'll be in touch.

I read it, read it again, and suddenly my knees give way and I'm on the floor, a strange ringing in my ears.

And so it begins, I think. And so it begins.

Chapter 33

The past two weeks have been a blur. I feel, in many ways, that my life is actually over. Do the newspapers, the reporters who write these stories, ever think about the consequences for those they write about, I wonder? Or is it just, 'well done, great story, pat on the back, on to the next'?

For me, everything has just ... stopped. Seeing my children, going to work, being with my friends, it's all on pause, indefinitely. I've barely left the house in a fortnight, and the thought of doing so gives me palpitations, as if I've suddenly developed agoraphobia. Even though I didn't film those videos, didn't send them to the porn site, didn't tip off the newspapers, I'm full of self-loathing, full of shame. And yet weirdly, at the same time, I still feel I've finally got what I deserve. I'm finally being punished in the most awful, public way for what I did to Lucy Allen all those years ago. I *deserve* this.

Knowing that doesn't make it any easier to cope with, of course, but the crying has stopped now. Instead, it's as if my mind has closed a door, the door to the room where all the questions are, the room where I've been wandering in circles, trying to work out who's behind this, who's done this to me.

It's almost as if I don't care anymore, and all that matters now is getting through each day and hoping that one day soon my life can restart. That one day Jacob will let the children come home, and the surgery will let me go back to work, and I can fade into the background again, and be a normal, working mother. That people will forget the sight of my naked body in the newspapers and the insinuations about my dark past.

The drinking needs to stop, though. Before, it was once a week maybe – with the girls in the kitchen or on the occasional night out, now and again a little too much and a hangover to pay for it. But now, despite Gabby's warnings, it's every night, and most days too, if I'm honest. Opening a bottle, taking that first sip of chilled white wine or warming red, I feel it hit my bloodstream and start to make my head swim; it softens the edges of my pain, calms me, numbs me. And numb is good right now. I don't want to think about it – any of it. I don't want to know which of the people I love has betrayed me.

For the first few days after that awful Saturday I forced myself to deal with the fallout. On the Sunday, I went to see Dad. He knew, of course. Holly Tree has all the papers delivered every day, broadsheets and tabloids all sitting on a polished side table in the lounge alongside an eclectic selection of magazines – *Country Living*, *Angling Times*, *Woman's Weekly*. He knew, but there was no anger, no judgement. Instead, he just looked sad, and even though he's the only person who really knows what happened back then with Lucy, the only person I could conceivably have a proper conversation with about it now, I just couldn't bring myself to burden him with my fears, with my certainty that this has all happened because of what I did to her.

'I didn't take those pictures, Dad,' I said. 'Someone hid a camera in my room; someone did it for a joke. And then somehow the newspaper reporter saw them and decided it would make a good story, and ... well ... It was a really stupid, really bad joke that got out of hand, and I'm trying to find out who's responsible. But I'm so sorry about it all, and so sorry you had to see it.'

He shook his head.

'S'lucky I'm half-blind. Couldn't shee them prop'ly anyway. Billy read the article to me though. He shed you looked crackin'.'

He raised a thumb, clearly attempting to lighten the mood. I tried to laugh, but inside I was shrivelling with embarrassment.

These old men ogling me, talking about me, looking at me now from across the room ... I see lecherous expressions on some faces and curled-lip disapproval on others. This is horrible ...

'Bloody shtupid joke. Some friend,' he said.

'I know, Dad. I know.'

He paused, then squinted at me, one eye red and watery.

'He knew, then, that reporter. 'Bout Lucy,' he said. 'Wonder how? At leasht he didn't say much, eh?'

He wiped a hand across his face, closing his eyes for a few seconds, and I knew that this had taken him back there, back to those bleak days. My stomach lurched with guilt and sorrow.

'Yes, at least he didn't say much. It'll be OK, Dad. Don't worry. I'm so sorry you had to see it, and it's been awful, but it'll pass. I'm handling it. And the kids are still at Jacob's by the way. But I'm sure he'll bring them in to see you soon. Hey, did you listen to *The Archers* this morning? Jolene's on the warpath, isn't she?'

I changed the subject and we chatted about our favourite radio soap-opera for a while. It seemed to distract Dad as his face brightened. I couldn't bear it for long though, and I made my excuses and left shortly after that, feeling wretched, sick at the thought of how much more of this there was to come. I'd already had the call from Gabby at work, her tone uncharacteristically sharp, her disappointment and frustration evident.

'We'd really hoped, as we hadn't heard anything else from that reporter, that this wouldn't happen, Beth. It's not good, not good at all. Obviously it's dreadful for you, but for the surgery too, our reputation ... and what's this about a suicide back in your school days?'

I told her the same vague story I'd told Mum and Jacob and she'd rung off muttering that she'd be in touch, though her unhappiness had been clear. Ruth had waited until the Monday evening to call me, to express the same shock, to ask the same questions. I was getting good at answering them by now.

'Is Deborah OK? I haven't heard from her at all since I was ... well, since I've been off,' I said, and there was a long pause on the line – so long I thought we might have been cut off.

'Ruth? Are you there?'

'Yes ... erm, she's on holiday,' she said. 'Had some days to use up. Think she's gone to the Lake District. It was all a bit last minute.'

'Oh,' I said.

They do have phones in the Lake District, I wanted to say, but I left it.

'Nadia was asking for you though,' Ruth said hurriedly. 'I popped over to take her some tea this morning and, well, she'd actually seen the *Daily Star*. Sorry, love. Apparently it was lying around in the hostel. Think she got the shock of her life, but she was asking if you were OK. She seemed really concerned. She likes you, I think.'

'I like her too,' I said. 'Oh, bloody hell, what must she think of me now?'

I pictured Nadia, chapped fingers in her tatty gloves, thumbing through the paper and seeing me like that. I shuddered.

Another person I'll never be able to face again. She must be appalled.

Mum, who had continued to be amazing, taking care of me, trying to keep my spirits up, went to her yoga class on the Tuesday morning and, realising after she'd gone that we were out of milk, I'd ventured out to the shop. I pulled on a baseball cap and slouchy sweatshirt, not making eye contact with anyone. I was almost home, feeling weak with relief that I'd got away with it, when suddenly there were Brenda and Barbara walking towards me, just feet away.

I glanced from one to the other and they stopped dead, but I kept walking.

'Beth! Beth, we—'

Brenda was holding out a hand as if to stop me in my tracks, but I lowered my head, unexpected tears pricking my eyes. I barrelled past them, desperate to get home. I couldn't, just couldn't, not that day. Maybe not ever. Those two, Deborah, Robin ... my suspicions still bounce around in my head, but I don't even care anymore. I just want to move on.

Since then, I've hardly been out, hardly spoken to a soul, other than my mother. My phone has buzzed repeatedly with messages from friends and acquaintances, and I've ignored them all. I can't face anyone. Jacob texts me brief updates about the children, and I've spoken to Finley on the phone, once or twice – short, awkward conversations that break my heart. My little boy sounds confused: he tells me he loves me but when I whisper, 'Do you want to come home? Tell Daddy, if you do,' he responds that no, he likes it here, and that Crystal might be getting a dog, a white cockapoo, and how exciting that would be. His ankle is much better, apparently, and he'll soon be playing football again; he's happy about that too. Eloise still won't speak to me at all though, and every day that she refuses to do so makes me shrink a little more into myself, into my misery. Into the bottle.

I've been trying to keep busy, trying to keep on top of the housework, not wanting Mum to do it all, but I've even struggled with that. I potter aimlessly around, occasionally summoning up the energy to put a wash on or water some houseplants, but it all seems to leave me exhausted. The other day I found the plastic bag of books Nadia returned stuffed into the hall cupboard. I took them as far as the lounge bookshelf, only to find that the effort required to put them back in their correct place (my shelves are organised alphabetically, by author) was too much for me, so I simply stacked them on a side table instead. It's pathetic, I know, but I don't know how to fix myself. And so I just drift along, somehow getting through each day, each minute.

Now, I sit here huddled in the corner of the sofa. The daylight is fading and the far corners of the room are already shrouded in darkness, but I can't even be bothered to get up to switch the lamps on. I take a long swallow from the wine glass on the table in front of me and think about how incredibly, how dramatically, life has changed for me. It's not even two months since Mum came back, since those wonderful early days of our reunion, before my life started to slowly, inexorably fall apart. And tonight I'm completely alone, for Mum's gone too – although not for long, she promised, as she hugged me goodbye earlier.

'My friend Gloria is sick, and she's been such a support to me over the years, love. She's going to be OK, but she's having an op on Monday and she doesn't have a partner or any children; I don't want her to be on her own when she wakes up. I need to go back to Cornwall, just for a few days. You'll be fine, won't you? Just promise me you won't drink too much. I'm worried about you, Beth ...'

I'd flushed at that. I'd thought I'd managed to hide my increased alcohol intake from her, pouring the wine into coloured beakers or coffee mugs for sneaky slugs during the day, topping up my glass in the evening when she nips to the loo, thinking she won't notice. I should have known better. She's not stupid. I'm the stupid one.

I dread being alone. I dread rattling around in this sad, empty house, but I'm glad she's having a break. It hasn't been easy for her, dealing with me over the past couple of weeks – my moodiness, my tears. I've noticed the new shadows under her eyes darkening and an unaccustomed slowness to her step. She's tired, wrung out with it all, and it will do her good to get away for a few days. My great fear, when she told me she was leaving, was that this was it; that she was going for good, that it was all too much; that finding me, her daughter, had not been at all what she'd hoped for; that she wanted no further part of it all. But before I could spiral into despair she said something so unexpected that I almost laughed.

'When I come back, I want us to have a party, love.'

'A ... a party? Did you say a *party*?'

'Yes.' She was checking her handbag as she spoke, putting reading glasses and keys into the side pocket. 'It's my birthday on Thursday, my sixtieth. And I don't want much – don't want to think about it really. Me sixty, good grief! But I'd like a small party, and I know that's probably the last thing you want to think about right now, but we're going to do it, OK? On Friday night though; that's always a better night for a do.'

She zipped her bag firmly shut and looked at me. I was staring at her, astounded.

A party? Now? It's ridiculous.

I'd almost forgotten it was her birthday this coming week too, and that made me feel even worse. Guilty. Selfish. I swallowed.

'Well ... what sort of party?' I asked.

'Early evening, cocktails and nibbles,' she said decisively. 'I've already started making plans, actually. I've spoken to Jacob, and he's agreed that the children can come ...'

'What? Really? Oh, Mum, that's ... that's amazing!'

I'd been sitting at the island, but I leapt to my feet at this, my heart soaring.

'Yes, he asked them and they said they wanted to be here for Grandma's big day. So that's sorted. And we'll ask some of your friends too, maybe make a fresh start, mend some fences. What do you think? I'll have to go home eventually and I want to leave you in good shape, my girl, so we may as well get going on sorting you out now – and my birthday is a good excuse. So, no arguments. I'll organise it all; you won't have to do a thing.'

She left shortly after that, and my initial elation at the prospect of the children coming home, of being here in this house with me again in less than a week's time, slowly faded.

Mum's a force of nature, no doubt about that. But really? Jacob isn't going to actually let the kids come, is he? Nobody's going to come, no matter what she says. And do I actually want them all to come anyway, when I know one of them has caused all this misery for me? Some party that's going to be.

I laughed a bitter little laugh, then looked at my wine glass, and at the empty bottle sitting beside it. I got up, slowly, and headed for the fridge.

Chapter 34

'Right, I'm just going out to pick up the bubbly. I won't be long.'

I pop my head into the kitchen where Mum is putting the finishing touches to a tray of canapés: little arancini balls and tiny lamb and feta burgers with mint sauce dip. They look delicious, and to my surprise I'm hungry; I'm looking forward to tucking in. Looking forward to this party. Because, somewhat miraculously, we *are* having a party. Mum's been vague about the final guest list, but I know that Jacob and Crystal are coming, and that they're bringing Eloise and Finley, and that's really all I care about. Ruth's coming too, and some of the others from work, apparently; I haven't really asked. Whoever turns up, turns up. I just want to see my babies again, and let Mum celebrate her birthday, and not think about the fact that one of these party guests is, almost definitely, the person who knows all about me and Lucy Allen. The person who's spent the past couple of months making me pay for what I did. Maybe one day I'll find out who was behind it, and why. Maybe I won't. I can't trust any of them ever again, I know that. I'm just hoping that it's finally over.

That what they did to punish me was enough. That we can all move forwards now.

And so I've painted on a smile for Mum, and weirdly, it's worked. Over the past couple of days I've felt better than I have in weeks. I've gone shopping to buy ingredients and balloons, ordered champagne, and cleaned the house until it sparkles. I'm looking forward to sipping a little bubbly tonight; I took a few days off the booze this week after scaring myself on Saturday night. Alone in the house after Mum went off to Cornwall, I drank far too much and fell asleep on the sofa, only to wake just after eleven, head aching, eyes dry and sore. I lay there for a few moments, trying to reorientate myself. I realised I hadn't even closed the curtains, and was slowly dragging myself into a seated position when a movement outside the window caught my eye.

A face, again, small and white, pressed against the glass. I screamed, shrinking back against the cushions, whimpering with fear, but just as suddenly as it had appeared, the face vanished again, melting away into the blackness of the garden. I sat there, shaking, eyes fixed on the dark space where it had been, but there was nothing. Eventually I got up, pulling the curtains across with trembling hands. It had been my imagination, I was sure of that. Too much wine, too much stress. I was hallucinating again, and that frightened me so much I stuck to water for the rest of the week and felt better for it. I didn't mention the reappearance of the face to Mum, of course, and I made a silent vow to be careful this evening.

'Not too much, Beth,' I said to myself as I laid out plates

and napkins, polished glasses, and found bowls to fill with nibbles. 'Not too much. Just a couple of glasses.'

Now, with just hours to go before everyone arrives at six-thirty, I head out to the off-license to pick up our order. The assistant is helping me load it into the boot of my car when he frowns.

'Got a flat tyre there, luv. Won't get far on that.'

I look at the wheel he's pointing at and curse under my breath. Dammit. The tyre is, indisputably, flat as a flounder.

'Bugger,' I say. 'I'll have to call the RAC. I hope they're quick; this party starts in less than two hours.'

The breakdown service does come relatively quickly – a smilingly efficient man in a luminous orange jacket. But by the time he's done and I'm on the road again, it's rush hour, so by the time I reach Prestbury it's after six-thirty and I'm in a panic. I haven't even changed yet, haven't wrapped the lovely silver wristwatch I've bought Mum, who insisted I keep my gift for her to open tonight. Now I'm out of time; this is *not* how I wanted this to go, and I feel furious at myself for not going out earlier, for leaving it all to the last minute.

Mum must be going crazy too, wondering where I am, I think, and I wonder why she hasn't called. I'm puzzled – *that is quite strange, actually* – and I glance at my phone on the passenger seat, but there are no missed calls showing on the screen, and then I forget all about it because I'm pulling into the driveway and—

Oh no!

There's a little huddle of people outside the front door. I cut the engine and stare at them for a moment, even more perplexed now. Jacob and Crystal and the children – my beautiful, beautiful children, dressed in their party finery – are standing there with Robin.

Robin? Why on earth would Mum invite Robin, after all the things she said about her?

Deborah's there too, with Ruth and Gabby. I look at her uneasily, and then I see Brenda and Barbara, and my stomach lurches. There's a cluster of other familiar faces, all of them clutching bags and bottles, all of them turning to look at me as I get out of the car.

Oh bugger. I'm not sure this was a good idea after all, but they're here now, I think. Why are they all standing in the driveway though?

'Erm ... hello!' I say brightly. 'What ... what are you all doing out here? Is the doorbell not working? I'm so sorry I'm late. I went to the off-licence and got a flat tyre, but Mum's here ...'

'We've tried ringing the bell and knocking and everything,' Ruth says. She's wearing a bright-yellow shift dress and her favourite string of coloured beads with a matching bracelet on her wrist. 'We even tried calling the house phone. No reply. Looks like nobody's in. And she told us not to be late too, which is why we all got here on time. She said she had some sort of special announcement to make?'

'Announcement? I've no idea ...' I say, wondering what on earth she's talking about. I feel horribly awkward now still in my scruffy jeans and trainers with my hair scraped back in a ponytail.

Where is Mum, for goodness' sake?

I want to hug my children, but everyone's watching me, waiting for some sort of explanation as to why nobody's opening the door at this so-called party, so I pull out my house keys and say, 'OK, don't worry, Mum's probably just got the music so loud she can't hear the door. You know what she's like.' I wink at Eloise who looks at me blankly, and I shrivel a little inside.

There's no music though. The house is silent and still as I push the door open and step into the hall, the others piling in after me. There's no music, no clattering of plates, no sound at all. There's something though, something that feels off, and as I move towards the kitchen I realise it's a strange smell, just a hint of something sour and musty, like when you've had a plumber or decorator in the house and they leave a faint, unfamiliar odour behind. The kitchen is empty. Mum's trays of canapés are sitting on the counter along with a baked cheesecake on a big white plate. I look around, bemused.

'Mum?' I call.

And then there's a scream, one I'd recognise anywhere. I whirl around, and it's Eloise, eyes wide with horror, hand outstretched. I turn to look at where she's pointing, towards the open-plan lounge area, and then I see it too, at the same time as everyone else does. And suddenly the room is a maelstrom of noise and panic, cries and gasps, and I stand there, frozen, unable to comprehend what I'm seeing.

It's my mother, though. I can see that. I blink and take a step closer, and now Gabby is rushing forwards, dropping to her knees and yelling for someone to 'call a bloody ambulance, quick!'

It's my mother, here after all, but instead of bustling around the kitchen, smiling, singing along to the music, and celebrating her sixtieth birthday, she's lying still and mute in the corner of the room. Still and mute, a pool of already congealing blood around her head, and trickling down her face like rain down a windowpane.

Chapter 35

'The doctor's on her way down now. Would you like a cup of tea or anything?'

'Thank you. And no, that's kind but I'm fine.'

The nurse who's popped her head around the door smiles and disappears again, and I watch her go, feeling lightheaded with weariness. The past twelve hours or so have been a haze of sirens, panic, questions, and fear. Now, after a night without sleep, I'm dizzy and nauseous, my back aching from sitting in this hard plastic chair. I turn back to the bed where Mum's lying, head heavily bandaged, eyes closed, an oxygen mask covering her face. On the small table to my right, a half-drunk cardboard cup of tea, now cold, sits next to a paper plate, the sandwich on it barely touched and curling at the edges. I can't even remember what sort of sandwich it is. Cheese, maybe? I found it in the vending machine down the corridor at about 4am after realising I hadn't eaten since lunchtime yesterday; I was trying to be sensible, trying to keep my energy levels up, but I had no appetite. How can I eat, sleep, do anything normal, when my mother's lying comatose in a hospital bed?

If I lose her now when I've only just found her again ...

I feel the panic rising once more and push the heels of my hands into my eye sockets, taking deep breaths. We're in a side room, private, quiet, and for that at least I'm grateful. The police, who arrived yesterday shortly after the ambulance and who followed us to Cheltenham General, spent an hour here with me last night, asking questions while Mum was whisked from A&E to CT scan to surgery. She'd been hit, hard, on the head, the resulting injury increasing the pressure inside her skull, but she's going to be OK, we think. They're keeping her heavily sedated, for now, and of course there are no guarantees, not with head injuries, as the kindly surgeon told me last night. But she's in as good a state as she can be, for now. I know this, and yet I can't seem to control the waves of dread and terror that keep sweeping over me, the cold sweat that breaks out on my skin, the trembling of my limbs.

Who did this? Who?

It's all I can think about, and the guilt is almost unbearable, because I know, without a shadow of a doubt, that although it's my mother who's now lying unconscious in a hospital bed, this attack was aimed at me. I took a daughter from her mother. And now, so many years later, my mother has – almost – been taken from me. The final part of my punishment. It's perfect, isn't it? Poetic, almost.

There was, as I told the police, no sign of a break in. No broken glass, no forced locks. Nothing missing either, as far as I could tell. Just my mother, battered and bloody on the floor, attacked by a ghost from the past who slipped in and out without leaving a trace. I didn't tell the police my suspicions, of course. I should have, but I didn't. I couldn't.

'She must have let them in, whoever did this – someone she knows, most likely,' the female officer said. She had red hair coiled into a tight bun at the nape of her neck and a freckled nose. She looked about sixteen.

'Is there anyone who might have a grudge of any sort? Had she fallen out with anyone recently, anything like that?'

I shook my head, swallowing a lump in my throat.

'Everyone loves Mum,' I whispered.

They went away for a bit then, leaving me alone to wait, shivering and terrified, for her to emerge from surgery. I'd jumped in the ambulance with her, asking Jacob to take the kids home and refusing Ruth's offer to come with me.

'I need to do this for her. Just me,' I told her, and she squeezed my hand and nodded her understanding. The others all stood around watching, white faces etched with shock. As the ambulance pulled away I glanced out of the window at them, this little group of people who were, just weeks ago, my closest friends and allies, and I thought about how everything had changed so monstrously much.

Did one of you do this? Did one of you come here earlier, do this, then slip away again? You must have, mustn't you? Or have I got this all wrong? I don't know. I don't know anything anymore, and I'm so scared, so tired of it all ...

Now my brain is too numb, too confused, to even begin to try and work it out. I no longer know what's true, or real, or who to trust. Suspicions and doubts chase each other around the dark corners of my mind then fade away again, leaving me dazed. Now and again, there's a sentient thought: *did someone say Mum had told them she wanted to make some sort of announcement? What on earth was that about?* But otherwise I just sit and listen to Mum breathing in and out, in and out.

The police returned briefly close to midnight, telling me they'd finished at the scene for now – a scene! My living room is now a 'scene' – and that the house was locked up and secure.

'We found the weapon used to attack your mother, by the way.' This was from the male officer who is tall and lean, his cheekbones sharp, his eyes deep blue.

'It was a lamp that was sitting on the side. It's in the shape of'—he looked down at the small, scrappy notebook he was clutching in his big, bony right hand—'a pelican. A pelican-shaped lamp.'

A hint of a smile hovered on his lips, just for a second, then vanished again.

'There's blood ... well, anyway, that was the weapon used, it seems. So probably not a planned assault. The attacker most likely grabbed whatever was to hand?'

He seemed to be asking me a question, and I stared at him for a moment then shrugged.

'I don't know ... I wasn't there, obviously. Yes, it's a pelican. The one with the blue velvet shade?'

He nodded and made another note in his book with a stubby pencil, and I cringed.

Why did I say that? What does it matter if it's a pelican or a frigging elephant? Someone grabbed my lamp and slammed it into my mother's head; that's all that matters.

'Mrs Holland? How are you doing?'

I jump. Two people have come into the room without me even noticing – one of them a doctor I vaguely remember from last night. She's petite with a brunette pixie cut.

'Oh ... hi,' I say. 'I'm fine. What's the latest? How is she?'

I gesture at the bed, and she looks at the nurse who's standing beside her.

'Celia's just going to do some bloods,' she says, and the nurse nods at me.

'Won't take long,' she says.

The doctor is sitting down now, pulling another chair a little closer to mine.

'Your mother ... well, she's not very well,' she says gently, and my stomach contracts.

'But ... I thought ... the head injury, the surgery ... I thought it went well?' I say, but she's shaking her head and my heart rate starts to speed up.

'It's not that. It did, and we do expect her to make a good recovery. It's just ...'

She's frowning, looking down at the clipboard she's holding.

'Well, when we asked you last night if she had any underlying health conditions, you didn't mention her cancer.'

'What? Her ... what?'

She sighs.

'I was afraid of that. You didn't know, then? We're having some trouble tracking down her medical records; I'm not sure why. I'm waiting for an update. And obviously we've only scanned her head at the moment, but we think she's probably been receiving treatment for renal cancer. Kidney cancer.'

My mind is racing and I'm finding it hard to catch my breath. The room suddenly feels hot, stuffy, and airless.

What's she talking about? Has she got Mum mixed up with someone else? My mother doesn't have cancer ...

'I ... I don't know what you mean,' I splutter. 'She hasn't ... She can't ...'

'You brought her handbag in with you,' she says. Her voice is gentle. 'There was a leaflet in it about what to expect from your kidney cancer treatment. And she's got radiotherapy tattoos. They're tiny little pinpoint marks the radiotherapist makes on the skin so he can line up the machine properly. You wouldn't have seen them, in the position they're in, under her clothes. She's probably had treatment quite recently ...'

'But ... I don't understand. Why wouldn't she tell me? Why?' I almost scream the words at her but she doesn't flinch; she just sits there, looking at me with sympathy in her eyes, and now I'm remembering how pale and tired Mum's looked at times recently, and how she went off to Cornwall to 'see a sick friend'. Now I'm wondering about that, wondering if that was true, wondering if what she was really doing was something entirely different. I look frantically from the doctor to Mum and back again, and then I start to cry.

'I didn't know. How didn't I know?' I sob.

'Some people just want to deal with things like this themselves. They don't want to burden their loved ones,' she says, and presses a tissue into my hand. 'We're going to do some tests, just to check, and when her notes get here ... Did she use any other name, do you know? Alice Armstrong isn't coming up, and as you weren't able to give us her exact address ...'

I shake my head.

'Well, she never married again. Her maiden name was Lacey; you could try that I suppose, but I don't think she's used it in decades. And I'm so sorry about her address. I know that seems really weird but as I said last night, we've been apart a long time until recently, so I've never had her home address and I didn't think to ask. It didn't matter because she's moved in with me for a while and ... I'm sorry. I'll call my half-sister and get it for you.'

'That would be useful, thank you.'

It had been a question I'd been asked last night. The nurse taking details from me had looked a little bemused when I couldn't give her my own mother's home address. I'd rung Liv but she hadn't picked up, and I hadn't wanted her to hear such horrible news from a voice message. I needed to call her again, and soon. I was sure she'd be on the next train to Cheltenham and I needed her.

Does she know? I think. Does she know, or did Mum keep it from her too?

'How serious is it? Kidney cancer?' I ask abruptly. The doctor's standing up, ready to leave.

'Until we do more tests and get her notes, it's hard to say what stage she's at,' she says. She looks at the nurse who's tucking Mum's arm back under the white sheet and smoothing it with her hands.

'But, well, radiotherapy in kidney cancer is generally used

when the disease isn't suitable for or hasn't responded to other treatments, or has spread to other areas – the bones or brain maybe. She may not have started it yet, possibly? The tattoos look new, so she may be just about to begin treatment; they usually do those in advance. I'm sorry, Mrs Holland. This must have been a dreadful shock, and as I said, this is just speculation at the moment, but, well ...'

She shrugs. I nod and thank her, and now I'm thinking about Mum's 'special announcement' again and I realise that this must have been it. This is what she was going to tell us all; this is why she wanted to get everyone I love and care about back together.

She knew I'd be devastated, I think. She knew I'd need their support. She was thinking of me, and look at her now. And if she's already sick, if she really does have cancer, then this is even worse. So very, very much worse than I thought it was ...

I'm crying again now, rocking backwards and forwards in my chair. I cry for a long time and then somehow I fall asleep, and when I wake, head drooping, neck cramping, the doctor and nurse are back in the room. I realise they're saying my name and that's what's woken me up.

'Oh ... I'm sorry. I need to call Liv and get that address. I fell asleep; I'll do it now,' I mumble, and try to get to my feet, but the doctor's holding up a hand.

'Don't worry. Take a minute. You must be exhausted,' she says. I sit back down gratefully, rubbing my eyes and trying to clear my head. Then I look at Mum, still lying silently in her bed. The nurse is gently wiping her face with a blue cloth, pulling down her gown to run it over her neck and chest. I watch for a moment, and then I lean forward, staring. Something's not right.

'Her tattoo,' I say. I stand up, moving closer to the bed and leaning over my mother. 'Her tattoo. Where's her tattoo?'

The nurse looks up at me, frowning, and I point, my hand shaking now.

'Her collarbone. She has a tattoo. Three little stars ... Where the hell is it? What's going on?'

The skin on her collarbone is bare, exposed, the green hospital gown pulled away from her body. There is no sign of a tattoo. I look at Mum's face and back to the nurse, and then whirl around to face the doctor.

'Where is it?' I shout.

I'm going mad, aren't I? This is a dream. It must be ...

'Oh, that.' The nurse is talking now and I spin back in her direction. She's looking confused, peering down at Mum's chest. 'She did have a tattoo when she came in – one of those temporary ones? I had one for a fancy-dress party once; they're pretty good. They last a couple of weeks nowadays. It came off when we were washing the blood off, but she'll easily be able to pop another one on when she's better.'

She's smiling reassuringly at me.

'No!' I feel frantic now. 'It was *real*. She had a real tattoo, there on her collarbone. She's had it for years, for decades, since I was a little girl. It's real. Where is it?'

They're both staring at me now, both looking bewildered.

'And this is definitely your mother, right?' says the doctor, and now there's an edge to her voice, along with a hint of suspicion.

'Of course it is!' I say. I know I sound rude and exasperated, but I don't care.

Does she think I'm making it up, that I'm pretending this poor woman is my mother?

'Of course it's my bloody mother. I just don't *understand* ...'

The doctor looks down at her notes, and then back at me. The nurse has moved to stand beside her now, and she's looking uneasy, her eyes flitting between me and her colleague.

'Look, this is really none of my business,' says the doctor, 'but if your mother has a tattoo and this lady doesn't, well, that's very strange. I'm not accusing you of anything here, Mrs Holland, but it's starting to sound as if you're not entirely sure about this lady's identity, and with the difficulty we're having in tracking down her medical records, well ... we need to be a hundred per cent sure of who she is, especially considering her serious health issues.'

'What?'

I think I might actually start screaming in a minute. What the hell is going on here?

'Look,' I say, and it takes everything I've got to say the words calmly because my throat is tight with anger and frustration. 'I don't understand the tattoo thing any more than you do but I can assure you that I am one hundred per cent sure that that is my mother. OK?'

The doctor's eyes bore into mine for a long moment, then she looks away, glancing at her notes again. And then, quite unexpectedly, she gasps, her eyes fixed on the page in front of her.

'Oh!' she says.

'What? What is it?'

She looks up, a strange expression on her face.

'Last night, when you came in, we took some of your details, do you remember? You were in deep shock, and we were a little concerned that you might need treating too, so we took a basic medical history?'

I nod, a vague memory of someone asking me questions resurfacing.

'Yes, I remember. And?'

She looks at me quizzically, then looks back down at her chart.

'Your blood type is O, is that correct?' she says.

'O, yes. Why?

'And you say this is your mother, your biological mother? You weren't adopted or anything?'

'No, of course I wasn't *adopted*.'

'Right.'

A pause.

'Your mother is blood type AB,' she says.

I shrug.

'OK. And?'

The two women exchange glances.

'Well,' says the doctor, then pauses again.

'So, this is the thing. A mother with blood type AB cannot produce a child with blood type O, no matter what the father's blood type. She can only produce a child with blood type A, B or AB.'

'What?'

I'm starting to shiver. Why is the room suddenly so cold? I look at the bed again, at my mother, and at the empty place on her collarbone where her tattoo should be. Then I look back at the doctor.

'What?' I whisper.

'Mrs Holland ...'

She looks back down at her chart again and sighs, and then her eyes meet mine.

'I'm so sorry, but if you're absolutely sure about your blood type, it's just not possible. This woman is *not* your mother.'

Chapter 36

My legs crumple. As I fall, the doctor and nurse each grab one of my arms, and then somehow I'm sitting in a chair, my head between my knees.

'Breathe. Deep slow breaths. You're OK,' the doctor is saying, and I try to obey but my heart is thumping and my body is bathed in sweat.

What did she say? Did she really say Mum wasn't my mother, that she couldn't be my mother? She's got it wrong; the blood types must be wrong. I've made a mistake, or she has. This can't be right ...

I gasp and sit up, swaying as a wave of dizziness hits me, then look across to the bed where Mum is still lying motionless, her gown back in place now, concealing the place where her tattoo should be.

'You're wrong,' I croak. 'You've got this wrong. That's Alice Armstrong, my mother. Please, help me sort this out.'

The doctor's kneeling in front of me now, her brow creased, the look in her eyes sympathetic.

'I don't think we've made a mistake, unless you're wrong

about your blood type? But I'm so sorry; this was not the way you should have found out about this.'

There's sweat running down my forehead and into my eyes, stinging them, and I blink.

'I'm totally sure. I've always known my blood type. I can't even remember why really. I know it as well as my shoe size. But this doesn't make any sense. I don't understand.'

I'm struggling to get the words out; my voice is a hoarse whisper. She nods and puts a hand on my knee briefly, then stands up.

'It's confusing enough for me. I can't imagine what's going on in your head. Look, I'm so sorry, I'm going to have to get on with my rounds, but I'll try and pop back later. Didn't you mention a half-sister? Could she shed any light on this, do you think?'

'Yes!' I sit bolt upright.

Liv, of course. I need to call her anyway and now, well, now I have so many questions. Could I be adopted and Dad's never told me? Would Liv know that, if so? And where is Mum's tattoo? Did she have it removed at some point maybe, after she left us, and decided to use a fake one when she came back? Why bother though? But what other explanation can there be?

My mind is racing; my thoughts are tumbling over each other.

I need to speak to Dad. But hang on, I'm not adopted; I can't be. I remember photos – loads of them – before he burned them all. Pictures of Mum pregnant, a neat bump under a long floral dress. Pregnant with me. A photo of her and Dad sitting in a hospital ward with me in her arms and both of them beaming.

'You're just an hour old in this photo,' I remember her saying to me, a dreamy look on her face. 'Just one hour. Can you imagine being that young, that new?'

She gave birth to me. She did. But the blood type thing, it makes no sense ...

'I'll call Liv now,' I say, and the doctor smiles and nods, lifting a hand as she heads for the door. When she's gone I grab my phone and dial Liv's number. Voicemail, again. *Where is she?*

'Liv, it's Beth. I'm so sorry to leave a message, but I can't seem to get hold of you and, well, don't panic but something awful has happened. I need to speak to you, urgently. Please call me as soon as you get this message. Thanks, Liv. Call me, OK? It's really important.'

I end the call and sit there, staring at Mum – or at what I can see of her. The sheets are tucked tightly around her and her face is almost completely obscured by the oxygen mask.

I need to speak to someone else who knows her, I think. Someone who can confirm her identity, who can help me prove that she is Alice Armstrong, my mother. That the doctor is wrong. But who? I don't know anyone else who knows Mum, not nowadays.

And then I have a brainwave.

The gallery. The gallery she works in. They'll have all her details, won't they?

I think of the personnel files I have in my office at the

surgery. Name, address, date of birth, education, qualifications, National Insurance number, bank account details ... it's all there for every member of staff.

They won't be able to tell me anything confidential, but maybe if I explain, if I tell them she's badly injured and that we need to track down her medical records ... But what's the gallery called, and where is it? She told me, I know she did. West something. West ... West Bercor. Yes, that's it!

I grab my phone again and put 'art gallery, West Bercor' into the search engine. There's only one, Callingford Studios. I find the contact page and dial the number with a new sense of purpose.

Right, let's get this sorted once and for all, eh Mum?

I give the silent figure in the bed a determined nod.

'Hello, Callingford Studios, Eleanor speaking.'

It's a refined voice – definitely not a Cornish native. A former Londoner maybe. I clear my throat.

'Hi, Eleanor. Erm, this is a slightly unusual request, but my mother, Alice, works for you, and I need to ...'

'Alison, you mean? She's away on a sabbatical at the moment, I'm afraid,' she says abruptly. 'But hang on, is that Liv?'

I pause, puzzled.

Alison? But she knows Liv ...

'Liv's my sister. Well, half-sister. I'm Beth. I'm older than Liv ...'

I pause again, suddenly realising that Mum may not have told Eleanor, whoever she is, anything about me.

Maybe they're not close; maybe she kept me a secret.

But what else can I do? Mum will forgive me, I'm sure she will ...

But Eleanor's speaking again, her voice sharp this time.

'Alison doesn't have two daughters, just Liv. Who is this? Beth, did you say?'

'Yes. My mum ... well, I'm a bit confused. Her name's actually *Alice*, not Alison. Maybe she uses Alison for work for some reason? She's Alice Armstrong. But yes, she's Liv's mum too. She moved away you see, when I was very young, and she's only just found me ...'

'Alice *Armstrong*? I'm sorry, but I don't understand. I don't know anyone called Armstrong,' snaps Eleanor.

'But ... you know Liv? I'm sorry, I'm not sure what's going on here,' I say.

I hear a sigh.

'Well, I'm not sure either. Yes, I know Liv. I've known her since she was a schoolgirl, and her mother's worked here for years, but her name is definitely Alison, not Alice. And Alison doesn't have any other children. Well, she did – a poor soul called Lucy, but that was many years ago, and—'

'What? What did you say?'

I freeze.

Did she say ... Did she say ... Lucy?

There's a cold sensation suddenly creeping up my body, as if someone's injected icy water into my veins.

'I said Lucy. Alison's late daughter. Look, I think we've got our wires crossed here somehow. Who are you again, and who did you say you're looking for? I don't know any Alice Armstrong. It's Alison Allen who works here.'

'Alison ... Alison *Allen*?'

'Yes. So you've obviously got the wrong place or something. I don't know. I'm sorry but I'm too busy for this. I have a sculpture delivery arriving any second and I'm on my own at the moment. Goodbye.'

And then she's gone, but I sit there, phone still jammed against my ear, listening to nothing. I can't move. I can barely breathe.

Alison Allen. Alison Allen, who had a daughter called Lucy many years ago. It can't be, it can't, and yet ...

Slowly, slowly, I put the phone down on the table beside me, rise to my feet and walk, step by hesitant step, across the room until I'm standing over the bed. I look down at her, at her closed eyelids which are almost translucent, at the tiny up-down, up-down movement of her chest under the sheet. And then I hear a howl, a guttural, animalistic roar, and to my surprise I realise it's coming from me.

This is Alison Allen, isn't it? This is not Alice Armstrong.

This is not my mother at all.

This is Lucy Allen's mother.

Chapter 37

Twelve hours later, she wakes up.

I've spent the day in a state of such confusion and fear that I feel feverish, almost delirious. The only person I've told so far is, weirdly, Jacob, and only because he called me minutes after I'd spoken to the art gallery, to tell me that the children were worried about their grandmother and wondering whether they could visit. There was a stunned silence on the end of the phone when I relayed what I'd just discovered, and half an hour later he was there, standing in the little hospital room in his weekend sweatpants and T-shirt.

'Crystal's taken the kids out to the wildlife park,' he said. 'Keep them busy for a few hours, while we work out how to break the news. Christ, Beth, what's going on here? Are you sure about this? She's really not your mother? Why on earth would *anyone* ...?'

And so I told him. I told him everything. I told him the truth about Lucy Allen, and what had happened twenty-seven years ago; about the events of the past weeks, and how I'd begun to fear that everything that had happened was, somehow, connected to Lucy; about how those fears had pretty much been confirmed when Daphne Blake had been mentioned in the Facebook post; and about how I'd suspected pretty much everyone I knew, even him.

'Seriously? Bloody hell, Beth. Is that how bad things have got between us? I would *never*, ever—'

'I know. I know that now. I'm sorry, but I've been so scared and so ... so befuddled by it all. I got to the point where I didn't trust anyone. Robin, Brenda, Barbara, Deborah ... there's a lot of stuff I still don't understand. But now, well'—I turned to look at the bed, where Mum ... No, not Mum. Where Alison Allen, Lucy's mum, was still lying, oblivious—'it was her, wasn't it? All of it, somehow. Or some of it, at least. I don't know. I can't get my head round it. I have no idea how she did it, or why she's waited so long to come for me. But you know what? I always knew she would, or someone would. Does that sound peculiar? My whole life I've been waiting for this to happen. And now it has.'

Jacob, who'd been listening with an expression that flitted between astonishment and incredulity, shook his head.

'Who attacked her though, and why? I don't get any of this.'

'No idea. Unless it *was* just an attempted burglary gone wrong. No sign of any break-in though. I'm hoping the police come up with something on that one because I can't explain it, Jacob. There's so much of it I just don't understand.'

'You and me both. It's like a film script,' he said. 'I can't believe this has actually happened to someone I know in real life. What happened back then, I mean, it was horrendous, and what you did, well ...'

'I know,' I whispered, but he was still talking.

'But this is *mad*. What you're saying is that she basically tracked you down after nearly thirty years to mess with your head and get revenge for what you did to her daughter? I mean, as you say, why the hell wait so long, and how did she do it? And ... shit, I mean *so* many questions. And how did you even fall for it in the first place? Does she *look* like your mother?'

I shrugged.

'I can barely remember my mother. All I have is that one photo, you know the one? She wasn't even twenty then. She was blonde and pretty, I remember that. But her face has always just been sort of vague in my head. When she'—I gesture at the bed—'when *she* came to the door, I had no idea who she was at first. I didn't recognise her at all. It was only when she leaned forward and I saw the tattoo ...'

I remembered then the way she had been trembling, clearly so nervous as she waited on my doorstep.

Not, as I assumed back then, nervous because she was about to be reunited with the daughter she abandoned. She was nervous because she wasn't sure if her ruse was going to work, wasn't she?

A little sob escaped me. I was grieving now, I realised. Grieving the loss of my mother all over again. The pain was almost unbearable; it was a physical ache inside me. How was I ever going to get over this?

'The *fake* tattoo,' said Jacob. 'Jesus. She's a clever one. Did she know your mother then? How would she know she had a tattoo like that?'

'I don't know. Old pictures, maybe? Maybe she knows someone who knew Mum ... Your guess is as good as mine. I never actually met Lucy's mum; I never even saw her close up really, just from a distance through her car window when she used to pick up Lucy from school. She was so bloody convincing though, wasn't she? She must have kept track somehow; she must have known that my mother was still missing. God, she even knew when her birthday was, everything. I've no idea how she did it, but ... it's almost impressive, isn't it?'

He nodded. 'It's amazing. And I suppose it wasn't just you who fell for it, was it? We all did. I mean, I'd only ever seen that one photo of your mother too, and as you say, Alison here is blonde, attractive ... close enough, considering how much time has passed. But we never even *thought* to question her, to ask for any proof of identity, did we? We're all idiots, every one of us.'

He slapped himself hard on the forehead and I managed a small smile.

'I'm the biggest idiot though. But I suppose I *wanted* to believe her, didn't I? When she said she was my mum, it was like all my birthdays and Christmases rolled into one. It was what I'd dreamed of for thirty years. I mean, I did notice that she was much less highly-strung, much more composed, I suppose, than I remember my mother being, but that comes with age, doesn't it? And all her yoga, and long walks, well ... I just thought she'd calmed down as she got older. And as you say, she does, to be fair, look a bit like what you'd imagine Mum to look like nowadays. About the right height, I think.

Blonde, West Country accent. Mum *could* look like that at sixty, and I wanted it to be her so much. I saw what I wanted to see, I suppose.'

'But your dad – I mean, how did she fool him?' he asked. Then he slapped his forehead again. 'Oh, his eyesight. Of course.'

I nodded. I'd been thinking about that.

'When I think back, she only agreed to come and see him after I told her he was virtually blind,' I said. 'And pretty much as soon as she got there she made sure he got a glimpse of her tattoo. That was enough for him. He didn't question it either. And of course nobody else here in Cheltenham ever knew her. If I still lived in Bristol, it might have been different, with old friends around and so on. But here she was able to get away with it.'

We talked about Liv then, and how she fits in to all this. She's Lucy's sister, if what Eleanor at the art gallery said was true, and my grief intensified, because of course now I don't have my longed-for sibling either. I am an only child again. We talked for two hours, me and my ex, longer than we've talked for a very long time, trying to work it all out and failing. When Jacob finally left, agreeing to keep the news to himself for now but telling me I needed to tell the doctors and the police, I nodded, promising I would. But since then I've just sat here, still numb with the shock of it all, paralysed with sadness.

My mother is still out there, somewhere. And she's never coming back, is she? My life is in ruins; it was in ruins yesterday too, but at least then I thought I had my mother by my side, helping me through it all. Today, everything's changed. This woman is not my ally, not my support. She's the architect of my demise, and I was so stupid, so gullible, so desperate for her to be who she said she was that I just opened the door to my life and let her in. I let her do it. I made it easy for her to do it. And yet, how angry am I allowed to be about this? Jacob's told me I must report her, that what she's done must be a crime of some sort – fraud, harassment, identity theft, something – but the problem is, she had every right to do what she's done. Finally, she's made me pay. Can I really blame her for that? And now that she's done it, and I know she's done it, what next? What happens now?

What actually happens now, right now, is that a sudden, tiny movement across the room catches my eye. Her arm, thin and bare, has, while I've been sitting here lost in thought somehow snaked out from under the covers; her hand is twitching on the thin white sheet, jerking as if someone is pricking her with a needle. I gasp.

And then she opens her eyes.

Chapter 38

'Hello, Alison. Mrs Allen,' I say.

I'm standing over her, watching, waiting. A strange calm has come over me now, and I feel oddly composed. My tears have dried and my legs are feeling strong and solid beneath me.

It's over, isn't it? She's done what she came to do and somehow I've survived it. She can't hurt me anymore.

She blinks once, twice. Her eyelids are crusty and her face is as pale as the bandage that's tightly wrapped around her head, and to my surprise I feel a wave of sympathy. This woman lost her little girl when she was just a few years older than Eloise is now, and when I try to imagine what that must have felt like, the agony she must have gone through, I just want to wrap my arms around her and sob. She must have hated me so much, for so long. What a way to live, with so much anguish and anger burning away inside you.

She's moving her hand slowly to her face, pushing the oxygen mask aside, and now I vaguely remember a doctor popping in hours ago saying they'd reduced her sedation, and asking me to push the call button if she showed any signs of waking. I will, but not just yet, I think. We need to talk first.

'Ahh. You've worked it out, then,' she rasps.

She swallows and clears her throat feebly, and I nod.

'I have,' I say. 'So. Want to talk about it?'

She blinks again.

'What happened to me?' she asks. Her voice is stronger now, her gaze more direct.

'I don't know. I came back to find all our guests standing in the driveway and you out cold on the floor inside. Don't you remember anything?'

There's a tiny shake of her head, and a wince.

'Only vaguely. Last thing I really remember is you going out to get the wine. I assume from the way my head feels that somebody hit me?'

'Hit you with my pelican lamp, apparently. Hope it's not broken. I love that lamp.'

Good Lord, I'm so calm I'm even making little jokes now.

But there's a flicker of a smile on her face too. We look at each other for a moment and then I turn away and walk across the room to pick up one of the plastic chairs. I put it down by the bed and take a seat.

'Right,' I say. 'I'm sitting comfortably. Shall we begin? Because I think you have rather a lot to tell me, don't you?'

She hesitates, but only for a moment.

'I suppose I do,' she says.

And so she begins. She's clearly in pain and her voice wavers from time to time, her face contorting with pain, but at the same time I feel she's revelling in her story. I find myself gripped, fascinated by the skill with which she wove the intricate web in which she trapped me, and then toyed with me, like a spider with a fly.

She didn't know my mother; I'd been right about that. But they did, it seems, have one mutual acquaintance in Bristol, and that acquaintance – a woman called Saffy – had become an unwitting source of vital information for Alison.

'I had this idea for years, to track you down. And then I remembered about your mother, and I wondered. I didn't know Saffy well, but I knew she'd known your mum. As time went by, I thought about her and wondered if she could give me a way in. And then, as if by fate, I went to a party back in Bristol a year or so ago, and there she was. I just brought it up in conversation, casually. *"Did that friend of yours who went missing back in the late 80s or early 90s ever come back? Anyone ever hear anything from her?"* When she told me your mother had never been heard from again, well, that was a gift. And when I told her I was fascinated by old missing-persons cases, that I fancied myself as a bit of an amateur detective and asked her if she had any more information, she was happy to tell me everything she could remember: Alice's birthday, bits and pieces about you and your dad, loads of stuff. Enough to make it work. When I asked for photos, and she emailed me one of your mother in a summer dress with her tattoo clearly visible, well, that was another gift. And it struck me then that actually we looked a bit alike as young women, me and her. And that was when I thought it might actually work. That I might be able to pretend to be her.'

She coughs, and I ask her if she needs some water. I hold

the cup while she takes a sip, all the time marvelling at how we're sitting here discussing this so calmly, as if it's something that's happened to someone else.

'I still had to find you though,' she says.

'And that was where Mike came in,' I reply. 'Why now though? Why wait *so* long?'

There are a few seconds of silence. Her eyes close briefly, then she says, 'I'm dying. I've got cancer, but you probably know that too now. It's not curable. I should have started treatment a while ago. I went to the hospital last week – that's actually why I went back to Cornwall, but, well, I'd thought about this for so long, you know? About finding you and making you pay. You got to live your life, Beth. My child died, and you got to live. And yes, I know you were only a child too, and a messed-up child. But that's no excuse, you know? I tried to find forgiveness. I couldn't. And then I got cancer, and I knew time was running out. So, what did I have to lose? It was worth a try. And my God, did it work out. Better than I could *ever* have hoped for.'

She practically spits the words at me, a spark back in her eyes and venom in her voice. A little shiver runs through me.

She really does hate me, doesn't she?

'I guessed quite soon after I arrived that you hadn't told anyone about Lucy,' she says. 'The fact that nobody ever mentioned it, and that you didn't tell me, your *mother*, during any of our *lovely* long chats. Your dad obviously moved you away for a fresh start, but I couldn't let that go on anymore, Beth. I wanted everyone to know what you'd done. I could have got somebody else to do it, you know? I could have done it a different way. But I wanted to be there myself. I wanted to watch as I slowly destroyed you, Beth. As you slowly destroyed *yourself*, like you destroyed me.'

I say nothing. There's nothing to say. She waits for a few moments, then inhales, exhales, and starts talking again.

'How good was my Liv though, playing your long-lost sister? With her blonde hair, I knew she'd get away with it. It's close enough in colour to yours, and you didn't even question it, did you? And of course, we both love acting. We both did a bit of amateur dramatics over the years; we were both good too, but that was nothing compared to this. Best performance of our lives.'

She smiles a satisfied smile and I remember the conversation Liv had with Eloise about her school play, how she told her being good at drama must run in the family.

'Bravo,' I say.

'I was going to confess all at the party – did you work that out?' she asks. 'I was going to tell everyone who I was, and what you did. Scuppered before the final act. That's annoying. Never mind. Can't have it all, I suppose.'

So that was your big special announcement, I think, and wonder again what happened in my house last night. Who attacked her? Who stopped her? But I haven't got time to dwell on that now because she's still talking.

'If you've been trying to get hold of Liv, she won't be picking up,' she says. 'I told her not to speak to you until I rang her and told her the deed was done. She'll be disappointed. She's the light of my life, Liv. I split up with Lucy's dad a year or so after we lost her. Our marriage just fell apart; our whole lives did. I moved away, travelled a bit, and ended up in Cornwall. When Liv came along ... I don't know. It was like I'd been given a second chance. It was true what I told you about her dad. He *was* an artist and he *did* scarper when he found out I was pregnant. It's just been the two of us since then, and when she was old enough, I told her all about Lucy, and about you. She's been on board with this from the very beginning. Yes, she'll be a bit disappointed the end of it didn't quite pan out, but still ... the rest worked rather well, didn't it?'

I shrug.

'It did.'

'Seeing your dad was a bit scary. That could have been the end of it,' she says, with a little laugh. 'Lucky he's almost blind. Took the risk when you told me that. Could hardly believe it when he fell for it too. Thank heavens for my stash of temporary tattoos. Got them designed specially – online place that copies real tats. Sent them the old photo. Worked like a dream. It all did.'

She coughs again, then recovers herself and looks at me steadily.

'Want to hear more?' she says.

I nod.

'Go on. Tell me everything. I'm intrigued.'

There's a hint of sarcasm in my voice now, but she doesn't seem to notice.

'With pleasure,' she says.

And so she does. She's on a roll suddenly, the words spilling out of her. There'd been rumours locally at the time apparently, gossip about the big age gap between my parents, about them falling out of love, about Mum being unhappy for a long time, according to Saffy. She'd been happy to share everything she'd heard, giving Alison what she needed to make the story she came to me with as convincing as possible. She had to invent certain things of course because nobody knows where my mother went when she left, but she stuck mainly to the truth about her own life and her work, knowing that the fewer lies she told, the easier it would be not to slip up. She'd been hugely relieved, she said, when she heard that Dad had never really looked for Mum after she'd gone.

'That made it so much easier,' she said. 'I could kind of say anything after I knew that because who would know if I was telling the truth or not?'

And, after all, she only needed to fool us all for a short time, didn't she? She started her 'campaign', as she put it, as soon as possible after I'd accepted her into my home, subtly making me self-conscious about my weight, buying me a top a size too small, starting to play with my mind. She made me distrustful of Robin, of everyone. She paid Mike to hang around (*it was him. I knew it, I knew it! He lied to me on the phone – of course he did*) to make sure I saw him talking to my friends.

'How did you manage that? How did you get him there just at the right time, every time?' I asked, remembering how he kept popping up wherever I happened to be.

'He knew what all your friends looked like from when he was tracking you down for me initially,' she said. 'After I moved in with you it was easy. With Robin, that was the day you were looking for your keys, and when Mike texted me to say he was about to nab Robin in the street – he'd been lurking, waiting for her to arrive for work – I told you to go out and check the driveway and the bit round the bins, to see if you'd dropped the keys there, remember?'

I did.

'At the surgery he just waited until he saw you come out to talk to your homeless friend and made sure you spotted him. And with your neighbours, well, that was the night we went out for pizza. I just texted him when the taxi arrived and he made sure he was still chatting to those two stupid women when you came out. He wore different clothes each time, made sure he changed his appearance a bit – one day a gardener, one day a plumber, you know – so you wouldn't be quite sure. Screwing with your head again. Nice touch, wasn't it?'

She grins widely, clearly pleased with herself, but I don't react.

'Oh, and those missing keys ... that was me too,' she says. 'I nicked them. Twice actually, but the second time was just for fun. You only gave me a front door key, you see, and I needed to get a full set of keys copied ...'

'Why?' I ask.

She keeps on talking then, telling me everything, explaining it all until my face is hot with anger, my body so tense I'm starting to ache. And then, finally, she's done. I can tell she's struggling now; exhaustion is etched on her face.

'Can you call a nurse, please?' she says. Her voice is weak

and I remember that this is not just a very sad woman but a very sick woman, and I feel ashamed all over again.

'Yes,' I whisper, and stand up. I'm just about to press the call button when the door opens and the two police officers from last night walk into the room.

'Mrs Holland, hello. We need to speak to you urgently. And actually, I believe you need to speak to us too? We've just had a call from your ex-husband. Something about some sort of fraudulent behaviour, about your mother not being your mother after all? The line was bad and we got cut off unfortunately, but that seemed to be the gist of it.'

The male officer looks from me to the bed and I curse silently.

Bloody Jacob. Couldn't you just have left this to me?

I glance at Alison but her eyes are closed now, her breathing fast and shallow. I know I need to call somebody, quickly. I turn back to the police officer, suddenly feeling oddly protective.

'It's complicated, but it's not a police matter. I mean, we still need to find out who attacked her, but, well ...'

The policeman interrupts me, waving a piece of paper he's carrying in his hand.

'Well, if she's *not* your mother, it helps explain something we're getting very confused about. We already have the initial forensics report, you see,' he says, and turns to his colleague.

'We do,' says the female officer. 'And the good news is that we have some of the perpetrator's DNA and fingerprints now, from the lamp that was used as the weapon. It's not a match to any on the police database unfortunately, so it wasn't left by anyone with a criminal record. But ... well, this is the strange thing. You'll remember we took a DNA sample from the victim last night, and you kindly gave us a sample of *your* DNA and fingerprints too, both for elimination purposes?'

I nod. Last night seems like a lifetime ago, a blur really, but I remember a swab in my mouth and touching my finger-tips onto an electronic tablet. It was some sort of digital scanner and I remember feeling surprised by that, having expected an inky pad like I've seen on so many television crime dramas.

'Well, Ian at the lab – he's a bit of a DNA whizz – noticed something about two of the samples: yours and one found on the lamp. So he did some sort of test – I can't remember what it's called. And it turns out the DNA sample on the lamp belongs to your mother.'

'My ... what?'

I stare at her and she stares back.

'I know,' she says. 'So at first we thought, hang on, the victim here *is* Mrs Holland's mother. So that would mean she'd bashed *herself* over the head with the lamp, which seems highly unlikely. But not all of the lamp DNA matches that of the victim; her blood is on it, obviously, but the attacker left a sample too, and that's the one we're talking about. And then your ex-husband called, telling us that this lady isn't your mother at all, but has just been pretending to be in some sort of scam. Ian at the lab confirms that the lady in the bed definitely *isn't* your mother. And your ex told us that in fact you haven't actually been in contact with your real mother for decades. Which is very odd, because—'

'Hang on, hang on.'

I'm completely lost.

'Can you start again? Yes, OK, I know *she*'—I point to Alison—'I know she isn't my mother. Her name is actually Alison Allen. I didn't know that last night, but I do now. But are you saying that the person who used the lamp to attack *her*'—I point to the bed again—'was my mother? My biological mother?'

'Correct. Ian's positive about that. I remember now; it's called a maternity DNA test. It's ninety-nine point nine nine per cent accurate, apparently. But Mr Holland says you aren't in touch with your biological mother, so we don't really understand how that's possible.'

A strange buzzing sound has started in my ears and I'm wondering if I'm about to faint. I reach out a hand and lean on the back of the nearest chair for support. I've never felt so confused in my life.

'I'm sorry, I just ... I just don't understand.'

The police officer looks at me quizzically.

'You do look pale, actually. Right, let me make this as simple as I can. The DNA tests have shown that this lady – Alison Allen? – was attacked last night by your biological mother. She left her DNA on the lamp, as well as in one or two other locations in your home – slightly older samples apparently. I don't understand how that's possible, if you say you're not in contact. But it looks like the victim here let her in, as there was no sign of any forced entry. Mrs Holland, your biological mother, was in your house yesterday. There's absolutely no doubt about that.'

Chapter 39

'Alison! You need to wake up, now!'

I hiss the words fiercely, poking her on the shoulder for good measure. She groans softly, eyes still closed.

'Alison! *Come on*.'

After dropping their bombshell, the police have left, saying they'll be back to interview Alison as soon as she's well enough to speak. I've had to give them details about my mother too, now that she's the prime suspect in the case – not that I've been able to tell them much. Her full name is about all I've got. Now I'm in shock; my legs are wobbly, my skin clammy.

'Alison!' I say again, louder this time, and finally her eyelids flutter. She blinks once, twice, and I lean over her, willing her to stay awake.

'Alison, I need to talk to you urgently, OK? Just for a minute, and then I'll call a nurse for you.'

'Ummm ...' she says, then swallows, blinks again and says, 'What is it?'

'OK, good. Look, the police have just been here and they've told me something incredible, something totally bizarre. They've now got DNA evidence and it shows that the person who attacked you last night was my mother. My *real mother*. Alice. And I know you said you can't really remember anything, but I need you to think, Alison. I need you to think very, very hard. The police will be coming back to talk to you too; they're going to want a description – anything you've got. So come on, *think*. What happened last night? What did she look like, the person who attacked you? You must have let her in ... so *come on*. I need to know. You have to tell me anything you can remember. *Anything* ...'

And then I stare at her in astonishment because she's grinning. Not just grinning, laughing. Actually laughing, a low, rumbling laugh, her chest heaving.

'What ... what the ...?' I splutter. She coughs and her laughter fades.

'Ahhh, this is funny,' she whispers. 'Funny, and so ironic, don't you think?'

I'm still staring at her, not understanding, and she rolls her eyes.

'So ironic that the person who stopped me pretending to be your mother was actually your mother,' she says. 'You're not very bright, are you, Beth? You let me walk into your life, no questions asked. And you let your actual mother do the same, didn't you?'

'What? Look, I have no idea what you're talking about.'

She smiles.

'I know, and that's what's so funny. OK, what the hell. I'm going to tell you something, Beth. But first, I want you to promise something. I'll tell *you* this, but I'm going to carry on telling the police I can't remember anything about last night, OK? And in return, I'm asking you not to make any formal complaint against me for impersonating your mother, or for any of the things I've done to you over the past couple of months. I haven't got much time left, Beth, and I don't have time for a police investigation, for possible charges. I want to spend my final days with Liv. With my *daughter*.'

I stare at her for a moment – *what on earth is going on here?* – and then I nod.

'I promise,' I say.

She sighs.

'OK. I lied earlier, Beth. When I said I only had vague memories of last night. I know exactly what happened. And yes, I did let her in. I didn't know she was your mother, not until a few minutes later, not until she told me. But I let her in because I knew who she was. As in, I recognised her. She wasn't a stranger.'

'You ... you recognised her? What do you mean you *recognised* her?'

I'm starting to feel dizzy, spots dancing before my eyes. She sighs again. Her voice is weakening; it is barely audible.

'I mean, Beth, that I knew who she was. Or who she's been *saying* she is, anyway. Your mother is someone you already know. Someone you've known for a while, actually. I'm not surprised you didn't recognise her, I suppose. I certainly didn't – she looks very different these days from the photos I've seen of her from back in the day. And I have no idea why she hasn't told you who she is. But you know what, I'm not going to tell you who she is either. I'm going to let you work that one out for yourself.'

Chapter 40

'I can't take this in. I just can't. It gets more bizarre by the day.'

Jacob shakes his head and takes another slurp of his coffee, and Crystal, who's sitting next to me while he paces up and down the kitchen, looks at me incredulously.

'It really does. You should write a book, Beth.'

'Hmmm. Well, I'm hoping I'll be able to go back to work soon now. But if that doesn't pan out, maybe!'

I laugh, and she does too. It's the Sunday morning of the most extraordinary weekend of my life, a weekend during which I seem to have experienced every possible emotion from terror and despair to utter bewilderment. But now I'm feeling ... OK. I'm still struggling to process the scale of Alison Allen's deception, and my own naiveness in falling for it, of course. Why I didn't even *think* to question her identity when she first arrived is something that will haunt me for a long time. But now that I know what's really been going on over the past couple of months, that I'm not, after all, delusional or having some sort of breakdown, the relief is overwhelming. And already, my life has taken a turn for the better. The children are home, both of them upstairs now and settling back into their bedrooms. They are calling to each other across the landing, the sound of their giggles floating down to where we're sitting and it makes my spirits soar.

'It's time they came back,' Jacob said when they arrived this morning. 'And I'm sorry, Beth. I should have trusted you. I should have realised something wasn't right ...'

'Shh, it's fine. I'm just so thrilled to see them,' I said.

He's done his best to explain things to Eloise and Finley, without going into too much detail; that the lady they thought was their grandmother was actually somebody else, trying to hurt Mummy because of something that happened a very long time ago. Amazingly, they seem to have accepted that for now, although I suspect Eloise will have some questions when she's had time to settle back in and think about things a little more. She appears to have forgiven me though, for all the things she was so mad at me about. The hugs they both gave me in the hallway earlier were long and warm, and as I wrapped my arms around them and kissed their beautiful faces, I thought my heart might burst. My babies, home again.

I've spent the past hour chatting to Jacob and Crystal, filling them in about all I've learned. After Alison's remarkable revelation that her attacker, my biological mother – *how the hell?* – was someone she already knew, she'd refused to say another word. She'd closed her eyes and her breathing had become shallow. I'd stood there staring at her for a full minute, my mind racing, my heart juddering. Then I called the nurse, picked up my bag, and left. On the way home I left another message for Liv, this time telling her I knew the truth, who she was and who Alison was, and told her to come and get her mother. It was over. Over. All of it.

I didn't call anyone else last night. Instead I came home, made a mug of tea and sat in the lounge, looking out at the darkening sky, thinking. And then I went to bed and amazingly, managed to sleep. I was physically and mentally exhausted after a day and a night at the hospital and the astonishing events of the past twenty-four hours. But my dreams were vivid and plentiful, plagued by visions of a faceless woman brandishing a lamp and peering in through my window. When I woke I remembered the times I'd thought I'd seen a real face outside my window, and lay there in the half-light of dawn, wondering. I'd asked Alison about that yesterday, and she'd shrugged.

'That was nothing to do with me,' she said. 'Still think you were seeing things.'

And so the question of who'd been lurking outside the house remained unanswered, for now. Weirdly, I believed everything she'd told me yesterday, for what did she have to gain by lying now? She'd done what she'd set out to do, and now she was dying. There was no point in lying anymore. Oh, she'd enjoyed it though, hadn't she, that last brief conversation? She'd enjoyed leaving me with this one final mystery. But the deal we'd made had been a single tiny kindness: I make no complaint about her to the police, and in return she gives me the chance to find my mother before they do.

What Alison had said had sounded ludicrous, impossible. How could my mother be someone I already knew, someone I'd already 'let into my life', as she put it? And yet, as she'd also kindly pointed out, *she'd* managed to fool me pretty easily. Was it so far-fetched to think that someone else might have been able to do the same? *Why* my long-lost mother would do that escaped me, but that was another question which would have to wait. I needed to work out who she was first. And so I started to think, really think about it, to think again about the people in my life who've definitely been acting oddly recently. Remembering too that all of their oddness began shortly after Alison arrived on the scene.

Robin. Barbara. Deborah

I thought about how Robin had reacted when I told her about my mum reappearing, how utterly shocked she had seemed. How she'd simply stared when I'd first introduced her to Alison, and then seemed to recover before bombarding her with questions. How when I'd told Brenda she'd shrieked with excitement on the other end of the phone, in stark contrast to Barbara, who'd responded with a stunned silence. It had been a similar picture at work: Ruth leaping from her chair, Deborah sitting open-mouthed, gaping at me. She'd said it was 'impossible' – that was the word she'd used, wasn't it?

Could I really be onto something here?

So I thought some more. Thought about how all of these women had appeared in my life in the past couple of years. How they're all about the right age, too. OK, so my mother's birthday was last week, at the end of April, and as far as I can remember Barbara's is in June and Deborah's in July, but people can lie about their birthdays, can't they? I'm not sure when Robin's is, and I wondered why I don't know and whether that's significant. And then I thought about how none of them *look* like my mother at all, not how I remember her at least, but also about the fact that I haven't seen her for thirty years and people can change so much as they age. What did I know about their pasts, their families, these women? Again, very little about Robin's. She's so private; she gives so little away about her personal life, and again that made me wonder. Meanwhile, Barbara is gay, and I thought hard about that.

If my mother was secretly gay, back then when times were so different, could she have married a man because she felt unable to be her true self and then realised she couldn't live a lie? Maybe.

And Deborah? She didn't marry her husband Gavin until her mid-forties, and has, she says, no children. Again, was that significant, I wondered? But then I carried on thinking and wondered again why on earth my real mother would arrive back in my life, make friends with me, and not reveal herself to me. I could come up with no rational answer to that, and so I gave up, busying myself with readying the house for the children's return. Now, Jacob and Crystal are as baffled as I am.

'It's *crazy*. And why did she attack Alison? I can't believe she won't tell you who she is. Well, I suppose I can, really ... What are the police doing to find her?' asks Jacob.

'Not sure. I couldn't give them much to go on,' I say. 'They want to interview me properly in the next day or so and talk to Alison again too, when she's feeling better. But I believe her when she says she won't tell them anything, I really do. There's no CCTV anywhere around here otherwise they could look at that to see who came to the house on Friday afternoon, maybe get a picture they could circulate. They're going to do some house-to-house enquiries to see if anyone noticed anyone coming or going, but if Alison let her in, well ... I mean it wasn't as if they were scuffling on the doorstep or anything.'

'So you really think it could be Robin? Or Deborah. Or Barbara? Seriously?'

Jacob's stopped pacing now and is leaning against the kitchen worktop, picking icing off one of the cupcakes sitting on a plate next to him – the cakes that had been intended for Friday's abandoned party.

'Well, they've certainly all been in the house recently,' Crystal says slowly, 'and they all know Alison of course, and could have talked their way in on Friday afternoon. The police said the DNA was elsewhere, too, not just on the lamp, didn't they? Do you know where they found it? That might help narrow it down.'

I shake my head.

'No, I don't. I was in too much shock to ask sensible questions like that. You're right, though. That might help. I can ask, maybe?'

'Do,' says Crystal. 'So ... what now? Are you just going to confront them, these women? Ask them if they're actually your *mother*? How weird is that going to be?'

'Don't,' I say. 'I have *no* idea how to go about it. I need to think a *lot* before I say anything.'

'OK, well ... come on, more detail about Alison Allen and her campaign against you. Shall I put the kettle on again?' Jacob asks, and I nod.

'Please. This might take a while,' I say.

And so, fresh cup of coffee in hand, I start talking, relaying the remarkable story that Alison told me yesterday.

'It was the so-called taxi driver who drove us when we went out for pizza that night, right at the beginning, who fitted the hidden cameras in my bedroom and bathroom,' I tell them. They're both open-mouthed, agog, like children at nursery story time.

'He was actually a friend of Mum— Gosh, it's still really weird not to call her that. Of *Alison's*, I mean, who does that sort of thing for a living. The taxi was just a ruse. She'd stolen my keys the day before – I was going mad trying to find them – and she got him a full set cut. He dropped us off in town and came back and let himself in. They were tiny little pinhole things, apparently. They connected to our wifi so he could access the pictures remotely. When he'd got enough, he came back when it was just Alison in the house and took the cameras out again, which was obviously why there was nothing here when I got the house swept.'

'Wow. Sneaky,' says Jacob.

'I know. It makes sense now that she didn't push it when I wondered if I should go to the police about the pictures too. That's the last thing she would have wanted. This bloke sent the footage to that horrible website and hacked my Facebook account to post the link. She told him to use the name Daphne Blake to try and freak me out, which of course it did. It was Lucy's nickname at school, you see. She guessed I'd remember that, and she was right; that was when I finally realised what was behind everything that was going on. She was the one who tipped off the newspaper reporter too. She'd been hoping he'd tell the whole story about what happened with Lucy but obviously he couldn't, for legal reasons. That was why she decided to out me at the party instead.'

I remember, then, how she'd cried that day the newspaper article came out. How she'd mentioned Lucy and sobbed. *She was crying for her lost daughter, not for me, wasn't she?* I think. And then I think of the day I asked her, weeks ago, if she'd kept in touch with anyone at all, if she knew anything of what I'd got up to in my school days; I think of her tears that day too, and my heart quivers. When she first arrived, she'd said something like: *'You never forget your child's face, do you?'* Now I know what she really meant: 'You never forget the face of the girl who killed your daughter, do you?'

We'd never actually met, not back then. But there would have been school photos. It wouldn't have been hard for her to find out what I looked like.

'Wow,' says Crystal. 'Beth, I do understand why you didn't confide in us earlier about that, I really do.'

At my request, Jacob had filled her in about me and Lucy Allen last night, and she'd been kindness personified, hugging me almost as hard as the kids had when she arrived this morning.

'But I really wish you had. We might have been able to help, to work out who was behind it all ...'

'I know. I was an idiot. Thanks, Crystal.'

For a few seconds, nobody speaks. Upstairs, Eloise has turned her music on, the *thump thump* of a Little Mix track drifting through the ceiling.

'She was so convincing in getting me to blame Robin for everything too,' I say. 'Making up all that stuff about her acting suspiciously in my bedroom and bathroom. She admitted none of that happened. She made it up to cover the fact that she'd moved some of my stuff around herself, trying to work out the best place for her mate to put those cameras. I believed her, because I'd seen Robin looking at papers on my desk and stuff once or twice, so I already had a few doubts about her. I need to apologise to Robin, if she'll let me. God, I even blamed her for messing with the central heating.'

'Alison, again?' asks Crystal.

'Yep. She told me she kept whacking it up to the hottest possible setting, and then making sure she turned it back down to normal again before I checked it. Robin was constantly asking her too many questions, she said, and she *wanted* me to blame her, wanted me to get rid of her. Gosh, so many things. She destroyed that letter of Eloise's, so I never saw it and so she missed her school trip. And then, of course, there was the trampoline incident.'

'Shit. Was that her too? The evil *bitch*!' says Jacob.

'Shh ... no swearing. Remember, the kids are just upstairs,' Crystal hisses.

'Sorry, but she could have bloody killed one of them,' he says. 'What did she do, tamper with it after you'd set it up?'

'Yep. First she hid the spring puller tool so I thought I was going mad. And then she loosened a screw or something, knowing it would probably cause an accident. She didn't even seem to care that Finley got hurt.'

'Christ,' says Jacob, and shakes his head slowly, his mouth set in a grim line.

I knew how he feels. A chill had gone through me when Alison had told me about that. There'd been a coldness in her eyes, and I knew exactly what she was thinking.

You took my daughter away from me. Why shouldn't I have at least tried to take one of your children away from you?

'She wrote an anonymous letter to Gabby at work too,' I say, and I tell them about that. They look horrified again.

'It was classic coercive control, when you think about it,' says Crystal. 'Slowly, very slowly, eroding all your self-confidence. Making you feel bad about your weight and your body. Making you think you were going crazy, humiliating you in front of your friends, making you feel like you were a bad mother. Getting rid of Robin, and even making things so bad here that Jacob took the kids, so you'd be even more isolated. What an actress though. BAFTA-worthy performance. Hey, you fell out with Brenda and Barbara as well, didn't you? Do you think she could have had a role in that too?'

'Oh. Flipping heck, maybe. I hadn't even considered that,' I say.

'So nasty,' says Jacob darkly. 'You must hate her. She put you through hell.'

'I don't know how I feel about her,' I say. 'She was so clever, always making it seem like she was on my side when everyone else was against me. She even told me she felt bad talking about her past because she didn't want it to seem like she'd had a great life without me. I know why she was sometimes so reticent now, don't I? I'm just glad it's over, and that I never have to see her again.'

It's true. I really don't know how I feel about Alison anymore. Yes, I'm appalled that she was able to fool me like that, to ruin my life so comprehensively. And yet, I understand completely. She needed to do it, and I made that possible. Now maybe we can both find a little peace. She's taken her revenge, and I've been punished, and now it's over. And, odd though this may sound, I *liked* her. I even have a tiny, sneaking suspicion that she liked me too sometimes, although I'm not a hundred per cent sure about that. But she was funny and glamorous and entertaining, and I liked her. I *wanted* her to be my mother; I was proud that she was my mother.

Except she wasn't, was she? And now I have to find out who is.

'So, what's your next move, Beth?' asks Crystal.

I hesitate for a few seconds, but I already know the answer.

'Today I'm spending with Eloise and Finley,' I say. 'But tomorrow, I'm going to start asking some serious questions, guys.'

Jacob and Crystal look at each other, eyebrows raised. Then Jacob grins.

'Fair enough. Good luck, Beth.'

'Thanks,' I say. 'I'll keep you posted.'

Chapter 41

It's Monday morning, and after I've dropped the kids off at school, asked Jacob to collect them later to give me some more time, and rung the surgery to tell Gabby I'm coming in later today for a chat, my first job is to go and see Dad. I tell him about Alison Allen as succinctly as possible, and at first he's shocked and disbelieving, then upset.

'I'm a fool, Beth,' he says. 'I thought it was her too. That tattoo ... I'm so sorry, love. The *disappointment* for you ...'

To my horror, tears spring to his eyes and I grab his hand, rubbing it gently and telling him it's fine, *I'm* fine, it will all be fine.

'I knew it would catch up with me eventually, Dad,' I say. 'Lucy Allen, and everything that happened back then. Now that it's finally happened, it's almost a relief, you know? It's not hanging over me anymore. I'm OK, honestly.'

And strangely, I really am. I feel freer somehow, even though I know what I'm about to do in the next day or so is, quite frankly, preposterous. As I drove to Holly Tree this morning, I remembered a book I used to read to Finley when he was a toddler, one of those big colourful hardbacks with lots of pictures and few words. It was by P.D. Eastman and was called *Are You My Mother?* It was the story of a baby bird who hatches while his mother is away from the nest and he goes off looking for her, asking first other creatures and then even a boat and a plane if they're his mummy.

That's me, isn't it? I thought. A lost bird, asking everyone and anyone. What *am* I doing?

I don't tell Dad anything about my real mum allegedly being the one who attacked Alison – it's too weird and too complicated to explain. If I find her I'll tell him all about it, obviously, but for now I'm on a mission and I need to focus. Sitting in the car outside the care home I text Brenda, knowing that Monday is one of her days off from the boutique. I tell her I need to see her, and Barbara too if possible, telling her something momentous has happened, something I *have* to talk to them about. I'm half expecting my text to be ignored, but within minutes there's a ping from my phone.

OK. Hope you're all right? We could both pop round in about half an hour, about 11.30?

To my surprise, I feel like crying. I've missed them so much, and now I desperately want to try to get back to where we were before. As I drive home though, I try to collect my thoughts, wondering how best to ask the questions I need to ask, which now seem even more ludicrous than they did yesterday.

'But my mother *is* somebody I know,' I keep telling myself. 'Remember that. I've *got* to do this.'

It's already eleven-fifteen by the time I open the front door. I turn the kettle on and assemble mugs, plates, and cake, grateful for the still-present party food. I bustle around feeling jittery and nervous while my stomach flutters, and when the doorbell rings I have to make myself stand still and take a few deep breaths before I answer it. They're standing there, shoulder to shoulder, Brenda in a floaty floral tunic and Barbara in a green jumper and jeans. She looks rosy-cheeked and noticeably fresher-looking than the last few times I've seen her, I notice.

Are you my mother? You can't be, surely? This is ridiculous …

'Hello. Thank you so much for coming.'

They look as on edge as I feel, with tight smiles and muted greetings, but Brenda is carrying a little posy of flowers which she holds out to me.

'Picked from the garden this morning,' she says.

It's lovely – pansies and freesias tied with red twine – and I feel my nerves easing a little. I make the drinks and we sit in the kitchen, and for a few moments there's an awkward silence.

'Well, here we go. Let me tell you a story,' I say. And then I tell them the whole incredible tale of Alison Allen, watching their faces carefully as I do so – Barbara's especially. They're both looking similarly astounded though, and I carry on, with growing anxiety, explaining *why* Alison did what she did. Because of what *I* did, to Lucy.

Alison wanted to do this, didn't she? I think. She wanted to out me to my friends, and now she's forced me to do it myself. She's won, but I don't even care anymore. No more secrets.

And so I tell them everything, and their eyes grow wider and wider as they listen, little gasps coming from slack-jawed mouths, and when I've finished Brenda leaps from her stool and throws her arms around me.

'Beth ... oh my goodness, I can't believe this! And honestly, what happened back then, I mean, it's awful, dreadful, so sad but, well, we all make mistakes. And you were so young and so unhappy. You're a different person now, aren't you? And— Oh gosh, now I'm wondering ... oh my goodness, did Alison lie to us too?'

She releases me, spinning round to look at Barbara who claps her hands to her face.

'Oh no! Bren, do you think so? I was *so* surprised, so upset by what she said, and it seemed so unlike Beth ...'

'What? What did she say?' I ask. They're both wearing horrified expressions now, and Brenda turns back to me and clasps both of my hands in hers.

'She said ... well, it was that last night when we came round, and you had a little bit too much to drink and fell asleep? Well, your mum'—she rolls her eyes—'not your mum. That *woman* ... When you fell asleep, she took us out here into the kitchen and said there was something she thought we should know. She told us that you'd been laughing about us, and saying how sad it was that you only had boring old women as neighbours, and that you only hung out with us because we were quite useful as babysitters and so on. She said she'd been a bit shocked by that, because she could see we weren't old; we were about the same age as her but she felt she should tell us because she didn't think it was right, her daughter disrespecting us like that ...'

'What? I didn't ... I would *never* ... Oh Brenda, Barb, honestly, how could you think that?'

I'm aghast. This is awful, *awful*, and now I'm remembering what Alison told me the next day and I realise that she gambled on playing us off against each other, and that it had worked.

'Listen, she said pretty much the same thing to me. She said that you two had told her how odd you thought it was that I didn't have friends my own age, and that you only hung out with me because you felt sorry for me, because I didn't have a mother, and that now that she was back you said that she could take over now, or something like that. And I was so upset because I thought we were friends, but she was so convincing ... Oh shit, why didn't we talk about this sooner? Why didn't we have it out with each other? We might have rumbled her!'

'Oh. My. God,' says Brenda dramatically. 'What. A. *Cow*.'

We all look at each other and we start to laugh, and suddenly everything in my world is just a little brighter, a little shinier, than it was ten minutes ago.

'What twits we are,' I say. 'We've wasted so much time.'

'We have. But the Busy Bees are back! Group hug?' says Barbara, standing up, and Brenda and I smile and stand up too. We have one of those lovely, silly, swaying-from-side-to-side hugs, and then we sit down again, all of us with broad grins on our faces.

'OK,' I say. 'So now ... well, now I have something else to tell you. To ask you, really.'

'Uh-oh,' says Brenda.

Again, I'm watching Barbara as I relay the news that my real mum was the one who attacked Alison, but again she looks no more and no less shocked than Brenda does, both of them open-mouthed again.

'But ... *how*? I don't understand,' splutters Brenda.

'No idea. But it was her. There seems no doubt about that, from both the police and from Alison,' I say. 'She was here, in this house, on Friday.'

Brenda looks around the kitchen with a wary expression, as if half expecting my mother to leap out of one of the cupboards.

'I don't get it. That's *so* creepy,' she says.

'Barbara ...' I begin, then stop, and she looks at me quizzically.

'Yes?'

I inhale and blow the air out again.

Just say it, Beth.

'Look, this is probably completely off the wall, but ... it's not you, is it? It's just that you've been acting really, well, *strangely* recently, ever since Alison arrived. You looked so shocked when you first met her, and then you were so quiet when you came round, just not yourself, and, well, it just made me think ...'

She clasps her hands to her mouth again, and my stomach lurches.

'Oh, Beth, I'm so sorry ... Brenda?'

She looks at Brenda, who nods.

'Better tell her, quickly!'

My heart has started to pound.

'Tell me what? You're not are you?'

'No! No, Beth. I found a lump. In my breast. I should have told you ages ago, but first I didn't want to spoil your reunion with your mother, and then after we fell out ... I was so scared, you see. My mother died from breast cancer and that should have made me go and get it checked immediately, but instead I did exactly the opposite. I was so frightened it was cancer that I buried my head in the sand and I didn't tell anyone. But it was eating me up, the fear and the worry, and that's why I was so distracted. I wasn't myself for weeks ...'

She's standing up now, looking flushed and agitated.

'Oh no, I'm so sorry, *so* sorry. And what now? Are you ... are you OK?'

She sighs and nods.

'I am. I finally told Brenda and she made me face it – even came with me to the doctor. It was just a cyst in the end; I'm absolutely fine. But, oh Beth, I'm so sorry that I made you think ... Well, I'm just so sorry.'

A tumult of emotions washes over me but it's mainly relief that my friend is OK. I swallow and try to smile.

'That's all right. And I'm so glad for you. That's great news.'

'Oh, Beth. What a big mess, eh?'

She takes a step closer. Her eyes are soft and she cups her hands gently around my face.

'My darling girl, I never had children. But if I had, I'd have loved to have one just like you.'

I touch my hands to hers, and I know I'm about to cry, and also that it doesn't really matter if I do. I'm safe here.

'You're not my mother. One down,' I whisper, and she smiles and shakes her head.

'And I'm not either, just for the record,' says Brenda. 'Two down then. Who's next, Beth?'

Chapter 42

Next is the surgery and I get there mid afternoon; the sun is warm on my bare arms as I pause outside the front door, bracing myself and wondering if I should have dressed more smartly. I'm just wearing jeans and a T-shirt, but it's too late now. I grit my teeth and push the door open, stopping at reception to ask Ruth if there's any chance I can speak to her and Deborah – ideally together – at some point in the next couple of hours.

'It's important. Really, really important,' I say, and she nods, looking alarmed.

'OK. I can make it happen,' she says, and I thank her and head for Gabby's room.

'You look better, Beth,' is the first thing she says to me, which surprises me. I've barely looked in a mirror since Friday night.

'Thanks,' I say. 'Gabby, I have some stuff to tell you. And I'm desperately hoping that when I do, you'll let me come back to work. But there's something ... well, there's something you need to know, something I never told you, which may have an impact on that, and ... oh gosh, I'm really nervous, I'm sorry.'

She looks intrigued.

'Okaaaay,' she says slowly. 'Well, take a deep breath, and just tell me, OK? I'm listening.'

And so I begin. As everyone has so far, she looks more and more dumbfounded as I tell the story, and when I tell her about Alison's reason for hunting me down in the first place, her eyes fill with tears.

'That's ... that's horrendous. I'm so sorry that happened, Beth. For Lucy, and for her mother, and her whole family. But for you too. To know that what you did had such terrible consequences, well ...'

I swallow hard. This was what I'd feared the most about telling Gabby: that she and the other partners would feel they didn't want me working here anymore, that they couldn't countenance employing someone with such a dark, evil stain on her character. I wouldn't blame them, of course, and so I sit and wait, watching her, feeling sick as she wipes her eyes and turns back to look at me, her eyes boring into mine.

'I think you've paid for it though, haven't you, Beth?' she says quietly. 'Not just recently with everything Alison put you through. But I'm guessing you've been paying for this your whole life, in here.'

She taps the side of her head, and the tears do come now, rolling down my cheeks as I nod.

'I've felt guilty every single day since,' I whisper.

'OK,' she says. 'I'm going to think about how we move forward with this. Is there any more you need to tell me?'

I sniff.

'There is, actually,' I say. I start talking again, and when I get to the bit about my biological mother she actually leaps from her chair.

'What? Are you *serious*?'

I shrug.

'I can't quite believe it myself, but yes, apparently.'

'But ... how? Beth, I'm flabbergasted. I don't even know what to say. And you're now trying to work out who it is? I can't believe Alison wouldn't tell you. Gosh, I have so many questions!'

She's walking backwards and forwards across the narrow space behind her desk now, shaking her head in wonderment.

'Not half as many as I have, I promise you,' I say, and she stops pacing and laughs.

'I'm sure. So you want to come back to work? I'll need to talk to the others about it, Beth. But I think it'll be OK. The past is another country, isn't it, or whatever the phrase is. I think it's time you tried to put it all behind you, and if you can do that, I think we can too. If you're sure you're up to it?'

'Oh Gabby, thank you so much.'

I feel weak with relief.

'Thank you,' I say again. 'And I am up to it, I really am. All of the things that happened, well, it was all her, wasn't it? OK, so I was drinking too much, and I can't blame her for that; that was all me unfortunately – a bad way of coping with everything that was going on. But I've knocked that on the head now, Gabby, I promise. I'm feeling good, and I want to come back, if you'll have me. But maybe next Monday?

That'd give me a week to try to get to the bottom of this mother mystery.'

She plants both hands on her desk and leans across it, looking at me silently for a few seconds. Then she smiles.

'Of course. As I said, I'll need to clear it with the others. But we've missed you. I'll give the temp who's been covering a week's notice. Beth, you don't think it's anyone here, do you? Your real mother? You're close to Ruth, aren't you? And Deborah? Alison had met both of them more than once, hadn't she?'

I stand up.

'Maybe. I don't know. That's my next job, actually. I'm going to go and talk to them now.'

She lets out a low whistle.

'Wow. Keep me posted, OK?'

'I will.'

I have to wait half an hour until Ruth and Deborah are free, so I go to the staffroom, grateful to find it empty, and make a mug of tea. I sit at the table and sip slowly, trying to stay calm, but I'm too nervous, too agitated, to sit still for long, and when Ruth finally pops her head round the door to say they're both ready, and that maybe we'd have more privacy in Deborah's room, I'm hopping from foot to foot and simmering with nervous tension.

'Do you need the loo?' Ruth says with a sidelong glance, as we leave the room. I shake my head.

'No. I'm just a bit anxious. You'll see why in a minute,' I say.

'Blimey. OK, come on then,' she says, and seconds later

we're in Deborah's cosy little consulting room, just big enough for her small desk, a filing cabinet, and a treatment bed. There's only one spare chair so I tell Ruth to take that and I perch on the bed, its paper covering rustling as I sit down.

'Right,' I say. 'Here we go.'

And I tell my story again, watching both faces carefully. I'm used to the reaction now. When I reach the part about Lucy, again starting to feel ill, Ruth visibly recoils.

'Beth ... wow. That's a bit of a curve ball.'

'I know. I'm so sorry. It was such a long time ago ... I'm not making excuses; I was a vile kid back then. I've never forgiven myself, and now, well ...'

I look from Ruth to Deborah. They both look shocked, and who can blame them?

'I just thought it was time to come clean with everyone. I've kept the secret for so many years,' I say. 'Maybe Alison did me a favour. Now you all know and you can decide whether you can still stand to be around me or not.'

There's a long silence, broken only by a ping from Deborah's computer – an email notification. She glances at the screen then turns to me.

'Well, I can't speak for Ruth, but the Beth I know is very different to what you've just described. You're kind and thoughtful and loving, and I for one am happy to leave the past in the past. Ruth?'

Ruth looks intently at Deborah, then gives me the thumbs-up sign.

'Me too. All good, babes.'

I exhale – I've been holding my breath, seemingly without realising it – and bury my face in my hands.

'Thank you,' I mumble. 'Thank you so much.'

I sit there for a few seconds, relief washing over me again, then sit up straight.

'There's more, I'm afraid,' I say.

'Oh, bloody hell,' says Ruth.

And off I go again. This time, I don't even have to ask the question.

'Well, it's not me!' Ruth explodes. 'Good grief, woman, you can't really think one of us is your *mum*? I mean, we're both turning sixty this year, but that's about the only ... I mean, how would that even have worked? We made up a whole new identity, and coincidentally both worked in the same field as you do? And then found out where you were working and deliberately got a job in the same practice, just to be close to you? And just didn't bother saying anything? That's the craziest thing I've ever heard. And working in this place, I've heard plenty of crazy things, let me tell you.'

'I know, I know! It sounds mad to me too, trust me. But Alison says she's one of my friends, someone I know. And only a few of you have been in the house recently, so ...'

I shrug.

'Deb?' I say. She laughs.

'No! Of course not. Beth, this is *insane*!'

'OK, so why ...' I hesitate, but I have to ask. 'Why have you been acting so oddly then, since Alison appeared on the scene? You've been so quiet and distracted. More than once you two stopped talking suddenly when I came into the room. And that day we went for lunch, for example, you barely spoke. I feel like you've been avoiding me, and ...'

Deborah's cheeks have been flushing red as I speak, and now she looks down at her hands which are tightly clasped in her lap.

'Tell her, Deb,' says Ruth gently, and my heart sinks.

Now what? Is she sick too?

'Do I have to?' she replies, not looking up.

'I think you do really,' Ruth says, and Deborah sighs heavily.

'OK,' she says. She sighs again and lifts her head.

'Beth, I didn't want to tell you this, partly because I was ashamed and partly because, well, I know we're close and all that but at the same time, you're the practice manager and I didn't want to put you in an awkward position. If you knew, you might feel you had no choice but to tell the doctors and then my job would probably have been in jeopardy. So I didn't confide in you, and now, well ... oh, this is so difficult. Give me a minute.'

She stands up and walks a few steps across the room, then turns round and walks back.

'Too small for pacing,' I say, trying to lighten the mood, and she gives me a little smile. 'Come on Deb, whatever it is it can't be as bad as what I've just told *you*?'

'I suppose ... OK, here goes.'

She sits down again, and Ruth pats her arm encouragingly.

'I've been gambling, Beth. Online. It started off with bingo, just a bit of fun to wind down after a long day at work, and then, I don't know really. It got out of control somehow. I never thought something like that could happen to me; it seems so weak. But it did. I was addicted, properly addicted, for a while, and ... well, I've stopped now. I'm getting help, finally. But Gavin's left me over it, Beth. I got myself into a lot of debt – got *us* into a lot of debt. Thousands and thousands. Even thought for a while we might lose the house, and when Gavin found out he went absolutely ballistic ... Anyway, he walked out, and ...'

She closes her eyes and takes deep breaths. I want to get up and hug her, but I make myself wait, my heart aching, remembering again the day we went out for lunch but now seeing it in a new light.

She brought her own lunch with her because she couldn't afford to buy lunch in the café.

Oh Deb, you should have told me ...

'I confided in Ruth, eventually, and she's been trying to help me. She's been amazing,' she says, and looks gratefully at Ruth, who smiles. 'I've even been to a Gambler's Anonymous meeting, which was so scary but actually fantastic. I know I can beat this now and I'm feeling so much better. I *would* have told you too, Beth – I hated leaving you out – but as I said, I was so ashamed and so worried about my job, on top of everything else. I mean, imagine it, a nurse with a chronic gambling habit. It would be a disgrace, and ...'

She takes a shuddery breath.

'Anyway, Gavin is coming round one night this week to talk. He's been staying at his brother's in Gloucester, but I've told him I've stopped and that I'm getting help, and I think ... well, I *hope*, I'm keeping everything crossed, that we can sort it out, that we can get back on track. So that's it, Beth.

That's why I've been so out of sorts recently, and I'm mortified and so sorry. It's up to you whether you tell Gabby and the others now. I'm not going to put any pressure on you, OK? But I'm so sorry too that this has been of no help to you. I'm not your missing mum, love.'

She gives me a sad smile and I nod and try to smile back, but inside I'm starting to feel something close to despair.

I'm running out of options here, aren't I?

'Well, thank you for telling me. What a couple of days of insane revelations, eh?' I say.

'Quite unbelievable,' says Ruth. 'Have you talked to Brenda and Barbara yet?'

'I have,' I reply, and slide off the bed. 'And no, it's not either of them. They had some interesting things to say too, but I'll catch you up on all that another time. Right now, I have to go. I have someone else to talk to, and I want to do it this evening, if possible.'

'Let me guess,' says Ruth. 'Robin?'

'Robin,' I say.

Chapter 43

I call Robin from the car. The fact that she showed up for the party on Friday gives me hope that she might meet me, if I stress how important it is, and I'm right. She's not exactly friendly on the phone, but she says she's actually at her friend's house in Prestbury and that she's happy to pop in in about half an hour.

I drive home as quickly as I can, still feeling that doing the rounds of everyone I know who's recently been in my house and asking them if they're actually my mother is just the most absurd thing I've ever done in my life. But I'm also thinking again about Robin, about how she first appeared in my life. I'd thought it was fate that brought us together, but maybe not.

Could it be her? She's so great with the kids, and they love her ... Imagine if she really is their grandmother?

She's already there when I arrive home, waiting outside the door. She's dressed in khaki-coloured running tights and a sleeveless vest today and her arms are tanned and toned.

If she's my mum, I certainly haven't inherited her body shape, I think wryly. I cut the engine, telling myself to stay calm and *breathe, breathe*, as I get out of the car.

'What's all this about, Beth?' she asks.

'It's kind of complicated,' I say. 'Come in, Robin. I really appreciate you coming over after ... well, after everything that's happened. And I really do owe you a massive apology, but I'm hoping that when I tell you what I'm about to tell you, you might forgive me. Things have been a little bit nuts around here, and not what they seemed.'

'Oh. Well, OK. I'm glad I came then,' she says, following me into the house. 'I'm intrigued.'

I'm half expecting her to say, '*I know, I know, Beth*' when I tell her that my mother is not actually my mother at all, but she doesn't, and so I carry on with the story. When I've finished she jumps from her chair and throws her arms around me.

'Holy frickin' bananas!' she says, and hugs me even tighter. I laugh and hug her back.

'Holy *bananas*?' I say. 'That's a new one!'

'Well, this whole thing's a new one on me,' she replies, letting me go. 'Phew-eeee! I was never sure about her, you know? There was always something a little odd; I couldn't put my finger on it. But this ... wow. I never suspected anything like *this*.'

'None of us did,' I say. 'She fooled us all. Quite the actress, eh?'

Robin nods, then grimaces.

'And what a cow, trying to make out it might be me behind all that stuff ... the heating problems, and the cameras in your room, and all the rest. Bloody hell, Beth. And as for the trampoline accident, that makes me feel sick to my stomach. I love those kids. I would never, *ever* ... I mean, Finley could have broken his neck; he could have *died*. I want to wring *her* neck for that. Is it awful that I feel a tiny bit glad she's so sick now?'

'No ... Oh, I don't know, Robin. It's all so confusing. I hate her for what she's done, but at the same time I kind of ... well, I understand. She went through hell, and that was my fault – or at least, I was certainly partly to blame. I don't know how to feel about it all. It's *weird*.'

She nods again and then reaches for my hand.

'And as for all the stuff back when you were a kid, you need to let that go now, Beth. It must be so hard for you, going around now telling everyone about it. We've all done things we wish we hadn't. I know you, Beth. You're a good person, OK? And if you want me to come back and work for you again, I'll do it in a heartbeat now. I've missed you all.'

'Thank you, Robin. Thank you so much.'

There's a lump in my throat suddenly, but I haven't finished yet, and I need to keep it together, so I gently slip my fingers from hers.

'Robin, there's one more thing,' I say.

Her expression changes from curious to astonished as I tell her that it was my real mother who attacked Alison, and when I relay what Alison told me about my mother being one of my friends, someone I already know, she can barely sit still.

'No! But that's *unreal*! Oh Beth, you're not telling me this because you think ...?'

'Robin, I don't know. I just have to ask everyone, you know? And I remembered that I caught you looking through my stuff once or twice,' I say. 'Things moved in my drawers, my passport, stuff like that. I wondered if that might mean something. I've no idea what, but ...'

She screws up her face, her cheeks flushing bright red.

'Oh *God*, I'm so embarrassed,' she says. 'I'm just nosy sometimes. I can't help myself. Other people's passport photos, you know; they're always funny. And the stuff on your desk, bits and pieces about patients' medical conditions, I just find it fascinating. I know it's confidential, and I'd never tell anyone any of it, but ... well, it's like those A&E programmes on telly; I can't stop watching them. But now I know that's made you think that I could be ... Oh, *shit*. It's not me, Beth. My goodness. Honestly I wish it was me; you'd be such a great daughter, but I could never have children. I had severe fibroids when I was in my teens. I was in so much pain ... Anyway, in the end I had a hysterectomy at eighteen. It was a pretty radical thing to do back then, and it took away my chance to be a mother, but I got my life back, and when you're that age you don't care. At least, I didn't. I felt differently later on, but at least my job means I have children in my life, and I'm an auntie too, and ... Oh Beth, I'm so sorry. It's not me.'

She shakes her head sadly, and again I get that hollow feeling of despair inside.

'I'm sorry you never had children. I'm sure you'd have been a lovely mum, and I really do wish ... but hey, it was a long shot,' I say. 'And now I'm running out of options, Robin.

Unless Alison was lying to me – and I honestly don't think she was – not about that. And there's the DNA thing, too. I'm a bit flummoxed, to be honest.'

'So what are you going to do now?' she asks.

'I don't know, Robin. I really don't know.'

Chapter 44

What I do is go to the police.

It was Crystal who pointed me in the right direction. Not long after Robin left yesterday saying she'd be back in the morning to do the school run so I could get on with what I needed to do, Crystal and Jacob arrived with the children. They'd already fed them and I sent them upstairs to get ready for bed while I quickly updated my ex and his girlfriend.

'So that's it,' I said. 'I can't think of anyone else who's been in the house recently. What do I do now?'

'Doesn't that just mean one of your friends is lying?' asked Jacob doubtfully.

I shook my head.

'I really don't think so. They all seemed so gobsmacked by the very suggestion,' I said. 'And if it *was* one of them, wouldn't now be the perfect time to admit it? I don't understand though. I've just run out of options.'

I groaned. This was impossible. Ridiculous. All of it.

'Right, well you need to go to the police and ask them about the DNA – remember what we talked about?' said Crystal. She was still in her work clothes – a navy pinstriped pencil-skirt and matching jacket, a white silk blouse, with her slim calves in sheer tights. It annoyed me sometimes that I liked her so much.

'The police said there was more of your mother's DNA, as well as the sample on the lamp – at least one older sample elsewhere, right? So tell them that you might be able to help them if you know where the other sample was found. *Exactly* where, I mean. Upstairs, downstairs? In your bedroom, in Eloise's room, in the kitchen? Wherever. If you know *where*, it might help you work out *who*.'

And so this morning, here I am, sitting nervously in a small, overheated Gloucestershire police interview room. Sunlight streams in through the row of small windows high on the wall and dust motes dance in the air around us. We've already had a preliminary chat, and it sounds as though Alison has been as good as her word.

'We've had absolutely no luck so far in tracking down Alison Allen's attacker,' the officer sitting opposite me says. He's the one from Saturday, the one with the intense blue eyes and pointy cheekbones.

'The search for your biological mother has drawn a blank so far, although maybe that's not too surprising, if nobody really has heard from her for thirty years. It's likely she's living under an assumed name, maybe with forged identity documents. Who knows? We still suspect that Mrs Allen might know more than she's telling us, as it does appear that she let her attacker in – and probably more than once, according to the forensic evidence, thus implying that they do know each other. But she says she can't remember anything, and since head injuries do sometimes erase memories, we have to give her the benefit of the doubt on that one for now. She's a very ill woman, unfortunately.'

He pauses, glancing at the notebook on the table in front of him, and I silently thank Alison for keeping quiet, for not revealing that she knows *exactly* who attacked her, while still wishing she'd bloody told me.

'So, Mrs Holland, can you give me some more detail now, about Mrs Allen and her *impersonation* of your real mother? We're finding all this very difficult to understand. How long has it been going on, for a start?'

I swallow. I've been dreading this bit.

'Not long. I think it was a bit of an experiment, really. She's very arty. She works in a gallery and she's into drama too – acts in am-dram productions. And I think she just wanted to see if she could pull it off – to become another person for a little while, to see if she could convince people she was someone else. A bit like a living art installation. I mean, it was cruel, yes. I fell for it, and so did everyone else in my life. But I don't think there was anything sinister about it. She wasn't trying to steal money from me or anything. She was on a sabbatical from work, and it was a project for her, a way to challenge herself. And she pulled it off, didn't she? Pretty impressive, when you think about it. She said she was going to tell me the truth at the party on Friday, and apologise and go home. But obviously something went wrong.'

The police officer's looking at me with a sceptical expression, and I know that as far as lies and cover stories go, it's about as weak as it gets.

I've blown it, I think, mentally cursing the idiocy of myself and Crystal. When we talked it through last night, we'd both decided it might just work.

'There's enough truth in there to make it stand up,' she said. 'The art gallery, the acting, the fact that she wasn't trying to steal from you ... well, she *was* trying to steal your life and your happiness, in actuality, but it wasn't for financial gain. Yes, it would be a very, very peculiar thing for anyone to do. But people do peculiar things every day, and if you just tell it straight, you might get away with it. And Beth ... if you ever tell anyone that I, a respected barrister, have been helping you to mislead the police like this, I *will* have to kill you, OK?'

She looked deadly serious for a moment, then a smile twitched at the corner of her mouth. I wanted to hug her, so I did. I was grateful, so very, very grateful to her, and to Jacob, for understanding and for not pressuring me to tell the police the truth about what Alison really did and why.

'What's the point?' Jacob said. 'She might go to prison, she might not, but if she's as sick as she says, well ... and if she is telling you the truth about your real mother, and you find out who she is, then she's done you the biggest favour ever, in the end, hasn't she?'

But now the police officer's nodding slowly, and it seems that by some miracle he's accepted my ludicrous story.

'Pretty horrible thing to do if you ask me,' he mutters. He makes some more notes on his pad. 'But if you don't want to press charges ...'

'I don't,' I say quickly. 'She's so ill, as you said. And while it was a shock when I found out, there's no lasting harm done. She was quite good fun to have around, a lot of the time.'

And she was, wasn't she? I think. Not everything I'm telling you is a lie.

Now he's wrapping up the interview. He closes his notebook and puts the cap on his pen, telling me to call him if I remember anything at all that might help the investigation. I know I need to get my question in now, quickly, before he ushers me out again.

'I was just wondering,' I say casually, 'about the location of the DNA samples? You said DNA from my biological mother was found on the pelican lamp, but that there were other samples, possibly older? I just wondered if you could tell me where exactly? Would that be possible?'

He furrows his brow, looking at me questioningly, then shrugs.

'Suppose it can't hurt,' he says. 'Hang on, I've got the full report here somewhere.'

He flicks through a cardboard file that's lying on the table and pulls out a sheaf of papers.

'Right, DNA, DNA ...' he mumbles, turning the pages slowly. Then: 'Ah. Here it is. There was matching DNA on the lamp, on the front door – probably from when she was entering and leaving the house – and on some books.'

'Books? Can you be more precise?' I say, puzzled.

He checks the report again.

'Yep. There were a few books in a pile, on a small table in the lounge. Agatha Christie books, it says here. Your biological mother's DNA was found on those.'

Chapter 45

I'm standing at the edge of the car park opposite the surgery, looking down the road towards Nadia's doorway. It's another warm morning, nearly midday now, and the sky is azure blue. The street is quiet. A man with a small, over-fed dog ambles along the far pavement and a mother with a pushchair walks briskly past me, her baby silent under a pink blanket. I'm almost too overwhelmed, too stupefied, to take the few steps I need to take now, and so I stand and I breathe and I look. She's there, as she always is, face tilted up towards the sun, her eyes closed. Even from this distance I can see that she looks calm – serene almost. And then, quite suddenly, as if she can sense my presence, she opens her eyes and turns her head. Our eyes lock and a shiver runs through me.

Mum? Are you really my mother? How can you be, Nadia?

And then she raises a hand, slowly, so slowly, and I know. And I know that she knows I know, and that she's been waiting for me, all this time. I start to walk, then somehow break into a run, and seconds later I'm falling to my knees beside her.

'Hello, Beth,' she says softly.

'Nadia?' I say. '*Mum?*'

'Nadia to most, these days. Always Alice Armstrong, deep down,' she says.

Her greeny-grey eyes are filling with tears now and I stare at her, really looking at her for the first time, remembering eyes like those filling with tears so often, so very long ago, when we were both thirty years younger. Remembering, but unable to comprehend any of it, terrified to believe it. I breathe in her stale aroma and remember the strange, musty smell in the house on Friday when we found Alison unconscious on the floor. I try to look past the straggly grey hair, the tattered clothing, the deeply lined skin, and try to see the woman underneath. Hope shivers like a baby bird inside me. With a trembling hand, I reach out to touch the baggy black sweater she's huddled in – no coat covering it in the warmth of this late spring day. I gently push the neckline down to expose a hint of pale collarbone. And there it is.

Three little stars.

One star for her, one for Dad, one for me.

Oh my God. It's her. It's really her.

'Mum,' I say, and now there are little firecrackers of joy and confusion going off inside me. I still don't understand any of this but it doesn't matter anymore because finally, *finally*, I get to say it, and this time to the right person. Because she is. I know she is.

'Hello, Mum. Welcome home.'

Chapter 46

'How will Father Christmas bring Nana presents, Mum? Will they unlock the doors for him?'

I'm sitting at my desk in my bedroom, writing a few final Christmas cards to deliver by hand this evening. Finley has sidled in, leaning his chin on my shoulder and pressing his warm little body against my back. He's eight now, and I'm not entirely sure he really believes in Father Christmas anymore, but I love that he still pretends to – for me probably. It's Christmas Eve tomorrow, and the presents are all wrapped and piled under the big tree in the corner of the lounge and the front door is decorated with a pinecone wreath. Downstairs in the kitchen, Eloise and Cleo, one of her friends from school, are singing along to Mariah Carey, their voices high and sweet.

I put my pen down and turn to look at my little boy, gently pushing an errant strand of blond hair back off his forehead.

'How does this hair grow so fast? I'm glad Daddy's taking you to the barber's this afternoon,' I say. 'Father Christmas would be leaving your presents somewhere else otherwise, 'cos he wouldn't recognise you.'

His eyes widen, then he grins.

'Don't be silly. He knows *e-ver-y-thing*. So will he? Be able to bring Nana presents?'

'Of course he will,' I say. 'Prison walls are no problem for him. The reindeer can fly right over them.'

He nods, satisfied, then turns and skips from the room. I watch him go, my heart swelling, and I marvel yet again at how accepting children are and how quickly they adapt to the strangest changes in circumstances. A grandmother who wasn't, and now a grandmother who is. She's not with us, not yet – she's currently residing in Eastwood Park women's prison in south Gloucestershire. She insisted, in the end, on handing herself in to the police, who charged her with grievous bodily harm for the assault on Alison. At the end of May she pleaded guilty in court, and was sentenced to three years in jail, which, I hope, means that with good behaviour she'll be out by this time next year. She's a model prisoner, by all accounts, content with her warm cell, regular meals, and the safety afforded by the prison walls. Despite her lifestyle of recent years it is, the police told me, the first time she's ever been in trouble, the first time she's ever been arrested.

'Pretty remarkable for a woman who's lived on the streets for as long as she has,' one of them said. I felt a rush of guilt mixed, weirdly, with pride and love.

Sixty years old and going to prison, for me. She did it for me. To protect me, when she finally worked out who Alison was and what she was about to do. She wanted to stop the party, to stop Alison before her final attempt to destroy me,

Her story was extraordinary, relayed that first afternoon as we sat together in my kitchen, before I drove her to the police station to make her confession.

'A clean slate, love. When I'm out, we can start afresh, if you want me.'

'Oh, I want you. You're not getting away from me again,' I said, and she smiled her gap-toothed smile, and nodded shyly.

It was almost eerie how comfortable I felt with her, and yet I had from the beginning, hadn't I? I'd sat there in a doorway with a homeless woman I'd known as Nadia, chatting about anything and everything, and I'd felt at ease. At home.

She cried a lot that first afternoon. I did too as we relived the past, gently raking over her final days with me and Dad. She explained how unhappy she'd been in the marriage. The rumours I'd heard had been true – the age gap had been just too big. She told me how she'd finally plucked up the courage to just walk away. How she'd moved abroad, travelling around Italy and France and Spain, looking for excitement and glamour. She'd had a string of boyfriends, none of whom gave her what she was looking for because she didn't really know that herself. She'd gone from low-paid job to low-paid job, drifted across Europe, and eventually found her way back to the UK, where she'd opted out of society, camping on beaches and sleeping in hostels. And that had continued for years.

'I started using Nadia instead of Alice because I didn't want anyone from my past to find me,' she said. 'The shame of leaving you never left me, Beth. And to come back as a homeless dropout, well, that made the shame even worse, because what was it all for? I thought about trying to track you down so many times, but I always talked myself out of it because I didn't think you'd want to know me. I didn't think you'd ever forgive me, and who would blame you?'

She'd found herself back in Bristol eventually, and that was when she'd bumped into Alan, an old friend of Dad's – one of the few he'd had kept a little contact with over the years. Somehow he'd recognised my mother when he'd passed her on the street.

'I don't know how,' she grimaced. 'He used to fancy me, you know? And look at me now. But he did; he stopped and we talked, and I begged him, *begged* him, not to tell anyone he'd seen me. He obviously felt sorry for me because he agreed. And so I plucked up the courage to ask him if he knew where you were these days, and he told me your dad had told him you were working at a surgery in St James Road in Cheltenham and, well, the rest was easy.'

She looked so much older than her sixty years, so wrinkled and so haggard, sitting there in her shabby, musty, oversized clothes. And yet, that day, she looked like the most beautiful thing I'd ever seen. My love for her was already brimming over.

'The first time I saw you, coming out of the surgery, my heart almost stopped,' she said. I thought about the day I'd first walked across the road to speak to her, and the way she'd stared at me.

'I could still see the little girl I left behind, and for a while I was content just to see you, to talk to you, to see how happy you were. And then you told me your mother had turned up, and I was stunned. I couldn't understand it. I knew someone was trying to con you – they had to be – but I just didn't know who or why ...'

I remembered then the day I'd told her about Alison and her bewildered expression.

If only she'd told me who she was then, I thought. All the trouble it would have saved ...

I had, it seemed, inadvertently left an old envelope inside one of the books I lent her, an envelope I'd been using as bookmark, and on it was my home address.

'Fate, maybe?' she said, and I had to agree.

And so it had been her, that face appearing outside my living room window, peering in, trying to get a glimpse of my 'mother', wondering if she was somebody she knew and trying to see if I was OK. She'd grown increasingly worried about me, she said, and when she saw the newspaper article about me which mentioned my link to a school suicide, she began to wonder. But when she saw me crying that day outside the surgery, the day I was suspended from work, she said she finally knew she needed to confront Alison.

'Ruth mentioned your party when she came over to see me the day before,' she said. 'She said your 'mother' was going to make some kind of announcement and I just got a bad feeling. I hid behind a bush across the road and when I saw you go off in your car I knocked on the door. She recognised me; she'd seen me by the surgery, of course. She was pretty surprised but she let me in, and then, well ...'

Alison had been in a state of high excitement, apparently, and had suddenly started talking, telling my mother that her friend Beth was not what she seemed, that I was a nasty, evil person. She told her what I'd done as a child, and what she had come to Cheltenham to do to me.

'I told her then that *I* was your mother,' she said. 'She was shocked, but only for a minute. She was sneering at me, laughing. She said it didn't matter anymore. She told me it didn't matter who knew she'd been faking it because it would all be over in a few hours, that she was planning to tell *everyone* the truth. And that was it, I'm afraid. I'm not a violent woman, Beth, but I saw red. I'm sorry. I'm not proud of attacking her like that.'

I was proud though, and I told her so. Proud too, and so, so grateful, that she confessed what she'd done to the police without telling them about my past, trying to ensure it wouldn't get into the newspapers. Trying to protect me, again.

'I just said I was angry at her for impersonating me,' she said.

It means I haven't had to tell Eloise and Finley about Lucy – not right now. I'll tell them one day, when I'm ready. When I think they'll understand. They're happy now; we all are, weirdly. All of my little group, my family and friends. Our lives are back on track.

Ruth, Deborah, and I see more of each other than ever these days. Our Cleeve Hill walks are now a Saturday morning must and our cocktail evenings are a regular fixture – often with Brenda and Barbara too. Deborah's stopped gambling, although she's still going to her GA meetings, and she and Gavin are back together. Robin's back in the fold too, of course, and we're closer these days – more friends than employer-employee, although I still secretly think she's a bit bonkers, with all her running. And as for Jacob and Crystal, we're getting on so well we've even talked about taking a joint trip with the kids somewhere at Easter, which would be a first.

And – and this is one of the smallest things, really, but it's given me *such* peace of mind – the porn website has taken down the footage of me. I'm still not quite sure whether it was my heartfelt email or Anna Reid's gentle threats that did it, but they've gone, and that's all that matters really.

Alison Allen died last month. I found out in a most unexpected voice message from Liv.

'Thank you, Beth,' she said. 'For not telling the police about all the things she ... we ... did to you. It meant we could spend her final days together. You won't hear from me again. Goodbye.'

And so now I'm looking forwards. I don't know yet where my mother will live when she comes out of prison; she says she wants somewhere small and snug of her own – maybe a bedsit somewhere close to me and the children. The streets have lost their appeal now. She gave me a letter for Dad and he cried. Maybe she'll even move in there, to Holly Tree, if we can make the finances work. Maybe they can be friends again. Maybe.

Dad took it amazingly well when I told him the remarkable story of Nadia and who she really was. He was astounded of course, as everyone was, but they've all taken their turn at visiting her in prison, and I've never felt more blessed, more grateful. Never felt happier, really. And so one long chapter of my life ends, and a new one begins.

I think about that now, as I finish the last of the Christmas cards and put my pen down. I'll never forget Lucy; her face still haunts my dreams sometimes. But I'll always be so thankful that I've been given this second chance, and I'm going to use it wisely – as wisely as I can.

I stand up slowly, turning to look out of the window, and my eyes widen. It rained heavily earlier, but now there's watery sunshine and, suddenly, a rainbow splitting the steel-grey sky with its arc of glorious colour. I stand there for a minute, drinking it in, all its impossibly brilliant, shimmering glory. In a minute I'll call Finley and Eloise and tell them to look outside so they don't miss this.

Because it's important isn't it, I think, to know that there'll always be rainbows? There will be more rain, more darkness, of course there will. But there will always be rainbows. You just have to weather the storm, and then lift your face up and look for them.

I smile, and head downstairs to find my children.

Acknowledgements

There are, as always, so many people to thank when you finally reach the point of releasing another novel into the world. This time, I'll begin with my friend and colleague Anne Dawson, one of the funniest women I know, who provided me with the "cheese in the dishwasher" story in Chapter 1. She didn't know I was going to put it in a book, so I hope she doesn't mind; and yes, it really happened to her, and it still makes me laugh so much every time I think about it. Thank you, Anne!

So many dreams came true for me in the year I spent writing *The Happy Family*. My 2020 novel (my fifth book overall) *The Perfect Couple* somehow became an international bestseller, something I'm still trying to process with joy and amazement. All the people who contributed to that success are still with me for *The Happy Family*, so here is a list of just some of them.

My incredible agent, Clare Hulton – you have genuinely changed my life, and I will be forever grateful. The lovely, committed, hard-working, super-talented bunch at HarperCollins One More Chapter, especially my wonderful editor Kathryn Cheshire (I could NOT write my books without you!), marketing geniuses Melanie Price and Claire Fenby, and Lucy Bennett who designs my gorgeous covers. Ladies – what a team. You ROCK, as do Kimberley Young, Charlotte Ledger, Fionnuala Barrett, Kelly Webster and my copy editor Lydia Mason. Huge thanks also to the HarperCollins teams in the USA, Canada and Australia. You're all amazing, as are Nicki Kennedy, Jenny Robson, Katherine West, May Wall and all of the team at ILA, who handle my foreign rights – I'm so excited to see the translated versions of my novels popping up around the world! And as always, so much love and gratitude to everyone who buys, reads and listens to my books, and to all the bloggers and reviewers who spend so much of their time supporting authors. We appreciate you more than we can ever say – thank you so much.

Beth in *The Happy Family* is a GP practice manager, so I want to thank my GP husband JJ, for everything always of course, but here for his insight into the world of general practice (and for reminding me to eat when I got so engrossed in writing this book I frequently forgot to come down for lunch). Huge thanks too to Dr Christine Thompson, who was also so very helpful.

Thank you to my beautiful hometown Cheltenham and specifically to Prestbury, where *The Happy Family* is largely set, for the inspiration. And to my friend Susan Blair, who has recommended my books to so many people, and who lives in Prestbury and asked me if I could write her into this story. (Susan, I did, but the book got too long and I had to cut some scenes, so I had to lose you again. I'm putting you here instead – hope this will do for now!) A massive thank you to the incredibly supportive author community, especially the lovely group I'm honoured to be a part of in Gloucestershire; and a special mention to author Karin Slaughter, who chose *The Perfect Couple* as one of her 2020 Asda "Killer Reads". And to *all* of my family, friends and colleagues, who continue to support me and cheer me on as I continue on this crazy writing journey – I love you all.

And finally, a big thanks to all those who join in with my monthly book club on Instagram. I started it as a little distraction during the first Covid-19 UK lockdown, never dreaming that more than a year later it would still be going strong with thousands of us sharing our love of books. Keep on reading!

Thank you, all of you, so very much.

Enjoyed *The Happy Family?* Make sure you've read Jackie Kabler's previous psychological thrillers!

I never thought it would happen to me ...

One moment I had it all – a gorgeous husband, a beautiful home, a fulfilling career and two adorable children. The next, everything came crashing down around me.

They said it was my fault. They said I'm the worst mother in the world. And even though I can't remember what happened that day, they wouldn't lie to me. These are my friends, my family, people I trust.

But then why do I have this creeping sensation that something is wrong? Why do I feel like people are keeping secrets? Am I really as guilty as they say? And if I'm not, what will happen when the truth comes out ...?

A devoted wife ...

A year ago, Gemma met the love of her life, Danny. Since then, their relationship has been perfect. But one evening, Danny doesn't return home.

A missing husband ...

Gemma turns to the police. She is horrified by what she discovers – a serial killer is on the loose in Bristol. When she sees photos of the victims she is even more stunned ... they all look just like Danny.

Who would you believe?

But the police are suspicious. Why has no one apart from Gemma heard from Danny in weeks? Why is there barely a trace of him in their flat? Is she telling them the truth, or is this marriage hiding some very dark secrets?